"Johnson introduces a vulnerable character who instantly wins your admiration with his humility, integrity, and humor. [Johnson's] sense of place and people drive a story in which you don't necessarily care who the killer might turn out to be; you just don't want the ride to end." —*Daily Camera* (Boulder, CO)

"Johnson evokes the rugged landscape with reverential prose, lending a heady atmosphere to his story."
—*The Philadelphia Inquirer*

"If you want a well-written mystery . . . this is your book."
—*Lincoln Journal Star*

"Johnson crafts great, imaginative mysteries with lots of twists, turns, and misdirections . . . [and] the author skillfully seasons his books with humor too often missing in his genre."
—*Billings Gazette*

"Pile on the thermal underwear, fire up the four-wheel drive, and head for Durant. Walt and his idiosyncratic crew are terrific company—droll, sassy, and surprisingly tenderhearted."
—*Kirkus Reviews* (starred review)

"[Johnson has] a sure-handed touch for jolting both his characters and his readers out of their comfort zones and deep into harm's way. It's hard to ask for more in a literary mystery."
—*Booklist* (starred review)

"Johnson weaves together city and country, Anglo and Indian, art snob and proud philistine and creates a laugh-out-loud, hard-to-put-down mystery."   —Book Sense

"There's genuine emotion and care in these pages, with humor and humanity to balance its undertone of imminent violence."
—*Mystery Scene*

A PENGUIN MYSTERY

THE DARK HORSE

Craig Johnson is the *New York Times* bestselling author of the Longmire mysteries, the basis for the hit Netflix original series *Longmire*. He is the recipient of the Western Writers of America Spur Award for fiction, and his novella, *Spirit of Steamboat*, was the first One Book Wyoming selection. He lives in Ucross, Wyoming, population twenty-five.

By Craig Johnson

CRAIG JOHNSON

THE DARK HORSE

PENGUIN BOOKS

PENGUIN PRESS
An imprint of Penguin Random House LLC
375 Hudson Street
New York, New York 10014
penguin.com

First published in the United States of America by Viking Penguin,
a member of Penguin Group (USA) Inc., 2009
Published in Penguin Books 2010

LIBRARY OF CONGRESS CATALOGING-IN-PUBLICATION DATA
Johnson, Craig, ———.
Dark horse : a Walt Longmire mystery / Craig Johnson.
p. cm.
ISBN 978-0-670-02087-4 (hc.)
ISBN 978-0-14-311731-5 (pbk.)
1. Longmire, Walt (Fictitious character)—Fiction.
2. Sheriffs—Wyoming—Fiction. 3. Wyoming—Fiction. I. Title.
PS3610.O325D37 2009
813'.6—dc22
2008054093

Printed in the United States of America
25   27   29   30   28   26   24

Set in Dante
Designed by Alissa Amell

For Sue Fletcher, the real Wahoo Sue, and for Juana DeLeon, whose heritage lives on in Auda, Marlen, and Benjamin.

ACKNOWLEDGMENTS

The origin of the phrase "dark horse" is based on a story about a nineteenth-century breeder who would arrive in a strange town and pretend to be riding an ordinary pack animal, which was in truth a very fast black stallion. He'd enter the dark horse in a race and, when the horse would win (much to the surprise of the locals), he would pocket the prize money and more than a few bets on the side and move on to the next gullible community.

The front-runners of the Absalom Trifecta, as always, are Gail Hochman, a handsome little Brooklyn filly with a sharp eye and a sharper tongue who taught me that the race may not always go to the swift or the victory to the strong but that's how you bet. Kathryn Court, a thoroughbred of fine breeding with an ability to go long in the back stretch and who taught me that horse sense is the good judgment that keeps horses from betting on people. For Alexis Washam, who tends to be fast out of the gate and who reminded me that you don't approach a bull from the front, a horse from the rear, or a copy editor from any direction.

My good friend Maureen "Donnybrook" Donnelly, who always comes up on the inside and instructed me from the get-go that life is generally six to five against but good days are around turn two. Ben "El" Petrone, who said that if an earthquake ever hit the Kentucky Derby while I was there to be sure to go straight to the ticket window where nothing ever hits. To Meghan "The Cincinnati Kid" Fallon, who, with the luck of the Irish, always seems to come in by a nose but says no horse can ever go as fast as the money you bet on him.

Eric Boss, who once bet me he could make the jack of spades jump out of a sealed, perfectly new deck of cards and squirt cider in my ear. I'm still cleaning the cider out of my ear.

Thanks to the Brannaman school of Oat-ology for all the inside tips.

Thanks to my buddy and track-side physician David Nickerson, who says racehorses are the only animals that can take a couple of thousand people for a ride.

A note of apology to Buzzy and the gang at "The AR," and the town of Arvada as a whole, which shares a geographic location but bears no resemblance to the environs of this novel. "The Arvada bar, where the pavement ends the fun begins." Indeed.

Most of all, to my wife, Judy, who took the greatest gamble in her life by betting on me.

dark horse: *noun*

1 a: a usually little known contender (as a racehorse) that makes an unexpectedly good showing b: an entrant in a contest that is judged unlikely to succeed

2: a person who reveals little about himself or herself, esp. someone who has unexpected talents or skills

1

October 27, 11 A.M.
It was the third week of a high-plains October, and an unsea-sonably extended summer had baked the color from the land-scape and had turned the rusted girders of the old bridge a thinned-out, tired brown.

I topped the hill and pulled the gunmetal Lincoln Town Car alongside the Pratt truss structure. There weren't very many of them in the Powder River country, and the few bridges that were left were being auctioned off to private owners for use on their ranches. I had grown up with these old camelback bridges and was sorry to see the last of them go.

My eyes were pulled to the town balanced on the banks of the anemic river and pressed hard against the scoria hills like the singing blade of a sharp knife. The water, the land, and the bridge were sepia-toned, depleted.

I told Dog to stay in the backseat and got out of the car, slipped on my hat and an aged, burnished-brown horsehide jacket, and walked across the dirt lot. I studied the dusty, wide-planked surface of the bridge and, between the cracks, the few reflecting slivers of the Powder River below. The

Wyoming Department of Transportation had condemned and, in turn, posted the bridge with bright yellow signs—it was to be removed next week. I could see the abutments that they had constructed off to the right on which the new bridge would soon rest.

A Range Telephone Cooperative trailer sat by a power pole holding a junction box and a blue plastic service phone that gently tapped against the creosote-soaked wood like a forgotten telegraph, receiving no answer.

"You lost?"

I turned and looked at the old rancher who'd pulled up behind me in an antiquated '55 GMC, the kind that has grill-work frozen in a perpetual sneer. The big truck was overladen with hay. I tipped my new hat back and gazed at him. "Nope, just looking around."

He kicked at the accelerator and eased the Jimmy into a lopsided idle as he glanced at Dog, my late-model car, and the Montana plates. "You workin' methane?"

"Nope."

He squinted at me to let me know he wasn't sure if I was telling the truth, his eyes green as the algae that grows on the tops of horse troughs. "We get a lot of them gas and oil people out here, buying up people's mineral rights." He studied me, sizing me up by my new black hat, boots, and freshly pressed blue jeans. "Easy to get lost on these roads."

"I'm not lost." I looked at his load, at the sun-dried, tiny blue flowers intermixed with the hay and the orange and cobalt twine that indicated it was weed-free; idiot cubes, as we used to call the seventy-pound bales. I stepped in closer and put a hand on the hay, rich with alfalfa. "Certified. You must have a pretty good stretch of bottom land around here somewhere."

"Good enough, but with the drought, this country's so dry you have to prime a man before he can spit." As if to emphasize his point, he spat a stream through the rust holes in the floorboard of the truck and onto the road, the spittle approaching the same tint as the river.

I nodded as I glanced down at the stained pea gravel. "A buddy of mine says that these small bales are what broke up the family ranches." I looked back up at the cargo—two and a half tons at least. "You buck a couple thousand of these in August and your mind starts to wander; wonder as to what the heck else you could be doing for a living."

His eyes clinched my words. "You ranch?"

"Nope, but I grew up on one."

"Where 'bouts?"

I smiled, stuffing my hands in the pockets of my jeans, glanced at his rust-orange, heavily loaded flatbed, and then at the dilapidated structure that spanned the distance between here—and there. "You gonna drive this truck across that bridge?"

He spat into the dirt again, this time near my boots, and then wiped his mouth on the back of his snap-buttoned cuff. "Been drivin' the car-bridge for sixty-three years; don't see no reason to stop."

Car-bridge; I hadn't heard that one in a while. I glanced back at the yellow WYDOT signs and the decrepit condition of the doomed structure. "Looks like you're not going to have much choice as of next week."

He nodded and ran a hand over his patent-leather face. "Yeah, I reckon they got more money down there in Cheyenne than they know what to do with." He waited a moment before speaking again. "The state highway is about four miles back up the road."

"I told you, I'm not lost."

I could feel him watching me; I'm sure he was looking at the scar above my eye, the one on my neck, that little part of my ear that was missing, my hands, and most importantly, trying to get a read on the insouciance that goes along with a quarter of a century spent with a star pinned to my chest. I nodded, glancing back across the bridge before he had a chance to study me longer. "Is that a town, down there?"

"Sort of." He snorted a laugh. "Halfway between woebegone and far away." He continued to study me as I watched the dust drifting across the warped and swirled surface of the dried-out planks. "Used to be called Suggs, but when the Burlington and Missouri came through they decided that it ought to have an upstanding, proper, biblical name."

I continued to look at the town. "And what's that?"

"Absalom."

I laughed and thought that one of those railroad engineers must have had a pretty good sense of humor or been from Mississippi. But then it occurred to me that Faulkner hadn't been walking, let alone writing, when the railroads came through here.

He continued to look at me through the collection of wrinkles that road-mapped his eyes. "Something funny?"

I nodded. "Do you read the Bible, Mr. . . . ?"

"Niall, Mike Niall." I noticed he didn't extend his hand. "Not since my mother used to make me. And there ain't nobody that makes me do much of anything in about seventy years."

Seven years longer than he'd been driving the car-bridge, I figured. "You should read it, Mr. Niall, if for no other reason than that historical reference. Absalom was King David's son—the cursed one who turned against him."

I started back toward the rental car, and there was a pause before he spoke again. "I wouldn't go down there if I was you; it's not a friendly place."

I opened the door of the Lincoln, tossed my 10X onto the passenger seat, and looked back at him from over the top, and especially at the .30-30 carbine in the truck's rifle rack behind his head. "That's all right; I'm not looking for friends."

I started to climb into the driver's seat but stopped when he called out to me again. "Hey youngster, I didn't catch your name."

I paused for only a second, continuing to look down the valley at the small town. "I didn't throw it."

I drove off the pavement to the edge of a dirt street alongside the railroad tracks and pulled the rental under the shade of an abandoned mill that read BEST OUT WEST, but maybe not so much anymore. It was true that they had changed the name of Suggs to Absalom in an attempt to elevate the town and pull it from a dubious past, but I couldn't help feeling that whatever its name, it had been surviving on borrowed time and the bill had come due. I left the windows down just a bit for Dog and got out across from the only obvious commercial establishment in the town.

The AR had been The BAR at some point in its past, but poor carpentry and the ever-prevalent wind had changed its name; that, or the B had decided to move on to a better hive. There were a few used-up motel rooms connected to the building on one side with a few unconnected cabins on the other, the entirety attached by an overhang that marginally protected the wooden walkway.

Through the opening between the main building and the cabins, I could see a propane tank in a weedy backyard and, attached to makeshift gutters with baling wire, cowboy boots that gently twisted in the breeze like loose appendages. There was a hand-printed sign that read ABSALOM BAR—WHERE THE PAVEMENT ENDS THE THRILLS BEGIN.

Indeed.

The truck I parked behind had a half-dozen dogs in the bed, border collie/blue heeler mixes that all came over to growl at me as I made my way around to the front of my car. The red merle in the corner snapped and missed me by only eight inches. I stopped and turned to look at all of them, still growling and snarling, and saw that Dog had raised his head from the backseat to balefully inspect the herding dogs the way timber wolves inspect coyotes.

There were still hitching posts in front of The AR, which was handy because there were horses in front of The AR. A snippy-looking grulla and a sleepy quarter horse stirred as I placed a boot on the wooden steps. The mouse-colored one had a cloudy eye and turned to look at me with his good one, while the grade went back to napping in the October sun, his right rear hoof raised in relaxation like some pre-Technicolor-era starlet being kissed. I stuck out a hand, and he brushed the soft fur of his nose across my knuckles. I thought about a circle around an eye and the last horse I'd been this close to and how he had died.

"In this country, we don't touch a man's horse without asking."

I dropped my hand and turned to look at the voice. "Well, technically, he touched me." I stepped the rest of the way onto the boardwalk and looked down at the cowboy, aware that a two-foot height advantage is always handy in dealing with antagonists, especially ones that are ten years old.

The little outlaw tipped back on the heels of his boots and looked up at me with dark eyes. "You're big."

"I didn't plan it."

He thought about that for a while and then looked disapprovingly at my new, pinch-front hat. "You lost?"

I sighed softly and continued toward the door. "No."

"Bar's closed."

He said everything as if it were an absolute that would brook no argument; I wondered if he was related to the green-eyed rancher at the condemned bridge. I turned to look at him with my hand on the doorknob. "Do you frequent this establishment a great deal?"

He placed a fist on his hip and looked up at me, as if I should already know what it was that he was going to say. "You talk funny."

I stood there looking at the black hair sticking out from all angles like a murder of crows trying to escape from underneath the stained cowboy hat. I thought about another kid from a number of years ago with a head like a pail—just as impenetrable and about as empty. "Is everybody in this town as polite as you?"

He paused for a second and stuffed the already chewed-on leather stampede strings that were dangling from his hat into his mouth, saving him from spitting on the road like the old rancher. "Pretty much."

I nodded, looking at the plastic sign in the window that read CLOSED, then turned the knob and stepped into The AR. "Must make for gracious living 'round these parts."

The AR was like most of the public drinking establishments in northern Wyoming, which bear a great resemblance to the establishments of southern Wyoming and everywhere else in the West, except that this one had a makeshift boxing arena to the left of the central U-shaped bar, with an elevated plywood platform, steel fencing poles in the corners, and two strands of calf-roping ropes strung around it.

On a shelf above the bar was a television set tuned to the Weather Channel with the sound off. Weather was always a safe subject in this part of the world—everybody was interested, everybody enjoyed the bitching, and nobody could do anything about it. A more-than-middle-aged man sat on a mismatched chair at one of the small tables to the right of the particleboard bar and smoked a cigarette. He was reading the Gillette newspaper.

"Bar's closed."

It was a female voice, with the same cocksure intonations as the kid's, so I ignored the man reading the *News-Record*, just as he ignored me. I looked around at the all-but-empty room. "Beg your pardon?"

"Bar's closed."

The voice had come from behind the counter, so I walked over and looked down; I could just see the punt end of a baseball bat, the butt of an old Winchester pump on one of the shelves, and a young woman. She was bantam-sized and was mopping up water from under the beer coolers with a dishrag. She looked at me beneath a confection of black hair pulled back with a wide elastic band. She had mocha-colored eyes, and her skin tone was the same as the boy's—maybe Indian, maybe, on closer inspection, from somewhere in Central America. "Bar's closed."

"Yep, I got that." I tipped my hat back and raised a hand in submission. "And before you ask, I'm not lost."

She threw the rag onto the floor with a plop of exasperation. "Then what do you want?"

It was silent for a moment. "I was wondering if there were any rooms available in the motel."

She rose to her feet and leaned on the bar, where she grabbed another rag from a pile and wiped her hands. "Nothing but rooms available. Nobody wants to stay here without air-conditioning and satellite television." She glanced at the man seated at the small table, who was still smoking and reading. "Pat? Man's wanting a room."

He didn't look up and continued to cover most of his face with a hand on which was an enormous, gold Masonic ring that seemed to hold the cigarette smoke in a sustained orbit. "Full."

The young woman glanced at me, then at him, and then shrugged as she went back to the leaking cooler. I turned to the man. He was overweight and dressed in overalls, a short-sleeved print shirt, and a trucker-style ball cap that read SHERIDAN SEED COMPANY.

"No rooms at all?"

He glanced up at me, but for only a moment, and flicked some ashes into the glass ashtray that advertised THUNDER-BIRD HOTEL, LAS VEGAS, NEV. "Booked up."

The young woman's voice rose again from behind the bar. "What about number four?"

He continued reading. "Toilet's busted."

She spoke again as I leaned against the bar. "We got a toilet in here, he could just use that."

He sighed and flashed a dirty look in her general vicinity. "S'against the law, room's gotta have a working toilet."

She stood back up, tossed the new now-sopping rag into a galvanized trash can, and ripped a half-dozen paper towels off a roll on the counter. "What law is that?"

He looked at her and stubbed the cigarette out in the ashtray. "The you-gotta-have-a-crapper-in-any-room-you-rent law."

"Whose law is that?" The quick-draw flash of temper in her eyes and the barest trace of an accent was significantly Latin.

He pushed his chair back and folded the newspaper, slipping it under his arm. "Mine."

She turned the entirety of her attitude toward me, and I was briefly reminded of my daughter. "You paying in cash?"

I blinked. "I can."

The attitude shifted back to the lawgiver, and I was just as glad to be relieved of it. "You haven't paid me in two weeks because you haven't had any money." He continued to look at her through sloped eyelids. "Well, here's money." She walked to the bar-back at the wall, plucked a key from a full rack, and slammed it on the counter between us. "Thirty-two dollars and ninety-five cents."

I nodded, looking at the key still covered by her hand. "For a room without a toilet?"

She glanced up at me from below the accentuated eyebrows and through the dark lashes. "You can forget about the ninety-five cents, and I'll eat the tax."

I reached for my wallet. "What the governor doesn't know won't hurt him?" She didn't say anything and ignored the older man completely as I handed her two twenties. "I might need the room for more than one night."

"Even better. I'll keep your change as a deposit."

I took the key and turned toward the door. "Thanks . . . I think."

"You want a drink?"

The older man hadn't moved; he still stood in the same place and was watching me. I turned and looked at her. "Thought the bar was closed."

She smiled a stunner of a smile with perfectly shaped lips. "Just opened."

October 17: ten days earlier, evening.

They'd brought her in on a Friday night. The jail had been empty. It usually was.

One of the ways we supplemented our budget allotment was to import prisoners from the overcrowded jails in other counties. They did a brisk business, especially in Gillette, which was in Campbell County, and I provided high-security, low-amenity lodging for a portion of their tax base.

Dog and I had slept the previous three nights at the jail. Sleeping in a holding cell was a pattern I had developed when I was feeling discontented, and I had been feeling this way since Labor Day, when my daughter, Cady, had left for Philadelphia.

I leaned against the wall and could feel my shoulders slope from their own weight as I watched Victoria Moretti. My deputy was easy on the eyes, and I liked watching her. The trick was not getting caught.

Vic filled out the transport of prisoner forms, dotted a vicious "i," and snapped the pen back onto the clipboard. She handed it back to the two deputies. "For them to send two of you, this Mary Barsad must be pretty dangerous."

The young man with the ubiquitous cop mustache ripped off the receipts and gave them to Vic. "Dangerous enough to fire six shots from a .22 hunting rifle into the right side of his head while he lay there asleep. Then, for good measure, she set the house on fire."

The other deputy interrupted. "Allegedly."

The first deputy repeated. "Allegedly."

Vic glanced at the papers and back at them. "That'd do it."

Wyoming law states that incarcerated females must be supervised at all times by a female docent or a matron, neither of which aptly described Vic, but she had the third watch and would until Mary Barsad was transferred back to Campbell County for trial in three weeks. It was an understatement to say that she wasn't thrilled.

She bid the two deputies an extraditionary farewell, and I waited with Dog at the door of her office, which was across the hall from mine. She handed me the paperwork, which was stuffed in a manila folder, crossed her arms, and leaned on the other side of the doorway. She stared at me. "I can't believe you're doing this to me."

"It's not my fault. If you want to yell at somebody, call up Sandy Sandberg and give him an earful." I reached down to pet Dog so that the beast wouldn't take the argument seriously; she reached down and pulled one of his ears so that he would. "He didn't tell me the detainee was a she."

"That douche-rocket is doing this because I outshot him at certification in Douglas two months ago."

I figured I'd divert her before she got really mad. "You want something to eat?"

She looked up. "Is this a date or just dinner?"

"Just dinner. I figured if you were going to be stuck here alone all night, I'd go get you something."

"What the fuck do you mean just me all night? Where are you going?"

I took a breath. "Well, I thought I'd go home."

She looked at the wall. "Great. You sleep in the jail all the time, but as soon as I'm here, you decide to go home?"

"You want me to stay?"

She looked back at me, the tarnished gold eyes shimmering. "Yes."

I didn't move. "You want me to go get you something to eat?"

"Yes." She thought for a moment. "What are you getting?"

I sighed. "I never know until I get there."

"I'll take the usual."

I slipped the folder under my arm and headed back to take

a look at the prisoner on my way to the café. Dog trotted after me.

Vic called out as I retreated down the hallway. "And be quick about it. There's a classic example back there of what happens when we women get frustrated."

Mary Barsad didn't look like one of my usual lodgers. She was tall with blond hair pulled back in a ponytail, with a face that had more character than pretty would allow. She looked good, which was a real trick in the orange Campbell County Department of Corrections jumpsuit she was wearing. She had narrow, long-fingered, capable hands and had used them to cover her face.

"Would you like something to eat, Mary?"

She didn't say anything.

"Dog and I are starved."

Her face came up just a little, and I looked into the azure eyes as they settled on Dog. She was terribly thin, and a trace of blue at her temples throbbed with the pulse of her thoughts.

"No, thank you." She had a nice voice, kind, very unlike the one with which I'd just been dealing.

"It's chicken potpies till Monday—sure you won't change your mind?"

Her eyes disappeared behind the hands, and I was sorry to see them go. I hung an arm on the bars. "My name is Walt Longmire, and I'll only be gone for about twenty minutes, but if you need anything I've got a deputy right down the hall; her name is Victoria Moretti, but she goes by Vic. She might seem a little scary at first . . ." I trailed my words off when it became apparent that she wasn't listening.

I watched her for a moment more and then slipped out the back door and down the steps behind the courthouse to the Busy Bee Café. Dog followed. We walked past one of the bright, red-and-white signs that read KYLE STRAUB FOR SHERIFF, A MAN TO MAKE A DIFFERENCE. I thought about the newest political slogan to sweep the county—a man to make a difference; what did that make me, a man against making a difference? Whenever I saw the slogan, I felt as though somebody was walking on my grave without me fully being in it.

Kyle Straub was the sitting prosecuting attorney and had been running a vigorous campaign with signs, bumper stickers, and pins; I had seen all of them with an unsettling frequency. When it had come time to choose a homily for my own campaign, I'd proposed a slogan from Cato the Elder, CARTHAGE MUST BE DESTROYED, but that platitude had been quickly shot down by the local council.

I had supporters. Lucian Connally, the previous sheriff of Absaroka County, had put in an appearance at the local VFW and had loudly announced to any and all, "If you stupid sons-a-bitches don't know what you've got, then you don't deserve a sheriff like Walt Longmire anyway." Ernie Brown, "Man about Town," was the editor in chief of the *Durant Courant* and had caught our dispatcher Ruby in an honest moment where she'd stated flatly that she wouldn't elect the attorney as dogcatcher. It seemed as though everyone was doing all they could to make sure I would be elected in November—that is, everybody but me.

The first and only scheduled debate at Rotary had been something of a disaster despite my friend Henry Standing Bear's support. Kyle Straub had made a point of lobbying for a new jail as the centerpiece of his future administration, and the fact that we didn't have enough lodgers to support the facility the county had now had done little to dampen the enthusiasm for a new building out along the bypass. I had failed to take into consideration how many contractors filled the rolls of Rotary.

It was the middle of October, and there was a star-filled twilight, with an evening that was cooling off nicely in promise of the cold to come. Autumn was my favorite season, but Cady had left and I was still unsettled by her departure—and now by the woman in my jail. I took a quick look at my pocket watch to see if I was going to make it before the café closed, and the brass fob with the Indian chief centered between opposed horse heads flapped against the pocket of my jeans. There were more than just a few leaves dropping from the cottonwood trees that surrounded the courthouse, and I crunched through a few piles on my way to the Bee.

Dorothy Caldwell had been keeping the café along Clear Creek open later to take advantage of the tourist trade, but all that might have dried up with hunting season almost over. If she'd already closed, it meant the potpies, which bordered on cruel and unusual punishment for the lot of the Absaroka County Sheriff's Department staff, never mind for Dog.

I paused at the open door of the all-but-empty café. "Can I bring him in?"

Dorothy, the owner/operator, turned from scraping the grill to regard me and beast. "It's against the law."

"I am the law, at least for another couple of months."

"Then I guess its okay."

I sat on my regular stool nearest the cash register; Dog sat in the space between the counters and looked at Dorothy expectantly. She reached into a stainless steel container, plucked out a piece of bacon, and tossed it. In one snap, it was gone. I looked down at the brute with the five-gallon shaggy red head, big as a bucket. "It's like the shark tank at Sea World."

"How many?"

I noticed she didn't bother to ask of what; I hadn't seriously picked up a menu in the place in years. "Three."

She took a frying pan as big as a garbage-can lid down from the hanger above. "You got a lodger?"

"Transport from over in Gillette." I glanced back out onto the deserted main street and could imagine how much the three of us looked like some high plains version of Hopper's *Nighthawks*.

She dumped a few tablespoons of bacon grease into the heating pan; like all things bad for you, it smelled delicious. She took out three large strips of round steak and began pounding them with a meat mallet, then dipped them in milk and dredged them in flour seasoned with salt, pepper, and just a touch of paprika.

I caved. "I take it chicken-fried steak is the usual?"

She tossed the strips of battered meat into the frying pan and dropped some fries into the deep fryer as Dog looked on. "The special. When are you going to get it right?"

I opened the file that I had put on the counter and studied the few pages that the Campbell County deputies had brought with the woman. "Make sure you include ketchup packets."

"Vic?"

"Yep."

The next question didn't sound completely innocent. "What's she doing working late?"

"Prisoner's female."

She leaned against the counter and looked down at the file, her salt-and-pepper locks hiding her eyes. "Mary Barsad?" Her cool hazel eyes reappeared and met with my gray ones.

"Ring a bell?"

She picked up an oversized fork and expertly turned the steaks. "Only what I read in the papers. She's the one that shot her husband after he killed her horses, right?"

I shrugged at the report. "The motivating factors are not mentioned, only the grisly consequence." I looked at the threadbare corner of my shirtsleeve—I had to get some new duty shirts one of these days. "What's the story on the horses?"

"The official one is lightning, but the rumor is he locked them in the barn and set it on fire."

I stared at her. "You're kidding."

She shook her head. "That's the story down the lane. He was a real piece of work, from what I hear. You must have been fly-fishing with Henry when the story broke; it was in all the papers."

"Where'd this happen?"

"Out your way, in Powder River country. She and her husband had that really big spread across the river near the middle prong of Wild Horse Creek."

"Rough country." I thought about it. "The L Bar X. I thought what's his name, Bill Nolan, had that."

"Did, but the rest of the story is that this Barsad fella came in a few years back and started buying everybody out. Took the old place and built a log mansion on it, but I guess that pretty much burnt down, too."

"The report says that he was shot while he was asleep. He set the barn full of horses on fire and then went to bed?"

She pulled up the fries, dumped them in the styrofoam containers along with the steaks, three small mixed salads, and the packets of ketchup and ranch dressing. "Seems kind of negligent, doesn't it."

"He burned the horses alive?"

She placed three iced teas in a holder, along with the requisite sugar, and slid them across the counter with the meals. "That's the rumor. From what I understand, the finest collection of quarter horses this country's ever seen."

I got up, and Dog started for the door; he knew full well that the real begging couldn't start till we got back to the jail. "Barrel racer?"

"Cutter, but I think she also did distance riding. I understand she was world-class."

"She looks it." I gathered up the movable feast. "What the heck was she doing with this . . ." My eyes focused on the file before closing it and placing it on top of the stack. ". . . Wade Barsad?"

I paid the chief-cook-and-bottle-washer, and she gave me back the change. I stuffed it into the tip jar. Like the usual, it was our ritual.

"They don't all start out as peckerheads; some just get there faster than others."

I paused at the door. "Is that experience talking?"

She hadn't answered.

October 27, 11:35 A.M.

The dark-eyed bartender's name was Juana, and she was from Guatemala. Her son, Benjamin, the little outlaw from the porch, was half Cheyenne and now sat on the bar stool next to me. He was nursing a Vernor's ginger ale and was hypnotized by *Jonny Quest* on the Cartoon Network. I didn't even know that such a thing existed. The lawgiver who passed the privy proclamations had disappeared.

"John; I bet you're a John." The young woman stole a sip from the straw of her son's soda and glanced at me. "Nope, too plain. William maybe, or Ben." She rested her elbows on the bar and looked at the boy. "Maybe he's a Benjamin, like you."

"He's an Eric." The child's voice carried so much certainty that even I almost believed him. He sidled up on one cheek and pulled a business card from the back of his kid-sized Wranglers and handed it to his mother.

I recognized the card—it had rested on the seat of my rental.

She read. "Eric Boss, Boss Insurance, Billings, Montana."

I looked at the little man and thought about the nerve it had taken to reach into a vehicle that contained Dog. His Cheyenne half was showing. "Did you get that out of my car?"

He didn't say anything but received a sharp look from his mother and a full Spanish pronunciation of his name. "Ben-ha-meen?!"

He shrugged. "It was unlocked."

She was on her way around the bar when he launched off the stool and was out the door like a miniature stagecoach robber.

She flung herself past me and across the room, yelling at

her son from the open doorway. *"Vete a la casa, desensilla el caballo, y vete directamente a tu cuarto."* The clatter of horse hooves resounded from the dirt street as she continued to shout after him. *"¡Escuchame!"* The young woman closed the screen door behind her and then crossed silently past me and back behind the bar. Once there, she slid the card across the surface. "I apologize."

"It's all right."

She gathered a remote and switched off the cartoon, where a giant eye with spider legs was chasing people around in the desert. She reached over to a burner for the coffee urn. "Well, that pretty much settles that mystery." I pushed my cup back toward her and watched as she refilled the buffalo china mug. "You're here about the house that burned down, the barn with the horses." She nudged the cup back. "That woman?"

I sipped my coffee—it was still surprisingly good—and collected the business card from the surface of the bar. "What woman is that?"

2

October 18: nine days earlier, morning.

The sheriff of Campbell County had laughed on the other end of the phone.

"Doesn't it strike you as odd, Sandy?"

"Everything in that Powder River country strikes me as odd. It's another world, Walt. Everybody's got police scanners; do you know what it's like to try and serve papers out there?" I could just imagine him seated in his luxurious leather chair in his wood-paneled office. What with all the energy development, I was beginning to believe the talk that Gillette would be the largest city in Wyoming in ten years.

I raised my eyebrows. "Yep, but setting your barn on fire and then going to sleep?"

Sandy Sandberg laughed again. He didn't take anything all that seriously—it was one of his charms—and being sheriff of a county as busy as Campbell would've given anybody ample opportunity for seriousness. "Yeah, well . . . they say it was lightning, but Wade Barsad was known to be kind of reckless."

I studied the thin, two-page report on my desk. "Not local."

"Oh, hell no. No man from around here would ever do that to a horse, let alone eight of 'em."

"Why kill the horses?"

"I think she cared more about them than she did him."

"That doesn't sound too difficult." Vic came in with her Red Bull, sat in my visitor's chair, and propped her tactical boots on the edge of my desk like she always did. "Sandy, you mind if I put you on speakerphone? Vic's here." I went ahead and punched the button; I knew Sandy Sandberg liked to work a big room.

His laughter tinkled from the tinny speaker. "How'd you like that little present I sent over for you, sweetheart?"

Vic looked up from her energy drink and raised her head a little so she could emphasize each word. "Fuck. You. Sand. Bag."

Sandy roared again. I interrupted before the two of them could get any further. "Where was he from?"

He took a breath to recover. ". . . Back east somewhere." The way he'd said it, he might as well have been talking about Bangkok, and I was sure it was for Vic's benefit.

"What about the woman—Mary?"

"Greenie from down in Colorado. She was one of those Denver Bronco girls, the ones that ride out onto the field after they score a touchdown? Not that the Donkeys have been doin' a lot of that lately . . ."

"Where'd the money come from?"

"Oh, she had some, but he had more. To hear him tell it, he had more money than the rest of the inhabitants of the Powder River area combined."

I stared at the receiver. "What makes you say, 'To hear him tell it'?"

Sandy laughed again. "You don't miss much, do you?" I waited. "We had a little visit from some investigators from the IRS about Wade owin' $1.8 million in taxes and penalties. We found about $742,000 in uncashed checks made out to him personally. DCI guys figured he was tryin' to keep it away from the revenue boys, but I think he was tryin' to keep it from his wife, since she'd already filed for divorce."

"She should have gotten herself and those horses out of there."

"Well, it was a race."

Talking with Sandy Sandberg was like sight-reading braille. "What's that mean?"

"Everybody in three counties wanted to kill that son-of-a-bitch—Bill Nolan bein' number two."

I'd gone to primary school in a one-room schoolhouse with a Bill Nolan; it had to be the same man. "What happened?"

"The bank was gettin' set to foreclose on the Nolan place, so he put the majority up for sale and saved a little spread for himself." I was sorry to hear that, knowing the L Bar X had been in Bill's family for four generations. "And do you know that rat-bastard Barsad wouldn't give Bill a right-of-way?"

"That's rough."

"They settled out of court, but Bill was home alone on his place the night somebody—and I mean anybody—could have ventilated Wade's head."

"I thought the wife confessed?"

"She did, but until we got the report back from DCI, it wasn't a sure thing."

"Anyone else on the short list?"

"Bill volunteered for a polygraph test and cleared it. There was another guy who showed up here recently and was working for Wade—fella by the name of Cliff Cly, who was in a bar over here tellin' everybody how he did it. Unfortunately for him, we happened to have an off-duty deputy in the bar at the time, and then fortunately for him we brought his ass in and gave him the lie detector, which detected that he was drunk and full of shit."

Sandy rustled some papers—I was getting the feeling the other sheriff was losing interest in a closed case.

"Hershel Vanskike might have been interested in killin' the bastard, too. He was looking after Barsad's herd, including what Wade had siphoned off the surrounding ranchers. From what we gathered, he hadn't paid the man in three months— just let him live in a trailer out by the old corrals and dipping tanks off Barton Road, where we're going to have the auction next week. Hey, do you need a tractor?"

"Anybody else?"

"What?"

"Anybody else who would want to kill him?"

"Oh, he screwed an old rancher, Mike Niall, by sellin' him a dozen barren cows. . . . Jeez, Walt, I'd tell you to just get out a Range Co-op telephone book and take your pick, but his wife confessed. Game over."

"What's DCI say?"

"The Damned Criminal Idiots say that her fingerprints were on the weapon, powder-trace elements on her hands, and that she signed a confession sayin' she shot him."

"Why use a .22?"

Sandy sighed. "It was handy? Hell, I don't know."

"Was it her rifle?"

There was a pause. "No, it was his varmint gun out of his truck—I think it was parked out front."

"He have any other weapons in the house?"

"Tons, but they were all locked up in a gun safe."

"Why would . . ."

"He was foolin' around with about three other women and that alone is enough to get your ass shot in that country." He laughed again. "Hey, Walt Long-arm-of-the-law, protector of lost women, lost dogs, and lost causes, I know what you're thinkin' and some rats need killin', but she made a mistake by getting caught—then she made a mistake by confessing, and now it's going to cost her the rest of her life."

It was silent, and I stared at the tiny, red light on the speakerphone. "Something just feels wrong." This was a sticky business and not my jurisdiction, so that was all I said.

Sandberg interrupted, as I hoped he would. "Walt?"

"Yep?"

"I don't have the time for this."

I looked up at Vic with her five sworn in the Philadelphia Police Department and her consequent experience in interdepartmental politics as she silently mouthed the words "Back off."

"I've already got one murder, one rape, two robberies, fifty-four cases of aggravated assault, forty-seven burglaries, and a hundred and eighty-six cases of larceny. I don't have time for mysteries that volunteer to solve themselves."

I had already formed an apology of sorts when the other

sheriff spoke again. "But hey, you wanna look into it, I'll pay your gas."

October 27, 7:32 P.M.
I stepped through the blackened timbers and tried to imagine what the ranch house must've looked like before it had burned. The binder that the real Eric Boss in Billings had given me said it was insured at over three million, which wouldn't come close to covering the cost of rebuilding the mansion, and there would be no money at all if the fire was deemed a case of arson.

Not that it seemed anybody would be rebuilding it.

Wade Barsad had spared no expense, but I figured the home's design had been his wife Mary's. The ranch homestead stood a mile and a quarter from the rough-hewn timber and moss-rock archways that trumpeted the entrance to the aspen-lined, red scoria ranch road of the L Bar X. The 7,516-square-foot "rustic" ranch house had been built with two-hundred-year-old timbers and two-foot-thick walls of golden-faced stone in a piazza-shaped plan that included a courtyard wrapped with verandas, open to a view of the Powder River.

I told Dog to stay on the rock patio as I carefully picked my way through the debris.

The nearest fire department was the volunteer one in Clearmont, and obviously they hadn't hurried in getting here; possibly they knew the man. The roof and supporting timbers were gone, but the majority of the heavy walls still stood with their windows blown out and shards of blackened glass scattered across the stone floors. I walked past the open front doorway, the side panels burnt and hanging loose on the hinges, the moonlight pulling the sheen from the flagstone walkway that led to where I'd parked the rental car.

Through an antique glass door that was curiously still intact, I crossed a greenhouse atrium that separated the public part of the house from the bedroom where the deed had been done. Burnt houses bring out the melancholy in me, but it was possible that burnt greenhouses were even worse. The withered, dead plants hung from the beds as if they had tried to limbo under the smoke to escape the flames. They hadn't made it. As I looked back from the door of the bedroom, I noticed the collective tracks of the Campbell County Sheriff's Department, those from the Division of Criminal Investigation, and those from the firefighters in the fine, black dust that covered everything.

The master bedroom suite was built over what must've been a root cellar, and most of the hardwood floor was gone, leaving only a vast hole that dropped to the charcoaled pit below. There was nothing left of the king-sized bed other than the inner frame and coils of the box spring. T. J. Sherwin and her DCI investigators must have had a time securing and processing the scene.

I stood there for a long while, looking into the abyss and wondering what the abyss was making of me. I tucked the folder under my arm a little tighter and turned, making my way back to the courtyard.

By the time I got there, I discovered that Dog's idea of "stay" was disinterestedly springing a few western cottontails from the brush. He wandered back in my direction when I called him, marking each stand of sage as he came, and finally rested his muscled behind on my foot. I ruffled his ears, my hand stretching a full octave across his massive head. I peeled some fur back to look at the bullet furrow across his thick skull. "Is that your idea of stay?" He smiled up at me, revealing rows of teeth that shone in the evening moonlight.

It appeared that with the prevailing wind from the river basin, the fire that was started at the barn had destroyed the main house, perversely leaving the courtyard. It was as if the elements had decided to ravage the enclosed areas but leave the open heart untouched.

It was not lost on me that the most obliterated area of Wade and Mary Barsad's house had been the bedroom.

There was an outdoor fireplace with firewood stacked nearby and a willow chair that yawned with an open seat, but I refused its invitation, walked to the edge of the patio, and carefully leaned on the hand-adzed timbers that supported the cedar shingles and copper gutters and downspouts. Part of this roof was still there and blocked the view of the thick stripe of the Milky Way that was just beginning to trace its girth across the twilight sky.

The courtyard wouldn't be a bad place to live; well, at least until a month from now when it would be filled with snow and the wind would attempt to blow the whiskers off your face.

It was getting chilly, so I looked at the fireplace again. It looked serviceable and almost as if it'd been used recently. Even if it hadn't, it wasn't like I was going to have to worry about burning the place down.

I glanced around, looking for a bit of fresh kindling, and

found a big bunch of tiny astrological scrolls that you see for sale in grocery-store checkout lanes. I noticed they were all Sagittarius—which was as far as my knowledge of astrology went—then wadded them up and tossed them into the makings of a fire. There were a few long-stem matches by the mantel in a tin container, and soon I had a blaze where no more than a month ago there had been far too much of the stuff to contain.

Dog, knowing a good thing when he saw one, curled up at the hearth and watched as I pulled the chair closer and unfolded the insurance binder to the middle where I had carefully concealed some faxed sheets from DCI. I was lucky that T.J., the wicked witch of the west, as she was known in some of Wyoming's law enforcement circles, had done the general on the deceased. She had included some disturbing and detailed photographs on how the rancher had gone not so gently into that dark night.

Six tangential shots from a Savage .22 automatic rifle had done the trick but, for all practical purposes, the first one had been enough.

Probably not a suicide.

Close range, but not that close—four feet to be exact—and there may have even been a little powder dispersal, but we would never know. The body of Wade Barsad had burned along with his home, his barn, and her horses. Dental records had hung the name on Wade's toe in lieu of upcoming DNA testing. I was just getting to the meat of the report when Dog growled with a sound as deep and resonant as a powwow drum.

I closed the report and listened to the soft pop of the fire and the chirp of the crickets. "Hello?" I placed a hand on Dog's back to keep him from disappearing into the darkness and into whatever it was out there. "I said hello."

The outline of a battered cowboy hat shifted from the partial shadow of the burnt juniper tree at the edge of the house, and I could see the octagonal barrel of a heavy rifle move in emphasis. "Make yourself at home, why don't'cha."

Dog growled again, but the repeater was cradled in the man's arms as he lit a hand-rolled cigarette, so I figured the threat from it wasn't too great. The glow showed orange on the large, flat face, stubbled with whiskers as prodigious as my own, and on a set of ears that pushed forward from an oversized, flat-brimmed, Powder River–style hat.

I rested the folder on my knee with the label facing out as he came closer. Dog continued to growl. I squeezed his neck and he stopped, even going so far as to sniff at the stained jeans of the stranger's leg as he stood there in the intermittent light of the fireplace. I tipped my own hat back and looked up at the fence-post-thin man, his clothes and entire body tapering down from the buttoned collar at his bobbing Adam's apple. "You burn my fortunes?"

"Excuse me?"

"My damn fortunes I had sittin' on that hearth, did you burn 'em?"

I remembered the tiny scrolls I'd used for kindling. "I'm afraid I did."

"Well, that's another trip to the Kmart." He said Kmart like it was Mecca and studied me for a while. "They told me you was askin' questions down at the bar, earlier tonight, and that you might be by."

"They?"

He didn't answer but leaned against a support timber with the old Yellow Boy wedged in his folded arms—I figured the Henry was probably a reproduction. "Lot of insurance money, I guess."

"Around three million for the house alone."

He glanced at the folder on my knee again. "Some racket, I'll tell ya." I waited. "That stuff, jus' a protection racket near as I can tell." He took a puff on his cigarette, cupped in his hand European style. It was a gesture he'd probably learned from the local Basque sheepherders—with a name like Vanskike, the chance that he was Basque himself was slim. "I guess it's all jus' a big protection racket, the government, the insurance companies." He looked straight at me. "So, how come you're up here sneakin' around in the dark?"

"There was more light when I got here, and I guess I didn't feel like sitting in a motel room."

He pulled the wrinkled cigarette from his lips, flicking some ashes into the dried grass. "I can understand that." He nodded and looked off toward the river. "It's a nice spot. I been coming up here since the fireworks when the weather's good—sit in that very same chair and drink beer."

I took a deep breath and started to rise. "Well, we'll get out of your way . . ."

"No, no." He looked genuinely panicked and motioned for me to stay seated. "I don't get too many visitors, and sometimes I forget how to behave."

We were both silent, then I apologized. "I'm afraid I didn't bring any beer."

He continued to smoke and then smiled with more than a few teeth missing. "'At's all right, I did."

October 19: eight days earlier, night.

I had been seated at my desk alone, having sent Vic home to grab a shower before she pulled the all-nighter.

I opened the windows in my office and had just leaned back in my chair to enjoy the unseasonably soft breeze when I heard Dog get up from beside my desk and thump his over-sized paws to the door. The beast paused in the hall but continued on toward the holding cells. Since I had adopted Dog, he'd almost never left my side, unless it was for Ruby, and I knew she was home and in bed, so I got up to follow his trail when I heard a low, steady noise.

I flipped on the kitchenette light. It didn't give the flat, antiseptic quality that the fluorescent overheads did and wouldn't disturb Mary too badly if she was only crying in her sleep.

She was crying but was not on the bunk; she was standing by the bars with her head down. She paid no attention to me or to Dog, who was looking up at her. I took off my hat and stepped forward; there was a lone streetlight across the road that illuminated the sidewalk in front of Durant Elementary, and its light spilled from the windowsill and splashed against the side of her light-colored hair. She was still crying very softly, and I turned to look at her as her shoulders twitched and her voice echoed against the concrete floor in a low moan.

She had a maiden name, but it wasn't on the two-page report. "Mrs. Barsad . . ."

I knew that people made noises in jail, whether they were conscious of it or not. Angry sounds, boisterous sounds, sad sounds—some even sang—but as she continued, I could hear it was the wounded sound, the one that caused the stillness in my hands and the cooling in my face.

The one I couldn't stand.

"Mrs. Barsad?"

She wailed softly, and I could feel that she was in a place that I could never reach. I felt it in me, and it clawed its way up the inside of my spine. I knew that it would come out of my mouth like a regurgitation of emotion, if I let it.

I thought about the missing lovers and the dead parents, the friends and strangers that I had seen behind closed doors and closed eyelids. I had lost people too and had grown used to those surprise visits of the mind that froze my thoughts and my heart.

I stood there, staring down at her, until I became aware of the welling in my own eyes. "Mrs. Barsad?"

She had paused for a second as she'd inhaled. I barely made out the words that she repeated over and over, and over and over: "So-o-o girl, no . . . Oh, God . . . So-o-o girl . . ."

October 27, 9:05 P.M.

Hershel handed me one of the tepid beers he'd retrieved from the spot in the river that he used as a refrigerator as he sat with his back against the post. "There ain't a pit in hell deep enough and dark enough for that son-of-a-bitch."

I threw a couple more logs into the fireplace and dusted off my hands on my jeans before taking the beer. Dog lay down between us as a conciliatory gesture to the old cowhand, even going so far as to allow Hershel to pet his broad back.

"Dante reserved the lowest rings of hell for the betrayers." I popped open the can and took a swig. "Rainier."

He looked at the fire. "Now, don't make fun of my beer."

"Mountain fresh, my favorite. Really." He nodded without comment, and I took a moment to study the Henry repeater leaning behind his shoulder. "Is that a real Henry?"

"Yes, it is." He smiled. "I found that gun back in the rocks up on Twentymile Butte at the Battlement."

"Can I see it?"

He continued to study me. "I don't know you that well, and my fortune is in this rifle."

I glanced at the fire. "You got a lot of fortunes."

"Used to."

I nodded and looked out toward the river. "Did you know Wade Barsad well?"

He sipped his beer with the cigarette still in the corner of his mouth and then let the can dangle as he supported his wrist on his bent knee. "Enough to not cross the street to piss on 'em if his guts was on fire."

I took another sip and thought about how much he sounded like my old boss, Lucian Connally; they would've been close to the same age. "Did you work for Barsad long?"

He sighed. "'Bout four of the longest years of my life." He reached down and stroked Dog's thick fur. "He didn't like animals, and I don't trust people that don't like animals. Hell, animals are the finest people I know." As if on cue, Dog rolled over and laid his head on the edge of the patio. The cowpoke smiled and talked to the nearest animal while rubbing the beast's belly. "You like to scare the shit out of me, you monster. I thought you was gonna eat me alive."

"Where was he from?"

"Youngstown, Ohio. Ever been there?"

"Can't say that I have."

"Me neither, but they must breed some true-to-life sons-a-bitches and that's good enough reason for me to never go." He took another long draught of his beer. "Made all his money in some steel mill, stole it probably." His eyes were drawn to the river and the star-dappled sky. "Always talkin' about how he hated all this cowboy shit."

I set the insurance binder on the hearth and leaned forward, my elbows on my knees. "He hated animals, and he hated the West? That kind of strikes me as odd for a fella who buys a ranch in Wyoming."

He looked at me pointedly. "Hers."

I nodded. "Seems like an odd couple. Where'd they meet?"

"Some cuttin' event down in Las Vegas; he liked Las Vegas." He took a deep breath and let it out slowly, belching softly at the end. "He was a handsome booger and smart. Don't get me wrong, he had a boatload of cash and he could turn the charm on like a bug light whenever needed."

"Why'd she do it?"

His hand stopped on Dog, and he looked out into the darkness. "I don't think she did, but if she did, she come to it righteous." He stayed motionless, and I got the impression that the Powder River and the high plains sky was not what he was seeing. "I knew a couple once, up near Recluse; fella was out irrigatin' and come in for his supper and said somethin' about his wife's biscuits. She pulled an old long gun off the wall . . ." He gestured to the big carbine in his lap. ". . . not unlike this one, and splattered his brains all over the dinner table." It was silent for a moment. "She'd had enough and, brother, believe-you-me, Mary Barsad had had enough."

"Were you here the night it happened?"

He motioned with the stubble on his chin toward the hills to our right. "My trailer, back at the loading chutes. Saw the reflection of the fire in the window and heard the horses a screamin' and come runnin', but it was too late."

I nodded. "Was there lightning that night?"

He begrudged the answer. "Yep."

"The fire from the barn caught the house?"

"Yep."

"Where is the barn?"

"Opposite side from where you parked your car."

"You go in?"

He looked at me incredulously. "There wasn't no goin' in there."

"Where was she?"

I glanced back at the blackened and cavernous rubble.

This time he motioned with the beer can and the cigarette. "Out there in the grass, with that varmint rifle across her lap." He took the last puff off the cigarette, stubbed it out on the ground beside the patio, and then stuffed the butt into his shirt pocket. Evidently, Hershel Vanskike was a respectful man, of what I wasn't quite sure, but I had suspicions. "Her head was down, and it was almost like she was asleep. I touched her shoulder and she looked up at me and said that the horses were dead and that she'd killed him."

"Did she show any remorse?"

"Nope, just said it like she was talkin' about the weather." He studied me for a moment longer. "You sure do ask a lot of questions about people, for a guy that's concerned with the insurance. You tryin' not to pay?"

"No."

"He's dead, and she's goin' to prison; who gets the money?"

"You tell me."

"He's got a brother back in Youngstown."

"Son-of-a-bitch?"

He nodded his head. "Most likely."

We both laughed. "I'm just curious." I took a sip and changed the subject. "She was good on horseback?"

He warmed to that line of conversation and smiled. "You ain't never seen anything like it. She was Junior Cutting Title in Las Vegas, National Cutting Horse Association Super Stakes Champion. Brother, she was the best I ever seen—and I seen some." He took the last swallow of his beer and crushed the can in his hand. "She could separate a horsefly from a cow's ass."

I took a breath of my own and was sorry to take us back to the sadness. "Why burn all the horses?"

The older man resumed petting Dog, then stopped and shook his head with his eyes closed. "I'll be damned . . ."

"What?"

His eyes opened, and he looked up at me. "You insured the horses, too, didn't you?"

I hadn't insured anything, but Eric Boss had. "Well . . ."

"And her?"

I strained to understand. "Mary?"

"No, *her*." I continued looking at him blankly as the fireplace crackled and popped with small explosions. "Them horses . . . Barsad didn't burn 'em all."

3

October 27, 10:30 P.M.

Her name was Black Diamond Wahoo Sue, and she was not your usual championship cutting horse; first off, she was a she and, secondly, she was dark as a starless night. A gorgeous and rare solid black in coat, mane, tail, and legs, the big gal had won every event in which she had competed and was the best in the cutting, reining, and reined cow-horse circles. The mark of a great mare is her ability to produce horses that are possibly even better than herself; Black Diamond Wahoo Sue had done so to the tune of more than twenty-five million dollars, which went a long way in explaining why she was underinsured at close to a cool five million.

Mary raised her, and she was the horse Mary had ridden at the National Cutting Horse Association championships, her pride and joy, and the thing that Wade Barsad had focused his considerable hatred upon before that fateful night when he'd burned alive not eight horses, but seven.

We walked our party around to the opposite side of the house and down a flat path that shone with mica in the moonlight. The beer supply had run dry; four for him and two for me, after which Hershel Vanskike produced a fire-damaged bottle of single malt Laphroaig, vintage 1968, from behind the fireplace. So far I'd declined, 1968 having not been the best of years for me.

The iron gate was soot-covered but still clung to the archway that framed the desolation of the burnt barn. It must've been something before the fire, but there wasn't much left. The photos in the insurance binder showed a log barn handcrafted with natural timbers and small, mission-style lights inset with amber glass that had given the place a friendly bronze glow. I'm not sure if it was the photography or the story, but the barn was more inviting than the house, or used to be.

The heat must have been terrific, and it was easy to see how the flames had jumped from the barn to the cedar shingles of the house. I stared at the charred timbers and piles of rubble.

It looked like a mass grave.

"Did they leave them in there?"

He socked himself another from the bottle and swung it toward me, a little of the precious, tawny liquor sloshing from the opening at the neck. I held out a hand in abstinence. "No, thanks."

"Don't blame you, stuff's horrible; needs a little Dr. Pepper." The old cowboy nodded with a liquor-soaked solemn that he'd probably never shown for any human being. "Smelled like cooked horse for days; I can still smell it." He weaved there for a moment. "I had my rifle 'cause I wasn't sure what was going on, but you couldn't even see to shoot the poor things."

Dog sniffed at the burnt grass, looked at the wreckage, then at the drunken cowhand, and backed up and sat on my boot. "And Wahoo Sue?"

He licked the paper on another cigarette and twisted it together a little unsteadily as I held the bottle for him. "Damn, she was a runner." He pulled another Blue Tip match from his hatband and lit the cigarette, cupping it in his hand again. "She won that forty-mile Durant-to-Absalom overland race, just run off and left the rest of 'em—first time a woman ever won it."

He took a puff, and I could hear the soft pop of his inhale. He brought his head up and took the bottle back, his voice taking on an animation that it hadn't contained before.

"She was a cutter, but that horse would race anything. I seen her race other horses, pronghorn antelope, even pickup trucks on the county road. She wasn't the biggest, she wasn't even the fastest, but she had something in her that wouldn't let her get beat. You can see that in an animal." He continued to look at me through the faint glow of the ember by his chin and the complex sugars racing through his veins. "And some people."

"What happened?"

"'Bout a week before . . ." He looked back at what was left of the barn and swigged down a mouthful of single-malt with a squint. "Before this, Wade loaded that horse up into a trailer, laid a .30-30 in the seat of his truck, and then drove off. He went out onto BLM land, south and east toward Twentymile Butte, toward the Battlement. He come back, but the horse didn't."

October 19: eight days earlier, night.

Mary Barsad's eyes had been open, but I wasn't sure that anyone was home.

I stepped around the partition wall and could see her perfectly framed in the illumination of the streetlight outside the window—she was standing at the bars, her slender fingers wrapped around the steel.

Her face had turned a little, but she spoke to the diffused light. "Somebody closed the gates."

I glanced down at Dog and noticed he was looking up at me. "Mary?"

"Did you feed Sue like I told you?" Her voice had a detached, otherworldly quality to it.

"Mrs. Barsad?"

"We'll have to wrap that tendon on her—it looks like she's favoring it." Dog woofed at her, and I gave him a nudge with my leg. She smiled but continued to gaze out of the cell and just to my left.

"Mary, are you all right?"

I watched as her lip trembled and a sob broke loose from her throat. "The horses . . . there's something wrong with the horses."

I didn't know that much about sleepwalking but had heard that it wasn't wise to awaken someone in that condition, so I decided to play along. "The horses are fine, I just checked on them." Dog looked up at me again, and I shrugged.

She turned and was looking me in the face now. "They're hurt."

I placed a hand on the bars. "No, I just checked and they—"

She came closer to me and trailed her hands across the surface of the bars as though she were playing a silent harp. "There's a fire."

"No, there's no fire."

"I smell it. . . . Can't you smell it?"

Her hand shot out and gripped my sleeve, and Dog mumbled a bark again. "Mrs. Barsad, there's no fire." She took a deep breath, and the air caught about halfway. "I just checked, and the horses are all right." She continued to pick at my sleeve, her eyes imploring. "I think Sue might have aggravated that tendon again, so I wrapped it like you said."

Her eyes stayed steady with mine and, with three consecutive blinks, the muscles around her mouth relaxed. She finally smiled and let out a cautious laugh. "She's okay then?"

"Yes, ma'am."

She let go of my sleeve and stood there. "That's good. She's tough."

"Yes, ma'am." She didn't move, and I looked into the shine of her eyes. "Maybe you should get some sleep?"

She nodded, turned, and crossed back to the bunk. "You'll let me know how she is?"

"Yes, of course."

She sat, tucked her legs back under the county-issued blanket, and turned away from me toward the concrete-block wall. "Thank you, Hershel."

There was a disassociated quality to the entire conversation, and I stood there thinking about what had been said. I finally nodded, patted Dog on the head, and turned to go back to my office. Vic stood in the doorway with two cups of coffee. "Who the fuck is Hershel?"

I shushed her, and we took our coffee into the reception area near Ruby's dispatch desk. I took a sip from my chipped Denver Broncos mug and sat on the bench. "She sleepwalks."

"No shit."

Vic sat next to me, Dog curled up in front of us, slowly rolling over onto his back. "Do you know anything about that stuff?"

"A little. My brother used to do it." She sipped her coffee.

"Which one?"

"Michael. When he was a kid he used to get up and walk around the house with this dopey expression on his face. He grew out of it, sorta." She lowered her mug and looked at me. "My mother says my uncle Alphonse says my father used to do it; it's supposedly genetic."

I leaned back and listened to the thin, wooden stays of the bench squeal. "Is it dangerous to wake them up?" I thought about the episode I'd just witnessed.

Vic shrugged. "I don't know. I don't think we could ever get Michael to wake up." She watched me. "I'm still not sure we have." I didn't laugh at the joke, and she continued to study the concern that rested on my face. "What'd she talk about?"

"Horses."

She petted Dog's belly with the toe of her boot. "That would make sense. There are environmental factors that can bring sleepwalking on—insomnia, tension, post-traumatic stress disorder, or dissociative states—"

"It all goes back to those horses that got burned alive."

"That'd be pretty traumatic." She nodded and took another sip. "For the sake of more than conversation, I'll ask again, who the fuck is Hershel?"

I chewed on the inside of my lip; it was a habit I would con- quer someday. "Sandy mentioned that the man who worked for the Barsads was named Hershel—Hershel Vanskike, to be exact."

October 27, 11:07 P.M.

Hershel Vanskike took two reasonably steady steps and then planted face-first into the dried grass off the pathway.

Dog turned and glanced up at me, unsure of the situation. I looked at the old puncher lying there, unmoving, and at the broken bottle on the flagstone. "Well, I think he's had enough."

Hershel had said he would just ride his horse home, but it was evident that he couldn't sit a horse let alone ride one. I saw that the aged gelding was tied off to a fence post as I carried the unconscious cowboy to my car. I stood him up against the side of the Lincoln and held him there while I opened the passenger door.

He started mumbling, but I ignored him, stuffed him into the seat, wrapped the seat belt around him, and clicked it in place. I tossed the insurance folder into the back with Dog and then shut the door and looked at the horse. I took a length of yellow nylon rope that the Campbell County sheriff's office had used to block off the drive and approached the bay. He crow-hopped, laid his ears back, and looked at me.

I stood there with the rope in my hands and tried to figure out what I was going to do when he lowered his head and stretched it out toward me. I didn't move and watched him as the big, prehensile lips approached my face. I had a brief moment of panic, thinking that he might bite, when he took in a great breath and sniffed at me. I thought he was just smelling me, but I noticed that his breathing was matching my own and that he was breathing my breath. He took a step closer as I threaded the rope through the bridle and looked him in the eye. "You are one weird horse."

After that, he seemed eager to leave, and I couldn't blame him, considering the recent incidents.

Dog sat in the back and watched as I drove slowly, keeping the car under five miles an hour, as the bay kept pace behind us with the nylon rope held in my hand, dangling by the door from the open window.

It took the better part of a half-hour to get to the Barton Road corrals, and once we got there, there wasn't much. An old sheep wagon was parked beside them, and the rounded top of the wagon gave off a silver sheen in the moonlight, bisected by the shadow of a pole where an electric cord was strung from an attached four-way plug. A soft yellow glow overhung the rear door where a few leftover miller moths battered themselves against the bulb inside the dish-shaped, porcelain fixture.

I parked the car and left Hershel sound asleep in the passenger seat.

I gathered the rope into a loop as I walked back to the bay and led him into the corral. After the same ritual of breathing my breath, I untied him. He stood there, waiting to be unsaddled, made a passing sniff, and then allowed me to pull the leather strap on the front cinch and the rear. I hooked the opposite stirrup on the horn and lifted the saddle onto the nearest pole. I took off the blanket and bridle and watched as the bay walked to the center of the fifty-foot ring and kneeled down to roll over, wiggling on his back with all four legs in the air. Half a roll, as the old cowboys say, and you've got a thousand-dollar horse; all the way over and you've got a fifteen-hundred-dollar one. Hershel's went over one way and then all the way back—a two-thousand-dollar horse.

It looked like it felt good.

I walked back over to the saddle and pulled the antique repeater from the scabbard. It was indeed the real McCoy. I examined the rough-worn weapon, the brass receiver glowing dully in the starlight as did a small plaque, screwed into the stock, which read CORPORAL ISAIAH MAYS, 10TH CAVALRY, CONGRESSIONAL MEDAL OF HONOR, JUNE 18, 1892. In smaller print were the words GALLANTRY IN THE FIGHT BETWEEN PAYMASTER ROBERT EDWARDS'S ESCORTS AND ROBBERS.

I studied the scratches, chips, and dents—it hadn't been treated like a museum piece, but it was one. I carried the historic rifle with me to the sheep wagon.

I'm smart about hauling people because I've done enough of it. I opened the door of the wagon so that I could carry Hershel to his bed unimpeded, propped the Yellow Boy in the corner, and started to go back outside to the vehicle to get the old cowboy. I stopped when I saw the far wall.

In the haloed light from the bulb behind my head, I could see pictures taped, pictures of Mary Barsad, hundreds of them. I leaned in and took a closer look. They were all from magazines, some dating as far back as the seventies: photographs of the woman when she'd ridden a white stallion during football games, some of her on cutting horses, and a few from when she must have been a print model. I studied the glossy surfaces and the stunning young woman. She had a broad smile and high cheekbones that were emphasized by her thinness, high-sky blue eyes, and long blond hair. She was a beauty, but I had to admit I preferred the edition who was in my jail. She was older and stiffer, but age had seasoned her and her grief had humanized her.

Mary had even starred in a Rainier beer ad. She was seated on a horse and trailed a six-pack tied off with a latigo strap. She had turned and looked at the camera and was all hair, teeth, and sex. Personal tastes notwithstanding, it was enough to stop your heart.

The wall was bordered with more of the little astrology scrolls that I'd used to start the fire at what was left of the Barsad ranch. I glanced around and clicked on a ceramic space heater. It was a desperate and lonely looking place, slightly smaller than the holding cells back at my jail, and the photos only made it worse.

He was still out cold. I carried him in, accidentally knocking his flat-brimmed hat off in the doorway, and laid him on the bunk. I pulled off his boots, shoved his stocking feet under a wool blanket, and pulled the scratchy fabric up to his chin. He sighed deeply as I retrieved his sweat-stained hat and carefully placed it over the pale forehead above the suntanned face and closed eyes.

I turned the heater on to medium and switched off the light, closed the door, and walked back to the car. Dog was driving. I had rolled all the windows down on the long trip over, and his head rested on the lip of the windowsill. I petted him and listened to his tail thwack the leather seat. "I'm tired; you tired?"

The tail thumped harder, and I looked at the sky and the condensation from my breath. It was going to get cold, and I was glad I'd turned the heater on for the old cowpuncher.

I was still watching the horizon when the bay in the corral snorted, and I followed his eye back, away from the river. We were both looking south and east, toward Twentymile Butte. It was big country in the thunder basin, a place where a person could get away with a lot and had. Like a giant, high-altitude frying pan in summer, it heated up during the day to well over a hundred degrees, but then, in accord with the extremes of its nature, plummeted past freezing at night. If you were going to kill, it seemed like the place for it.

I could hear the noise of a large vehicle coming up the road behind me. I turned and waited as it crested the hill and slowed to about twenty. The brights clicked on and, with the curve of the road, the headlights were pointed straight at me.

It was a new truck, big and red, a one-ton duellie with an extended cab. It bristled with oversized wheels and tires, fender flares, and a grill guard. It looked for a moment as if the truck were going to stop, but the big Dodge accelerated slightly at the curve, the Cummins diesel clattering along on the gravel road toward the Powder River, and I looked at the reflection of myself in the tinted window as the truck disappeared over the next hill, the next, and the one after that.

It didn't have any plates.

I tossed the rope onto the passenger-side floor and made Dog move over. As we drove back into Absalom, I mused on the thin line between smitten and stalking. It was obvious that Hershel had some kind of crush on his former employer and I figured it was innocent, but it wouldn't hurt to have Ruby run a check on the old fellow.

The outpost of a town along the Powder River was still awake when I parked the rental alongside the railroad tracks.

I was tired, but I had work to do and it was possible that a portion of the work might be in The AR.

I reached in the open window to get the insurance binder and popped it into the trunk to keep company with my large duffel and a small hard case. I rolled the windows almost up, leaving an opening for Dog, and massaged my temples in anticipation of the headache that was beginning to hit me like a short-handled shovel. I'd have to make an appointment with Doc Bloomfield about these headaches one of these days.

I locked the car, set the alarm so that it wouldn't go off with movement inside, took a deep breath, and told Dog not to play with the radio; it was our joke—he knew he could play with the radio if he wanted.

It was a mixed lot in The AR, and I had to admit I was a little disappointed to see the middle-aged lawmaker in the Sheridan Seed Company hat behind the bar rather than the young woman. He ignored me as I took the stool nearest the door and propped my elbows on the particleboard. Mercifully, the jukebox was turned down low, and the television was tuned to the weather and on mute.

There were a couple of old ranchers sitting in the gloom at one of the tables, two younger fellows playing eight-ball near the boxing ring, and a large, surly-looking individual in a two-day beard, sunglasses, and a stylish black straw hat at the other end of the bar. He was talking to an elaborately tattooed young woman who held his arm and pressed her hip against his. I smiled and nodded toward them, and they smirked at me.

"What'a ya want?"

I turned, looked at the bartender, and my headache worsened. "The simple, gracious companionship of my fellow man?" He didn't say anything and continued to stare at me. "Rainier."

He fished a can out of the cooler and set it on the counter. It was common to have can-only bars in the rougher areas of Wyoming—nobody ever got hurt throwing a can, and nobody in this part of the world ever threw a full one. "Buck-seventy-five."

I pulled two ones from my jacket pocket and flicked them onto the bar. "Keep the change." He glanced at me without altering the look on his face and then took the bills and walked away. I'd meant it as an insult, but I wasn't sure he'd taken it that way. "What happened to the girl who was here this afternoon?"

He punched the numbers on the cash register, and the drawer came open. He shut the drawer and stuffed the money in his shirt pocket. "She don't work here no more."

"She quit?" He didn't answer but continued back to the area I assumed was the kitchen and disappeared.

I sighed and kneaded the back of my neck. There was a piece of paper taped to the bar's surface announcing the Friday Night Fights, Powder-River-Pound-Down-Tough-Man Contest that had a list of about a half-dozen names.

Jesus wept.

The can was cool, and I held it to my left temple in an attempt to stall the headache that continued to surge there. I wondered if I was doing any good with all of this covert stuff. Then I started wondering about the dubious judgment and apparent difficulties of going undercover in a town of forty people.

"You lost?"

I turned and looked at the surly-looking fellow with the woman attached to his arm and hip, and they both smirked again. I lowered the can. "Nope."

"I wouldn't drink that horse-piss on a bet."

I popped the tab on the can and raised it in salute. "Expense account—don't want to cost the company too much."

He lowered his sunglasses and stared at me from under the brim of his stylish hat. With half-eyes evident, he looked like one of those drugstore cowboys who sing shitty songs and sell pickup trucks. "Those insurance companies make enough money, why don't you buy all of us a drink?"

I sipped my beer. "I'm only here for one."

He glanced at the bottle blonde. "Seems like I've paid enough money in premiums for one lousy drink."

It was quiet in the bar except for some of the aforementioned modern country music that couldn't decide what it wanted to be when it grew up and moved to Branson. I put the can back on the stained surface of the cheap bar and looked at the names listed on the sign-up sheet for tomorrow night's fights—the first name was of interest. "Like I said, I'm only here for one."

I heard the stool's legs rub against the floor as he pushed out and then walked toward me. I waited as he pulled the next seat over and sat facing me. "I can't believe I have to beg a man to buy me a beer." He turned and looked back at his girlfriend as she continued to smile with only half her face. "Shit, it's common decency and western hospitality to buy a round."

I continued to study the bar and, absently, the sheet of paper. My head was killing me now, and this character wasn't making it any better. "Well, then, why don't you?"

He was silent for a second and then continued. "I did . . . earlier."

"Well, I'm sorry I missed it."

"Leave him alone, Cliff."

I recognized the voice and turned my head just a little to see the green-eyed rancher that I'd met at the bridge earlier in the afternoon.

"Oh, he looks like a big boy. I bet he can take care of himself."

Mike Niall countered as I looked down and closed my eyes in an attempt to loosen the grip of the pain in my head. "Yep, I bet he can. As a matter of fact, I bet he could stick his boot so far up your ass, your breath'll smell like Kiwi shoe polish, but you work for me now and if you think I'm going to buck bales by myself tomorrow morning, you've got another think comin'."

I could feel the drunken cowboy's breath on the side of my face. "Are you a fighter, mister?"

The blonde still looked straight ahead but spoke up. "Kick his ass, Cliff."

I finished off my beer in one swig and placed the empty can back on the bar. There wasn't anything here for me, my head hurt, I was tired, and it was possible that I'd lose my patience, so I figured the best thing for it was to go get Dog and duffel and head for my bed, which was only four doors down.

I tried to remember if I had any aspirin in my suitcase.

I started to rise and turn, but he placed a powerful and young hand on my shoulder. I continued up as he stood, and we were very close. I was sober and he wasn't, and that was probably something he was used to, but I was bigger than he was, and that he wasn't.

You always register the hands. His were occupied, one on my shoulder and the other hitched in his pocket. And register the eyes. One was focused on my face, and the other a little right.

The mechanics of twenty-four years on the job fall into place in these situations, and you don't have to think about taking the hand on your shoulder by the base and twisting it in a reverse wrist lock that plants his face suddenly and securely on the surface of the bar, about the second hand that pins his neck, and the boot that kicks his feet out and spreads them so that he has no leverage to resist.

Drunks can be amazingly intuitive, however, and as I stood there thinking, I was sure he could see the entire scenario playing out in my tired face. His eyes widened a little and then stayed set on mine, his hand still on my shoulder. The bottle blonde had turned and was looking at both of us and it dawned on him that he couldn't back down, not now. "I'm a fighter."

The rancher spoke again. "Cliff?"

I didn't say anything, so he repeated it. "I'm a fighter—" He didn't sound so sure about it this time and pulled his hand off my shoulder. He stabbed a finger at the piece of paper Scotch-taped on the bar. "That's me, right there, Cliff Cly. Number one on the list, and you know why that is?"

I still didn't say anything.

"'Cause I'm the toughest bastard on the Powder River." The rancher behind me snickered, and the self-proclaimed toughest man on the Powder River with the weakest lineage shifted over to get a look at him. "What the hell are you laughing at?"

It was silent for a second. "I'm gettin' a head start on laughing before you get licked. You're drunk, Cliff. Sit down."

"Screw you, old man."

I heard the chair move and could just make out the shot glass Mike Niall had out on the surface of the bar to my right. "Barkeep!" I could see him approaching from the kitchen as the older rancher continued. "Cliff, if I was you I'd save myself for tomorrow night, 'cause I think you got your work cut out for you."

The young man breathed a response. "I can kick the shit out of every man on that list." His eyes shifted back to mine. "You wanna put your name on that list, mister?"

"Is there a problem?" The bartender was just at the other side of the particleboard now, and I could see his hands resting on the shelf that held the baseball bat. I was relieved it wasn't the next shelf down that held the Winchester pump.

Niall was the first to speak. "Gimme another shot, Pat." The bartender looked at the two of us for a moment more and then reached behind him for a bottle of Wild Turkey. "There's a couple of those boys you might have a little trouble with."

"Like who?"

Pat poured, and Niall sipped his shot and returned it to the bar. "Well, that big buck that came in here this afternoon and gave everybody the hard eye for one." His eyes drifted toward me. "Big Indian fella came in, didn't say a word to nobody— just put his name on the list and turned around and walked out."

I smiled, and Cliff Cly misinterpreted. "You think that's funny, mister?"

I looked down at the list and continued smiling as my headache lessened just a little. It figured that the other toughest bastard on the Powder River with a lineage that stretched back into the history of this country before there was a country would find a way to provide backup even when it hadn't been requested.

"I asked you a question."

I looked at the cowboy for a moment more and then stepped past him and toward the door. I left behind the piece of paper on the bar that announced the Friday Night Fights, Powder-River-Pound-Down-Tough-Man Contest, where the last name on the list was Henry Standing Bear.

4

October 20: seven days earlier, late morning.
I had read the report that'd been faxed from the FBI field office in Denver.

Vic stood over my desk and fidgeted as I looked up from the eighteen pages. "You want me to read aloud?"

"I've already read it."

"So, what does it say?" My undersheriff's distillation was always more entertaining than the reports from the Feds.

She crossed around the desk and sat in her usual chair. "If she hadn't killed him, it looks to me like somebody else would've, or he would have been spending the rest of his life in a place where there are no light switches and you have to ask to go piss."

"He was in trouble with the Department of Justice?"

She sipped her coffee but didn't put her feet up like she usually did; instead, she sat there with her knees bobbing up and down. "Worse."

I sighed and forced more coffee into my system. "What's worse than the FBI?"

Vic pushed her nose to her cheek with her index finger.

Her voice was nasal, and she emphasized her South Philly accent. "He was made—the operative term here is *made*—the accountant in charge of operations for a casino operating firm, and in a matter of five years was able to siphon close to three million dollars out of the place."

"From the mob?"

She released her nose and smiled; she always smiled when she was relaying information like this, the way sharks smile when they see snorkelers wearing yellow. "Makes you wonder if he was dropped on his head as a child or if he was eating fucking paint chips like they were Cool Ranch Doritos, doesn't it?"

"Or he was a lot tougher than anybody gave him credit for." I flipped to the photo on page two; the deceased was inordinately handsome and could've been Italian except for his name. "Barsad doesn't sound particularly Italian."

She shook her head. "Wannabe. He started out as Willis Barnecke and worked for an accounting firm that did business for a number of casinos in Atlantic City, where he comes in contact with Joey 'Suits' Venuto and was offered a job. He took the job and the three-very-very-large, but when the Fed turned up the heat after a waterfront-based racketeering investigation where a competitor ended up shot to death in the trunk of his own car in Union, New Jersey, Willis's name started popping up on FBI wiretaps like Whack-A-Mole."

"He killed somebody?"

"Inconclusive." She set her mug on my desk and laughed. "He gets locked up for a DWI in Atlantic City but as thick as he was spreading it, you'd have thought he was the capo of capos. He drove around with an Italian flag on his car, for Christ's sake, and had Sinatra sound bites on his cell phone."

"How did he end up in Ohio?"

She continued to smile the saltwater crocodile smile. "This is the good part. Now, just on the offhand chance, the feds bring Willis in and tell him that they know he was the one that did the guy in Union—and lo and behold, Willis 'Canary' Barnecke starts singing like Frank at the Stardust. He names names from exit 9A to 16B on the Jersey Turnpike and assists the DOJ in obtaining about a half-dozen convictions. He gives up a lot but not everything because I guess he's just a certain brand of moron. Evidently, he had a list somewhere, and the DOJ wants it ever so bad."

"A list?"

"In his short time in the slam, he got in the habit of making kites—notes on tiny pieces of paper. The agent I talked to in Denver said Barsad never got out of the habit and that they found a lot of them, but not the one with the names." She paused, looked at her coffee, but didn't pick it up. "Now, what do you do with someone like that once they've finished testifying as much as they're gonna?"

The hand that was holding up my chin slipped over and covered my face. I peeked at her from between my fingers. "Witness protection?"

"Hello, Youngstown, Ohio, where Willis, now known as Wallace Balentine via the Feds, gets a job accounting for Central Ohio Steel, wears a tie, and reinvents himself as a pillar of midwestern society. Gets in touch with some of his old buddies in an attempt to make good, and in three years he accumulates another tidy nest egg before being fired and sued by the owners. Wallace Balentine settles out of court for an undisclosed amount, which the owners say is far less than the amount he embezzled, but that puts him in the papers and soon he has to reinvent himself once again, just a little farther west. First Las Vegas, then here."

I sighed the words. "Rancher Wade Barsad?"

She picked up her coffee. "Powder River, let'er buck."

I played with the handle on my mug. "It all makes sense; people have been hiding in that Powder River country for over a hundred years."

She stood when I did and walked out to the dispatch desk where Ruby was going over the reports from DCI. I leaned against the counter, and Ruby started to hand them to me. "Did you read them?"

She batted her neon-blue eyes over her lowered glasses with the pearl string, more than giving the impression of a second-grade schoolteacher. "Yes."

I nodded and then crossed to the wooden bench beside the steps, I preferred audio most times. "Let's have it, Sparky."

Ruby frowned—she disliked nicknames. "She doesn't stand much of a chance."

Vic had taken the report and was silently reading. She looked up. "His body was incinerated." She crossed her legs and leaned an elbow on the counter. "But they found all six melted slugs in his skull." Having sensed my dissatisfaction, Dog ambled from behind Ruby's desk and came around to rest his head on my knee. "The report said that the fire, possibly started by lightning, possibly not, actually began with the barn and then drifted over and burned the house."

"That must've been a fun one for T.J. and the bag boys."

I petted Dog's broad head. "Where was the confession taken?"

Ruby blinked and watched me. "At the scene."

I nodded and stared at the pattern of the old wooden floor and at the sway in the marble step at the landing. I thought about how many times my boots had hit that step, having first noticed it when my daughter had picked it as the favorite place to sit her six-year-old butt.

Cady hadn't called recently, and it was weighing heavily on me. She and Michael, Vic's younger brother, were seeing a lot of each other, and I was thankful for the attention the Philadelphia patrolman was lavishing on her, but I wondered where it was all leading. She'd been in an extremely bad relationship before Michael, one that had ended in her being severely injured. "And the statement was?"

Vic read from the file. " 'I dreamed of shooting the son-of-a-bitch, I dreamed about it every night and I finally did it. I shot him, I shot him six times.' "

It was quiet in the office as I repeated the words to myself. "I dreamed—"

I'd come to terms with the fact that Cady had gone back to Philadelphia, but it didn't make it any easier. I'd once again grown used to her company: the coffee in the mornings as I tried to get her to let me fix something for breakfast; the workouts at Durant physical therapy; the way she'd breeze into the office like Venus on the half-shell and pull everybody out of their bad moods; the way my deputies, Saizarbitoria, Double Tough, and Frymire, looked at her when they thought I wasn't watching them; the afternoons in my office where she would sit with her legs curled under her to read another book in her read-a-mystery-a-day plan; the quiet dinners at home.

"Walt . . ." I continued to pet Dog and glanced up at my undersheriff's unforgiving eyes. "The last part—she says she shot him. She says she shot him six fucking times."

I nodded and looked at the two of them. Ruby weighed in, and it made me a little irritable to see how quick they were to gang up. "Walt, she repeated the statement en route to the Campbell County jail and once again to the investigators and then to DCI. All in all, she confessed four times."

Vic shook her head at me. "Walt, this is a forcible felony with purposeful and premeditated malice." She paused for a moment. "Back in Philly, we used to call it a whack-job."

It was two hours later in Philadelphia but still early enough for me to make a phone call. I was being tough and not calling as much. I was doing really well and had held myself in check for a day at a time, only phoning her every other day. At least, I *thought* I had been doing really well, until the irritated Daaaa-dee on the other end told me otherwise.

I went back to studying the floor and quoted the passage of the legal description of homicide that Vic'd omitted. "You forgot of sound mind and discretion."

She interrupted, tossing the report back onto Ruby's desk. "Mary Barsad could be nuts, and I'm sure that's the tack that the defense attorneys are going to take, but she shot him in the head six times; she shot him till she ran out of bullets, and she shot him just to watch his head bounce on the mattress."

I studied the veins in the marble step and thought about the veins in Mary Barsad's temples and then about the thoughts that resided there, the things that visited her while she slept. I could feel words creeping into my mouth, words that weren't my own. ". . . But then begins a journey in my head, to work my mind when body's work's expired." I thought I'd said it to myself, but when I looked up they were both looking at me like I was the crazy person in question.

Ruby was the first to say something. "Walter—"

"Twenty-seventh sonnet."

"Christ." Vic had redirected her look from Ruby back to me. "Look, Shakespeare, I know you're looking for something to do since Cady left, but this isn't it. I hate to be the one to break the news to you after twenty-four years in law enforcement, but some people are in jail because they did it."

They had continued talking to me but their voices had diminished as if I were falling away from them even as their siren song continued.

October 27, 11:36 P.M.

Dog stood on the wooden walkway with me and stared into the empty motel room. I held the hollow-core door back with my right hand and looked around. There was a sagging single bed to the left and a dresser to the right, but what was of more interest was the bathroom door at the far end of the room, which was partially shut with the light on.

There were noises coming from the bathroom.

I stepped into the room and set my bag on the only chair beside a wobbly round table. Dog started toward the half-closed door, but I made a noise through my teeth that stopped him. There was the sound of metal on metal, a clanking of something into something, a shuffling noise, and then the door opened.

Juana, the young woman from the bar, stood there silhouetted in the backlight of the bare, sixty-watt bulb. I smiled as I flipped the light switch, illuminating dead flies in the childish cowboy-and-Indian sconce above the bed. Dog wagged. She blinked and didn't smile back at me or Dog. She held a toolbox in one hand and a pipe wrench like a weapon in the other. "Does he bite?"

"Nope."

She continued to look at the beast as he did his best to convey an even disposition by continuing to wag. She still held the wrench, which looked massive in her small but steady hand. "I don't like dogs."

I picked my bag up by the handles and tossed it onto the bed. It landed against the peeling painted headboard. "That's too bad; he likes pretty girls."

She didn't move. "I fixed your toilet."

I sat in the empty chair and listened to its recitative of creaks; I took off my hat and rested it on my knee. My head still hurt, and I massaged my eyes in an attempt to drive the headache down my neck. "Glad to be in compliance with the you-gotta-have-a-crapper-in-any-room-you-rent law."

"I felt guilty about charging you full price—figured you should have a bathroom that works."

I took a deep breath and looked up at her. She was placing the wrench into the toolbox. Dog sat on the worn, somewhat green carpet between her and the door. "I heard you didn't work here anymore."

She smiled and stiff-armed a lean on the dresser; it shifted. "Pat fires me about once a week, but nobody else'll work for him, especially for the nothing he pays."

I worked my jaw, lay the back of my head against the cool plaster surface of the wall, and rolled the dice of nationalism. "So, what's a nice Guatemalan girl like you doing in a place like this?"

"I'm not legal, and this place is under the radar."

I nodded and looked around. "It's that."

She continued to study me. "Are you okay?"

I took another breath. "I've got a headache."

She opened the toolbox and pulled out a small plastic bottle of aspirin, uncapped the container and tapped six small orange tablets into my outstretched hand. "Children's, so you'll need three times as many."

"You keep aspirin in your toolbox?"

"Plumbing gives me headaches." She started to turn. "They're chewable, but I'll get you some water."

"No need." I popped the pills into my mouth and swallowed.

She made a face. "How can you do that?"

I half-smiled, which probably looked more like a smirk. "Practice. At a certain point in life, aspirin becomes a major food group."

She carried the bottle over and sat on the corner of the bed; she was careful to avoid Dog. "You're making everybody around here nervous."

"Why's that?"

A rounded shoulder shrugged. "You just are." She flipped her hair. "Maybe it's because they think you're an insurance man."

"Hmm . . ." I swallowed again, feeling the aspirins finally hit bottom. "Do I make you nervous?"

"No, but I don't think you're an insurance man."

"What do you think I am?"

"A cop."

I nodded. "And what does Benjamin think?"

"He thinks you're a cop, too."

I yawned and covered my face with my hand. "How do the two of you figure?"

She put the bottle of aspirin on the bed and reached out to take my hat from my knee. "When you're a fugitive, you get a feeling for these things." She examined the inside of the black fur felt: "7 ¾-LONG OVAL. TEN X, H-BAR HATS, BILLINGS." The mahogany eyes, young but deep-stained with experience, looked back up at me. "If you're federal, and I'm hoping you're not, you flew into Montana and bought a hat so that you could blend in—or you're from the FBI field office in Billings or Cheyenne."

I stared at her, the pain in my head resurging. "What, you taking a mail-order course in how to become a private investigator?"

"Almost two years of law enforcement classes at Sheridan College." Both shoulders shrugged this time. "Ran out of money." I sat there without saying anything. "You could be state, maybe an investigator from DCI, but they were already here."

I nodded. "You and Benjamin have very active imaginations."

"Or you could be local, but I doubt it—the sheriffs around here couldn't find their butts with GPS."

"Really?"

"Yeah, strictly Barney Fife."

I smiled, this time with my whole mouth. "So, bringing the vast experience of two years of law enforcement education to bear—"

She placed my hat back on my knee and focused on my eyes. "Oops . . . maybe you are local."

I laughed. "So, did you know her—or him?"

"Both. I cleaned house for them for the better part of a year."

"What were they like?"

"Night and day." She leaned forward and rested her folded arms on her knees. "She was great. The house was always spotless when I got there, so I'd help her with whatever she needed help with, painting, planting—she had a greenhouse."

"I've seen it."

"She had orchids; I've never seen anybody around here with those."

"What about him?"

She made a face. "Loudmouth. If you were around him, you got to hear about just how wonderful he was. No matter what you'd done, he'd done it better. No matter where you'd been, he'd been there. That kind of stuff."

"I understand he had his fingers in a lot of pies?"

"He owned this place at one point—the motel and the bar. It got to where if you came in for a drink you'd have to listen to him, so people stopped coming. After he died, Pat opened it up again."

"Who owned it before Barsad?"

"Pat."

"Were they partners?"

She thought about it. "I'm not sure. Wade's business dealings were always a little complex."

"In what way?"

She shrugged. "Wade was involved in everything but had this habit of making lists and stuff on little pieces of paper he called kites."

"Is that what you called him, Wade?"

She studied me. "Sounds like you already know a little about what he was like."

"A little."

"He came on to me one time at their house; I passed, but he got more persistent and I got out a digging trowel to convince him of my lack of interest."

"Did it work?"

"For a while, but then you had to remind him; he was like that."

"I heard a few gals weren't exactly uninterested."

She was silent for a moment. "A few."

"Let's say I was interested, just for argument's sake; where would I find those women?"

She studied me more closely. "I'm not naming names because I'm not sure, but if I was so inclined I'd check the immediate vicinity of the ranch. Barsad wasn't one to go out of his way to look for female companionship; looking the way he did, he didn't have to."

"Kind of like a journeyman outfielder—he'd catch it if it came near him, but he wasn't going to stretch for it?"

"Exactly." She smiled. "There's an auction over at Bill

Nolan's tomorrow morning at ten—I'd imagine everybody'll be there. Might be an opportunity to meet all the players."

I leaned forward and rested my elbows on the armrests of the chair. "You still haven't answered the big question. Did she kill him?"

She sighed deeply and stood, looking down at me. "Are you from around here?"

"Hereabouts."

"There's a myth about this place."

I didn't try to hide my confusion. "This town?"

"No." She crossed to the dresser, fetched the toolbox, and stood there holding it between herself and Dog again. "More like the West, or maybe it's the world."

"Maybe it's my head; I'm not following."

"The myth is that you're supposed to be independent— you know, cowboy-up and all that stuff?"

"Yep?"

"I don't think they mean for that to apply to everybody, especially women." She nudged toward the door, but Dog didn't move. She gave me a side glance. "You wanna call him off?"

I made the same noise through my teeth, picked up the bottle of aspirin, and patted the swale of the bed; he was on it in an instant, wagging and smiling. "He was never on." I extended the plastic bottle toward her. "You want your aspirin?"

She held the door, and I watched her think about what she was going to say and what she wasn't; then she spoke again, her voice carrying with the soft buzz of the yellow bug fluorescents outside. "Definitely local, or Billings; how else could you have the dog? Either way, you're a dark horse, that's for sure." She closed the door, and I listened to her footsteps in a pair of leather sandals as they became a diminishing echo on the wooden walkway.

In town seven hours, and I'd already been made by an associate degree.

October 20: seven days earlier, noon.

I had rested the DCI file on my desk.

"What the fuck are you looking for?"

"She was diagnosed with chronic insomnia."

"So?" Vic came in and sat in the chair next to Saizarbitoria, who was eating his lunch on his lap. The Basquo was one of the newer additions to our little high-plains contingency and was still attempting to get over having one of his kidneys filleted only a couple of months ago.

I was easing the young man back, but the going was slow after his injury. I'd assigned him court duty and a number of other less strenuous jobs, but it seemed as if a certain light was missing from the Basquo's eyes, as if the dark at his pupils was overtaking the spark that had lived there.

Sancho wiped some gourmet mayonnaise from the corner of his mouth with an index finger. His wife, Marie, packed his lunch every day and made what looked like incredible sandwiches. He took a sip of his Mountain Dew. "She was prescribed both Ambien and Lunesta."

I returned to the faxed sheets in the report as Ruby appeared in the doorway. "Joe Meyer is on line one."

We all looked at each other—it wasn't every day you got a call from the state attorney general's office, let alone from the ranking officer himself. I picked up the receiver and punched the button. "Hey, Joe—"

"What the heck are you up to?"

I liked Joe; he was old-school Wyoming and one of the few appointed individuals in the state who still exuded integrity. "I'm watching one of my musketeers eat his lunch on his lap and am thinking about how I've gotten to the age where skipping a few meals won't hurt me."

It was quiet on the line for a moment. "Since when did your jurisdiction encompass parts of Campbell County?"

I leaned back in my chair, careful to slip my foot under the edge of the desk so that I wouldn't flip over backward; a safety measure I'd adopted after hard-won knowledge. "Aw, c'mon Joe. I'm just curious."

"Well, I've got two investigators down here at DCI that are as mad as a couple of wet hens." I looked at the faxed report Saizarbitoria had requested from the Division of Criminal Investigation. "They want to know why it is the celebrated Walt Longmire has taken such a sudden interest in this case."

Vic watched me with more than a trace of amusement on her face. "Well, I've got her in my holding cell for the next two weeks and—"

"I'm going to have a word with Sandy Sandberg about that."

"Now, Joe."

There was a loud sigh from the state capital. "You and I both know that's why the Powder River dry-gulcher sent that woman over to you." The thought had occurred to me. "Haven't you had enough to do lately?"

In the last twelve months, Joe had run interference for me with the Department of Justice, the Philadelphia Police Department, and the California attorney general's office. It was my turn to sigh.

"Maybe you should stick a little closer to home in the next few weeks."

I set the folder on my desk. "I was born in that Powder River country."

"I know that, Walt." It was silent on both ends of the line. "You know we have the highest regard for your abilities here in Cheyenne."

"Have you met her?" It was quiet again. "Mary Barsad, have you met her?"

"No, I can't say that . . ."

"I have, and I don't think she did it."

It was the longest silence of the conversation, and I sat there waiting. My two deputies stopped chewing and watched me as I argued with the highest sworn official in Wyoming law enforcement. "Walt, you need to be careful. I got another call from the Department of Justice, wanting to know in exactly what capacity you were involved with this case."

"What?"

"I told them to go piss up a rope, but in state there are some folks who're thinking about pouring some serious money into Kyle Straub's coffers—television ads, radio, and the like. I know that it seems like neither of these things has anything to do with the price of cattle in Crook County, but if you're going to stick your neck out for that woman, you better know what you're risking."

I looked at my two deputies, one of whom I was hoping to hand the reins off to in two years. "What the hell does the FBI have to do with all of this, other than that before he was dead they were spreading him over the country like a venereal disease."

"You didn't hear this from me, but there's been talk about the federal marshal's position that's coming up."

I laughed; the idea was ridiculous. "Joe, I'm not even sure I want to be sheriff of Absaroka County anymore."

"All I'm saying is that if you're going to do this, you better make sure you do it right."

"Well, that's pretty much how I approach all my investigations." I looked at the floor. "Is this what you called to tell me?"

"Pretty much."

I laughed at the absurdity of it all. "Well, I appreciate you looking out for my back, but you can tell anybody that'll listen, including the Department of Justice, that my political ambitions begin and end here, in Absaroka County."

"I'll do that, but in the meantime you watch yourself. All right?"

"I will, Joe. Tell Mary I said hey."

"You bet."

I hung up, and my two deputies stared at me—Vic, of course, was the first to speak. "What the hell was that all about?"

I studied the phone and thought about the conversation I thought I'd just had. "I believe I just had a warning shot from the Department of Justice fired across my bow." They both studied me, but I changed the subject. "Ambien and Lunesta?"

Sancho nudged his ball cap back. "What?"

"I'm assuming they're sleeping pills?"

Vic glanced at Sancho and then at me, unwilling to let it go. "What the fuck is going on?"

"Nothing—just a bunch of political foolishness." I picked

the file back up and began studying the notations in the margin. "What's this stuff about the FDA?"

Saizarbitoria glanced at Vic, who continued to watch me, and then spoke. "Ambien was pulled by the FDA as unsafe, and then they suggested stronger warnings. They're called sedative-hypnotics and they have a side effect known as 'complex sleep-related behaviors.'"

"You hear about this stuff in Rawlins?" The Basquo had been a corrections officer in the state's extreme risk unit.

"The Internet. When we got the report from DCI, I looked it up. Technically, it occurs during the slow-wave or deep stages of nonrapid eye movement sleep. The subject is usually incoherent though the eyes remain open, and there are cases where people dress, undress, cook, eat, and even drive cars—completely unaware."

I sat forward. "Wait, you have a computer?" Sancho had taken the office next to Vic's but kept his door shut most of the time, an act I felt was somewhat antisocial, considering I didn't even have a doorknob. I looked at Vic. "He has a computer?"

She shrugged. "He knows how to use one."

"I could learn." I studied the file. "Do you need a prescription for this stuff?"

Sancho picked up his sandwich again. "Yes, but there were about twenty-seven million prescriptions written last year."

I flipped the sheets but couldn't see anything about any prescribed medications. "Where did Mary Barsad get hers?"

"There's no mention of it in the report, but it was in her bloodstream."

I looked up at the Basquo; it was important information, but the young man seemed uninterested. "You figured that out from the blood tests?"

He shrugged. "Yeah."

"At any point, did you call down to Cheyenne and ask the investigators at DCI about this?"

"Yeah, they seemed pretty upset that they hadn't caught it."

I had gone back to the report. "I bet they did."

5

October 21: six days earlier, afternoon.

It had meant a great deal that Eric Boss had driven down from Billings just to have this conversation.

"I know it's a lot to ask, Walt, but you'd be doing me a big favor. We're into this one to the tune of close to nine million dollars, and if there's any funny business I just want to make sure we're not the ones footing the bill."

I sipped my coffee and slid it across the counter for Dorothy to refill. "What, exactly, is it you want me to do?"

The insurance man pushed the bone-white, cattleman-style hat back on his head, and I noticed the golden crucifix hat pin that glinted in competition with Boss's grin. "Well, nothing illegal." He shifted the smile to the chief cook and bottle washer. "How good's the pie today, honey?"

She looked back at him more than just a little askance as she poured coffee. "Are you trying to get our sheriff in trouble?"

"Nope." He picked up his mug and winked at her from over the edge. "Just got a tough job and need a tough guy for it."

She placed the pot back on one of the burners and dumped

the grounds from the other, readying it for a refill. "You get him hurt, and you're gonna know what tough is."

Boss ignored her and reached down to pull up a leather satchel that was engraved with the words COWBOYS FOR CHRIST across the hand-tooled leather. He retrieved a thick file from the bag and put the pile of papers on the counter between us. "You know me, Walt, I don't mind paying on a righteous claim, but I need to know if this one's on the level."

"Don't you have investigators who do this sort of thing?"

"We do, and the last one I sent barely escaped with his life." He sipped his coffee. "They are a regular bunch of outlaws out there. The law of the land has left Absalom, and I need somebody to go out and reintroduce it."

"To the tune of nine million dollars."

"Exactly."

"A feast is made for laughter, and wine makes life merry, but money is the answer for everything?" I didn't see any reason to tell the insurance man about the phone call with Sandy Sandberg or the one with Attorney General Joe Meyer, for that matter, figuring there was nothing like getting offers for more marching orders on a march you'd already decided to make. "Ecclesiastes 10:18." I slid the folder beside my mug and looked up at the blond man's nonplussed face. "Who's the beneficiary in all this?"

It took an instant for Boss to respond. "Barsad's got a brother in Youngstown, Ohio, who sounded on the phone like he was just as glad to hear Wade was dead."

"He hasn't shown up?"

"Nope, but I don't think there was any love lost between 'em."

"What'd he say about the wife, Mary?"

He thought about it. "Didn't say anything."

"No questions about why she did it or how?" Boss shook his head. "Doesn't that strike you as odd?"

"Some, but they sounded estranged, so maybe he never met the wife." Vic swung open the door of the Busy Bee and sat on the stool beside me. Boss glanced at me and then at Vic. "Hello, young lady."

I continued to study the file without looking up. "It's all right, she's with me."

Taking his chances, Boss ordered the pumpkin chiffon pie and looked back at Vic. "We were just discussing that people do all kinds of horrible things to each other, young lady, but I figure that's between them and God. I'm more concerned with the work at hand."

From the corner of my eye, I could see Vic nodding. "Amen."

I flipped to the contact sheet. There were a couple of numbers for Wade's brother—work, home, and a cell. "You mind if I give him a call?"

"Be my guest."

I read the figures and tallied up. "So, you think he burned all those horses with the intention of insurance fraud?"

"I don't know, but I'd say it was pretty telling of his character if he did so."

I flipped some pages. "The problem being DCI didn't find any signs of arson?"

The insurance man grinned in Vic's direction, the effect being halfway between a snake-oil salesman and a snake. He watched her closely as Dorothy poured her a cup of coffee.

She doctored it with the requisite cream and four sugars. "Exactly."

"You want whipped cream on that pie?"

He was still looking at Vic when he answered. "Yes, ma'am. That would be fine."

I followed the insurance man's eyes and then gazed up to the crucifix on his hat. "Maybe your boss was trying to hit him with a lightning bolt and missed."

His face colored a little, embarrassed at getting caught staring at my deputy. "My boss doesn't damn well miss." He leaned forward and tipped the brim of his hat to Vic. "Excuse my French, young lady."

The coffee cup had stalled out, just in front of her lips. "Yeah, well, you watch your fucking mouth."

October 28, 12:48 A.M.

I lay there listening to the loud voices and country music and thought about how much energy it was going to take to put my clothes on, go next door to room number three, and tell them to turn it down and quiet up.

There wasn't a lot of space with the two of us on the bed, but the beast had insisted. He was sprawled across the bottom, so I'd attempted sleep with my feet hanging off the edge diagonally. It didn't work, so I made use of the only reading material I could find in the room.

I stuck an index finger in the Bible I'd found in the bedside drawer, left for travelers in need of salvation via the Gideons; Absalom was seemingly prime territory. There was a loud thump against the wall, and Dog sat up at the end of the bed, a low growl beginning to emit from his pulled-back lips.

"Easy, easy—" I took a deep breath and rolled my head over so that I could see the partially melted clock-radio's plutonium-like green numbers.

12:52 A.M.

The headache was still lingering, and I started thinking that I should've gotten some of Mary Barsad's medication myself. The party in the next room had started at a little after midnight, and an hour later the soirée was in full swing.

I retrieved my index finger, stared at 2 Samuel, and read aloud: "And unto David were sons born in Hebron: and his first born was Amnon, of Ahinoam the Jezreelitess, and his second, Chileab, of Abigail the wife of Nebal the Carmelite, and the third, Absalom the son of Maacah the daughter of Talmai king of Geshur—" I paused and looked at Dog's big brown eyes. "Are you getting all this?"

His head lowered back to the stained bedcover.

"That's a lot of begetting." I skipped ahead to the juicy part. "Absalom was riding upon his mule, and the mule went under the branches of a great oak and his hair caught fast in the branches and he was left hanging between heaven and earth." I nudged the beast with my foot, but he ignored me. "That's what you get for riding a mule." I continued my theatrics. "And Joab thrust three darts into the heart of Absalom while he hung, still alive in the oak tree. And ten young men, Joab's armor-bearers, surrounded Absalom and struck him, and killed him." As if the three darts hadn't done the job. I nudged Dog again, but he didn't move. "Seems like all they do is beget and slaughter people in this book. In the Old Testament part, at least."

The volume of the radio next door increased. It was a

station out of Durant, and I recognized Steve Lawrence's voice as he introduced the next song. "This is an oldie but a goodie, 'Cattle Call,' from that Tennessee plowboy, Mr. Eddy Arnold."

I remembered that it had been one of my mother's favorites. A fellow by the name of Tex Owens had written it while waiting to do a radio broadcast. It had begun snowing in Kansas City that night, slowly at first, but then it had blotted out his view of the buildings across the street.

1:05 A.M.

Owens had grown up on a ranch, not unlike myself, and had done a lot of cattle feeding in the winter; knew what it was like for the animals out in the weather, the wet and cold. He'd felt sympathy for all those animals and just wished he could call them all in and break up a little corn for them to eat.

1:06 A.M.

Thirty minutes later he had written the music and four verses. I could still see the little 45 turning on my mother's suitcase of a record player on hot afternoons in August. I was in high school and thought the tune one of the corniest things I'd ever heard, referring to it as goat-yodeling music. My mother knew I hated the song, and so she played it constantly. She might have been the reason that I was considered by some as a bit of a wiseguy.

1:07 A.M.

I found my lips moving along with the lyrics. I'm not a very good singer—as a matter of documentation, I'm horrible, but I can be loud. My father used to call it my field voice and forbade me to use it in the house. As I started singing, Dog turned and looked at me with an ear cocked. In the short time we'd known each other, he'd never heard me sing. Encouraged by his attention, I sang louder.

Then I sang even louder.

I'm pretty sure I was shaking the walls when Dog joined in. "Ooooooo, oooooooo, dooooooo dee dee—ooooooooooo, doooooo, doooo doo-doo-doo-dee . . . For hours he'd ride on the range far and wide / When the night winds blow up a storm. / His heart is a feather in all kinds of weather, / when he sings his cattle call . . . Ooooooo, oooooooo, dooooooo dee dee—Ooooooooooo, dooooooo, doooo doo-doo-doo-dee . . ."

I gave out with one more chorus of yodeling, and Dog howled with me when I noticed that they had turned the radio off next door. There was a certain amount of conversation, and I could hear a number of expletives as somebody thrashed around the adjoining room. He was cursing and threatening as a woman laughed. Then she laughed again.

Five seconds later, the somebody was hammering my door. Dog barked, and I rested the Bible on the nightstand, got up, and slipped on my jeans and boots.

I ignored the .45 Colt in my duffel and opened the door.

"You some kind'a fuckin' comedian?"

As I'd suspected, it was Cliff Cly. I guess he had decided to take his party to a room. He was still wearing the same droopy potato-chip straw hat, sunglasses, and the two-day beard but had stripped down to a sleeveless T-shirt that read PRO BULL RIDING TOUR. He was holding a bottle of Jack

Daniel's and leaning a shoulder on my doorjamb for support. Dog growled from behind me, and I turned my head to shush him, then turned back to the ranch hand. "Excuse me?"

He leaned in a little closer and, with the strength of the alcohol fumes, I was sure I didn't have any hair left in my nose. "I said, you some kind'a comedian?"

I studied his face, the wobbling intent of his eyes, the elongated nose. "I don't take myself all that seriously, if that's what you mean."

He cocked his head and tried to focus his eyes on mine, and I could see just how profoundly drunk he was. "You . . ." He belched. "You take me seriously?"

"Right now? Not so much." He stood there for a moment more, then pushed off from the doorway. He staggered a second and started to raise the bottle, but the movement was so slow and clumsy, I didn't even bother to raise a hand in defense. Instead, I watched as he lost his balance.

"Oh, shit—"

I reached out and tried to grab him, but I was too slow and he sprawled backward and landed on his back with a liquid thump, the bottle of whiskey skittering down the slight gravel incline toward my rental car.

I took a step forward and crouched down on the walkway as Dog trotted out and joined me in looking down at the semi-unconscious Cliff Cly. I glanced back at Dog. "I know this is twice in one night, but people don't usually act like this." Dog looked at me, unsure if I was telling the truth or just defending the species. I gathered Cliff, sitting him up and leaning him against my shoulder. "Are you all right?"

His hat fell off, his head leaned against me with sunglasses askew, and he belched again. "I'm kind of fucked up in general, so it's hard to gauge."

I had to smile. "Well, let's try and get you into your room."

He was heavy, and I could tell that the majority of his weight was muscle, but I was able to put one of his arms around my neck and lift him to a partially standing posture by grabbing his belt, which was made out of some kind of chrome timing chain. The door to his room was still open, and the lights were on, so I moved us in that direction. Dog sniffed at him but then moved away. He definitely didn't smell good.

When I got to the doorway, I recognized the Rubenesque tattooed woman from the bar. She was seated on the bed in a bra and panties, and she looked to be about four months pregnant, a fact that had been hidden by clothes earlier. Her mouth, which was outlined with very dark lipstick, made a perfect O.

"Can you help me with him?"

She looked past me with black penciled eyes. "Where's the Jack?"

I carried Cly toward the bed and sprawled him there, face first at her feet. "I'm just guessing, but I think he's had enough."

She got off the bed and walked past me toward the door; there was a peacock on her back with feathers that exploded in greens and blues toward her neck. "Yeah, but I haven't even got started."

I rolled Cliff over and figured he could sleep it off where he lay when I heard a yip come from the young woman. I turned and saw that Dog, standing in the open doorway, had frozen her. I walked over, shooed Dog with my leg, and led her through the door. He looked hurt, and considered us like a disgruntled Grendel.

"Where's the bottle?"

Before I could catch myself, I glanced toward the car and down the slight incline.

She looked up at me, her blond hair shifting to the left. I think the dark roots were a fashion statement. "You're the guy from the bar."

I reached for my hat but then remembered it was sitting on the table in my room. "Yes, ma'am."

"Do I know you from somewhere?"

"I don't think so."

"You look real familiar—"

I couldn't place the face, and it was unlikely I'd forget the tattoos, so it was possible that I hadn't ever arrested her. "Guess I've just got one of those faces."

She smirked in an attempt at a smile. "It's a good face."

"Thanks, it's a little tired right now, so I'm going to take it to bed."

She walked down the incline, tiptoeing on the gravel with bare feet, stooped and picked up the bottle, and crow-hopped back to the wooden walkway; she held the whiskey and her stomach with her left hand. The other she stuck out—it had a locomotive amid floral designs and a jack-o-lantern, which trailed up her arm in blues, purples, yellows, and reds. "Name is Rose."

By any other name. I stood there for a second, then extended my hand into hers. Her grip was strong.

"Did you hit him?"

"No, he passed out."

"There wasn't any fight part?"

"No, the passed-out part came before the fight part could get started."

She shook her head. "That's Cliff all over. These rodeo cowboys all think that eight seconds is a good ride." She raised her other hand, which had a lacelike design inked on the fingers that became snakes that intertwined as they climbed. "Most people wouldn't stand up to him like that."

"Seems like you were rooting for a fight just a couple of hours ago."

She smiled fully this time. "Boring night in the big town. I was just looking for a little excitement." She glanced into the room she shared with Cliff and then looked back to me. "He's only been around for a couple of weeks, but I can tell you, he's crazy."

I nodded. "I'll remember that."

"You strike me as one of those guys who doesn't forget much."

I watched as she brought the bottle up and noticed there was a good two inches left. I thought about a young woman I knew, an Indian princess, who had been born with fetal alcohol syndrome. "How 'bout you not do that?"

She paused. "What?"

"Just do me a favor and don't drink." For the next five months, I thought—but you've got to start somewhere.

"Why?"

"You're pregnant."

She looked down at her belly in mock surprise. "Wow, wonder how that happened?"

There's a bone-weary quality to putting on your white suit in these kinds of situations, but you do it anyway. "What's your baby's name?"

Her hand dropped to support the girth as she grinned. "Wiggle."

This was going to be harder than I thought.

She tossed a shoulder and then leaned it against the T-111 siding of the motel's exterior wall, closed her arms around herself, and shivered. "It's what it does." I stood there looking at her and said nothing—I had probably said too much already. I reached a hand out for the bottle, but she pulled it behind her, and a look of anticipated defiance streaked its way across her face. "Hey, no way—"

I took a deep breath and marveled at my ability to find a place even more tired than the place I'd been. "Okay." I turned and started into my own room.

"Whatta ya mean, okay?"

I looked back at her and then gestured to the front of The AR. "If I take that away from you, what's to say that you won't just go back over to The AR and get a full one?"

She studied me for a while, an even more puzzled look on her face. "The what?"

I shook my head just to clear it a little and make sure I was the only one in there. "The BAR."

Her head cocked to one side, and the blond pageboy swayed just a little as her eyes stayed steady with mine. I stood there for a moment as she turned and began closing the door behind her with her foot. The bottle was still in one hand, and her belly was supported with the other—where worlds collide. "Mr. Good Samaritan, you're in the wrong town."

The door shut softly.

Boy howdy.

I stood there thinking about Wiggle, about what kind of chance he or she had, and wondered, in a place like Absalom, what kind of chance any of us had.

I was about to go back to my room when I noticed that the truck parked in front of The AR was a new, red Dodge duellie with no plates. I motioned for Dog to go in and then plucked my shirt off the chair. "Stay, and this time I mean it." He looked after me as I closed the door.

I circled the backside of the empty truck and couldn't see any temporary tags taped to the inside of the back window that I might've missed. It was probably some young rancher having made his first, second, or third pile of money from coal-bed methane, or one of the local boys coming back to show off a little to the hometown crowd of forty. There were a million reasons for the truck to have been there, another million for it not to have plates. I wasn't sure why I was fixating on the Dodge, other than the oldest trick in the lawman's repertoire—the hunch.

I walked the rest of the way around the truck and paused at the passenger door. It was locked, but on close inspection through the tinted windows, I could see a Winchester lever-action .30-30 propped up against the dash.

I looked back at the bar—the lights were out in the main room, but it looked like there were still a few on in the kitchen in back. I thought I could hear voices and decided to circle and see who might be inside. I walked to the right and went around the final unit and up a small rise to the roadway behind the motel. There were no streetlights in Absalom, and along with a smear of clouds, it was a moonless night that made it hard to pick through the high grass, garbage cans, and automobile parts without making a racket. I finally found a path that led to the back of the establishment's kitchen.

There was one light on in the short hallway connecting the bar with the kitchen, and it looked like there were two men talking. I edged a little closer and could make out Pat's profile beside a pay phone on the wall—he was leaning back with his arms folded as a taller man in the shadows gesticulated passionately. They were keeping their voices low, but it was a heated conversation and I could just make out the gist of the thing.

The owner of the bar lifted his head and looked at the other man defiantly. Neither of them said anything for a few moments, and then the taller man began speaking again, in an even lower tone, with his index finger in Pat's face.

There was a mudroom leading into the kitchen, and I carefully opened the screen door and slipped inside, or slipped as gracefully as I could. The floorboards bleated and complained under my weight.

I stood there without moving, but the conversation stopped.

I waited for a moment and then leaned forward to get a better look, but the light was off now and both men were gone. I pulled back into the corner and stayed where I was, waiting for the next sound, which was the pump-action of the shotgun I had seen on the shelf under the bar.

I could run, but I don't do that very well. I could waltz through as if I were just looking for a little midnight snack and get a serving of a few ounces of lead for my trouble, or I could just stand there quietly like a buffalo in a stand of year-old aspens pretending that if I can't see them, they can't see me.

I heard footsteps in the bar. Whoever it was, either Pat or the tall man, they weren't playing fair. The first thing we always tell people who have to deal with burglary is to make your presence known by flipping on all the lights, scream at your wife to call 911, and turn loose the dogs while you get the .38 from the closet. Never, but never, go sneaking around in your own house at odds with some stranger.

Nobody was talking, nobody was turning on lights, and I had that hunch feeling that nobody was calling 911.

There was some more whispering, and I could hear someone coming down the hallway, through the kitchen, and toward the mudroom where I stood; he was moving slowly and carefully. I could see the barrel of the shotgun first and could even register the diameter—20-gauge—in the direct cast of the moon that had, of course, chosen to come from behind the clouds.

If the thing shifted four inches to the left, it would be pointed directly at my gut.

The shooter stepped forward, and I could make out the hands holding the scattergun and the gold Masonic ring.

The owner of the bar and maker of the crapper laws stepped full into the moon glow, blinked, and looked out the screen door to my right. The barrel wavered for a second, at which point he took two steps closer, still looking out the doorway and into the overgrown back of the place.

I could see his face clearly. His hat was missing, and it looked like there was some swelling around the nearest eye; blood was palmed from his nose to his hairline. I looked at his hand again and could see the still-wet blood there.

Evidently, the taller man had struck him.

I hadn't breathed since he'd entered the tiny mudroom and still didn't. I watched him lean his face forward to get a better view of the back bushes. The swelling at his eye certainly wasn't helping in the search, but he must have seen something because he suddenly turned toward me and looked directly up to my face.

The sound was already coming out of his mouth when I grabbed the shotgun with both hands and pivoted the butt up and into his chin—it sounded like a cleanly hit baseball. After a brief moment of teetering, he started to go over backward, but I was now practiced and grabbed one of the straps of his overalls and pulled his collapsing body into me.

I lowered him to the floor with one arm and leaned him against the wall with his legs folded underneath him, and then checked his pulse, which was rapid, but there.

Out cold.

I wondered why he hadn't fired. I checked the Winchester and discovered that the reason he hadn't was that he must've automatically clicked the safety on, something a lot of inexperienced shooters do. I was happy with his inexperience, clicked off the safety, and stood. More footsteps echoed from the silence, and I took the two steps that would give me a clearer view of the short hallway leading toward the front of the building. I could only see a small portion of the bar.

Nothing.

I unfocused my eyes to adapt to the dark and allowed them to become motion sensors as I stepped into the kitchen proper. There were a few BLTs on two plates on the cutting board along with a couple of cans of Coors. One of the sandwiches had a single bite taken out of it, and the other had been eaten, except for the crusts. Evidently, business had interrupted dinner, and then there was me.

The floor continued to complain under my weight as I took the first step into the hallway. I kept my eyes on the surface of the bar, fully expecting someone to flip over the counter with a two-handed grip and pop a few into my chest.

I raised the pump-action to my shoulder and tried to remember which way the front door of the bar opened, settling on left to right, and chose the right and larger side of the public room on which to concentrate. Television and movies would have you believe that the proper way to do this type of thing is to leap into a room, first directing your weapon one way and then the other, but without backup, it's a fifty-fifty proposition that you'd enter said room dead.

In the dark, if you're alone, the rule is reveal low and very slow. I crouched at counter level, slid along the wall, and scanned the area where the makeshift fight ring stood ghostly and empty. I pivoted the shotgun to my left, keeping it level to the bar and looking into the area where there were the few tables and mismatched chairs.

Still nothing.

I was sure I hadn't heard the front door open and equally sure that the other man must still be inside when the big Dodge chirped and the interior lights came on in the truck. I started around the bar, quickly moving toward the front, when something moved to my left, raised up, and fired.

I staggered back, tripped over a loose chair, fell to the floor, and scrambled to put the bar between us. His aim had been high. He stood and continued forward, around the bar and toward me with what sounded like a 9 mm. The rounds from the semiautomatic blew through the beer poster on the wall and tore into the ceiling as I found the baseboard and turned the 20-gauge back toward the shooter. I decided to shoot high as well, since all I really wanted to do was back him off long enough to get a look at him.

I pulled the trigger and listened to the loud crash as the front window of the bar exploded onto the walkway out front, immediately followed by the roar of the Dodge as its engine dieseled to life.

I abandoned the thought of a remote starter and figured he'd just been throwing down cover fire long enough to get himself out the door to his avenue of retreat.

I struggled up from the floor and grabbed the corner of the bar as I ran toward the jagged glass shards of the now-shattered front window; I slid to a stop in the full illumination of the truck's high beams.

I brought the Winchester up in a half-extension, the barrel pointed directly at the darkened driver's side. Old habits die hard, and the words were out of my mouth before I could re-assess. "Sheriff, freeze!"

There was a brief second when absolutely nothing happened, except the second, third, fourth, and fifth helping of guessing; you don't know who they are, you don't know if they're going to comply, you don't know if they're still armed, you don't know if they're still aiming at you, you don't know if they're involved with the case, and you don't want to shoot even after being shot at, unless you absolutely must.

Then the big full-ton shifted, and the reverse lights illuminated the rear of the truck. I lowered the barrel of the shotgun, aimed at the radiator, and pulled the trigger. There was a sharp click.

Nothing.

I jacked the pump-action as the Dodge flew into reverse, sprayed gravel in a murdersome arc, and was jammed into a forward gear. I took aim at the rear tires and pulled the trigger again.

Click.

Nothing.

The truck disappeared over the hill at the edge of town and then reappeared on the next hill, hell-bent for diesel leather as it continued down the Powder River Road, the smoldering running lights like tracers in the darkness.

I turned back and heard noises from the rooms in the motel—people shouting, people running, and probably now people dialing 911. I rested the shotgun on the particleboard surface, jacked the pump-action back but not forward, and looked into the empty chamber of the Winchester.

I raised my head and could still see the unconscious owner of The AR propped against the mudroom wall in the pooled moonlight. I spoke quietly to the two of us as I lay the scattergun on the bar and watched my hands shake. "Who the hell puts only one round in a shotgun?"

6

October 28, 6:11 A.M.

I waited quietly in the back of the Campbell County sheriff's cruiser, tried not to concentrate on the multitude of stains on the seat, and watched as the former and now retired Absaroka County sheriff and the current and very active Campbell County one explained to a deputy why it was he couldn't arrest me. The deputy didn't seem happy with the turn of events but, with less than a year on the job and facing close to a half-century of experience, he didn't have much recourse.

Sandy laughed with Lucian, and they came over to the parked car where they both got in the front. They turned and looked at me through the wire mesh that divides the arrester from the arrestee, both grinning like possums.

My old one-legged boss shook his head. "Jesus H. Christ."

I shrugged as best I could with the handcuffs on, nodded toward him, and looked at Sandy. "What, you decided you needed backup?"

He smiled and glanced at Lucian. "He said you were most likely lost, and we should go look for you." Everybody liked Sandy, and if you didn't, all he had to do was smile and you would. "He also said it was likely that people would be shooting at you." I didn't say anything, and he continued. "That deputy of mine wants to put you in jail some kind of bad."

"I refused to give him any ID and didn't offer a whole lot of information. I told him I'd just wait for you. I take it he doesn't know who I am?" The young man was watching us from the walkway of The AR.

Lucian interrupted. "He thinks you're Dillinger, but then he couldn't find his pecker in a pickle jar."

Sandy folded his arms over the back of the front seat. "So, what happened?"

I told them.

"Holy crap." He sighed.

I leaned forward. "What'd Pat say?"

"The owner?" I nodded. "He says he was closing up the place and that he heard something in the back and went to check it out."

"With the shotgun?"

The sheriff of Campbell County snorted. "He didn't mention that part, till we asked him how the window got blown out and onto the road."

I looked at him. "And?"

Lucian laughed. "He says somebody drove by, threw a few shots into the bar, and kept going. Says it happens periodically when he makes folks pay up their tab—said he always throws a few rounds back at 'em just to dissuade 'em of the activity."

I readjusted my weight. "And the part about being unconscious when the deputy got there?"

"Says he slipped and hit his head."

"In the mudroom. In the back?"

"Said that's where he usually goes when folks are shootin' up the front."

I pushed my cuffed hands to the side. "Well, since he's not saying anybody hit him, do you think he has any idea who did?"

Lucian chimed in again. "Hard to say, but since you displayed yourself in a rather dramatic fashion and announced to any and all, including the fella in the truck, that you were a sheriff, it might be time for you to get the hell outta Dodge— red, white, or blue."

I looked at Lucian and thought about the woman in my jail as it grew silent in the cruiser. "Have you been to the jail?"

"Mine?"

"Mine." Our eyes met, and I was always struck by the darkness in his pupils; maybe I needed to get him and Saizarbitoria together. "You meet her?"

His voice changed, growing softer. "Yes, I have."

"Do you think she's guilty?"

He took a deep breath and blew it out of his nostrils like a shotgun blast. "She's burnin' bridges in her head; I'm just not sure if he was one of 'em." He studied me. "What's that got to do with horseshit and hat sizes?"

"Everything." He made a noise in his throat. "Somebody taught me that, a long time ago."

It was quiet, and neither of them looked at me.

"Well." The ex-sheriff of Absaroka County sniffed and thumbed his nose. "Never did any of this undercover crap— you've got a lot of people worried that you're gonna fool around and get yourself killed out here."

I thought that the old sheriff had been sent out to check

on me, but I didn't figure on him admitting it. I changed the subject to save him any further embarrassment. "What's everybody else in the motel say?"

There was a pause as Sandy prepared to speak; Lucian and I both looked at him. "Not a whole heck of a lot." He scratched his neck and placed one of his sun-leathered hands on the dash, the heavy, curved, Cuban bracelet on his wrist blinking in the morning sun. "There's a little tattooed girl that says you beat up her boyfriend, but other than that it's business as usual out here on the Powder River—ain't nobody sayin' nothin'."

"Who called 911?"

"Anonymous, female, from the pay phone outside the post office/library up the hill."

I thought about it and could only come up with one name. "You'll run a check on the Dodge?"

"Yep." The hand on the dash reached for the mic.

"One more thing?"

He and Lucian turned back to look at me. "Yeah?"

"Get these damned handcuffs off."

October 21: seven days earlier, evening.

I'd followed Dog, who had made a habit of trotting to the holding cells.

Mary Barsad was running her hand across his back. She was sitting on the floor beside the bars and looked up when I came in. "Nice dog; where'd you get him?"

"From a friend."

"Didn't they want him anymore?"

I thought about what to say. "Um, no." It was still early, and

Vic was going to be back soon, so I pulled one of the folding chairs over and sat.

She looked back to study him. "What kind of dog is he?"

I shrugged. "When there's bacon around, I'd swear he was part wolf."

"St. Bernard and some German shepherd, I'd say." She scratched under his neck. "Something else, but I'm not sure what."

"You know a lot about animals."

She breathed a soft laugh. "Yes, but evidently I'm a poor judge of human beings."

I leaned forward, elbows on knees. "Which brings to mind a question."

The more-than-blue eyes came up. "Please don't ask me why I got mixed up with Wade."

We sat there looking at each other. "You know, my daughter was in a bad relationship back in Philadelphia, and I've developed a theory on that." She continued to gaze at me. "I think our hearts are the most fearless organ we've got, considering how often they'll make the same mistake, over and over again."

She continued to study me. "You do know the heart is just a muscle, right?"

I smiled. "Then maybe we're getting stronger from the exercise."

Her eyes had broken contact with mine. "Or you just lose another piece."

October 28, 10:10 A.M.
The first cup of coffee I could get was at the auction at Bill Nolan's place. It was from a catering service out of Wright

called the Chuck Wagon, and thankfully they didn't know me. I took my two ham and egg sandwiches and my coffee back over to the rental car and fed Dog his breakfast through the window.

The majority of the items to be auctioned were in a large, tin-sided indoor arena with the heavy equipment parked in a row along a fence line. I wandered up and took a look. I wasn't alone; there was a pretty good crowd of ranchers who had arrived early. It was late in the season for an auction, and the majority of the chores that these newer-looking implements would be used for were already done for the year. Prices would be low, and if you needed a swather, baler, or tractor for next year, now was your chance.

I exchanged a few nods but thankfully didn't recognize anybody. I kept an eye partially peeled for a red Dodge duellie—so far, nothing.

I was always generally ill at ease at these types of things, feeling as though auctions were like picking over bones. I couldn't help but remember the one at my parents' place after they had passed. I'd gone through their things and hadn't kept much, but when it came time for the auction I'd had a strong impulse to bid on everything like some museum curator attempting to keep the collection whole.

I still owned the place but hadn't been back there much since.

"See something you like?"

I turned and found Juana and Benjamin watching me as I mindlessly fingered a Massey Ferguson model 775 swather—at least, that was what was decaled on its peeling side. "No, this looks too much like work."

"Didn't you say you were born on a ranch?"

I looked at her. "Not to you."

She smiled and watched me as Benjamin studied the equipment. "Did you sleep okay?"

"No, but the toilet worked magnificently and so did the shower." I inclined my head toward the little outlaw. "How are you this morning, young man?"

She nudged him with her hip, but he ignored both of us and pushed his hands deeper into his jean pockets. "He's mad, because I won't buy him and Hershel a horse trailer."

"Hershel's here?"

She nodded toward the tin building. "Inside, inspecting the trailer."

I bumped Benjamin's ever-present hat. "You two outlaws run together?"

He nodded and began speaking quickly. "He says we're going up to the Battlement someday; it's a butte where the dinosaurs are buried and the teepee circles are and where the secret graves are for the buffalo soldiers and the Indians that—" He quieted suddenly, remembering that he was in midpout.

I watched him as he looked at his mother. "Hey, I was just getting interested."

He ducked his head and stared at the ground. "We can't get there without a trailer; it's too far for the horses, and there's no water."

"I've heard of the place; its south and east of here, isn't it? Out on Twentymile Butte?"

He was chewing on the stampede strings again but spit them out to answer. "Yeah."

I nodded, and we all walked along the equipment and toward the indoor arena, Benjamin hanging back. After a few moments, Juana spoke again. "I understand there was some excitement down at the bar last night?"

"I don't know; I slept through most of it."

She continued to watch me. "And that would be why they arrested you?"

I didn't say anything; she continued to stare at me. "They released me on my own recognizance."

She raised an eyebrow, but let it go at that. "You look tired." I nodded again as we walked toward the more recreational items that were to be auctioned later in the morning. "Are you coming to the fights tonight?"

I laughed, because I'd forgotten all about it. "I thought I saw someone on the list I know."

"The Indian?" I turned and looked at her as more than a little mischief played in her baking-chocolate eyes. "He asked about you, or somebody who looked like you." She pulled herself up to a towering five-foot-four and quoted with a flat Cheyenne accent, mimicking Henry's down to the excluded contractions: "A large man with a large dog who probably looks like he would rather be somewhere else."

"That'd be me. What else did he say?"

She smiled the perfectly formed grin; her lips were pink today. "He said that you used to be his sidekick but that you had gone bad."

"Uh huh."

"That you had stolen his dog."

"Hmm."

"And that he had tracked you from the Northwest Territories and was now going to have to kick your ass."

I sipped my coffee and glanced at a '60 short-bed half-ton that looked like a refrigerator on wheels and was remotely familiar. There was a man standing with the hood up, talking to a maybe thirty-year-old. I casually steered our path in that direction.

"Rebuilt, with only thirty-two thousand miles on her, floor shift and a heavy-duty suspension. I bought her off a rancher north of here."

Juana leaned on the fender and looked up at the man who was speaking, as I stood a little away. "Hi, Bill."

"Hey, *chica*." He grinned right back at her. "How are you?"

The younger man, seeing an avenue for escape, wandered off.

Bill Nolan watched the man walk away. "Kids. If it ain't got a satellite radio and cruise-control, they ain't interested."

She turned partially toward me. "Bill, do you know Eric Boss?"

He paused for the briefest of seconds and then stuck out his hand. "You're the insurance guy that's got everybody all worried."

It didn't fully appear that he remembered that we'd gone to a Powder River, one-room schoolhouse, classes separated by three years and a long time ago. "Why do you suppose that is?"

"Oh, any kind of authority makes 'em nervous around here." He hadn't changed enough that I wouldn't have known him; still thin as a fence rail but with a few more years. A born car salesman, his father, Sidney, had owned the Powder River Red Crown Service Station along the river and to the north, and his mother had made peach ice cream that she sold for a nickel a cone.

I remembered that Bill had had an uncanny ability as a child: he could imitate coyotes. It was a talent he'd acquired when his father built two guest cabins near the service station on the banks of the river. The dudes were always disappointed whenever the animals weren't making noise every night, so Sidney sent his son out to the riverbank to imitate them. He was good at it, and I wondered whether he could still do it.

The years had carved fissures and grooves in his face; he was about a head shorter than me and weighed about a third. His hair had gone a becoming silver, but the eyebrows were still jet-black and probably his most predominant feature. "You lookin' for a truck, Mr. Boss?"

"No, I'm afraid not, but I would like to ask you a few questions, if I could?"

"Well, now I'm worried."

I glanced at Juana and Benjamin, but she was determined to stay; she folded her arms and leaned against the old truck. "I was just wondering if you could tell me a few things about your relationship with the Barsads?"

He looked around from beneath the bushes of eyebrow, and the meaning was clear. "This sounds like it's going to be a lengthy conversation, and I'm kinda busy today with the auction. . . ."

"We could talk some other time?"

Juana moved Benjamin away as Nolan closed the hood on the truck. "That'd be handy. I've got some more stuff to get packed up over at the house, so I'll be there later in the after-noon. I've got a couple of cans of iced tea in a cooler—refrigerator should be gone by then."

"That'd be fine."

He was already looking past me to where the auctioneer was setting up inside. "Around two then?"

"You bet."

He nodded a perfunctory nod and walked past us; Juana hadn't moved so far as to be out of earshot. "Still rounding up all the usual suspects?"

I gave her a long look with a smile at the end. "Why don't you give that almost–associate degree of yours a rest."

October 22: six days earlier, morning.
It had been the third number with a Youngstown area code that I'd tried. The first was a home phone where I'd left a mes-sage, and the second was an office answering service where I'd left another.

"I'd like to speak to Wendell Barnecke?"

"Speaking." There was a mumbled pause, and I got the feeling I'd interrupted the dentist's lunch.

"Mr. Barnecke, I'm sheriff of Absaroka County, Wyo-ming—"

"Is this about my brother?"

Vic and Ruby were in my office and were listening and watching me from across the desk; the dentist was on confer-ence, which might've explained the bad connection, but the connection didn't muffle the fact that Wade's brother sounded officious.

"Well, yes it is."

"Then I really don't have anything more to say. I told the detectives that he . . ." There was a pause, and I listened to the noise that accompanied the man's voice along with what sounded like gusts of wind. "Who did you say you were with?"

I reached down to ruffle Dog's ears; touching the beast was a comfort. "Sheriff's Department, Absaroka County, Wyoming."

"Sheriff, look . . . you're the sheriff of what county?"

"Absaroka. I'm assisting—"

"That's not the county Wade lived in."

"No, but—"

"Look, I don't know anything about my brother's business dealings, his life, anything, okey? So I wish you people would stop contacting me. I've told you everything I know. I haven't even spoken to him since he was here in Youngstown, six years ago."

"Then how is it you know what county he lived in, Mr. Barnecke?"

There was a longer pause, and I looked across the desk at the two pairs of female eyes watching me. "Sheriff, I've been doing nothing but answering questions about my brother with the FBI and the Ohio state police investigators—not to mention your own DCI people and detectives from the *Campbell* County Sheriff's Department."

I looked down at the report on my desk. "Wendell—do you mind if I call you Wendell?"

"Yes, I do." An even longer pause, and I could hear the ten-note song of a meadowlark. It sounded nice, wherever Wendell Barnecke was having his lunch. I pictured him sitting on a bench beside some pond in a park where the deciduous trees had just begun to change to red and yellow; then I started hoping that a maple would fall on him. "No, you may not use my familiar name. You don't know me, and I don't know you—"

I cut him off before he could get much further with his tirade. "Did you know his wife?"

"Which one?"

"Mary, the one we have in custody?"

His voice changed tone. "No, I'm afraid I've never met her."

"Well, the situation being what it is—"

"Sheriff, can I tell you something, a little hard-won knowledge?"

"Sure."

He spoke slowly. "Just for the record, I don't know who killed my brother, but whoever did probably had a pretty good reason for doing it." I could hear the rustling of what must have been the wrappings from his lunch. "I grew up with him and, at the risk of incriminating myself, I'm glad he's dead."

"I see."

"I never met his most recent wife, but I'm sure she's a fine woman." His tone changed again but stayed prim. "I'm sorry for her situation, and I'm even sorrier that she ever met my brother, but people get what they choose in life." He sighed, and there was more paper rustling. It sounded like he was packing up his food; evidently, I had ruined his lunch. "Now, if there isn't anything else?"

"Are you aware that there was a large insurance claim that could result in a substantial amount—"

He laughed, and it was not kind. "Are you joking, Sheriff?

Whatever amount of money Wade might've made from all his wheelings and dealings out there, he most assuredly owed more than that to somebody, somewhere. I'm still paying off some of his debts here. He owed everybody, and I'm sure that when all the parties concerned are through picking the financial carcass clean, there will be nothing left but debt for anyone who had anything to do with my brother. That was the way he did business."

"Mr. Barnecke, you mentioned your brother's other wives?"

"Sheriff, do you mind if I ask what all these questions are about? My understanding was that there was pretty conclusive evidence that his most recent wife killed him and that she had confessed to the crime."

I thought about Mary Barsad, who was only two rooms away. "Well, the evidence is inconclusive, but Mrs. Barsad did confess—"

He interrupted. "Then what is this all about?"

Saizarbitoria, holding a cardboard tray of food from the Busy Bee, appeared in the doorway. "There are some questions that—"

There was a loud sigh. "If there are questions, then why hasn't the FBI asked them, or the state police investigators, or the *Campbell* County sheriff, for that matter?"

I glanced up at Vic, who shook her head. "Well—"

"Why am I talking to you?"

I stared at the red button. "I thought you might be interested, concurrent with the investigation—"

"Sheriff, I've got a news flash for you—I don't give a shit. Okey? Wade's dead and from all the information I've been getting, it sounds like his wife did it. Now, unless you've got some more information that I don't know about?"

Vic, Ruby, Saizarbitoria, and Dog all looked at me. "No, I don't."

"Then I'd like for you to copy down this phone number." I picked up a pen and dutifully jotted the number. "That's my attorney, Sheldon Siegel, any more contact you wish to have with me can be done through him. Now, if there isn't anything else, I've got to attend to an impacted molar and a root canal."

After bidding a not-so-fond farewell, I was glad I wasn't having any dental work done in Youngstown, Ohio, this afternoon. I looked up at my attentive staff and, as I'd expected, Vic was the first to speak.

"What a fucksicle."

Ruby adjusted her reading glasses. "Doesn't appear to be a great deal of love lost there, does it?"

Sancho looked at all of us. "I take it the brother was less than cooperative?"

I stood but left my hat on my desk. "You could say that." I crossed to the doorway and took the prisoner's lunch from him.

The Basquo handed the receipt to Ruby and looked at me. "You going to try today?"

Despite our brief conversation, Mary Barsad was on the fourth day of trying to starve herself. Dog followed me back to the holding cells and to the bag of food that would most likely go uneaten.

She was sitting in her usual position when I turned the corner, and I pulled the folding chair over to sit with her.

She momentarily uncovered her face from her hands to glance at Dog but then once again disappeared behind the long, thin fingers.

"Lunch." I opened the bag on my lap and looked inside. "Grilled cheese sandwich, fries with seasoned salt, a salad, and an apple." Dog looked at me expectantly, having been the beneficiary of Mary Barsad's resistance so far. "You know, I'm going to stop giving your food to Dog—he's getting fat."

She didn't say anything.

I took a breath. "Mary, if this situation continues I'm not going to have any choice but to have you transferred back to the Campbell County jail and then to Lusk and the women's prison, where you will be forcibly fed with a tube."

She still said nothing, and her hands remained covering her face as I sat there holding her lunch. Maybe it was the phone conversation I'd just had, or the situation she was putting me in, but I was getting a little irritated. "You don't talk, you don't eat—what exactly do you do?"

To my surprise, her hands slipped down a little. Her voice was perfectly reasonable. "Haven't you heard? I shoot people in the head."

The unearthly azure eyes had focused on me for the first time in ninety-six hours; I thought about another tall blonde I'd been unable to save and swallowed a little of my past.

October 28, 10:33 A.M.
Hershel was looking at the horse trailer Benjamin wanted that neither of them could afford. "How you feeling?"

A somewhat unfocused picture of hung over, he turned

and looked at me as he rolled himself a cigarette. "So, why did you let my twelve-year-old horse step on my head?"

"I think it was that twenty-year-old scotch that stepped on your head." I looked at the powdered paint that was flaking off of the four-stall horse trailer. "What's it worth?"

The old cowboy shrugged, and I think it hurt. He pulled the trademark Blue Tip match from his hat and lit the hand-rolled cigarette. I counted six matches in his hatband and figured Hershel was pacing his cigarettes these days. "'Bout a thousand, maybe."

Two shotgun stalls with butt-bars and a rotten wooden floor, questionable tires, and broken plastic windows—I figured the auctioneers would be lucky if they got seven-fifty. Benjamin scuffed a boot in the sand of the arena. "I heard you were thinking of taking this little outlaw up to the Battlement?"

Hershel looked at the boy and then back to the faded cobalt paint of the vintage trailer. "Might as well be a million." He smiled bitterly at Benjamin with his missing teeth. "I'm so stony broke that if they was sellin' steamboats on the Powder River for a dime apiece, all I could do is run up and down the bank yellin' ain't that cheap."

I glanced at Juana and she rolled her eyes, and the two of us watched the auctioneer attempt to get another twenty dollars out of a manure spreader before moving on to the object of our two cowboys' affection. "Why do you suppose Nolan is selling his place?"

She leaned against the trailer and pushed her hair back behind her ears. "He was going to get rid of it because he didn't want to deal with any more of Wade's crap."

I joined her and leaned against the trailer. Bill looked pretty satisfied; evidently the sale was going well. "Has anybody told him that's not much of a problem anymore?"

"Yeah, but I think he got used to the idea of selling the place, so he's just going ahead with it."

The familiar auctioneer's voice echoed in the confines of the building. "Now we have a prime example of a nineteen-and-sixty-eight, dubya-dubya brand, straight-load, bumper pull trailer. What do I hear, what do I hear! Gimme a thousand to start, a thousand to start! Here we go!"

We weren't particularly going, because no one was bidding.

Larry Brannian was the auctioneer. He was from my county, and from where I stood I could read BRANNIAN AUCTIONEERING SERVICES, DURANT, WYOMING, on the PA system. He was a comfortable old cowboy and the best auctioneer in the state, with a turquoise and coral bolo tie that bobbed up and down on the freshly starched opening of his white dress shirt when he spoke. He was a little embarrassed at having opened the bid too high. "Eight-fifty, do I hear eight-fifty, eight-fifty, eight-fifty, eight-fifty—"

The crowd remained unmoved.

"Seven-hunerd, seven-hunerd dollars for this fine piece of equipment with tires that . . ." He peered to get a better look at the bald and dry-rotted tires to our left. "Tires that hold aieeer!" There was a smattering of laughter from the crowd as his eyes caught mine, and he laughed. "Well, we must have some trouble around here somewheres." I ducked my head and pulled my hat down just a little; I looked behind me as if Larry must've been talking about somebody else. The auctioneer was nothing if not quick on the uptake and rapidly changed the subject back to matters at hand. "Seven-hunerd?"

Another disaster averted, I watched the abject misery that passed between Benjamin and Hershel as the old cowpuncher started to raise his hand but then thought better of it. A spotter raised his arm and pointed toward an area we couldn't see, which was blocked by the trailer itself. "Hup!"

"I got seven-hunerd, seven-hunerd, gimme seven-fifty?"

Mike Niall, who was leaning against the far wall, raised his head and nodded. Another spotter caught the gesture. "Hup!"

"Seven-fifty. Do I hear eight-hunerd?"

He looked back at the party we couldn't see to the right, and the spotter rang out again. "Hup!"

"Eight-hunerd. Eight-hunerd. Do I hear eight-fifty?"

Mike Niall raised the brim of his sweat-stained straw Resistol and spat on the sand-covered floor.

"Hup!"

"I got eight-fifty." Brannian looked toward the mystery bidder, and his spotter cried out again. "Hup!"

"Nine-hunerd, nine-hunerd! Now we're talkin'! Rubber mats, padded walls, hay manger, and a tuck-under saddle rack!" The spotter swung back toward Niall, but you could see the rancher's will was rightly weakening.

I watched Hershel and Benjamin, cowpokes separated by a good sixty years but joined in a brotherhood of horseback and by a thing we all shared, the want of a journey to a mystical place.

"Nine-hunerd once!"

There was a lesson my mother had instilled in me at an

early age, which had been reinforced by my experience in Vietnam and by my twenty-four years as sheriff of Absaroka County. She said that I should protect and cherish the young, the old, and the infirm, because at some point I would be all of these things before my own journey ended.

"Nine-hunerd twice!"

So far, I was two for three.

I raised my hand above the crowd.

"Hup!"

I left it there as a tall, handsome Cheyenne man peeked around to see who he was bidding against now. The young woman and the two cowboys looked up at me in surprise. Henry Standing Bear glanced at our little group and shrugged. Hired on faith, one is obliged to be more than expected.

7

October 28, 3:17 P.M.

It looked like UPS with all the boxes in the kitchen of the old Nolan ranch house, and it was all I could do to find a place to sit down. I chose a foldout stool, which was leaning against the wall, and sipped my can of iced tea. I turned down a slug from the bottle of rye whiskey that Bill had offered before he spilled himself a double shot into a tumbler—it was his second since I'd arrived. I wondered what it was that caused old cowboys from around here to resort so readily to drink. He alternately sipped and wrapped plates, stacking them in cardboard boxes.

"I tell you, if you ever want to talk yourself out of buying anything ever again, just be forced to pack up everything you've already got." He held up a dish for my inspection. "You need any dishes, Mr. Boss?"

I shook my head no and thought about all the boxes still in my own life that were lined up against the walls of my cabin. "Where you headed?"

"Believe it or not I bought a condo in Denver, down in

LoDo." He stopped packing for a moment and toasted the Queen City. "Thought I'd try urban life; see if it agreed with me. Eat in restaurants, drink five-dollar cups of coffee, and see if the Rockies can ever win the big one." He smiled.

I felt a little guilty about raising the next subject. "Being neighbors with Wade Barsad turn you against ranching?"

He thought about it. "Oh, there wasn't much of the ranch left after I sold the majority to him. All I had was this old place, two hundred and sixty acres, and the new house." He glanced around. "I got it all listed in Gillette and Sheridan, and it'll probably be sold by next week."

I sipped my tea. "You ever think about buying the other part back instead?"

The look on his face hardened, but it was having a difficult time combating the liquor. "Not really. My family had this and an old gas station up on the east side of the Powder River forever, but it always seemed like they were working three jobs just to make ends meet." There was a resignation in his voice I recognized. "I guess I'm just tired of it."

"No family?"

"Nope, I'm the last one stupid enough to stay. I had a wife." He looked around as if she might be in one of the boxes. "But I must'a misplaced her somewhere." His eyes finally rested on the tumbler of rye, with more than a little meaning.

"Kids?"

"Yeah, but it appears they went the way of their mother."

I studied him. "Footloose and fancy-free."

"That's the way of it." He continued to gaze at the amber liquid intermixed with the ice cubes for a while longer, then rattled the tumbler, sat it down, and began wrapping more dishes. "You don't have to dance around it; you can ask me about Wade, I don't mind. I got nothing to hide."

"General consensus was that he needed killing."

He breathed a short laugh. "I've heard that from more than one source."

"You don't seem overly bitter toward the man."

He folded the flaps on the box, pulled up another one from the floor, and glanced at the large and mismatched stack of dishes on the counter. "Hey, you sure you don't need any dishes?"

"Yep, I'm sure." I continued to look at him.

He picked up the bottle from the counter, refilled his glass, and took another swig for emphasis. "I got my money out of him."

"Meaning?"

He shrugged. "Most of the people around here who hated his guts, hated him because he cheated 'em in one way or another. I got my money up front, when he bought the ranch. Maybe I just caught him at the head of the curve, while he was still flush."

"Lost it quick?"

He sat the bottle back on the counter and gazed at the unwanted dishes, but his enthusiasm for packing seemed to be waning—mine would have. As he ruminated, he reached up, unplugged, and plucked from the wall one of the ugliest metal sunburst clocks from the fifties that I'd ever seen. "Oh, yeah."

"He didn't know a lot about ranching?"

He looked at the clock, greasy from years of ticking above the range, its cord dangling to the floor, and it was like time had died. "You need a clock?"

"Nope."

He looked disappointed. "You don't start taking some stuff, I'm going to stop talking to you."

I held out a hand for the clock—it was even uglier on closer examination.

He smiled, satisfied that there was at least something in the kitchen he wasn't going to have to pack. "He didn't know heifer from steer as near as I could tell, but he came rolling up in that big, black Cadillac of his at a time when it didn't seem like anybody else was doing anything but leaving."

I rested the clock on a box and hoped he wouldn't notice if I left it. "He wanted your place?"

"Hey, he was a godsend to me. The bank was getting ready to foreclose; damn right I was glad to see him."

"Where did the money come from?"

"Out of state, both times."

"Both times?"

"He bought half of my ranch about four years ago, and the other half about a year or so back." He sipped his refreshed whiskey, set it on the counter with the bottle, and began packing dishes again. "But you know all this stuff." He glanced up at me. "I mean, you insured him, right?"

I didn't answer the question. "Did he ever say where the money came from?"

He reached for the packing tape. "There was a lot of talk about that. Some folks puzzled over the fact of how such a lousy rancher could keep coming up with money."

"What'd they say?"

"Oh, the usual stuff. Some said drugs, some said the mob, and others figured he was in the witness relocation program."

"Really?"

"Wouldn't be the first one who showed up out here." He finished taping the last box and put it with the others on the linoleum floor. "He got sued about a half-dozen times, once by the hospital in Gillette, once by the propane delivery people, once by Mike Niall, once by Pat down at the bar, and twice by me."

"What was the hospital one about?"

He picked up the bottle of rye and refilled the tumbler, which was four times, by my count. "That was tied in with Niall, who 'bout kicked his ass over some cattle Wade sold him. There was a fight, and Wade went and got a rifle out of his truck and Mike broke his hand takin' it away from him."

"That would be the rifle that his wife Mary used to allegedly kill him?"

His eyes avoided mine as he picked up the glass. "I'd rather not comment about that."

"What about Pat at the bar?"

He leaned against the counter and propped an elbow on a folded arm, glass by his head. He was still staring at the floor. "Pat owed Wade a small fortune and rather than pay him money, he just gave him half the bar."

"You?"

He opened the closest drawer and gazed at the mismatched utensils. "You need any silverware?" I didn't say anything, and he closed it with the extra care that an almost drunk man would. "We had a little right-of-way problem, but I want to go back to something you mentioned about Mary."

I waited, but he didn't say anything. "I'm listening." He didn't move for a long time, and I was almost sad the greasy, old clock was unplugged; at least it would have given us something to listen to.

He finally spoke again. "You wanna take a little ride with me?"

"Excuse me?" I waited, but he didn't say anything else. "I don't think I'm following you."

He put the tumbler down but picked up the almost half-full bottle. "I need to run up the road a minute, and I was hoping that you'd come along."

"Now?"

"Yep, if you don't mind drivin', 'cause I'm about three sheets to the wind." He pushed off the counter, the rye in his left hand, and stood there staring at the concrete pad of the porch with the propped-open screen door in his hand. "One thing I'm gonna miss."

"What's that?"

He gestured with the bottle. "Somebody's been leavin' me a fifth of whiskey every couple of days." He smiled. "I guess I've got a secret admirer." He called back to me as he continued out the door, and I got up from the stool. "Hey, don't forget your clock."

October 22: six days earlier, afternoon.

I had looked at her eyes, washed out like an old pair of Wranglers, and it seemed to me that the color there had gone through the wringer.

"I have these dreams."

I already knew what the dreams were about, but there were other things I wanted to tackle, and I thought a little backstory might help with the context, so I asked her. "About?"

"Horses."

I nibbled on a triangular portion of the grilled cheese sandwich that we were sharing. I'd already eaten lunch, but a deal was a deal. This was the first real response I'd gotten from her, and I knew I had to go slowly. "What horses?"

She brought her part of the sandwich up to her mouth but just held it there without eating. "Everything is orange, and there are these flares of circular light that keep expanding toward me—it's hot, but I can see them in the distance, looking back at me." She took a deep breath, and it was like she was still in a trance. "They're all dead."

I didn't say anything.

"That night . . . I'd been at a friend's house; he'd been sick. When I got home, he wasn't there."

"Your friend?"

"No, Wade."

I paused. "This was the night of the fire?"

"No, before." I waited. I was confused but didn't want to disturb the flow. "When I got home, he wasn't there. Neither was my horse."

"Wahoo Sue?"

She stared at the floor and still held the sandwich at her lips. "He said he killed her, but he didn't. I know him better than that; know how he liked to torture things." Her eyes came up again, and she smiled. There was no happiness in it. "Look at me."

"Who was the friend you went to visit?"

She stopped smiling. "I don't think I want to tell you that."

I waited as she took a bite of her sandwich—the first—and chewed without enthusiasm. "Why?"

She handed the rest of her portion of the grilled cheese to Dog through the bars. "Don't you think enough people are in trouble with all this?" I watched as Dog carefully extended his muzzle and took the bite from her tapered fingers.

"No, I don't." I looked out Virgil White Buffalo's window. He had been our lodger for a week or so in the summer and while here was intent on watching the children at day care play in the school yard. "See, here's the thing." I looked back at Mary. "I don't think you did it, and that means somebody else did. And in a roundabout way, it's become my responsibility to find out who that is." I took a deep breath and figured if I laid all my cards on the table, maybe she would see them, too. "I've got a killer out there, somewhere, and I have no intention of letting them get away with it. Now, who's your friend?"

October 28, 3:30 P.M.
Small-man-big-truck syndrome was what Lucian called it.

There, sitting in the now-empty arena, sat a sparkling red Dodge duellie. I stopped as Dog moved ahead of us and sniffed the tires and then turned around and looked at Bill and me. I glanced at the ex-rancher, and he smiled as he took another slug from the whiskey bottle. "Ain't she a beauty?"

I only nodded and said nothing, wondering what he hoped to gain from introducing me to a vehicle I'd already met twice, once at the Barton Road Corrals and again early this morning, when I'd attempted to shoot out the radiator with an empty shotgun. It had plates now, but it assuredly looked like the same truck.

"A lifetime of ranching and this is the first brand-new pickup I ever bought."

I gauged the size of the thing. "It's going to be kind of hard to parallel park this at Larimer Square."

He shrugged, and it honestly appeared that he didn't have an underlying motive in showing me the truck. "You can take the boy out of the big-sky country, but you can't take the big-sky country out of the boy."

I noticed he walked to the driver's side, before remembering that he had asked me to drive. "Sorry, the last thing I want to do is pilot this thing after too much 'who-hit-john.'"

I circled around and peered in the tinted windows—the same Winchester was still leaning against the passenger seat.

Same vehicle. Had to be.

Bill was watching me when I looked up. "New truck—are you sure you want my dog in there?"

He studied me for a second more and then shrugged as he pulled the passenger-side door open. "It's a truck."

I opened the door on my side and listened to the buzz indicating that the keys were in the ignition, then opened the back door and watched as Dog leapt onto the pristine, slate-gray seat and set up sentinel at the middle. The thing was a showcase for modern electronics, with a GPS navigation system, a DVD player, and a satellite radio. The furry beast gave me a quick look that said, How come we don't have a truck like this? It was not the first of Dog's disenchantments with a life of public service.

I glanced around the interior again and didn't see the 9mm pistol, but just because I couldn't see the semiautomatic, that didn't mean it wasn't there, either in the door compartment, the center console, or the escarpment of the dash glove box.

Bill climbed in and centered the .30-30 between his legs along with the booze. He looked puzzled and made a face as I hesitated. "C'mon, let's go." He reached back and ruffled Dog's ears as the barrel of the Winchester leaned over and casually pointed at my head. "What's your dog's name?"

"Dog."

He looked at me, caught my eye on the rifle, and pulled it back upright. "That's convenient."

I turned the key, watched the coil indicator light up and turn off, and started the big diesel. For the first time in a very long time, I regretted having to fasten my seat belt.

He motioned me through the double doors, down the ranch road, and onto the Powder River Road. We were headed north and drove silently through town past the old mill. They were nailing masonite over the front window of the bar as we passed. Bill didn't wave, upholding the it's-not-a-friendly-town motto, and we continued up the grade to where some WYDOT trucks were parked at the condemned bridge.

He did wave at the few workers who paused to look at the general prosperity that the new truck signaled as we drove across the tire-worn smooth planks. He motioned for me to stop at the dirt lot at the other side, and I reached for the key. "No, leave it running. I just want to ask a quick question." He rolled down the window and yelled to a redheaded and mustached man who stood at the back of the Range Co-op trailer. "Hey."

The man turned and walked over. He was another rail-thin individual and looked a little incongruous wearing the massive electrical tool belt at his waist and the broad-brimmed black cowboy hat on his head. I recognized him as Steve Miller, the man who had hooked up the phone at my cabin and whose daughter, Jessie, had deep-sixed a Datsun pickup in an irrigation ditch about a year ago.

I was wondering how to keep my cover as the telephone man spotted me and started to speak, but Bill cut him off. "Hey, Steve, how long are you guys gonna leave that emergency phone over on the pole?"

Steve nodded at me for just a second and then glanced over his shoulder at the blue plastic receiver still connected to the junction box. "Not long; I was just using it until they remove the bridge."

Nolan reached out and grasped the lean man's elbow. "Do me a favor and leave it up there till after the weekend? I'm cut off back at the house, and that thing's pretty handy."

Steve glanced at me again, and I diverted my gaze in hopes that he wouldn't say my name. "Well, you're not supposed to be using it, Bill." He looked my way again. "It's against the law."

I assumed that was for my sake.

"I ain't usin' it for long distance. I just need you to leave it over the weekend, all right? In case of emergency." Without waiting for a response, he hit the button and the tinted window rolled up.

Steve stepped back. I gave him a brief nod as I slipped the Dodge in gear and pulled out.

Bill threw an arm over the seat and looked past Dog to see if the telephone man was making any move to go toward the utility phone on the pole. From the rearview, I could see him watching us, but then he turned and went back to the trailer.

Nolan looked straight ahead. "They're gonna tear it down."

I glanced at him. "The bridge?"

"They shouldn't rebuild it; they should just leave that town over there, stranded."

It was almost the exact same thing that Mike Niall had said. "Why is that?"

He took a stiff draught of rye and licked his lips. "S'cursed." He settled his back against the seat and gestured with the bottle toward the bow in the river behind us. "You know, the town used to be on that side of the river."

I faked ignorance. "Really?"

"Yep." He fiddled with the foresight on the .30-30 and collected his history. "Camp Bettens was out here somewhere, about five miles east of Absalom—used to be called Suggs, about a century ago." He paused again. "You look like you were in the military. Were you?"

I continued to study the road. "Was."

He sniffed and nodded. "You got the look."

"What look is that?"

He smiled to himself. "A precision of movement, and you don't seem to miss much." He cleared his throat. "There was a night back in 1892, when these two buffalo soldiers wandered into the saloon at Suggs and were met with more than a few racial slurs." He shook his head and laughed, contemplating the liquor bottle. "Can you imagine that bunch of barflies, whores, and outlaws suddenly considering their watering hole as exclusive?" He laughed again. "Well, these ol' boys were 10th Cavalry, companies G and H, and had just come back from Cuba and the Philippines—and let me tell you, they were not unserious individuals."

"Hershel Vanskike has an old Henry rifle from—"

"Do you believe that ol' coot has that thing hanging in a saddle scabbard out there in a sheep wagon on Barton Road?"

"He says it's his fortune, and that he's going to retire on it."

The rancher nodded. "If somebody doesn't run off with it first."

We crossed Highway 14/16, which was the main paved road, and since Bill made no move to indicate another direction, I continued north on the Powder River Road. I navigated a long straightaway where the gravel changed from gray to shale-red and glanced up to see a sign that read YOU ARE NOW ENTERING THE NORTHERN CHEYENNE RESERVATION. There were stunted juniper bushes and mountain mahogany, some stretching into miniature trees but most just shrubs, and strong embankments of rock jutting from the valley that the Powder River had carved. "I take it those buffalo soldiers quietly departed, choosing to take their custom to another and more liberal establishment?"

"Well, sorta." He took another but smaller sip—I guess he was trying to slow his intake. "They escaped a shoot-out but got sniped at all the way back to Camp Bettens. The next night, twenty of the troops got together and rode back into Suggs and set up a standing and kneeling position on the main street and threw one massive volley into the saloon."

I glanced over and watched as the Winchester continued to bounce between his knees. "I bet that livened things up."

He nodded and closed his legs together to support the rifle as I wound my way along the cliffs at the riverbank. We were climbing. "As you might imagine, there was a considerable amount of return fire, but the only person in the bar who was hurt was the bartender, who was hit in the arm, and he got a shot off that killed one of the troopers. The squad from the 10th departed, leaving one of their dead in the street, and the locals sniped at 'em again all the way back to their post. There was a court-martial, and the whole batch of 'em got reassigned in short order to Coeur d'Alene, Idaho."

I glanced back at Dog in the rearview mirror, and even he was watching the man with the rifle. "End of story?"

"Not exactly." He glanced out the side window at the river, still flowing a tired, watery chocolate milk. "Two months later, one 'a them buffalo soldiers came back, walked in that saloon, and raised up the barrel of a big Colt Walker .44 and shot that same bartender in the left eye."

"I take it he didn't survive that one?"

"Nope." He took a deep breath and let it out slowly with a belch. "They put together a posse and went after the trooper, but they never found him. Some people say he mingled on the reservation here, but others say he got help from a local rancher and got away."

"Interesting."

He turned in the big, leather seat and looked at me with more consideration than he had so far. "It is, isn't it?" He continued staring at the side of my face, and I registered where his hands were, one idly on the barrel of the rifle, the other holding the bottle. "There's history all over these hills—some of it people know, some of it they don't." He didn't move. "I wonder about that."

"About what?"

"About history, when it dies." He leaned back into the seat

but still regarded me. "Kind of like the tree that falls in the forest when nobody's around? I mean, if nobody remembers the history, did it still happen?"

I studied the road ahead, looking like a red ribbon stretched through an extended bolt of khaki cloth, and thought about the Indian notion of the black road and the red road. According to Native spirituality, the black road was one of selfishness and trouble, while the red road was one of balance and peace.

I smiled and shook my head as I noticed a vehicle parked at the end of the long stretch, and a tall, dark man leaning against the truck bed with his face turned upward like a sunflower.

I let off the accelerator and gave Bill an answer. "History's history—it doesn't change."

He shook his head as I slowed. "Not really. Think about all the history in this area that never got witnessed, never got written down—isn't it dead?"

I stopped the Dodge a little past the battered green three-quarter ton and slipped the new truck into park. "Nope."

Bill leaned to look past Dog and through the back glass at the tall man who hadn't moved, still sunning himself and ignoring our arrival. "Hey, isn't that that big buck you were bidding against on that horse trailer of mine?"

I ignored the slur and nodded. "Yep, I think it is."

My hand was on the handle of the door before he spoke again. "You sure you wanna do this? Those ol' boys can be pretty concerted, especially when they don't get what they want."

"I'll risk it; he might be broken down."

He glanced back again. "Drivin' that shit-box, I wouldn't be surprised."

I left Dog in the truck so he wouldn't greet the Cheyenne Nation with too much enthusiasm and noticed that Bill didn't offer me the rifle or accompany me as I walked the ten yards back in the shale dust; the red road stretched to the blue horizon. I stopped about six feet away, as if I didn't know the Bear. His head stayed back, and his eyes remained closed as he spoke softly. "What seems to be the problem, Officer?"

"Careful, you'll blow my cover." I glanced back, but Bill hadn't moved and continued to occupy the passenger seat. I turned around. "You broke down?"

He still remained motionless. "We are resting."

I noticed the rolled-up sleeves and the grease and dirt on his folded arms. "So, you're broke down."

"Resting."

I nodded and approached a little closer, leaning against the wavering flanks of Rezdawg, the green and white paint looking as though it had been applied with a spatula. "What are you doing out here?"

"It is the Rez. I live here."

"Here. Specifically."

One eye opened slightly to regard me. "Waiting for you."

"Uh-huh, and how did you know I'd be out here?"

He looked irritated that I was ruining his sunbath and finally opened both eyes and swiveled his neck to look at me. "I did not." He flicked his eyes at the truck. "She did."

"I see."

"Where are you going?"

I glanced north, where the country got wilder and the breaks of the river more jagged, then at Bill, who had turned with the rifle now up and on the seat. "I think I'm being driven out into the country to be executed."

Henry nodded, and the eyes closed again. "Nice day for it."

"Yep."

We both enjoyed the sun for a moment, the pale surface of the rocks reflecting a dirty, almost white chalk. His voice rumbled in his chest again. "So, are you ready for the fights tonight?"

I shook my head and felt a little anger. "What in the world possessed you?"

He smiled just a little ghost dance of a smile. "It is something to do."

I shook my head at him. "You're not as young as you used to be, you know."

"Neither are you, and you are riding around with someone who is going to shoot you."

I grunted. "When I get back to town—"

"If you get back to town."

"If I get back to town, I'm going to grab that piece of paper from the bar and cross off your name."

He closed his eyes again. "I would not do that."

"Why?"

"It is the best cover we have so far; there is no way an upstanding citizen would ever do anything as stupid as be friends with someone who was fighting in The Powder-River-Pound-Down-Tough-Man Contest."

He had a point.

I glanced back at the Dodge; Bill had probably locked the doors—it was Indian Country after all. "I gotta go, or he's going to get suspicious."

"Do you want me to follow you?"

I shot a look around at the open country. "I would, but I don't think you could do it without being seen."

"My people, we have a way with these things. . . ."

My ass, along with my head, was beginning to ache. "Uh-huh."

The dark eyes closed again. "As you wish."

I patted the mottled surface of the ugliest pickup on the high plains. "Anyway, he's pretty drunk, and I don't want to overwork Rezdawg."

The one eye glanced at the truck and then at me. "She is almost through resting." I pushed off and started to turn, but he spoke again. "Rezdawg is only obstinate when you are around. She hears your words, and it hurts her feelings; you should apologize."

I leaned in for a little emphasis. "I'm not apologizing to your crappy truck."

He shrugged and closed his eyes again. "When she won't start and you are executed, do not blame us."

"I won't. I'll see you later."

"You know where he is taking you, right?"

I stopped and looked at him. "Maybe."

He sighed, and I got a slight wave from under the arm. "*Wacin yewakiye.*"

Good luck, indeed.

*   *   *

When I got back to the truck, it was locked. I knocked on the window and watched as Bill searched his new vehicle for the button to allow me to open the door. "What was that all about?"

I started the diesel. "He says he'll trade you. Even up." The Winchester was now lying across Bill's lap but still pointed toward me; I was fully aware that the lever-action didn't have a safety. I pulled the selector back into D. "Where to?"

He looked back from the big Indian to me, had a moment of hesitation, and then pointed in the direction we had been headed. "Down there about two more miles in the breaks, then right at the draw, and there's an old two-track."

I pulled out slowly, so as to not blow too much red dust on Henry, and continued alongside the river at just under forty miles an hour. As he'd said, there was a draw that led northwest, but there were two drooping strands of barbed wire hung across the road ending in one of the old levered hoops.

I looked at him, and he shrugged. "I know it's against the code, but could you get it? I'm so drunk, I'm liable to pinch a finger off." It is a western tradition that the passenger always gets the gate, which is why cowboys generally fight to sit in the middle, where you have no responsibilities other than to avoid the odd scrotal meeting with the gearshift.

I got out of the truck, walked toward the makeshift gate, and listened to hear if the passenger-side window rolled down along with the fumbling sound of the .30-30 being laid over the sideview mirror.

Nothing.

I undid the levered hoop and then dragged the post with the two strands of wire attached to the side of the little-used road. Bill motioned for me to climb back in, which I did. I eased the massive truck through the narrow gate and started to stop so that I could go back and close it, another western tradition, but Bill motioned to drive on. "Go ahead, there isn't any stock in here."

I noticed he wasn't drinking from the bottle any longer.

We came up on a rise and then took a knife's edge turn away from the river to where the trail, covered with cactus and sagebrush, edged along some of the rocks that Henry and I had been looking at from the road.

The two-track path ended in a scrabble field and then slowly climbed into a dry pasture that rolled with the hills. When we got to the top of the nearest one, I could see slight depressions where the road continued north and west and some larger rocks to our right, jutting out from the ground beside us like molars—the perfect place to kill someone, if you were so inclined.

I looked at the rancher. "What now?"

He cleared his throat and gestured toward the depleted vista. "Jus' keep going that way, toward the mountains."

The hills became more pointed as we drove, and the tall, dry grass rolled like waves crashing against the foothills of the Bighorns. Gradually, the road became more apparent and I could see a ranch gate in the distance, a big one made from rough-hewn 12×12s, with a bent sign chained on the top and sides.

There was a brace of structures in a meadow of bottom-land below the pale yellow cliffs, which were the same shade as the ranch house, barn, and outbuildings. The stone of the buildings, the shadows of the giant cottonwoods that just had turned dusty gold, and the deeply overhung cedar-shake roofs felt cool even from a distance, and I could feel emotion pulling in my chest as I took it all in.

I stopped the truck at the gate. We sat there for a moment, then Bill got out, and I opened the door for Dog. The three of us met at the cattle guard, and Bill gestured for me to continue toward the gate, which I did, even though he still held the .30-30. He held the bottle too, if unsteadily, but I wasn't too afraid of being shot in the back anymore and reached down and ruffled Dog's ear. "C'mon. You've jumped these things before."

Bill followed us over to the thick rails that made up the pivoting double gate. The hardware was handmade, and I could see all sorts of finishing touches in the forged steel, a talent which was far beyond the abilities of most ranchers. Even the chains that held the sign above us looked handmade.

Bill leaned on the top rail with the Winchester lying parallel, his forearms covering the rifle. "The fella that built this place was a blacksmith by trade, but he dabbled in masonry."

"Uh huh." I propped up an elbow of my own on the worn spot just where you would have gripped to pull the custom latch. I could see that the four-inch rails were smoothed, where horsemen had sidled against the gate for more than a half-century, so that they could open it without dismounting, saving themselves the ignominy of becoming a cowboy afoot.

"Knew what he was doing: back to the cliffs, easy access to water, and those beautiful mountains off in the distance." Bill stood there for a moment, breathing in the flavor of the changing wind as it followed the bottomland and climbed the cliffs that surrounded a perfect basin where the homestead was located and where the air was sweet and heavy with the life-affirming humidity of the river. "He had a wife who was probably the prettiest thing in the Powder River country—musical, too. Played the piano, as I recall."

There were a few juniper and some cottonwood trees growing up from the fissures in the rock along the cliff, the volunteers mimicking the shimmer of the big guys by the ranch house. There was an old road that led down to the huddle of buildings, but until you were almost upon it, the place was completely concealed from the outside. You had to know it was here to get here.

I turned as Dog circled the perimeter, taking in the smells, and I could feel a little of the moisture collecting in my eyes. "Whatever happened to them?"

Bill stood with his back against the gate, the rifle now propped against the fence, and gestured with his chin for me to join him. He scratched his neck where his protruding Adam's apple strained as he continued to look up at the ranch sign. "They had a boy who played ball, offensive tackle for USC, but I don't think he ever amounted to much."

The chains that held the sign racked against the eyelet bolts with the wind and then relaxed, the sound like spurs jingling on a hardwood floor. Memories were crowding in on me now, and all I could do was stand there and take the hits like a tackling dummy.

He finally lowered his head and took a sip of the rye as I

stared at the sky and read the name I knew as well as my own. Because it was my own.

The gusts pushed against the wooden plank, but the letters that my father had carved deep into the whorls of the ironwood were still highly legible and read,

LONGMIRE.

October 28, 5:40 P.M.

I handed the bottle back to him and stood there, still feeling the burn in my throat as I thought about what Henry had said alongside the red road, about knowing where we were going. "You remembered my family after all these years, Bill?"

He blew out a deep breath that pursed his lips. "Yeah. I heard about Martha getting the cancer and I know I should've gotten in touch, but I didn't, and after that it just kept getting harder and harder to work up the nerve." He readjusted, still in search of a comfortable spot for his butt on the top rail, and tossed a small pebble into the roadway that stretched down to my father's house. "I figured I'd see you again." He laughed. "I don't mind telling ya, I was getting worried thinking I was going to have to write you a letter from Denver. Hell, I'd rather take a bullet than write a letter."

I walked away from the gate toward the edge of the cliff and stared at the reflections on the water as Buffalo Creek twisted its way to the reservoir that I had helped my father build. I stood there on the bluff overlooking the place where I'd grown up, trying to deflect the flood of history and emotion. "After they died, I just stopped coming out this way."

"I know." He took another swig of the liquor and gestured toward the tidy ranch house with the stone archways shading the front porch and to me with both hands, his voice echoing off the rock face. "Funny how you can have your life some place and then just pick up one day and walk away."

"How long did you know it was me?"

He smiled. "I met Eric Boss before, and he wasn't what everybody was describing. I read the newspapers, and you've been in there a lot lately."

"I suppose so."

"Then I got a look at you at the bar last night."

"You were there?"

"Nope. I started to come in but saw you and turned around and went home."

"What time?"

He smiled. "You sound like a sheriff now."

I didn't smile. "What time?"

He cleared his throat and spit to the side, wobbled a little, and paused. He looked like he might puke, but he only belched and turned back to me. "'Bout eleven-thirty. It looked like you were havin' a little scrape with that Cly fella."

"Who else knows who I am?"

He made a face. "Nobody."

"Nobody?"

His eyes stayed steady underneath the brows. "Nobody that I know of."

I took a deep breath and looked at the homestead and then at the sign again.

His eyes narrowed as he watched me but then widened as he followed my gaze. "I'll be damned. There aren't that many Longmires around these parts, and I've heard the stories about your grandfather and that fugitive buffalo soldier."

"Did you recognize Henry back there on the road?"

He waited a minute, aware that I'd changed the subject. "Yeah. I think more people know who he is than know who you are. He's kind of a celebrity around these parts. . . . He played ball, too. Didn't he?"

"Running back for the Cal Bears, appropriately enough."

His head nodded, maybe a little more than it should have. "Both of you were good—what happened?"

"Vietnam." I looked back toward the house, my eyes unable to leave it alone. "Do you think anybody's made any connections?"

"Well, nobody's said anything, but you've got 'em nervous." He shook his head. "What the hell are you doin' out here, Walt?"

I plucked the .30-30 from its resting place and examined the breech—it was loaded after all. I held it and looked at him. "You know, I thought you might have some other reasons for bringing me out here."

It took a long time for him to respond but, when he did, he looked confused and then just a little shocked. "Me?" We both looked at the Winchester. "I bring that thing with me everywhere I go anymore. With all the things goin' on out here, I figure a man ought'a have some protection."

I walked back through the gate and leaned on the grill guard of his truck. "Who else has a red Dodge like yours?" He sat there, looking at me blankly. "Your new truck—anybody else have one like it?"

"No, don't think so."

"When did you put the plates on?"

He thought about it. "This morning. I got 'em in the mail yesterday."

"Anybody else use your truck?"

"No." Then he reconsidered. "I let Hershel use it to haul some of the equipment over for the auction, but that's it."

I thought about last night, when I'd carried the cowboy home. "Were you driving out on the Barton Road by the corrals last night?"

He laughed. "That was you that brought Hershel back?" He laughed again. "I always make a loop to make sure he gets to his trailer all right." He shook his head. "I was on my way home."

"When I saw your truck at the corrals, it passed me, then headed south and east."

It was silent for a bit—we both knew his place was north and west. He sniffed and covered his face with a hand. "I sometimes take Barton down to Middle Prong and then circle back on Wild Horse—just cruisin'." He slid the palm of his hand down and rested his chin. "You'd be amazed at the things you'll do if you think you're never gonna see a place again."

I looked over my shoulder and could see someone on horseback on the road leading up to and alongside the cliffs. "How about at the bar?"

"When?"

"Afterward."

He sounded honestly confused. "Like I told you, I went home and hung my keys by the door like I always do."

"So, you weren't at the bar in Absalom at about one-thirty this morning?"

"Hell, no. Like I said, I was at home asleep. I was in bed by midnight—I can guarantee it." He fished in his shirt pocket, pulled out a plastic medicine vial, and rattled the contents. "Took two of these—boom, boom, out go the lights."

I held out a hand, and he threw me the bottle. I read the paper label and looked up at him. "Where did you get Mary Barsad's medications?"

He studied me. "It's not what you think."

I didn't say anything.

"It's not." He started to reach for the container, but I tightened my hand around it. His hand dropped. "She gave 'em to me. I was having trouble sleeping, and she thought they might help."

"Did they?"

"Like a pole-axed steer." I waited. "We were just friends, that's all." He watched me, trying to gauge my reaction. "I'd see her out ridin' and we'd talk; pretty soon she'd stop by and have a cup of coffee. We got to talkin', and if I was to tell you the truth, I think she felt sorry for me—and shit, Walt, I let her."

"Then I take it that you knew her pretty well?" He nodded. "Do you think she shot Wade?"

He took a deep breath. "God, I don't know—" He slipped off the fence, stretched his muscles, and walked toward the middle of the road with his palms at the small of his back. He spoke to the cliff. "I'd like to think that she didn't do it but she says she did, so what the hell do you think?"

I decided to keep a few hole cards where they belonged. "I'm not sure."

"I mean, they found her with the gun—"

I knew the story. I'd heard it from Hershel and had read it in the Campbell County reports, but I figured I'd play along. "Who did?"

"Well, Hershel; then he came and got me."

"Did he bring her?"

"Nope, left her sitting there in the yard, but he took the gun and came and got me."

"He left her sitting in the yard with the house burning?"

He turned to look at me. His voice was strained and was carried away by the wind. "Only the barn was burning when he came to get me, but by the time we got back over there the house had gone up, too. We found her sitting right where he'd left her."

"Hershel didn't go in before and check on Wade, to see if he was dead?"

"Yeah, now that I think about it, maybe he did." He shook his head. "I couldn't have done it."

I tossed the container of pills in the air, caught it, and held it up between us. "In the kitchen, you mentioned something about Mary, something you wanted to show me. Was it this?"

He nodded and smiled. "Yeah, I figured it was the only guaranteed way to get you to come along with me."

I nodded. Dog had been sitting on my foot but raised his

head to look at me when he noticed that the rider, who had a small child seated with him on the horse, was only a hundred yards off. I looked at the mounted young man in the cowboy hat. Tom Groneberg, to whom I leased the place, and the two-year-old boy who was sharing his saddle both recognized me and began waving. "You mind if I hang on to these?"

"Not if you think it'll help, but can I have two for the road?" I walked over, popped the cap, and tapped two of the white, oblong pills imprinted with "S421" into his open palm. "You never know when you might have a rough night."

Or a rough day. Boy howdy.

October 22: six days earlier, night.
Her eyes had reflected the streetlights that shone through Virgil's window. She never seemed to really sleep, and I had begun to think she should try it standing up, like a horse.

I stood, but she didn't move, so I quietly patted my leg for Dog to follow. We slipped back into the main hallway and walked toward Vic's office, where I could hear her softly tapping her keyboard.

Her office was small, with the Wyoming law binders covering the walls, but she liked it crowded. Her legs were stretched out with her naked feet crossed at the ankles on the edge of her desk, the keyboard in her lap. Dog settled on the floor, his big head between his paws, and I occupied the gray plastic chair. "What's the word, Thunderbird?"

She waved for me to hold on a second, continued typing an e-mail message, and pressed send. She mumbled in response to my question. "What's the price, forty-four twice. What's

the joy, nature boy. What's the reason, grapes are in season."
She turned and sighed—an undersheriff's work is never done.
"The toxicologist in Cheyenne is flirting with me."

"On state time?"

She shrugged an eyebrow. "Hey, I get it where I can."

I ignored the comment. "I thought Saizarbitoria was going
to research this—"

She interrupted. "I sent him home."

"—medication."

"No thanks, I've got plenty." She stared at me as I waited,
finally glancing up at the ceiling and reciting, "Eszopiclone is
a nonbenzodiazepine, nonimidazopyridine, cyclopyrrolone
hypnotic sedative. The stuff was developed in the eighties,
refined and tested in the nineties, and is now a widely available prescription drug."

She placed the keyboard back on her desk but kept her
shapely ankles on display. Her boots and socks were on the
floor by the wastebasket. It was a warm night, so she had
taken them off, which revealed her perfectly pedicured feet.
She had rolled up her jeans to make Wyoming culottes, something she did a lot in the summertime—I guessed this ward-
robe decision was her swan song—and her muscled calves
showed to perfect advantage.

"It works by binding to the GABA receptors in the brain,
but beyond that connection they're really not sure how the
stuff works." She glanced at the computer screen, hit another
button, and the drug company's logo and active screen commercial came up. Vic knocked the syrupy music down and
looked at me. "Most of these hypnotic and sedative drugs are

still a mystery to the companies that produce them—all for people with chronic insomnia like your friend back there."

"So, the pills are legit?"

She nodded. "DCI ran every test they had and guess what?" He waited. "They're sleeping pills." She glanced back at the computer screen as a couple frolicked on a beach at sunset. "The only effect that most people notice is a bitter, metallic taste in the mouth called *dysgeusia*." She considered me, with her head slightly cocked. "Do you believe they have a fucking scientific term for bitter metallic taste?"

I nodded. "We used to just call it fear."

"Five to ten minutes after dosing, you get the taste." She threw a chin toward the computer screen. "Ten to fifteen minutes and you're out, REM sleep within the hour."

"Can you OD on it?"

"Oh, yeah. Anything more than about thirty-six milligrams and you're looking at an activated charcoal cocktail or the pump, and you're also likely looking at renal or liver damage; then, depending on that damage, you go to operation bank account."

"Which is?"

"Going through pockets for loose change."

I sighed.

"There is one important note concerning our case though, and that is that the medication is for temporary usage." She stared at me. "Sleeping Beauty's been using this stuff for almost two years. Who knows how much of this crap is backed up in her system or what effect it has."

"Illegal use?"

"There's a small niche in the drug culture of addicts that use the stuff since it's DEA Schedule IV and easy to get. They use it for the come-down phase after cocaine, meth, LSD, MDMA, and all the 'upper' drugs. ADD and ADHD patients use the stuff to come down after spending the day on amphetamine variants." She pointed at the screen as the happy actors collapsed in giant feather beds, surrounded by huge, sleepily floating butterflies hovering over them. All in all, it was kind of creepy. "Do you believe this crap? I mean, if you're to the point of drugging yourself into a stupor to go to sleep at night, you're probably not leading an idyllic life."

"An extra Rainier usually works for me."

I started to get up, but she swung her chair around, hooked the aforementioned naked calves behind my legs, and pulled herself in close, grasping my thighs with her capable hands. "I usually rely on hot, sweaty, jungle monkey sex." She leaned in, and our noses were about eight inches apart. "Works every time."

I didn't move. "I hear that can be very addictive, too."

Her face grew closer, and her voice lowered to a rough whisper. "Oh, yeah."

"I'm still thinking about going out to Absalom."

She leaned in, even closer than before. "You know, I think we're developing an unhealthy pattern here. Every time I talk about the job, you talk about sex, and every time I talk about sex, you talk about the job." I watched as the smile hollowed under her cheekbones and traced her grin.

"Kind of a passive-aggressive thing?"

I could feel her hands running up and down my thighs,

building heat. "I'm okay with either, and I have my own hand-cuffs." I leaned back in my chair and broke the spell as she looked at me. "What?"

I took a breath. "I've got a question for you, a serious one."

"Okay."

"Do you want to be sheriff in two years?"

She leaned back in her own chair and thought about it. "This is a serious offer?"

"Yep."

She took a breath and studied me with a hard look. "Why are you asking me this now?"

It was a fair question, but I'd been giving the election con-siderable thought. "Well, the vote is next month and up to now I've only put in a halfhearted attempt."

She smiled at me with that oversized canine tooth. "Seems to me you're giving everything a halfhearted attempt." She dropped her legs. "What, you worried you're not going to get reelected?"

It was my turn to take a breath. "We're not talking about me." I slowly let it out. "We're talking about you."

Her eyes went down to her hands, which still held my knees. "Look . . . I know my limitations."

"What's that supposed to mean?"

"I'm not an administrator."

I shrugged. "Neither am I; that's why I have Ruby."

"I won't have that luxury because as soon as you retire, she'll leave skid marks." She looked around the room as if the staff had suddenly assembled and then departed. "They'll all leave, and I'll be sitting in this fucking mausoleum alone."

"I think you might be underestimating yourself."

"Really?" Her head nodded in emphasis, the way it did when she had more to say than one mouth would allow. "The Ferg is, for all intents and purposes, retired. Double Tough will bail as soon as one of these methane outfits offers him sixty thousand a year. Frymire, the international man of mystery—who the fuck knows what Frymire is going to do? And Saizarbitoria? You think he's going to be happy being a deputy for the rest of his life?"

"He just switched over from corrections—he's not ready to be a sheriff."

"He will be in two years."

"Maybe not." I wanted to put a little more distance between us, so I contemplated the books on her shelves and the one space left for the light switch. "Does the Basquo seem a little odd to you lately?"

Her head inclined. "In what way?"

"Since he got stabbed?"

She thought about it. "Maybe a little. He's quieter—why?"

"I've been trying to work him back on the duty roster, but he's not showing a great deal of enthusiasm."

She sighed. "Well, he lost a kidney, so maybe he's got a right to a little bullet fever." She leaned back, cocked an elbow on her armrest, and placed a fingernail that matched her toes between her teeth. "And you?"

"What about me?"

"I'm going back to the original subject of this fucking conversation. Are you going to be my deputy if I'm sheriff?"

I leaned forward and took her finger out of her mouth and put my hands over hers. "Like I said before, we're not talking about me, we're talking about you."

"I asked you a very simple question."

I didn't answer, and she'd nodded some more. "That's what I thought."

October 28, 7:25 P.M.

Bill dropped Dog and me off at my rental car and said he'd see us later this evening at the fights. I drove the lonely gravel road back toward Absalom. A fantail of ochre dust plumed twenty feet tall behind me before it was lifted by the prevalent wind and carried off toward Twentymile Butte and the Battlement. The two-hundred-foot front face of the topographical landmark stood like some sort of Powder River Monte Cassino along the wide valley of Wild Horse Creek, which reflected the autumnal glow as the scoria shone like carved platinum.

When I was about Benjamin's age, I'd read Arthur Conan Doyle's *Lost World* in the back bedroom of the ranch house we'd just been surveying and had secretly suspected that dinosaurs roamed the elevated and unapproachable twenty square miles that I saw almost every day. I was right in a sense but wrong in a chronology that was off by a couple of million years.

The college in Sheridan had had a dig up on the butte where they had found the intact, fossilized skeleton of not a dinosaur but a birdlike creature about eight feet tall. I'd seen the *Diatryma* in the museum over there and had dutifully read the little brass plaque that had labeled it as one of the dominant predators of the Eocene period, when Wyoming had been a dense jungle of subtropical climate at the edge of a western interior seaway.

Geologically, I'm sure there was a lot that had gone on there since then, but socially I don't think much had happened. There were the occasional antelope and plenty of modern birds that made their homes in the rock, but the plateau was too high and the wind too forceful to allow for cattle grazing, and there wasn't much to hunt, so not many people made the trip.

There was a new road where an energy exploration firm had tested for gas and oil, and which might have provoked more exploration, but in keeping with the Battlement's inhospitality, all of the seventeen-thousand-foot wells had come up empty.

Secretly, I was glad. I still had hopes that there might be a few dinosaurs up there lingering about.

Just outside of town, I pulled the rental car to a stop at the railroad crossing and watched a fully loaded Burlington Northern & Santa Fe coal train rumble over the dark, shiny rails that gleamed like quicksilver in the twilight. My mind matched the pace of the train, each thought snagging the next and hauling it in tow.

I had explained to Tom Groneberg and his son, Carter, that we were just out for a ride and had taken the old ranch road by habit. He'd asked if I'd gotten this month's check, and I assured him that I had. He said that he and his wife, Jennifer, had purchased the property to the west and still had hopes of having a place of their own someday. I assured them that my place was theirs as long as they liked.

I glanced back up the hill toward the cemetery and thought about two of the graves that were up there.

I reached over and scratched Dog's ears as the last railcar passed and snaked its way in a gradual arc along Clear Creek south toward the Bighorn Mountains. "Thomas Wolfe says you can't go home again." He watched me with his big, soulful eyes and then glanced back down the gravel road to the hills beyond, perhaps looking for his own long-dead ancestors.

There was a great deal of bustle in The AR in anticipation of the big fight, and I was hoping that Juana would be working so I could get Dog and me some dinner. It was as she'd said, and Pat had rehired her; then, after giving her all the work, he had gone home to take a nap before this evening's festivities. She was loading auxiliary coolers behind the bar, and there were sixteen more cases to carry in from the porch. I volunteered to stock the beer if she would grill up a few hamburgers for us.

The food was ready by the time I finished setting up the coolers, and she even allowed Dog to come in and sit at the end of the bar. She broke up his two hamburgers and started to carefully feed them to him. I guess her opinion of the species was softening. "He likes me."

I ate my one cheeseburger and suspected that it might've been a little larger than The AR usually served. "So, you called the cops last night?"

She fed another bite to Dog, and I could tell she was surprised at how gentle he was. "Yeah, even as an illegal I figured that was too much gunfire to not call in. Anyway, I was incognito." She glanced at me. "How come they arrested you?"

I swallowed and took a sip of my iced tea. "They didn't."

"Why'd they put you in the cruiser?"

I plucked a fry that had fallen from my plate onto the surface of the bar, dragged it through my puddle of ketchup, and gave it to Dog—waste not, want not. "They just said they wanted to go over a few things."

She gestured a graceful chin toward the now-boarded-up window. "Like who blew out the front of the bar?"

I nodded. "Things like that."

"Pat's got a pretty wicked scuff on his chin, and he says his jaw isn't working so hot."

"Really?"

"Yeah." She continued to watch me as I ate. "He says that he was closing up and that somebody came in the back and surprised him."

I turned to look at her as she fed Dog another bite. "Somebody was breaking in the back while somebody was shooting up the front?"

"That's what he said." She shrugged with one shoulder and again with just a bit of attitude. "What do you think happened?"

I had to smile at her two-year, textbook procedure. "I really wouldn't know."

"I found about fourteen nine-millimeter casings scattered all over the floor, and a twenty-gauge shell behind the bar with wadding out on the porch."

I ate a fry. "Really?"

"Yeah." She fed the last of the burger to Dog and wiped her hands on a dishtowel hanging from her back jeans pocket. "You wanna know what I think?"

"Sure."

"I think there were three people involved. I think Pat and somebody else were meeting here in the bar, and then somebody came in the back. I think whoever it was that came in surprised Pat, hit him with his own gun, and then went toward the front." Her face grew flushed, and I could tell she was very excited about giving me her account of the story. "Then, whoever was out here didn't really want to see who-ever it was that took Pat out and started shooting at them."

I nodded. "Took Pat out?"

Her smile bunched to one side as she considered me. "It's cop-talk. Don't you ever go to the movies?"

"Not since 1974. It was a double feature—*Ulzana's Raid* and *Bring Me the Head of Alfredo Garcia*."

She swatted my words away. "Evidently, nobody got shot since there isn't any blood."

"Evidently."

She folded her arms and looked at me. "There's just one thing I can't figure out, and that's why the guy with the shot-gun didn't just shoot the guy in the pickup truck?"

I took a sip of my tea and sat there watching her in the si-lence. "And what pickup truck was that?"

It was silent some more. "I didn't tell you about the red Dodge pickup truck?"

"No, you didn't."

"Oh." She reached down and petted Dog's head. "After I called 911, I ran down the road by the church and saw a truck back away from the bar and take off down Wild Horse Road." As an afterthought, she added. "It didn't have any plates."

"Uh huh."

She leaned in on the bar, conspiratorially, and stole a fry. She chewed and watched me. "Bill Nolan's got a truck like that." She made a face and shook her head. "But he's not the one you're looking for."

"Oh?"

"No, he might be a law bender, but he's not a lawbreaker."

I sighed and finished my tea. "I wasn't aware that I was looking for anybody."

She leaned in even closer, and her voice was barely a whisper. "Okay, but a lawyer from Philadelphia by the name of Cady Longmire called looking for her father, the sheriff of Absaroka County, and described a guy who sounded an awful lot like you." She stole the last fry and looked very satisfied with herself. "I told her that I was working for you, and I could deliver a message." She put her elbows on the bar and looked to the right and to the left for dramatic effect, then at me directly. "I told her you were undercover."

I stared at her. "What was the message?"

"She said that some guy named Michael asked her to marry him."

9

October 28, 8:45 P.M.

"How am I supposed to know you're *undercover*; you're never *undercover*!"

Cady emphasized the word like I was playing spy.

Ruby, unaware that my activities in Absalom were of a covert nature, had given my daughter the number of the motel office, which was also the one for The AR. Luckily, Juana had been the one who had answered. "It's okay. I trust the person who got the phone."

"The man or the young woman?"

I took a breath. "Who answered the phone when you called?"

"Some guy, sounded like a real piece of work. Funny name, like something you'd hear in a bad television show."

"Cliff Cly?"

"That's it."

"What'd you tell him?"

"Nothing. I just told him I was looking for my father and then asked if he worked there. Then he handed me over to the woman."

"Juana."

"Who is she?"

"You're sure that's all you said to him?"

Long sigh. "Yes, Man From U.N.C.L.E., that's all I said. Now, who is she?"

I looked down the bar at the young bandita who'd allowed me to use the wall phone in the hallway of the empty establishment. "She works here."

"She sounds foreign."

I cupped the receiver against my face. "She's Guatemalan. She's an illegal—"

"She said her name is Juana."

"It is."

"She said she worked for you."

"She doesn't work for me."

"She said she did."

I sighed. "She has an overly active imagination and a potential two-year degree in criminology from Sheridan College. You know what they say about a little knowledge being a dangerous thing?"

"Speaking of—you're a sheriff. What are you doing working *undercover*?" She continued to say it as though I were in the school play.

"Sandy Sandberg called and needed a little help."

"Oh, God."

"What?"

"Daddy, you know he is such a character." She and Sandy went way back. When she was a toddler, he had taken the time to play with her at the law enforcement academy in Douglas, and they had become fast friends. Even through her protests,

I could hear the admiration she had for the man. "He could get you killed."

"It's not that dangerous a case." I leaned a shoulder against the wall and tucked the big Bakelite receiver against the side of my head. "What is this about you getting married?"

There was a pause, the first in the conversation. "Michael asked me to marry him."

The second pause. "When?"

The third pause. "Yesterday."

The fourth pause. "What'd you say?"

"I told him I needed to think about it."

I nodded at the wall and rested my forehead there. "I think that's smart." I waited for the critique of my response.

"Aren't you going to congratulate me?"

I cleared my throat. "For thinking about it?"

"For being asked."

"Congratulations."

"Thank you."

I listened to her breathing and could tell she was holding the phone close to her mouth. "What are you going to do?"

"I'm not sure."

"It's awfully soon."

"I knew you were going to say that."

I paused again; if only I could find a way to parent *undercover.* "You've had a lot of things in your life lately."

"I know."

I thought about the Philadelphia patrolman, Vic's younger brother. It wasn't that I had reservations about him, but it had only been five months since they'd met and a tumultuous five months at that. And even though it wasn't fair, I thought about her previous relationship and how that had left her un-conscious on the steps of the Franklin Institute. "Why do you think he asked?"

"Well, I think it has something to do with him loving me."

"I mean now."

Silence. "I don't know."

I nodded at the wall. "Have you guys discussed this?"

"A little, just talking about what we could do. . . . Just pie-in-the-sky stuff."

"I guess he's decided he wants his dessert now."

"Daddy."

I stared at the army-green wall. People had written and scratched things so deeply that re-paintings had only height-ened the sentiment. I wondered if Custer really wore Arrow shirts, if DD still loved NT, if the eleven kids that got left at the parking lot were still beating the Broncos twenty-four to three, or if 758-4331 was still a good time. I thought about the love, heartbreaks, and desperate passions that had been played out through the phone in my hand and wondered if emotion held like the scent of honeysuckle in late August—sad and sweet, hopeful and tragic. "I think he loves you. I think he's crazy about you."

"Yeah."

"It's not hard to do, you know." I could hear the smile.

"Yeah?"

"Yeah." I ran my fingertips over the wall. "I think you need to follow your heart, kiddo." I took a deep breath and let it out slowly, allowing my emotions to join all the others that had sighed through the pattern of black holes in the mouth-piece. My heart, which was two thousand miles distant, pulled away a little bit farther. "Is he okay with you taking your time?"

There was a sniff. "He says he'll wait forever."

I nodded at the wall again, aware that something had changed in me a few months ago and that now I seemed to be battling a sort of grief aversion—the emotional backwash of Cady's narrow escape. During her crisis, I had been in a kind of present-tense, protective mode that got me through the danger without wasting energy or emotional resources, but now it was past tense and I was uneasy.

We do everything we can to protect those we love, whatever it takes, and it's not enough. Unlike bone, once that illusionary magic circle of safety is broken, it can never be completely repaired and it is not stronger at the break. When Cady had left to go back to Philadelphia, I had hours and days to think and feel. I was supposed to be happy, but I wasn't, and I hadn't been sleeping well—having Mary Barsad in my jail hadn't helped. Like an addict, I was taking it one day at a time.

Dog was still seated at the end of the bar, and Juana was feeding him the remainder of my cheeseburger now. "I figured you didn't want the rest?"

"No."

She studied me. "Are you okay?"

I took a deep breath, cleared my throat, and swallowed. "Yep." I extended my hand. "Walt Longmire, sheriff, Absaroka County."

She wiped her hand on her jeans, took mine, and smiled. "I know. I looked you up on the Internet at the library in Gillette.

There was a big article about you in the *Billings Gazette* and the *Denver Post*—something about you breaking up a human trafficking syndicate in California?"

"I had a very small part in an investigation."

"There was a photograph of you on the steps of some big building, but your hat covered up a lot of your face."

"That's my best side." I reached down to pet Dog. "Was Cliff Cly the first to answer when Cady called?"

She nodded. "Yeah, but I grabbed it away from him pretty quick. He was in here drinking his lunch and got to it faster than I could." She thought about it. "It was like he was waiting for a call."

She seemed pretty sure of the situation, so I decided to let it drop. The undercover thing was wearing me out. "Is there anything else I can do to help you?"

"Nah, I'm just going to arrange some of the food in the freezer out back to make it easier for tonight, but I think we're ready."

I reached over and took one last sip of the melted ice in my tea. "Then I think Dog and I are going to go to our room and take a nap."

She let Dog lick the plate. "Is that Indian friend of yours really going to fight?"

I shook my head at the absurdity of it all. "Yep, I suppose he is."

"He looks like he can take care of himself."

"He can."

She nodded. "Watch out for Cliff Cly. He hasn't been around here very long, but I bet he cheats."

I patted my leg for Dog to follow. "I bet he does, too."

* * *

I get asked sometimes about what it is that makes a good cop. Of course, typing is handy, but really it's as simple as noticing things. Ask a good cop into your house once, and a year later he'll be able to tell you the layout of the furniture, what pictures are on which walls, and whether the toaster is white or stainless steel.

Somebody had gone through my room.

Juana had cleaned and straightened it, but I was pretty sure she wasn't the one who had gone through my things; it was a professional job and, if you hadn't thought to notice, you wouldn't have. Everything had been put back exactly the same way, except that my sidearm was now unlocked. I couldn't detect any smudges without high-powered assistance and whoever had searched had probably worn gloves, but I know the Colt's slide-action had been pulled when I'd put it away.

I made a quick search and found that the paint had been pulled apart where the bathroom window had been pried open. There was an open lot behind the motel with a couple of ramshackle houses facing the other way and a weedy, overgrown hillside that would have provided easy ingress to my room without exposing the intruder to a great deal of public scrutiny.

Who would have been interested and professional enough to leave almost everything as though it had not been touched? Couldn't have been Benjamin, and I didn't think that Pat had the dexterity to slip through the high window, especially after last night's altercation. There was that mystery man who had been driving Bill Nolan's truck or one that was remarkably similar.

Cliff Cly didn't match the stranger's profile—maybe Mike Niall and possibly Bill Nolan himself, despite his assurance that he had been asleep. If Bill was involved, you would have thought that he would want to keep away from me, not take me to my father's house. Besides, all his motivations seemed pure and what would he have had to gain in Wade Barsad's death? Mary? Possibly, but he would have to have figured that she would be facing a life sentence. Was that something they hadn't taken into account—that somebody would have to take the fall? And what about her confession to Hershel, Bill, the Campbell County investigators, and just about anybody who would listen?

I tried to see Mary as a Campbell County jury would see her; it didn't bode well. She lacked the one quality the populace expected in an accused killer, guilty or not—repentance. I had the feeling that if it came to it, Mary Barsad would be a woman who was tried for a crime but judged for her persona.

I took my hat off, placed it brim up on the wobbly table, and sat in the only chair. I glanced back at the Bible on the nightstand; I figured I'd had enough religion for one day. Dog leapt onto the bed, curled up, and looked at me. I always wondered if he knew more about what was going on than I did; some sort of innate canine ability to read people and situations.

"So, who dunnit?"

October 23: five days earlier, afternoon.
Mary Barsad had been at her best about the middle of the afternoon and, in an attempt to get her to eat, I'd moved the schedule back about two hours.

She still wouldn't eat breakfast, but at least I could get her to nibble on lunch and a nominal amount of dinner as we sparred. She sipped her soup and watched me as though I were the one in jail and not her. I'd uncrossed my legs and put my empty bowl of chicken tomatillo soup on the counter; Dorothy Caldwell's chicken tomatillo soup took all prisoners. "There's a difference?"

"Of course there is." She shook her head, and she dismissed me with a wave of her hand as she looked out the window and into the opaque sunshine of fall. "How long have you been a sheriff?"

I ignored the question. "I guess I see justice as the framework, and right and wrong as the philosophy behind it."

Mary turned, and I had the feeling I'd just stepped into a theoretical quagmire. She smiled a thin, hard smile that didn't reach her eyes. "Can't you do justice by doing wrong?"

"No, because then it becomes an injustice in itself."

She looked doubtful. "And who judges that?"

"We all do."

"Easy for you to say from that side of the bars." It was a bitter laugh. "Some judgments, it would appear, carry more weight than others."

I wanted to work the conversation around to her particular situation again. Previously, whenever I'd tried she'd clammed up; here was another opportunity, and I was going to have to go at it gently. "It's a collective framework, and I'm not saying that it's perfect by any means—but considering the alternative—"

"And what's that?"

I shrugged. "Chaos."

She looked at me intently. "And you've seen chaos?"

"I have."

"Where?"

"Vietnam . . . and a few other places." She took another spoonful of soup, but it paused at her mouth. "Mary, I need you to tell me what happened that night. I need you to tell me everything you remember or else I'm not going to be able to help you."

She had looked at me, quietly put the rest of her soup at the opening at the base of the bars, and placed the can of diet pop beside the bowl. She had slipped off her sandals, curled her knees up, and rolled over to lie on the bunk to face the concrete block wall.

October 28, 9:00 P.M.

When the gladiators died in the Coliseum, men in costumes came out and sprinkled sand to soak up the blood between bouts. The word for sand in Latin is *harena*—hence, arena. It's thoughts like this that occupy my mind when I probably should be thinking about more pressing matters. It was a five-hundred-dollar buy-in for each contender, and I was surprised at the number of individuals who had the financial resources to sign up. I was not surprised at the number who had the lack of judgment to fight, including the Bear.

Henry Standing Bear was resplendent in a white T-shirt with the logo FIGHTIN' WHITIES on it and below, in smaller script, EVERY THANG'S GONNA BE ALL WHITE. Somewhere, he'd scrounged a pair of actual boxing shorts, red silk with gold piping. The bar owner I'd coldcocked last night had acquired a few new mouthpieces and had boiled the ones left over from the previous bout. It was a free-for-all grabfest, but Henry was one of the quickest, so he'd gotten a new one.

I tried to think of the last time I'd seen gloves on the Bear, let alone seen him in a ring, and was coming up with eras when cars first started having seat belts. It was during a Rosebud County fair in Forsyth, when a traveling show had brought in the largest black bear we'd ever seen, and for five bucks you could climb over the ropes and "box" with Buster. Buster was muzzled, had had his claws removed, and was attached to a harness that could be pulled by two very large men so that he could be separated from the human contestant after he'd won, which Buster did every time that velvety Montana night.

Buster the Bear's technique had been pretty simple—he'd lumber out and straightforwardly envelop his opponent in his giant arms and smother him to the canvas. He was only about six feet tall on his hind legs but held the weight advantage in that he tipped the scales at close to seven hundred pounds. Henry and I had consumed several Grain Belt Premium beers and had rapidly risen to the sporting life, as only drunken teenagers can.

We watched about a dozen denizens of the high plains get crushed before it was Henry's turn. He had a strategy, which utilized the little-known fact that bears had notoriously crappy eyesight, and that, with the added weight, this one was a tad slow. He figured the thing to do was come out quick, give Buster everything he had in one punch, and then tackle him before he had a chance to see and recover.

It didn't work.

Buster the Bear's head snapped with a roundhouse punch to the muzzle that would've killed any man, but by the time

Henry Standing Bear tried to grab Buster by the middle, the black bear had already lifted him from the canvas and flung him aside, at which point he pounced on him with a verve yet unseen that night. It took four men, one of whom was me, to pull the chains to get the bear loose from the Bear, and by the time I got to Henry, he was the whitest I'd ever seen him. He said another little known fact about black bears was that they had forty-two teeth—he said he counted them as the muzzle pressed against his face.

I'd done a little Golden-Gloves work in my youth and had risen to the top of interplatoon competition in the Corps by virtue of size, youth, and skill—one of which I still had, one of which I didn't, and one on which the jury was still out. I'd competed well enough at Camp Pendleton to continue boxing at Camp Lejeune and then at the Armed Forces Boxing Championships at Lackland Air Force Base, where "Jacksonville Jake," a bundle of bailing wire from Florida with skin the color and toughness of tanned saddle leather, had bounced me like a Super Ball. Those three minutes had taught me a special and lasting respect for chief petty officers with middle names from the cities where they'd been born.

I was older now and looked back at those episodes as if they had been a part of some other man's life. I'd engaged in earnest only a few times, sinking to that primordial depth of instinct to destroy and then call it a game. I'd seen and sworn to never look upon that kind of savagery in myself ever again.

In the history of bad ideas, however, this had to be the thesis statement. The first indication that you're in the midst of a bad idea is that people stop making eye contact with you and you with them. When I saw him entering the standing-room-only bar, Henry Standing Bear didn't make eye contact with me. Juana served him a canned iced tea and also avoided his eye.

They were lined up four deep at the bar, and Pat's entrepreneurial skills had been tested when the bleachers borrowed from the Gillette American Legion baseball team had collapsed under the weight of the faithful. No one had been hurt; after all, God looked out for children, animals, and drunks. They'd brought in all the folding chairs from the community hall and had even torn the particleboard from the broken window so that more patrons could be seated on the porch.

I scanned the place for somebody who might blow my feeble cover but didn't see anybody I knew except Bill Nolan and Henry, who had continued to ignore me until I volunteered to corner for him, seeing as how no one else seemed to be willing.

The bag gloves didn't provide too much protection for Henry's hands, but he could get them in where regular boxing gloves wouldn't go, and the Bear advanced through his first match. In his second, he landed a return punch in Gary Hasbrouk's left side, which continued his theory that he could systematically left-hand his opponents to death. He then caught the man with an uppercut from out of Lame Deer that lifted him a solid eight inches from the plywood platform. In a model of sportsmanship yet unseen in the Powder-River-Pound-Down, the Cheyenne Nation stepped back to allow Hasbrouk to stretch his jaw and to try to remember what planet he was on, after which Henry sighed and reapproached his opponent.

Hasbrouk swung and missed the Bear by two feet and

then squared off with one of the towel men. Henry stepped back again and looked at the referees. Mike Niall, Pat, and some thin man I didn't know decided to call it a technical knockout as the crowd roared with disapproval.

Their behavior would have disgraced the Circus Maximus.

I ushered the Cheyenne Nation to the narrow hallway where I'd earlier talked with Cady on the pay phone and watched as the redoubtable Bear hid his swollen paw by keeping a shoulder between his hand and me. He'd made it to the final round as had Cliff Cly, who was standing in the ring and was exhorting the crowd.

In his first match, the rodeo cowboy cum ranch hand had knocked D. J. Sorenson out with one punch. In his second, a quick feint to the right kidney, and Ken Colbo let his guard down. Cly hammered him with a sweeping roundhouse that caught the wide-faced man in the side of the head. Colbo's jaw grew slack for a blink, and then he crumpled forward on his knees. Cly unceremoniously pushed him back with a knee of his own, and the sound of the back of the man's head hitting the plywood platform carried across the crowded and noisy room.

I led the Bear farther into the hallway and spun him back by grabbing his shoulder. "All right, if you're bound and determined to do this, he drops his right when he pulls back from a jab—" He wasn't paying attention and continued to keep his left hand where I couldn't see it. "Let me have a look."

He held the afflicted hand under his armpit. "No."

In the entire evening so far, it was the first moment our eyes had met. "Henry, enough."

He made a face. "What?"

I leaned in close. "Stop this before you get hurt."

He turned his shoulder so that I couldn't see and smiled at my glare. "We may be too late."

"Why are you doing this?"

"What?" He continued to smile at my discomfort and his. "I am helping."

"You're not."

"I am, whether you are aware of it or not."

You could always depend on Henry to be the straw that stirred the collective drink. I shook my head. "If you don't stop, I'm going to take you out back and beat the crap out of you myself. Let me see your hand."

"No."

For the second time in the conversation, our eyes met. "Let me see it."

The smile faded, and his face became cigar-store-Indian immobile. We stood there like that, unmoving, and then I turned back toward the makeshift ring with the white bar towel in my hand.

I caught the eye of the three unofficial officials as I sidled against the crowd. Niall leaned over and spit in the nearest spittoon and then looked up at me with a questioning look on his face.

"His hand is broken."

He shook his head. "What?"

I leaned in a little closer, watching as Cliff Cly approached, sipping a beer from his gloved hand. He gargled a little and then swallowed. I continued to speak to the rancher in a low voice. "The Indian's hand is broken. He can't fight."

"You're shittin' me." He gave a worried glance around the room. "That's not good."

Cly trailed his elbows on the top rope and looked down at us. "What's the holdup?"

Niall looked at the soon-to-be champion by default and nodded toward me. "He says the Indian's hand is busted, and he can't fight."

He swallowed the beer in his mouth, the sneer spreading across his lips. "That's bullshit."

I kept my eyes on the rancher. "His left is useless; there's no way he'll be able to continue."

Niall shrugged. "Well then, he forfeits his five hundred dollars, and Cliff here becomes champion."

I felt something nudging me in the side and turned to see the toe of Cliff Cly's boot poking me in the ribs. "He's a chickenshit—just like you." He took another gulp of his beer and looked down at me.

I thought about what good a quality, grade-A ass whipping would do the man. "Another time." I turned back to the ring judges.

"That's what I told your daughter." I ignored him and started to speak to Niall, but Cly interrupted again. "On the phone, she was coming on to me pretty hard, so I told her the next time she was in state I'd give her the high hard one."

That's when he spit the beer on me.

I stood there for a second, hoping that he hadn't done what he did, but the persistent tickling of used beer and spittle dripped off my hair and onto my shirt.

I can't be sure, but I guess it was about then that I looked back up at him and thought about Henry, the election, Mary Barsad, the investigation, my father's homestead, but mostly about Cady, all of it ganging up on me—and something just broke.

My hand was on the ropes before I could think about what I was doing, and it was like my muscles were intent on a little trip and my mind was just along for the ride. Cly backed away as I ducked under the top rope, and he watched with a cocky interest as I wrapped the corner towel around my right hand.

As I wrapped my other hand, he kicked his head sideways, stretched the muscles in his neck, shuffled a few steps, and moved to my left. "C'mon, old man."

The crowd was going nuts, but I could barely hear them. I felt the familiar coolness in my face and the steadiness of my hands as the rational qualities of my nature and the extended panic attack of the unimaginable deserted me.

I stepped in close to keep him from getting the maximum leverage of his swing and then watched as he bobbed and weaved into a Dempsey roll. He slipped to his right with my jab and then delivered a powerful undercut to my unprotected side.

I grunted and then reset my footing, lowering my elbow to block the punch that immediately followed. Cly ignored my footing and applied both hands into my ribs, and that was a mistake.

The clacking of Cliff Cly's jaw sounded like the snap-shuffle of a deck of cards, and he staggered back. I stood there in the center of the ring, and he moved toward me with a great deal more caution this time.

The temptation to pound the living daylights out of the

younger man was great, but I was betting I'd drawn enough attention to myself by just being in the competition.

Cliff came barreling in, maybe thinking that if he got in tight I wouldn't be able to use my greater reach. He crouched, and I figured he was going to put it all on the line with one good, solid strike. I was right except that he did so with his head and not his hands, swiftly flinging the back of his skull up and into my face in a debilitating head butt.

I had seen it coming in that last second and turned, but the majority of the force deflected from my nose and into my left cheekbone and brow. The effect was a blinding amount of blood that flowed from the cut at my cheek.

I backed away, swiping at my eye with one of my toweled hands. It hurt and felt like half my face had ballooned to the size of a softball. I smeared the blood back with the shoulder of my shirt, and I was relieved to make out shadows moving in the rapidly closing eye, but for now I was effectively blind to my left.

He had come out better in the impact, but not by much. He shook his head—evidently he had come close to knocking himself out with the illegal move. When he looked up and could finally get a read on me, he smiled at the damage to my face.

Cly stepped forward and feinted with his left but brought a jab back up with his right; when he withdrew from the punch, he dropped his guard just as I'd told Henry he would.

I responded with a quick jab from my left. He was off balance and started to fall away. I could have just let him go, but I was tired and angry and wanted it really over. I stepped after him and watched with my one eye as he raised his right to block the anticipated left that had stung him twice. It was another mistake, and his last for the evening, as I'd anticipated his move and had already brought a roundhouse haymaker down into the side of his head.

You can hit a man in a lot of different ways, ways I'd learned in the rough-and-tumble high-plains bars as a boy, ways I'd learned in the inner trenches of Big Six football, in the Marine Corps, and in more than a quarter-century in law enforcement. You can hit a man to embarrass him, hit him to blood him, hit him to knock him down, or you can hit a man to lay him out.

To my absolute dishonor, I hit Cliff Cly with the intention of the last.

His jaw bounced off his chest, and I could see that his neck muscles didn't work just before he pitched over backward, taking the metal pole at the corner, three lengths of rope, and at least two other people with him.

There is a sound that bodies make when they hit the ground, and there is no way to describe it. I've heard that sound in motels, bars, football, and battlefields, and it is this sound that brought me back.

There was a great deal of screaming, yelling, and confusion as I approached to see if he was still breathing; he was, but he lay still, with only his chest moving. I guess he had been the crowd favorite and there must have been a lot of money placed on his potential victory, because as I stood there a folding chair clattered against the back of my head and a few more flew onto the platform. I stumbled out of the ring and started pushing my way toward the back hallway, but even with my limited view from one eye, I could see that the entire crowd was now involved in nothing short of a melee. I tripped over another folding chair and went down as the mob swallowed me.

I started to get up, but a familiar hand planted itself against my chest, and the Bear ducked as more chairs sailed into the ring. There was a crash of glass near the bar, along with more screaming and yelling, and I could hear fighting that didn't sound like the kind sanctioned by the Powder-River-Pound-Down. Henry crouched guard over me and pushed some-one away while dodging an airborne bottle that smashed on the floor and showered us with shards.

I was staring at his hand as he continued to smile like the Cheyenne always do in battle. I tried to blink my left eye but couldn't tell if I had, and then allowed my head to fall back to the floor as he asked in a perfectly conversational tone, "Did you know your daughter is getting married?"

10

In 1948, at the Jimtown Bar, two hundred yards north of the Cheyenne Reservation, Hershel Vanskike killed a man. He was involved in a side-room billiards game when two traveling gentlemen from Chicago noticed the sport and asked to buy in. It was inquired as to whether they had the wherewithal to join the game, and they assured the local cowboys that they did.

The cowhands, not assured, asked them to exhibit the funds. The gentlemen from Chicago displayed over two thousand dollars in small bills.

Thus assured, the locals agreed to let them participate, but after a few hours of losing and drinking too many whiskeys, the Chicagoans grew irritable, and one of them, whose name was John Boertlein, began abusing an Indian rancher who was seated at the bar. He poked the Indian with a pool cue and asked the "chief" what the locals did for fun around these parts.

The middle-aged Cheyenne ignored him and continued

drinking, slowly bringing the pungent liquid to his lips with his elbows seemingly attached to the bar.

The man from Chicago told the "chief" that he had plenty of wampum and jabbed the Indian with the pool cue again, leaving a small, blue chalk dot on the Cheyenne's white shirt-sleeve.

The bartender took a step away, bracing his hands on the bar.

Boertlein prodded the Indian again and asked if he knew where he and his friend, whose name was Bud Ardary, could find a few squaws for the night. He left another blue mark.

The Cheyenne remained silent and took the final sip from his shot glass.

Bud Ardary, the other gentleman from Chicago, broke from the pool table to join in on the fun. Boertlein poked the Indian on his other arm but still didn't get any response. Instead, the Cheyenne put his empty glass back on the bar surface, tipped his hat to the bartender with his right hand, and rose. Boert-lein, sensing that he was about to be totally ignored, grabbed the Indian by the shoulder as the Cheyenne turned toward him, but the Indian stepped by him and headed for the door.

John Boertlein had a puzzled look on his face as he stood there.

Ardary pulled his friend toward him in time to see a thin line of red blooming across his buddy's dress shirt where the blade of a knife with an edge like a scalpel had sliced the Chi-cagoan's abdomen.

Ardary pulled a pistol as the Indian opened the door, and Hershel Vanskike, realizing that the last man to draw his gun in these situations was likely the first to end up dead, snatched a natty little .32 from his own waistband. Ardary fired at the Cheyenne as he stepped through the door. He missed. Sensing some movement to his right, he then extended his .38 toward the pool players, and Vanskike pulled the trigger on the .32.

I looked up at the big Indian seated next to me. "Damned Indians, they always get you into trouble."

He nodded. "I think that was my Uncle Art, the one who moved up to Rocky Boy."

I looked back at the report. "I can see why he moved."

It was viewed as a clear-cut case of self-defense, and the autopsy revealed three more bullets from previous altercations, but Vanskike still received nine months in the county jail. There were also the usual amount of D&Ds on his record and public intoxications with a smattering of aggravated assaults, but most of Hershel's criminal activities had tailed off a good thirty years ago when the old outlaw had grown accustomed to painting the town beige. Other than the incident at the Jimtown Bar, the only really troubling item was the one involving a rented house in Clearmont.

As for our involvement in the present altercation, no one questioned why Henry and I were arrested by the Absaroka County deputy and not the Campbell County one.

Just north of town across the condemned bridge, Victoria Moretti pulled the Bullet off to the other end of the dirt lot that WYDOT and Range Telephone were using, along a fenced pasture and to the side of what appeared to be an abandoned, yet familiar, green pickup.

The Cheyenne Nation and I sat on the tailgate of his truck as Vic doctored his and then my broken face from the first-aid kit from my truck. My undersheriff squinted at my swollen eye and pulled at my cheekbone, her investigation inflicting a considerable amount of pain. "Does it hurt?"

I leaned back a little, trying to get away from her probing fingers. "It didn't till you started fussing with it."

She stood her ground with her arms folded and looked at me. She wore a light fleece jacket, and she had the collar turned up against a repeated tide of cool air floating down from across the Bighorns. You could almost see the slight trails of breath leaving her mouth—almost. "He needs to get that hand X-rayed, and you need stitches."

"Just pack it full of that antibiotic stuff and bandage me up."

"You need stitches." I didn't say anything else, just continued to look at her through one and a half eyes. "Walt, you're being an asshole."

I took a deep breath, sighed, and I think I might've even smiled. "I do it rarely, but you've gotta admit that when I make an effort, I'm pretty good at it."

She shook her head as she delved through the kit for the requisite supplies. "What in the hell came over you?"

"I was feeling manly." I listened as the breezes played the dry, burnished grass like a mandolin and thought that maybe it was the oncoming winter, or maybe it was what Henry was reading in the file, or the fact that my left eye was almost completely swollen, but even though I felt tired, I was still willing to rise to the occasion. I sighed deeply and looked up at the Cheyenne Nation. "He supposedly burned a house down in 1992?"

"He was charged, but then it was dropped."

Henry read further in the glow of Vic's Maglite, which he held in his good hand as she continued to assess my injury. "He was supposedly out of town, but according to the Sheridan County sheriff there was reason to believe that he was the arsonist."

Vic knocked my knees apart to get better access, and I listened to the creaking of her gun belt as she pushed against my legs.

The Bear read aloud. "'Large, high-relief alligatoring of charred wood, crazing patterns of irregular glass, and depth of charring indicate the use of an accelerant. . . . Line of demarcation and spalling of the masonry indicates suspicious point of origin.'"

Vic looked up. "What? They had Sparky the fuckin' arson expert working over in Sheridan?"

He snorted. "It gets better. Guess who the investigating officer was?"

He held up the manila envelope with the arson report on top. Vic snatched it off his lap and read the scribbled signature at the bottom of the faxed sheet. "It says Frymire. Fuck me."

I looked back up at her and remembered that Chuck had been employed by Sheridan County before us. "Our Frymire?"

Henry nodded. "In the personal notes, he says that it was such a clear case of deliberate fire that he tried to run it down, but as soon as the owner got a check from the insurance company, he dropped the charges."

The Cheyenne Nation sat forward to hold the flashlight for Vic as she squeezed a worm of topical antibiotic onto her index finger.

Vic leaned my head back and removed the gauze pad she'd

been using to sop up the blood, careful to keep the medication on her finger from getting smeared off. I spoke to the sky.
"Who's watching the store?"

"Ruby, and she says to tell you that the next time you're
working undercover, would you please leave a note or something?"

"I'll leave a sock on my office doorknob."

"You don't have a doorknob."

I looked at Henry's hand as he held the flashlight, and Vic
smeared the goop under my eye and into the cut. "Oww."

She smirked. "Good. I hope it fucking hurts." She peeled
the wrapper from a large gauze-backed Band-Aid. "I'll ask
again: what in the hell possessed you?"

I continued to look at the Bear's hand. "The Indian started
it."

She dismissed him with a glancing blow from the Mediter-
ranean eyes and pasted the bandage onto my cheek. "From
him I expect it."

"Why?"

She smiled, the canine tooth sparking in the beam of the
flashlight. "He's a savage."

Henry's voice rumbled in his chest. "Look who is talking."

After Vic finished, I stood and walked away from the bridge
toward five horses. They stood just over the crest of a hill
alongside the river and watched us, probably wondering if
there was any chance of getting fed. I made a kissing sound
and watched as the lead bay raised his head. He came toward
us, and the others followed. They expected something to eat
but settled for nosing my hands.

I scratched the big bay behind his ears and then ran my

fingers under his chin where the bugs usually bit along the soft flesh beneath the jaw. The short hair was pebbled with small swellings, and he rocked his head back and forth, using my hand as a scratching post like some thousand-pound house cat.

I glanced back at Vic and Henry. "He's got pictures of her all over his sheep wagon."

"Who?"

I pulled my hand back, and the bay nibbled at my knuckles. "Mary Barsad. When I dropped Vanskike off at his trailer last night, I saw that he had pictures of her all over his walls."

They looked at each other before resuming their communal looking at me, Henry the first to speak. "That is significant."

I brushed the horse's nose and stretched my other hand out to pet a roan. "Maybe. He also believes in the divine accordance of Kmart." They both were still looking at me. "He buys these astrology scrolls at the checkout line at Kmart, and I think he really believes in them."

Vic pushed off Rezdawg and walked over. She kept her distance; she didn't much like horses. "He was on Sandy's short list; we know he killed a guy, and he might've set a house on fire."

"So?"

Her snort startled the little remuda. "Somebody once taught me that if you're looking for a murderer, you start with the people who've killed people." She took a step closer, and I could just see her in my bad eye, past the gaggle of horse noses. "I don't know if you've noticed, but it's not like we've got a suspect behind every fucking tree." She glanced around with purpose at the plains stretching to the horizon. "Not that there are a lot of those around here either."

Henry stuffed the folder under his arm. "What are you thinking?"

I took a breath and watched the roiling of the over-grazed sweetgrass in the pasture; it was as if someone was stroking it just as I'd petted the horses. "I'm not getting a feeling for any of it, and that worries me." The bay extended his muzzle and breathed in my breath as I laughed. "Hershel's horses."

Henry joined us, handing Vic back her flashlight. "What?"

I palmed the bay's head slightly out of the way. "These horses must be some more of Hershel's; they always want to identify you by sniffing your breath."

"OIT."

I glanced at him—Old Indian Trick. "Really?"

He nodded and extended his good hand to a dun mare. "I have heard of it done when gathering horses on the open range."

I nodded. "Maybe Hershel has more Indian connections than we know about."

Vic stuffed her hands in the pockets of her fleece. "So, how does that help us?"

"Damned if I know, but I don't think it's Hershel."

"I thought it's only women who have intuition." She sighed in exasperation. "Then what about this Bill Nolan character?"

I thought about it. "He's up to something, but then he's been up to something ever since I've known him. I don't think he's a killer, even in the more abstract sense of setting the house or the barn on fire."

Vic risked getting closer to the horses so that she could get into my line of sight. "So, now we're thinking that Wade Barsad might've not set the barn fire?"

I ran my hand down the bay's muscled throat. "I don't know."

"Then why did she kill him?" I turned and looked at her. "Walt, she's the only one left."

I shook my head. "Nope."

"Then who? That's everybody who was there the night of the murder."

I reached out to pet the bay between his ears, but I guess he figured we didn't have anything in the way of treats and decided to move on; the others followed. Henry started digging in his shirt pocket. He extended his unswollen hand with one of the high-grain sorghum treats—the kind that horses will walk through hell in a napalm saddle to get. The bay turned on a heel and took the horse cookie from the flat of the Bear's palm. The others crowded near as he distributed a few into my shirt pocket where I'd hidden my star.

"Then it was someone who was not there."

October 24: five days earlier, late morning.

Frymire had sounded irritated.

"I walked in here, and the prisoner was gone."

I leaned on the counter at the nurse's station and held the phone a little away from my ear. "We're at the hospital. Mary's getting a mandatory checkup; Vic and I brought her."

"I thought that was supposed to be at two o'clock?"

"Isaac called and said he could fit her in sooner, so I figured we'd get it over with."

"What's the verdict?"

I glanced at the closed door that led to the examination room. "I don't know, but Isaac, Vic, and Mary are still inside."

"Well, I'm here serving and protecting. There was a drive-off at the gas station south of town, but the guy came back and paid while I was there."

"Must've known that the International Man of Mystery was on his trail."

Frymire hung up. My deputies did that to me a lot.

I was bored, and Ruby's niece was working on the computer at the next desk, so I ambled over and looked down at the sandy-haired young woman. "How you doin', Janine?" I was particularly proud of myself for remembering her name; it seemed as though I was forever forgetting it.

She didn't look up. "I'm busy, Uncle Walter, so stop bothering me."

I decided to take a walk down to the bank of machines by the door and get a bottle of water, seeing as how they didn't have an apparatus that dispensed Rainier. I dropped in a few quarters, pushed the button, and retrieved the plastic bottle below. It was a nice day, so when the automatic doors that opened to the outside automatically swung wide, I took it as an invitation.

I stepped onto the sidewalk outside the emergency room. There was a grassy hillside that the hospital board had recently landscaped and dedicated to Mari Baroja. There was a conveniently placed bench that had her name inscribed on a small brass plaque, so I sat, sipped my water, and thought about Mari and her granddaughter.

Lana had stopped by the office a week ago to say hello, but I'd been out. Word was that the young baker was buying up a remarkable amount of property on Main Street with the millions her grandmother had left her, along with a large tract of land leading up to the mountains. The buzz was that she was attempting to gather enough land for a ski resort, but I was hoping for a Basque restaurant.

The locals had been predicting, with resigned and doom-filled voices, that Durant was the next Jackson before Jackson had been Jackson. I didn't see it.

Jackson's geography was a lot like that of Manhattan in size and restriction—the City of New York because it was an island surrounded by water, and the town of Jackson because it was a valley surrounded by state and national parks. There was a limited amount of land in both places, and a lot of people who wanted to live in either or both.

A ski resort would change things, but I doubted we'd be seeing espresso stands and full-length coyote coats on the sidewalks of Durant—other than the one on Omar, that is.

I sipped my water and looked across the parking lot where another of Kyle Straub's signs proclaimed A MAN TO MAKE A DIFFERENCE. What the hell did that mean, anyway? It wasn't even particularly good English. The sign still made my ass hurt, but I was cheered by what was sitting on its top. A large, very yellow meadowlark periodically lifted its head and sang out with the gurgling, flutelike notes of its song.

A hardy bird that nests in the grasses of the plains, famous for that song, the meadowlark is the state bird of Wyoming, North Dakota, Montana, Kansas, Nebraska, and Oregon. As a state bird choice, original it was not. The birds always arrive in the spring, but then seem to disappear in July until they come back in fall, like sentinel bookends for summer.

The glass doors slid open to my right, and I turned my head

just in time to see Janine run by and down the hallway toward the examination room. I was up and through the doors after her. We reached the room at the same time, and I blew through the door in front of her.

The treatment table had fallen over, and Mary Barsad, still attached to an ECG monitor, was lying on the floor beside a series of small, glass-doored cabinets. Vic was holding both her hands against the woman's throat as the pulse of the blood from her carotid artery pushed with Mary's pulse through my deputy's fingers in a one-and-a-half-foot arc. Vic was the only one speaking. "Fuck, fuck, fuck, fuck."

There was blood everywhere, and what appeared to be one of those disposable scalpels was lodged in Mary's throat with the wrapper still half on. Isaac Bloomfield, who sat on the floor across the room, was tangled in an overturned utility cart with his thick glasses askew.

I grabbed a large roll of gauze from the counter and knelt to wind it around Mary's neck; then I slid my arms under her back and legs. I used my foot to flip the table back upright and placed her on the flat surface as a fresh stream of blood streaked across my uniform shirt and badge.

Vic continued to apply pressure, but the blood loss was catastrophic. "I turned my head for a split fucking second." She was literally shaking with anger. "Fuck!"

Mary lay with her head turned to the side, her mouth gulping air like a landed trout. It seemed as though the pulse in the veins at her temples was beginning to still. My voice was loud but sounded far away. "Isaac . . . I need your help."

The small man, assisted by Janine, slid up the wall and

partially settled his glasses while approaching with hands extended, hands that had saved my own life. I hoped they would save hers.

"Vertebral arteriovenous . . ." The doc's face turned only slightly toward the young nurse. "I need a transvascular embolization kit. Quickly, please, Janine." She slipped past us to the cabinets on the wall as he continued to speak, almost as if he were reminding himself of the procedure. "Neurologic deficits coincident with the fistula should resolve with the reestablishment of flow—" Janine brought back a balloon device as Isaac's hands took over for mine, and I was stirred by Isaac's sudden switch to his native Teutonic tongue. "*Gottverdammit!*"

I held Mary's head and looked into her eyes, the blue dulling with each pulse of blood. I knew that we were in a race as to whether the woman would die of blood loss or of suffocation from the mounting hematoma of coagulating blood that was forming in her throat. Isaac called for a number of paralytic drugs to be administered through the IV that Janine had nervously pushed into Mary's arm.

The choice was brutal but necessary, and for the remainder of the episode, no matter how short that might be, Mary would be aware of what was happening and feel everything as we attempted to save her life.

Isaac took the endotracheal tube and began feeding it into the stricken woman's mouth. He handed Janine the plastic that was connected to the balloon device and to a one-way valve. With hands shaking, the young nurse screwed a syringe without a needle but full of air into the valve and depressed the plunger on the syringe, effectively holding the tube in place as Isaac listened to Mary's chest and stomach with a stethoscope.

He nodded, and Janine passed the bulb to me. Isaac looked directly into my blood-spattered face. *"Einmal alle fünf Sekunden."*

I stared back at him and smiled grimly at the concentration camp survivor. "English, Doc."

Bloomfield swallowed. "Once every five seconds."

One.

I was now Mary's lungs.

Two.

Her lips quivered, and she continued to try to gulp air— pushing out silent words past the tube in her throat.

Three.

I allowed Isaac's hands more access to the wound, and I brushed her bloody hair back from the high cheekbones, driving my eyes into hers. I spoke from only inches away.

Four. "Not today you don't."

Isaac continued to dig into the wound with a hemostat in an attempt to find the artery responsible for delivering the bright red blood to her brain, as Vic conceded him her portion of the wound.

Five. I compressed the bulb again.

"Got it." The old man's voice was tired but steady. "Clamp, please, Janine." Mary Barsad would no longer die from blood loss or strangulation. He looked up and through the still-crooked glasses, and maybe because the circumstance had been so dire, it was funny. "She kicked me."

I smiled, but it didn't hold for long. "I bet she did." I looked down. Mary's eyes were wide with the pupils contracted to tiny tunnels. She was trying to get to a place to which I wasn't going to let her go.

I'd lost too many, and I wasn't losing another.

October 30, 1:00 A.M.

I was tired when Vic dropped me off at the motel room in Absalom, but she sat there, lounging against the seat, and watched me. I leaned in the window and met her eyes with my one good one. "You're driving my truck."

"Yeah." She ran the palm of her hand over the leather steering wheel. "Thought I'd see what it felt like."

"Well, don't get used to it too soon."

She paused for a moment, and I had to admit that the big, three-quarter-ton truck suited her. "You want to give me a straight answer this time?"

I turned so that she would see the undamaged side of my face. "What?"

"Have you lost your fucking mind? A tough-man contest?"

I cleared my throat, which made my eye hurt—not a good sign. "I wasn't an official entry."

"And that makes it better?"

I fessed up. "I think Henry wanted me to get in a fight."

"Why?"

"I'm just guessing, but I think it was his way of getting me all unballed-up from Cady, the election, the investigation—"

"And me?"

I nodded, and that hurt, too. "And you."

"Wily devil, isn't he?" She snorted and covered her face with her hand. "Unballed-up. Is that a technical term?"

She shimmied over and raised her hand, putting the cool of the back of her fingers against the skin next to the wound on my left cheekbone. It felt really good, and I was carried back to that night in Philadelphia when we'd become intimate in a way with which I was still unsure I was comfortable. As a symptom of that discomfort, I changed the subject to her brother and my daughter. "I assume you've gotten the word on the latest from our respective households, both alike in dignity?"

Her eyebrow cocked like a revolver. "I think Romeo's being a tard, but who am I to stand in the way of true love?"

"So, if they get married, does that mean that we're—"

"I don't want to think about it." She summarily pulled her hand away and rested it on my shoulder. "You know, I'd come in if I wasn't afraid of blowing your cover."

"Uh huh." I folded my forearms on the passenger doorsill. "I'm not so sure I've got much of a cover to blow."

She inclined her head and looked up at me through the open window and her dark lashes. "I could always come in and blow something else."

I didn't move for a minute, and I don't think I'd been at a loss like that since junior high school.

I was saved by a loud crash. Juana had carried out a garbage bag of empty bottles and deposited them onto the boardwalk. She looked over at the two of us with a hand on her hip. "I let your dog out, twice."

"Thanks." I leaned against my truck and introduced the two women. "Juana Balcarcel, this is Undersheriff Victoria Moretti—Vic, Juana."

She started over but then stalled out when she saw me.

"*¡Ay, mierda!*" She took the step down to glance at Vic, but her eyes kept returning to the side of my face. "Are you all right?"

"Yep, I'm okay. How's my adversary?"

She shook her young head, the dark hair swinging. "He was still unconscious when the EMTs loaded him out with a neck brace, but when he woke up, they gave him the cash, since you weren't an official entry. I think that made him feel much better." She reached in and extended a hand to Vic. "Hi."

Vic shook her hand and smiled. "How you doin'?"

I felt compelled to continue. "Juana's almost got an associate's degree in criminal justice from over in Sheridan."

They both ignored me.

La bandita flicked her eyes at my caved-in face and then looked back at Vic. "Is he really the sheriff?"

The Italian beauty's head dropped in silent laughter, then raised and considered me. "Yeah, and believe it or not, most of the time he acts like one."

Juana looked at me again and then back at Vic. I felt like sonar readings were being made, but I wasn't on the same frequency, even though I could see the pings bouncing back and forth between the two.

"If you're going to stay, I'm going to have to charge you the double rate for the room."

11

First there was pounding on the door, then Dog started barking, then my head fell off and rolled across the stained carpet and lodged itself in the corner against the chipped baseboard—at least that's what it felt like.

I got up in my boxer shorts, appropriately enough, pulled on a T-shirt from my duffel, and stumbled over Dog toward the door. If it was Cliff Cly looking for a rematch, I was going back to my bag, pull out my .45, and just shoot him.

I swung the door open and looked at a man with glasses and a graying beard with mustache to match who was wearing a ball cap that read COFFEEN DYNO-TUNE. The name *Jim Rogers* spiraled in white thread across the left chest pocket of his dark blue coveralls. "You Eric Boss?"

I stared at him. "What?" He looked at some of the other doors, and the number on mine, sure he'd made a mistake. I cleared my throat; what could it hurt? "Sure, I'm Eric Boss."

"No, you're not; you're the sheriff from over in Absaroka County." He studied my face, which still felt like it had fallen off. I glanced at the corner next to the baseboard just to make sure it hadn't. "At least, you used to be."

"And how do you know that?"

"I got a speeding ticket last year—it was that nasty little brunette deputy of yours nabbed me."

The voice behind me was sharp. "You were doing seventy-three in a fifty-five." I turned to look back at the bed I'd just vacated. "And you had no taillights."

I turned back and looked at the mechanic, who was desperately trying to see around me. "Can I help you with something?"

He focused on me and threw a thumb over his shoulder. "Steve sent me over; I've got a horse trailer out here—we repacked the wheel bearings, fixed the brakes, rewired, and put new tires on."

I reached up and cradled my face before my cheekbone reminded me about the pain. "Right, right . . ." I took a deep breath and recalled having the vehicle towed into Sheridan for a makeover. I looked over him and could see they had cleaned the old trailer off, and she wasn't looking half bad. "Uh, you can just leave it out there, Jim."

He didn't move.

"Is there something else?"

He nodded. "Ya gotta pay for it."

"Oh . . . you bet." I closed the door. He was still trying to see who it was that had spoken to him from the bed. It was lucky that the wind was blowing and that he seemed just a bit hard of hearing. I dug into the jeans that I had left on the chair for my wallet as Vic rolled over and luxuriously stretched, revealing a perfectly rounded breast and alert nipple. She propped herself up on an elbow and used her red-nailed hand to support her tousled head; she made no effort to cover up. I stood there, unable to move, then remembered my mission, opened the door, and handed the guy my credit card. I stepped forward and got between him and the provocative room.

I closed the door behind me as he finished writing down the numbers and totals. He handed the card back and ripped off a receipt. I took the slip of paper and looked at him. "Anything else?"

He shifted his weight and gestured with the thumb again. "Just leave it out here?"

"Yep." I waited until he got the trailer unhitched and had climbed back in his truck before I turned and sidled into the room, closed the door, and looked at her.

She was still lying on her side with one leg pulled up ankle to calf, one hand still supporting the mussed hair; the other was lazily making circles on the flat of the sheet. More than a little of her body was still exposed, and I took that extra second to take in the swoops and swallows of her general physique.

I felt like I should carve a statue.

I tossed the transaction papers and my wallet in my open bag, stepped over Dog, and sat on the corner of the bed as she watched me with the tarnished gold, vulpine eyes. "A horse trailer?"

I nodded, and it still hurt. "It's a mercy mission."

"You don't even like horses."

"I do too—it's just that they're big, dangerous, and a poor form of transportation."

She bit her lip. "Two of the three could be said about you."

I reached out and pulled the sheet over the portion of her anatomy that was distracting me as the knocking began at the door again. "Jeez . . ."

"You're popular."

I stepped over Dog, who didn't even bother barking this time, and cracked the door slightly open. I expected to see the mechanic: instead, it was Benjamin who stood there. The four-foot cowboy looked over his shoulder at the trailer.

"Are you ready to go?"

I squeezed through the doorway, drawing the door closed behind me again. I could see Hershel backing Bill Nolan's red Dodge pickup to the horse trailer. I looked at the little bandito as his eyes traveled up and down my frame from underneath his sweat-stained cowboy hat.

"I never seen anybody in their bedclothes at ten o'clock in the morning—you sick?" He studied my face a little closer. "Boy, that's a shiner."

I held up a finger. "Just a second, okay?"

He nodded. I turned, shut the door, and gazed at the exquisite female stretching luxuriously on the bed of the squalid motel room. I cleared my throat and felt the pain in my head increase. "After one of the best nights of my life, I think I'm about to pay for it with one of my worst days."

October 26: four days earlier, afternoon.
She had been petting Dog, who had rested his head on the hospital bed, but she continued to ignore me.

"Mary, if you don't tell me what happened that night, then I can't help you." She looked up, and her expression made me wonder why I was trying. "If I go through the report, would you at least give me an indication as to what you agree with and what you don't?" She continued scratching the dense fur behind Dog's ears near the furrow of his bullet scar. "I know it hurts, but Isaac says you can talk." I slumped back against my folding chair, picked the report up from my lap, and flipped the page. "In your initial statement to the investigators in Campbell County—"

She rolled over on her side and continued scratching Dog under his chin. I watched her for a moment, then stood and patted my leg. "Dog." The beast was by my side in an instant and followed me. I pointed toward Janine's desk at the end of the hall. "Go."

I backed into the room, closed the heavy door behind me, sat in the hospital chair with the report in my lap, and tipped my hat back. "No talk, no Dog."

She looked up at me. We sat there staring at each other.

I took a deep breath, thought about Cady and another hospital bed, and relied on my last, most secret approach when confronted by female opposition—I begged. "Please help me; I can't do this alone."

The muscles in her face softened just a touch. She considered me, finally clearing her throat and licking her lips as if she hadn't spoken in years. I stared at the bandages at her throat and thought about how she'd looked on the floor of the examination room just yesterday.

When my eyes met with hers again, she barely nodded, and her voice was a fragile whisper. "Okay."

"I've got some questions about the timing of that night." I

carefully avoided actually mentioning her husband's murder. "Do you remember leaving the house?"

She nodded, almost imperceptibly.

"Do you have any idea when that was?" She shrugged and then lay there looking at me. "Before midnight, after?"

"Before." She didn't wheeze quite so much with this answer.

"You don't have any idea when?"

She shook her head and swallowed carefully. "Why?"

"The volunteer fire department in Clearmont didn't get a ten-seventy fire alarm until almost one o'clock in the morning." I lowered the report and looked at her. "That seems like an awful lot of time between the fire in the barn and the anonymous call."

"I could have been confused about the times."

"I don't think you were." I allowed the pages of the report to fall against my chest. "Mary, you stated in the report that the hired man, Hershel Vanskike, was the one who found you." I let the image sit there with her for a moment. "Was there anybody else there that night?"

"No."

"You're sure?" I leaned forward, closed the file, and dropped it flat on the floor between my boots as a symbolic gesture. "Mary, for me to really know what happened to you that night, I need you to think about it clearly—and tell me. See, I'm beginning to think that there were a lot more people there than you're willing to say and possibly more than you know about." I rolled my lip under my teeth. "Let's start with the ones you do."

"Why is this so important to you?" Her voice was stronger with this question, even if it was without emotion.

I stared at her and then nodded toward the manila folder on the floor. "This is your life we're talking about."

I stood up and walked over to the window. I could see the back of Kyle Straub's sign, where another meadowlark was singing. There was something about the sign that was bothering me, and not just because it was a reminder that the thought of Kyle Straub or his grammar made my ass hurt. I let it submerge in my mind and shifted my weight from one size 14-E to the other.

"It's going to happen like this: the statements that you've made to the Campbell County investigators are enough to—" I stopped speaking and turned to look at her. "They don't get many high-profile cases like this one. Generally, it's Bubba shot Skeeter while they were drinking beer in the cab of Skeeter's truck and trying to figure out if Bubba's Charter Arms revolver was loaded." I leaned back and sat on the windowsill. "You see, the mechanism that I'm a part of—it feeds on high octane, and that's what this case is. Everybody is going to want a piece of it—of you." The sun cast shadows on the crown of my hat. "They'll call for a change of venue, and they'll get it; possibly Casper, maybe Cheyenne, and you'll get a jury trial—and that won't go well for you. I've stood through a lot of trials, and I can tell you that those prosecutors are going to tap into something—a virulent little strain of human nature that's going to sway that jury into getting somebody, somebody rich, beautiful, and powerful—somebody they've never had a chance of getting before. It's going to be you, Mary, and not just because you confessed."

She watched me intently. "Why then?"

"Because you are incapable of showing the one thing that

they are going to demand, whether you're guilty or not—repentance. They want you to feel sorry; it makes them feel better about themselves." I couldn't look her in the eye, so I turned my face and gazed at the pillow beside her head. "Most people . . ." Her head dropped a little, but with my peripheral vision I could see she kept her eyes on me, on my polyester shirt and my dull and unpolished badge still with traces of her blood in the engraving. "They go through their lives believing in things that they never have much contact with—the police, lawyers, judges, and courts. They have an unstated belief in the system; that it'll be impartial, fair, and just."

I could hear normal conversations through the door. It was good to know that normal conversations could still happen while I was engaged in this one. "But then there's the moment when it comes to them that the police, the courtroom, and the laws themselves are just human, vulnerable to the same shortcomings as all of us, that they're a mirror of who we are, and that's the heartbreaking dichotomy of it all—that the more contact you have with the law, the less belief you have." I took a breath. "Like some strange little religion all its own, the one thing that makes the whole system work is the one thing it robs you of—faith."

I turned my face and looked at her directly. "But you have to believe that justice is truly blind, and that those scales aren't tipped."

She had taken a breath of her own. "Or what?"

"Or else you're in a dark place."

She looked at the sheets covering her legs. "But you haven't answered my question: why is this important to you?"

I smiled sadly. "This is important to me because I believe you're innocent. And I've spent most of my life defending and protecting the innocent." I crossed to the door and opened it. "I'll let you in on another little secret—the sheriff of Campbell County believes you're innocent, too. Otherwise he never would've sent you over here to me."

I allowed Dog to enter the room. The beast was waiting outside the door. He looked at her, then at me. I nodded, and he crossed to the bed and placed his broad head next to her hand. "Mary, tell me about that night."

She had laughed a sad exhale and scratched the fur on his muzzle as his big tail fanned in a counterclockwise circle the way it always did when he was happy.

October 30, 2:20 P.M.

We drove across the railroad tracks and headed south on Echeta Road, which went past the local cemetery. It was an odd place with an iron archway and two bands that went across the drive to which the words ABSALOM CEMETERY were attached. There were lights on either side, a ranch gate below that was closed to keep any stray cattle from grazing between the markers, and a cross affixed above, which was black against a sky so blue it hurt my eyes. Most everything hurt my eyes this morning, so I closed them and nodded off.

It was a good thing that Hershel was driving. I woke up when we hit a rough stretch on the only road leading to and from the Battlement's flat mesa, and I hoped we wouldn't meet another truck as there was only room for one and a half. It was the kind of road where, if you met anybody coming up or going down, somebody was going to have to put it in reverse.

My headache was subsiding but only commensurate with the increasing pain of my eye socket. I'd tried to cradle my face in my hand with an elbow resting on the truck's windowsill, but the constant jolting of the uneven road only resulted in my periodically punching my damaged face with the palm of my hand. It was an ongoing battle, which had not gone unnoticed by Benjamin, who was seated on the bench seat between Hershel and me.

I stretched my jaw and felt the unsettling pop in my temple.

"I bet that hurts."

I glanced down at the little bandito as he leaned forward to get a better look at my face. I pulled my Ray-Bans from my shirt pocket and slipped them on in an attempt to hide the evidence. "You'd be right."

He nodded. "Have you decided what your name is today?"

I shrugged. "I thought we'd all go by aliases."

"You mean nicknames?" He seemed excited by the thought and turned his attention to Hershel for approval.

"Sure." The older cowboy's face remained immobile as he negotiated the grade, the oversized pickup, and the two tons of trailered horseflesh behind us.

The boy struggled against his seat belt, which was my dictate, and peered over the dash at the road ahead. "I'm going to be *El Bandito Negro de los Badlands.*"

I waited a moment before replying. "You don't think that's a little long?"

He looked dissatisfied with my response. "Why?"

"Well, if I have to say *El Bandito Negro de los Badlands* look out for that rattlesnake, you're likely to already be bitten."

He swiveled in the seat back toward Hershel and pulled the stampede strings into his mouth. "Are there rattlesnakes up here?"

The puncher shrugged. "Rattlesnakes everywhere."

We topped the mesa and turned northeast. The top of Twentymile Butte looked like a pool table for Jack of beanstalk fame. If there had been dinosaurs up there, you'd be able to see them from a long way off.

Hershel pulled the caravan to the left and slowed.

The boy looked at him. "Why are we stopping?"

He growled. "Because my nickname is *Pequeña Vejiga*." Benjamin laughed as Hershel climbed out, unzipped, and began watering the broken rocks at the edge of the road.

Thinking a little air might clear my lingering headache and figuring Dog could always use a leg-lifting opportunity, I decided to get out and stretch my legs. Benjamin followed us as we walked into the middle of the rutted and powdery two-track that stretched to the horizon; the only other road curled off to the right and disappeared into the distance as well.

I thought about how we tilled and cultivated the land, planted trees on it, fenced it, built houses on it, and did everything we could to hold off the eternity of distance—anything to give the landscape some sort of human scale. No matter what we did to try and form the West, however, the West inevitably formed us instead.

I watched the dust collect on the left side of my boots as the constant wind kicked up a dust devil about seventy-five yards down the road. Dog looked up at me and Benjamin took a few steps past us, and I could feel the palpable urge in him to go chase the miniature twister. "This is the biggest butte in all of Wyoming."

I had to smile at the absolute assurance of all his statements. "No, it's not."

He looked up at me and pulled the stampede strings into his mouth again; I was beginning to see a pattern. "Is too."

"No, because technically it's a mesa." He turned his head and searched the horizon for justification. "Mister *Bandito Negro de los Badlands*, you want to know what the difference is?"

Maybe I had dampened his enthusiasm, because his voice mumbled as he chewed the braided leather and a hand crept down to pet Dog. "Nope, not really."

I started to raise an eyebrow, but it hurt my eye, so I settled for nudging him with my elbow. "I shudder for the fate of future generations if your scientific curiosity is indicative."

He shook his head at my funny talk. "You gonna feel better if you tell me?"

I thought about it. "Yes." He didn't deign to look at me but threw out an open palm as if to accept the unwanted knowledge. "A butte is taller than it is wide, whereas a mesa, like this one, is wider than it is tall."

"What's Devil's Tower?"

I thought about it. "That'd be a butte."

He looked puzzled. "Then why did they call this Twentymile Butte?"

"With respect to all the knowledge that our frontier forefathers carried, a steadfast understanding of geological terms may not have been a strong suit."

He nodded, and we listened to the wind. "You ever been up here before?"

I kept my eyes on the edge of the world, which was to the south. With the vastness of the plateau, it was difficult to tell if we were looking at the edge, but I had my suspicions. "Once or twice."

"When?"

I glanced down at the top of his hat, thankful for a view that didn't pull at the corners of my eyes, especially the sore one. "When I was about your age."

He looked up at me with the stampede strings still in his mouth and continued to pet Dog, who now sat on his foot. "Really?"

"Yep."

He looked around. "Is it the same?"

"No." I shrugged back at the dirt path we'd just driven on. "There weren't any roads, and the only way up was a horse trail that they must've built this road over."

"Were you hunting Indians?"

I smiled down at the half-Cheyenne boy. "Nope, as a matter of fact it was Indians who brought me up here."

I figured I'd finally hit upon a subject that truly interested him, since he spit out the stampede strings, and looked up at me. "Cheyenne?"

"Yep."

"I'm half Cheyenne."

"I know."

He now turned toward me fully, forcing Dog to reseat himself. "My father was Cheyenne."

"Was?"

"He's dead." I nodded, and his next statement was as if we were discussing the difference between buttes and mesas. "He got run over by a train."

I stopped nodding. "I'm sorry."

He stood there for a while without moving. "Why do people say that?" He took as deep a breath as his young lungs would allow and sighed. "It's not like I think they drove the train."

"Well . . . maybe they're just sorry for your loss."

He nudged Dog and walked past me to the edge of the road. "He lived in Chicago with my mom, that's where I was born." He took his frustration out on a few rocks with the toes of his scuffed boots, his hands stuffed tight in his jeans as if he didn't trust them. "He was a construction worker; he built big buildings and bridges." I nodded, even though he still wasn't looking at me, and patted my leg for Dog to come over. "My mom was mad at him because he took me up on one of the bridges he was working on one night. He carried me up on the girders and stood with me over the water, and it was really far down."

Dog sat on my foot, and we both looked at the boy. "The water?"

"Yeah and you could see the reflections in the river from all the lit up windows 'cause it was nighttime." He turned to look at us. "We flew that night."

I didn't say anything.

"I mean, we didn't really except for maybe one second, but he held me out over the water and told me to not be afraid because even if he dropped me I'd just fly." He kept looking me in the face, the way only children can without becoming self-conscious. "I closed my eyes for just a second when he held me out there—and I think I really flew, for just a second. Really." His dark eyes seemed remarkably familiar for just a moment. "Do you think I'm crazy?"

I laughed. "No, I don't think you're crazy."

"You aren't going to tell my mom about me flying, are you? 'Cause she doesn't know about that part."

"No, I won't tell her."

He continued to study me. "Why'd you laugh?"

It was a time for truth telling and with children, if you didn't make the reach, they might learn to stop asking. "I have dreams like that."

He smiled back at me, and something passed between us, something old and powerful.

Hershel approached from around the truck, placing his palms at the small of his back and stretching. "Did you fellas know this is the biggest butte in Wyoming?"

Benjamin, Dog, and I continued to look at each other and we smiled, but none of us said anything.

October 30, 4:30 P.M.

We drove the truck as far as the first high shelves of rock that rose above the plateau, which created a giant series of sedimentary steps leading north. Hershel paired me off with a big bay, about seventeen hands, and watched as I tightened the belly cinch with a quick yank before the gelding could expand his lungs. Satisfied that I knew what I was doing, he assisted

Benjamin in saddling the same grulla that I'd seen in front of The AR, as his dun waited patiently by the shade of the horse trailer along with Dog.

"I give you that big'un so you'd be comfortable, and so he would be, too."

I checked the bedroll he'd provided, and the saddlebags I'd brought along. "I appreciate it."

"Only one we got bigger is a Percheron from up in Montana, but he can get wonky when you put a saddle on him."

The thought of a wonky draft horse on the high plateau was one my rear end was just as happy not to contemplate. "This one got a name?"

The old cowboy replied with a well-worn sentiment. "Don't like naming things I might have to eat."

"You got any rawhide? Some of the saddle strings on this one are broke off a little short." He motioned toward the rear end of the trailer, so I walked back and took some strings from a hook inside the door. Hershel had already established squatter's rights. There was an antiquated McClellan saddle, along with an old cavalry canteen with the number 10 and the letter G stenciled onto its canvas side. It would appear that Hershel was quite the collector.

I fixed the strings on my horse's saddle and tied my horsehide jacket to the bedroll. I found a neckerchief in the inside pocket and knotted the bandana at my neck, slipped a foot in the stirrup, and stepped up, gently flinging a leg over the bay. He took a slight counter to the left but then planted and turned to look at me, probably wondering why it was I was riding him and not vice versa. Then his long face turned south, almost as if he were looking for something in particular.

I searched the horizon along with him but saw nothing and turned him along with the others.

After getting the boy saddled and seated, Hershel checked the sawbuck rigging on the packhorse and the canvas bags filled with supplies, oats, and two five-gallon containers of water, which we especially needed since there wasn't any on the entire mesa.

Benjamin gigged his horse and yelped as it crow-hopped a little to the right and shot out about twenty feet before stopping and craning its long neck to inspect the foreign ground.

Hershel laughed and climbed aboard his own mount, where he readjusted the Henry Yellow Boy in his rifle scabbard and draped the old cavalry canteen I'd seen in the trailer off the horn of his saddle. "You know what they say about a horse bein' only afraid of two things?"

"What's that?"

"Things that move, and things that don't."

I smiled at the old joke and followed as he trailed the packhorse from a lead position. The horses fell into a walking pace with Dog going up ahead to stay with Benjamin.

There are people who prefer the spring and summer on the high plains, but I'm not one of them. My blood quickens, and I begin to sleep better when the cottonwood leaves begin their weekend turn to a varsity gold and a slight skim of frost surprisingly appears on your windshield one morning. I was glad I'd brought my jacket, and only hoped the bay, whatever his name was, didn't notice that it was made out of horsehide.

The sky was fading in and out of blue with wide bands of diffused clouds, and it was possible that we'd get a shower or even a blowing skiff of snow from the front that was promised by morning.

"How's your head?" Hershel, who had allowed me to ease up on his left, thrust his chin forward and peered at the bandage at my cheekbone and the discoloration around my eye.

"Still on."

He pulled his head back, shook it, and adjusted his reins and his hat. "I sure didn't take you for the bull-at-the-gate kind of fella."

"I haven't been myself lately."

He nodded and the next words carried a little more weight than perhaps they should have. "That's what I hear." I turned in the saddle, enough so that I could see him with my good eye and could watch the shifting shadows disappear in the afternoon sun. Benjamin was hanging back, and I could almost hear him listening to our budding conversation. He wasn't much of an undercover kind of guy either. Hershel pointed with his chin toward the rocky expanse of the trail ahead. "Ben, why don't you ride on a little and check things out?"

Recalcitrant even when told to do what he really wanted, Benjamin turned completely in the saddle till both legs draped off one side, his horse continuing to clop forward and paying him no mind. "Why me?"

The older man squinted into the sun and at the boy like some B-movie support player. "Because you're the Indian. Go scout."

Without another word, the half-Cheyenne warrior leaned back and rolled his leg over the bulletproof horse's withers. He nudged him with his heels into a slightly faster pace, snugged up his stampede strings, and left us behind. Dog looked back at me; I gestured with my chin and he trotted after the boy.

I had the feeling I'd just been afforded a glimpse of what the country had been like around a hundred and fifty years ago and turned to look at Vanskike, aware that he'd dismissed the boy for a reason. "What's on your mind?"

He spat over his horse's shoulder and looked at me again as he pulled up his canteen and took a deep swig. "Couple'a things. When you dropped me off the other night?"

"Yep?"

He wiped his mouth and hung the canteen back on the saddle horn. "All them pictures on the wall of my trailer?"

"Uh huh?"

I watched him as we rode, and it was as if he and the horse were inseparable, with all the hours, days, and years they had most likely had together. He held the reins in one fist while the other hand, trained to rope or relax when there was no roping to be done, lay limp in his lap. "I just didn't want you thinkin' I was some kind of pervert."

"I don't, honest." I stood in the stirrups to stretch my legs. "But if you think your future lies in those little scrolls you buy in the checkout line at Kmart, then I do think you're crazier than a shit-house rat."

He shrugged and then patted the stock of his museum-piece rifle. "My fortune is in this rifle." He glanced over to see if I had a smart-alec remark about that, and when I didn't have one, he took a deep breath and let it out slowly, as if it were practice for something he was going to have trouble saying. "I got a buddy in the Campbell County Sheriff's Department—"

I let a moment pass. "Okay."

"I don't wanna tell you his name, for obvious reasons, but he told me a few things."

"Like what?"

He readjusted and leaned forward to counter the rise in the path. "He said there was this sheriff from over in Absaroka County—a big fella that's supposedly one tough customer, but fair."

I didn't say anything.

"He also said he knows for a fact that the powers that be made sure that Cliff Cly didn't have to take no lie-detector test about killing Wade Barsad."

12

October 30, 6:50 P.M.

I tried to remember the last time I'd camped out but finally gave up. Then I tried to remember the last time my posterior hurt this bad and couldn't come up with that, either.

We'd trailed along the northern edge of the plateau and had made camp near the precipice of the stacked shelves of sedimentary rock that had seemed so far away when we were starting out. They formed a sort of natural amphitheater, which is where we set up the tents, careful to keep away from the eight-hundred-foot drop-off that was nearby. We'd put the horses on a picket line, had made and eaten dinner, and were quickly running out of wood to keep the campfire going.

"There's a couple 'a old truck skids down where that well-head is, from where they abandoned the methane, along the second ridge southeast."

The young cowboy tipped his hat back, looked into the gloom of a cloudy sunset, and then back at Hershel as he stoked the few remaining pieces of lit wood. "How do I get 'em apart?"

"They're old; just break 'em with your boot." Vanskike watched the boy stand there. "What?"

Benjamin sniffed. "Wouldn't it be faster if we all went, then we could get it in one trip?"

Hershel tossed the last piece of wood into the fire. "What in the heck is the matter with you?" He nodded toward me. "He took care of the horses, I fixed dinner, now it's time for you to earn your keep." The boy remained immobile. "What?"

"I'm goin'."

The old cowboy shook his head in incredulity as the boy started off. I yelled after him. "You want a flashlight?" The small figure at the very end of the campfire stopped and walked back as I fished in my saddlebag and handed him the five-cell Maglite. "You run into anything, hit it with this." I turned and looked at my trusty companion, sprawled beside my bedroll. "Dog."

He raised his oversized head and looked at me.

"C'mon." He slowly rose and stretched as I put a little more emphasis in my voice. "C'mon." He came over, but I didn't feel too sorry for him since he'd had his dinner and the camp's collective scraps, followed by a considerable amount of my water ration. I nudged him toward the boy with my leg and watched as Benjamin marveled at the weight of the tactical flashlight, clicked the button, and the two of them followed the beam off and into the night. I watched as the flashlight's single ray cascaded across the rock shelves and over the next rock-strewn ridge. "I don't think they're going to be surprised by anything."

The old man shook his head and pulled out a small bag of fixings and some papers. "Nope, don't think so." He tapped the tobacco into the paper and rolled one and then two cigarettes. A callused and worn hand offered me one. "No, thanks."

He nodded, then stuffed it into his mouth and lit it with the last of the Blue Tip matches from his hatband. "This friend of mine I was tellin' you about back at the trailer, he's an ol' boy playing out his string as a special officer here in Campbell County—one of the two that runs the lie-detector for 'em. He only works about two days a week." He scooted back and sat against a slab of rock that leaned at a perfect thirty-degree angle, and smoked. "I run into him at Mona's, that little Mexican place down by the highway, this morning while I was puttin' diesel in Bill's truck."

"What'd he say?"

The old cowboy rolled to one side and drew up a knee on which to rest his hand, flipping his ashes into the fire. "He asked about that shiny new truck, and I told him it was mine. He said that was bullshit, so I told him about the trip we were taking; told him about you, and he described you right back, down to that chewed-on part of your ear."

The bandage under my eye was distracting, so I started peeling it off. "Mike Smith?" I studied the bit of blood seepage on the gauze and tossed it into the fire.

He smiled and didn't look at me. "I can neither confirm or deny—"

I figured that Hershel hadn't learned the neither/nor rule. "What about Cliff Cly?"

He took another deep inhale from the cigarette cupped in

his hand. "Said they called him in on a Sunday morning, real early, and told him to get set up. He said pretty soon they brought Cly in and sat him down, so he hooked him up to the machine and started askin' him what they call—"

"Control questions."

"That's it." He nodded and looked into the fire. "Well, after he verifies that the lights are on in the room, his name is Cliff Cly, and that yes, the smirking son-of-a-bitch has lied to people that are close to him, the sheriff comes in with some guy in a suit and has Mike unhook Cly."

I tried not to smile, since without the bandage my cheek hurt even more.

"I just said Mike, didn't I?"

"You did."

"God damn it." He shook his head and took another drag from his cigarette. "I'm not really good at this undercover stuff."

"Welcome to the club."

"Well, they unhook Cliff, and Sandy Sandberg tells Mike that the three of them weren't ever there."

I sat up a little. "Sandy?"

"Yep."

"What about the guy in the suit; Mike have any idea who he was or who he was with?"

"Nope." I looked at him and thought about it just as a scattered beam of light wavered from behind us and then down the rocky path. Benjamin dropped an armload of gray, splintered lumber beside the fire, and Hershel looked up at the lad as Dog came over and sat. "That'd be about a third of what we need for the night."

"A third?"

The old puncher's voice was certain as he flicked more ashes into the fire. "A third."

His thin shoulders slumped, and the miniature cowboy trudged away only to stop and look back at Dog. "You comin'?"

Dog lay down and placed his head on his massive paws. I nudged him with my boot. "C'mon, earn your keep."

The boy patted his leg, just as I had. "C'mon." He slowly got to his paws.

"Good boy." Dog trotted off after him as I pushed my hat back and came clean. "Not as if you didn't know, I'm not Eric Boss. My name is Walt Longmire, and I'm sheriff of Absaroka County."

Hershel turned, and I watched as the flickering light planed off the hard surfaces of his chin and cheekbones. "Longmire did you say?" I nodded. "By God, I think I know your people—your father have a place north of here?"

"He did."

"Passed?"

"Quite a while back."

"You got the place leased out to the Gronebergs?"

"Yep."

He shook his head some more and flipped the butt into the fire. "Well, I'll be damned . . . you've come home." The old cowboy pulled the second of his cigarettes from his shirt pocket. "So, what are you doin' out here after so long?"

I thought about how much I wanted to reveal to Hershel, how much the cowboy already knew and, if I trusted him, how far did that trust go? If Cliff Cly didn't take a polygraph, which Sandy Sandberg said he did, and somebody stepped in to keep it from happening—there were only a few possibilities of what that could mean. It was either Sandy, who wasn't playing fair, or it was the Feds who had taken a hand. If it was the Feds, then in what capacity? Wade Barsad had been under the auspices of the witness protection program, but why would they have brought an agent in? To pressure Wade on the names and money he'd absconded with from his business associates along the Garden State Parkway and in Ohio?

I figured a good offense was the best defense and decided to try a little lie detecting of my own. Seeing as how clinical psychologists had come to the conclusion that the machines were only correct about 61 percent of the time—only slightly better than random—I took a chance with the police officer's best friend: instinct. "Hershel, are you involved in any way with this foolishness?"

"No." He seemed shocked that I'd ask. "No, I'm not."

I believed him. "Good." I gathered my legs beneath me and stood. I walked a little stiffly to the edge of the precipice and looked out over the Powder River country. The harvest moon was just beginning to stare at the hills, and the long shadows from the rocks and few junipers cascaded through the draws and gulleys toward the Bighorns.

It was a stark beauty, but you can't come home again, no matter what Hershel said. I could feel an urgency to get back to my proper place in the rolling hills under the mountains. Before I could, though, I was obligated to Mary to find the truth. She had become my trust when Sandy had sent her to my jail, and I was bound to find out what happened the night that Wade Barsad was killed.

Something felt wrong, and that itch without an ability

to scratch was needling me from somewhere in my subconscious. "I need you to tell me everything that happened that night."

"I already did."

I pulled my hat down against the wind and turned to look at him. "No, you didn't really, and when we talked, no offense, you were drunk." He pulled at a long earlobe, stuck the cigarette that he'd been holding into his mouth, and lit it with a piece of smoldering firewood. "I know that Mary was there. I know that you were there, and I know that Bill Nolan was also there. Now, was there anybody else there?"

He looked up at me. "No, nobody." Then his eyes dropped to the fire as he thought about it. "I mean Wade but he was dead."

"When you got there, Mary was in the yard with the rifle on her lap?"

"Yep."

"The breech was open on the .22, and the magazine was empty?"

"Yep."

"Then what?"

He flipped the half-smoked cigarette into the fire. "I took the rifle away from her and went into the house." He looked up at me to make sure this is what I wanted to hear, but I said nothing. "He was in there."

"Where?"

"Layin' across the bed."

"He was dead, you're sure?"

"God, yes. She'd shot him in the head." He corrected himself. "He'd been shot a half-dozen times, and there was so much blood that it soaked the mattress and poured off onto the floor."

"Did you touch him or anything in the room?"

He was adamant. "No, I just backed out of that room; I mean, Jesus, the barn was on fire, she was sittin' out in the yard like it's all a dream—"

"You had your gun with you, didn't you say?"

He gestured toward the repeater lying across his saddle. "I had that Henry. When I got woke up by the fire, I brought it along 'cause I didn't know what the situation was, and I learned a long time ago that unknown situations with a gun are better than unknown situations without one."

Boy howdy. "What'd you do with the Yellow Boy?"

"Left it in the scabbard on my horse, tied out at the fence; that horse wasn't goin' anywhere near that fire."

I crossed my arms and looked into the flames licking up and around the broken and splintered wood, which reminded me that Benjamin and Dog were due back soon. "So after you left him in there, and her on the lawn, what'd you do?"

"I ran over to Bill Nolan's and got him."

"You didn't think to use the phone at the Barsads?"

He looked genuinely discomforted. "I didn't—"

I interrupted, saving him the embarrassment. It wasn't unusual in just such a situation for any of us of a certain age to forget about modern conveniences, or mistrust them, and simply run for help. "You wake Bill up?"

"No. He was in his kitchen."

I looked up on the ridge at the horses milling about. "Had he been drinking?"

"No."

"You're sure?"

"Yep, why?"

I leveled with him. "I've known Bill for an awfully long time, and in this current reincarnation I think it'd take three men and a boy to get a bottle away from him."

Hershel nodded. "He drinks, there's no two ways about that."

"Do you have any idea who might be leaving fifths of whiskey for him on his porch?"

He looked honestly surprised. "Nope, but if you find out, sign me up."

I looked past our camp and beyond the horses on the picket line, back over the rocky hillside, and spoke mostly to myself. "Why would he be sober that one night?"

October 26: four days earlier, afternoon.

I had watched as the words stuck in her bandaged throat, finally tumbling from her half-opened mouth.

"It was as if I wasn't alone, like somebody was there, leading me to where I needed to be, helping me to do it."

I got up from the windowsill and approached the hospital bed with my hat in my hands. "Do you remember getting the rifle from the cab of Wade's truck?"

Her head remained still for a moment and then shook in a hesitant manner. I didn't think it was her lacerated throat that caused her to be careful. "I remember walking to the truck, but then it was as if the gun just appeared in my hands."

I looked down at her profile and pondered the stark difference between the uncertainty of her story and the clarity of the sunshine that made a perfect trapezoid on the tile of the hospital floor on the other side of the bed. "Then what happened?"

"There was a storm, and the wind was blowing." She paused and cleared her throat with the words that spilled out again. "The door was open, banging against the side panels, and I thought about how it was probably going to break, but that I didn't care." She shook her head, a piece of her blond hair getting in her mouth. She tried to wipe it away but the leather restraints at her wrists would only allow her hand to go so far. I leaned over and helped her, my hand looking large next to her fragility. "The fire was reflecting off the glass, and I was tired. I wanted to just drop the rifle, but he kept telling me to keep it in my hands; that I was going to need it."

"He?"

She lifted her head a bit too quickly, and I could tell the effort was hurting her throat. "It was like somebody was there, keeping me moving."

"Who?"

"I don't remember—I mean, they weren't there, not really."

"You said *he.*"

She dropped her head and had spoken softly, looking at the sunshine that was still pounding through the window. "A voice, from my dreams . . ."

October 30, 7:52 P.M.

Hershel glanced over his shoulder. "What's the matter?"

I continued to allow my eyes to play over the star-sprayed

horizon. There weren't as many as usual and the Milky Way didn't show its whole stripe, but I felt like I always did when I looked at the night sky, as though I were falling backward. "That boy's been gone too long."

Hershel stood and joined me on my side of the fire. "Probably just dawdlin'."

I raised my fingers to my mouth and whistled long and clear. "Dog!"

Nothing.

I walked over to my saddlebags and pulled out my .45 and a handheld radio. I handed him the radio, and he stared at the walkie-talkie. "You stay here in case he comes wandering in, and if I don't get back in twenty minutes, dial that thing up and call the Sheriff's Department."

"Which one?"

I called over my shoulder. "Mine!"

I scrambled my sore legs and rear end up the pale, moon-glowed surface of the rocks, thankful I'd worn my rubber-soled boots but wishing I had a flashlight of my own. At the top of the ridgeline, the horses stepped back, reading my mood, but then nosed toward me, eager to be a part of whatever was going on and hoping for treats.

I walked past them, reaching a hand out and steadying the nearest, who was my bay. I stood there for a moment, listening to the soft caress of the high-altitude breeze and then, in the distance, to the unwelcome sound of a great horned owl.

As I made my way to the left, over the first ridge, I thought about the messengers of the dead and the owl feathers on the rifle that Henry Standing Bear had entrusted to me. I remembered how Dena Many Camps had unbraided her hair in the presence of the old Sharps, and another who, for a different reason, didn't want the old rifle in her home. Owls were supposedly not a sign that death was imminent, but were envoys from beyond, and I sometimes felt as though I was on their regular delivery route.

In the faint moonlight, I could see the boy's boot prints along with the tracks from Dog, whose paws could've easily been mistaken for a wolf's. Benjamin had followed the draw where a few scraggly stands of sage had valiantly attempted to grow, but where the odds and annual rainfall were against them.

The trail curved further to the left and played out into an open area with a two-track path leading east and, eventually, south and west to join the only road off the mesa. There was an old wellhead on the flat with the usual refuse left from a wildcat operation. There were loose stacks of rusted pipe, lathe, and wire snow fence that gave an indication of the era in which the drilling must have taken place, and a sealed slab where the actual rig must have been.

The truck skids that Hershel had earmarked for firewood were piled against one of the rock walls, a few of them scattered across the chalky ground and broken apart from the boy's efforts.

No Benjamin.

No Dog.

I slipped a little on the scrabble of the downslope and started toward the broken woodpile where it looked like the boy had been. What if he'd lost his way and fallen over the steep cliffs of the mesa? What if he'd slipped into one of the deep crags or fissures in the surrounding rock? What if he was hurt? Wouldn't Dog have returned? Shouldn't I be yelling his name? Why was I holding my sidearm?

I knew the answer to all of these things before I saw the dull glow of the Maglite buried in the pile of splintered wood. I crouched down and pulled the flashlight from the debris. I shook it once, and the beam grew brighter as I shined it around the surrounding area. There were prints, a lot of them. The boy's boot trail led to the woodpile along with Dog's, but there were others from a pair of running shoes, about a size 11, and a pair of boots, maybe a size smaller. I stood and shined the beam forward and could see that there had been some kind of altercation where someone had fallen, and there had been a struggle and more of a fight leading away.

The footprints ended at tire tracks left by a large four-wheeler, which must have been parked along the edge of the rock wall. The fat marks of the ATV followed the road heading southeast, and Dog's prints followed.

October 30, 8:22 P.M.
The radio wouldn't reach the repeater-tower across Antelope Basin and only mocked us with a crackling static; maybe it would get reception farther south. I clicked it off to save battery power and handed it up to the old cowboy.

Hershel watched me from horseback as I finished saddling the bay and tied off my saddlebags. I pulled a large-frame clip-on holster from the closest bag and slipped it at the small of my back. It was getting gusty and almost cold, so I put on my jacket. "You're going to be a hell of a lot faster than I am across broken ground; just don't break your neck in the process."

He looked apprehensive but nodded. "I've got a tough neck."

I steadied the bay and checked the reins on the packhorse and Benjamin's pony. Hershel had already had the majority of our gear loaded up and ready to go by the time I'd gotten back to our camp; evidently, he had come to the same inklings I'd had. "The service road from the abandoned drilling site appears to go southeast but turns and arcs back toward the main road where we parked the truck and horse trailer?"

He nodded. "Yep. It'll take longer for you, especially trailin' a pack line."

I pointed at the device. "Then check that radio and see if you can raise my department. If you can't get anything, load up your horse, get in that truck, haul your ass down to Absalom, and start making phone calls to get us some backup."

"What about you?"

"I'll follow the tracks and see where they took him. I've got a suspicion Dog trailed after them."

He looked down the ridge that fell toward the dark and endless surface of the mesa, his hand playing on the old brass receiver of the Henry, still in its sheath. "That's a lot of territory."

I slipped a boot in the stirrup and saddled up, the bay pivoting right but not so much this time; apparently he was getting used to my weight. "I've got tracks, and there's only one way off this rock."

The old cowboy sat there in the saddle. "Well, there's two, but let's try and stick with the one." He didn't look up and, after a second, he slapped the worn leather reins against the gelding's rump and the powerful horse leapt forward, the shoes on his hooves raking sparks from the rocks as he disappeared across the ridge west and into the night.

I led my horse forward, along with the packhorse and the silent reminder of the riderless pony, and they steadied only when I pulled us east along the rocks in the opposite direction. We picked our way down the same draw that I had covered on foot, past the struggling sage, and I think the horses were as relieved as I was when we got to the flat area at the wellhead. I strung us toward the woodpile, just to make sure I hadn't missed anything, but the site looked just as it had.

I pulled the flashlight from the saddlebag and checked the far side of the well where the pipes were stacked and a few fifty-gallon drums lay rusting on their sides. I circled back to the tracks to my right and stopped where the four-wheeler had been parked. I shined the Maglite along the patterns in the dirt, and I could see that the driver had hit Dog, but not badly enough to keep him from following. I could see the spot where he'd rolled and then where he had righted himself. He must have hurt his right rear leg, but a contract is a contract and he had limped off after the ATV.

October 30, 8:40 P.M.
About a mile down the two-track and between the buckshot breaks, it had begun to snow—not hard, but enough so that if it increased, the ground would be covered and the tracks would be lost. I spurred the horses forward.

I thought about the running-shoe prints at the wellhead and tried to think whom I'd seen lately with that style of foot-wear. Cliff Cly had on motorcycle boots the first time I'd met him in the bar but was wearing tennis shoes during the fight. Bill Nolan had worn boots the entire time I'd seen him and, as near as I could remember, Pat from the bar had also worn hard shoes.

I rode on and thought about the latest turn of events. Why take the boy? Had he seen something? Was he leverage against Juana because she'd seen or done something? Was it about Hershel, since he and the boy were so close? Was it about me?

One thing was for sure, it was an open declaration of war. Whoever was doing these things wasn't locked up in the Ab-saroka County jail, and whoever it was couldn't stay behind the scenes any longer. I'd turned up the heat, and now a boy was missing, and possibly dead due to my efforts.

I turned and looked at the empty saddle on the grulla.

I felt miserable, cranked my hat down against the increas-ing wind, and followed the single road that emptied itself onto the hardpan surface of the dry, endless stretch of flat badland called the Battlement.

I had to admit that in my current mood, it was the perfect place for me.

My horse's ears pricked and something blew up from one of the clumps of sage and came straight at us in a monumen-tal burst of gray feathers and talons. The bay went berserk and reared on his hind legs and the two other horses tried to bolt, but I held on and was able to withstand that little ro-deo. After I got them turned and settled a bit, I watched as the great horned owl I'd been hearing flapped his way south and across the hardpan of the Battlement with a five-foot wing-span.

I took a deep breath and watched him, the messenger from beyond, as the Cheyenne called them. "Hold all my calls, will you?" The bay was still a little skittish but settled back into a steady walk as I rolled my hips and tried to gain a new seat that would give my own seat a little relief.

It was a partially moonlit night; the pale deadness of her heavenly body pitched back and forth between the clouds, one minute illuminating the scrub sage and sparse tufts of buffalo grass, and the next, hiding her face completely. The snow had slackened for the moment, but I was betting that wouldn't last.

The road was slightly rutted and nothing had attempted to grow again in the running depressions that the oilmen had grooved in their hurry to drill. Environmentalists had pointed out just how fragile the crusted surface of the high desert is and how it would take hundreds of years for the land to repair itself. I could see where the drillers had forged new roads across the tundra in an attempt to make money in a place where time equaled cash and expedience meant jobs. I hoped that they had blown an engine.

The four-wheeler had made my tracking a little easier by staying on the main road, but I figured with the advantage of an internal-combustion pace, they had a good forty minutes on both Hershel and me. Dog's prints came and went as if he'd been trailing the ATV but hadn't wanted to be seen— that, or I'd watched too many episodes of *Rin Tin Tin*.

I let out a deep sigh and watched as my breath joined with

that of my horse and trailed southeast, following the road. My hands and face had gotten a little numb, which at least made my cheekbone feel a little better, if nothing else. It was snowing harder and the flakes stuck to the right side of everything, including the horses and me but, with the perversity and volatility of Wyoming weather, it seemed to be getting a little warmer. There were flashes of lightning in the clouds to the west, and it was possible that the wet snow would turn to rain.

I switched hands and discovered an old pair of buffalo gloves my wife had given to me decades ago in my between-seasons jacket pocket. I pulled the gloves on, tied off my scarf at my throat a little tighter, and cranked my hat down again, dipping my head a little to protect my exposed ear and busted cheek. Now I looked the part completely and remembered why I didn't like cowboying.

I pulled at the stiff collar of my jacket to try to protect the side of my face and could feel the ache at the top of my once-frostbitten ear.

The road turned west after a few miles, and it was a relief to be facing the wind. I dipped my head down and rocked back and forth as the bay plodded on. The urge to hurry ran through my blood like fractured streaks of lightning imitating the bursts overhead, and I thought about Benjamin and the dust devil; but the packhorse couldn't take speed, and all I'd find was an empty trailer for my troubles anyway.

We continued on, and I could just see something in the sporadic lightning that continued to illuminate the mesa.

It had to be the horse trailer.

I nudged the bay, and we came to the wide spot of the road at a trot. The trailer was as we'd left it, except that there was a pile of blankets, some feed buckets and ropes, a half bag of oats, and Hershel's prized canteen near the back of the end stall. The rear door of the trailer was held open with a hooked rubber strap, but not enough to stop it from rhythmically tattooing against the metal flanks.

Upon closer study, there was also a fluttering piece of paper on top of the blankets with a large rock holding it as a paperweight.

Something moved on the top of the trailer, and the bay spooked again. I reeled him in with a wrap on the reins, my free hand on the Colt at my back. The next uneven streak of lightning revealed the horned owl. He was seated on the sliding rail of the horse trailer, and he was about half the size of Benjamin. He turned his gigantic head and stared at me with eyes as gold as others I knew.

"Hello again." He didn't move and continued to stare at me for a moment; then he looked disgusted and flew off. I watched and listened to his wings slap the air as he circled south. "I was just kidding about holding my calls."

There was no dun horse tied off or inside the trailer.

The tiny alarms began ringing in the distance in my head, and I could feel the familiar cooling of my face and the stillness of my hands. I pulled the big Colt from the small of my back and wheeled the bay into a tight circle where I could see the surrounding area.

The packhorse balked along with the pony, but then they both circled around and looked off into the darkness south, just as they all had when we'd first arrived and saddled up. I didn't know what to look for as I peered into the remoteness of the south mesa. I knew that they couldn't see as well as I could but that they could feel more.

I wondered what, or who, they were feeling.

13

October 30, 10:00 P.M.

The pencil was blunt and Hershel's handwriting and spelling was pretty bad, but I could still make out the gist of it.

Sherif,

Raydio did not work and truck was gone when I got here. Dropped off the xtra stuff and went down hill and back to town. I spose Bill decided he needed his truck after all. Your dog was here, his leg is hurt, and he's limping bad so I threw him over the saddle and took him.

Hershel

PS: I lef the canteen for you but took the radio just in case it works, and will be back soon with the calvry.

I studied the note. It was odd that he'd misspelled the word "radio" the first time but then spelled it correctly in the postscript.

I tied my bay and the grulla off to the trailer and unloaded the packhorse. There wasn't that much water left, so I just emptied the plastic containers into the buckets, collected the canteen for myself, and took the flashlight over toward the head of the trailer. There were boot prints and ones from running shoes, and I shined the Maglite in the granules of gritty snow that had collected in them. I placed one of my feet beside one of the boot prints—it was definitely from a shoe that was a couple of sizes smaller than my own.

I circled around the other side of the trailer and picked up the four-wheeler's tire marks, which circled to the left and back to the road. When I got to the two-track dirt road, I could see that Hershel had made for town, but the ATV and duellie both turned and went east.

Dog's prints were everywhere, and it was difficult to tell which were new ones and which ones were from before.

I stood there for a moment, registering what it all meant.

I walked past the back of the trailer to where Benjamin and I had stood earlier. I looked off to the south and remembered the turnoff that we had seen that was just ahead. I started walking and pulled Hershel's canteen from my shoulder, unscrewed the top, and took a swig. It tasted like a Civil War mud puddle, and I was immediately sorry I'd given the horses all the water. I screwed the cap back on and slung the canteen over my shoulder.

The tracks continued to the cutoff and then abruptly turned. Whoever had the boy had gone south, but had the truck met the four-wheeler, followed them, or gone ahead?

No matter what had happened, the boy was south.

I went back to the trailer with the idea of writing a note but then couldn't find anything to write with. I hung the canteen over the horn of the bay's saddle, pulled the extra ammunition and clip I'd brought in the saddlebags, and dumped it all into the pockets of my jacket. The wind had stopped but the cloud cover was getting heavier, and it looked like there might be more precipitation.

I buttoned up my jacket, re-gloved, put a foot into the stirrup, and saddled up. I hadn't been on horseback this much in years. I felt the weight of the large-frame Colt against the small of my back and started off. I followed the road with the flashlight beam leading the way. I looked into the darkness south and watched as the lightning continued to pound the Battlement like artillery fire.

I clicked the Maglite off, flipped up the saddlebag cover, and dropped it inside.

No sense advertising.

October 26: four days earlier, afternoon.
I had placed my hat on the handle of the semiautomatic, crossed my arms, and softly exhaled, afraid I would break the spell.

"The voice told you to go in the house?"

Mary Barsad studied the bedsheets, her eyes wide and staring, as if she was seeing that night over again. "Yes, he said for me to go into the house."

"You said 'he' again."

She thought, and I watched her. "It's always the same voice, a male voice."

"Do you recognize it?"

"Yes. I mean, it's familiar."

"Who is it?"

She took a deep breath of her own, and you could see the

frustration tensing her body. Her eyes searched the sheets, and her brow furrowed, the lines deep between her eyes. I was afraid that she would lose the story, and she almost panicked at losing the story herself. "I went into the house, and I remember that he'd killed my horses—Wahoo Sue, my horse." There had been a catch in her breath, and she plucked at the blanket before she spoke again. "The bedroom, I remember going into the bedroom, and it was strange because the lights were off."

I spoke gently. "Was he asleep?"

"Yes."

Even more gently. "But if he was—"

"No. He always slept with the lights on, because he said he could. It had something to do with the time he'd spent in prison, like those little lists of paper he kept."

"The kites?"

"Yes, there was a particular one that he accused me of taking, and I think I did. . . . Once, just to see what it was."

October 30, 10:35 P.M.

There's nothing romantic about a dead body, and the romantic poets notwithstanding, there's nothing romantic about death.

About thirty minutes down the road, the bay skittered to the left and tried to rear. I was getting tired of his nervousness and was prepared. I wrapped the reins again and stayed put, allowing the big horse to back away but not turn and run. Something was out there a little ahead, something the horse didn't like. I didn't want to chance riding him closer, but I didn't relish the idea of walking around out here, trying to find him in the dark, either. The closest thing I could find to tie him off to was a sprig of dead blue sage—it was brittle but looked strong enough to hold the bay unless he was really determined.

I stepped off, comforting him with my voice and wishing I knew his name. "Easy, easy boy—"

I thought of reaching into my saddlebag for the Maglite, decided against it, and then changed my mind, figuring that if there were someone out there, they probably already knew I was here. I got the flashlight and then unclipped and slipped the .45 from the pancake holster at my back. I clicked off the safety and spoke to the horse again, looking into the white of his eye. "Easy, easy now."

I ran my eyes over the surrounding area, left the horse, and continued down the dirt road. Twenty yards further, I could see that there was a spot where the big Dodge had slid to a stop and then continued. I clicked on the tactical flashlight and could plainly see that there were running shoe prints again. It was the driver who was wearing them, and I could see where he'd yanked the truck to a lurching stop, jumped out of the cab, and run around the back.

I followed his tracks into the scrub weed and Johnson grass. There were boot tracks now as well, and it appeared as if the booted man had jumped from the passenger side and then been chased by the man in running shoes.

There wouldn't be anybody coming to my rescue tonight.

I found his hat first, lodged against one of the skeletal hands of dead sage. The battered beaver fur was brim up and the hat struggled against the dry branches, unable to escape their grip. I could see the stained, white sateen of the liner beckoning like the whites of the horse's eyes I'd just left.

I picked up the hat, rescuing it from the cruel, punishing wind of oblivion.

He was another twenty yards from the road. He must have been trying to angle toward the trailer. He'd been shot in the back and then again in the back of the head at close range, both, from the look of the wounds, 9 mm. His hands were duct-taped together.

I squatted by the old cowboy and nudged my own hat up, running my gloved hand across my face and placing the other on his shoulder to steady myself and maybe to provide some solace to his soul. I suddenly felt very tired. "Well, hell."

Evidently, Hershel had jumped from the truck and tried to run for it, but whoever he was attempting to escape from had chased after him and placed one of the 9 mm slugs between the old cowboy's shoulder blades and slightly to the right. As the puncher had tried to crawl away, the shooter had calmly walked over, lowered his weapon, and finished the job.

"I'm so sorry, Hershel."

I crouched there for a while, because it was the only thing I had the energy for. I watched one of the stark flashes of lightning strike no more than a mile away, the quick succession of explosive noise and reverberation through my boots telling me to move. I sighed and took one last look at the old cowboy, wondering how much blame I carried for his demise. It wasn't how the old fellow should've passed, on the mesa, executed. I made a promise to myself.

October 30, 10:52 P.M.

I piled some rocks on top of Hershel's hat and sat there on the side of the road. Who would've wanted to do such a thing? I felt another wave of sadness and that peculiar weariness that only overtakes you with the weight of a world gone bad. I took a deep breath and pushed off from the ground. I felt like the stack of rocks.

I looked back in the distance and thought about how easy it was to lose a body in this country, how quickly the scavengers and the weather could dispose of it, and scatter you. I also thought of something Bill Nolan had said in his truck about personal history—if nobody remembered you, were you ever really here?

I made a silent promise to not forget Hershel and then slowly approached the bay that had grown more skittish with the proximity of the lightning. "Easy, easy now—"

Despite recent developments or maybe because of them, I again felt a wave of exhaustion as I hooked a hand on the horn of the saddle and draped the .45 Colt over the seat. I pushed my hat back again and placed my damaged cheek against the cool leather of the saddle and just stood there. I could smell the rich, earthy scent of the leather, the horse, and the strong ozone of low-slung clouds.

Something was troubling me, something that tied all these events together dot to dot like one of those games that kids get on restaurant menus.

I turned my face and saw something move to the south. Probably the owl again. Maybe he had been delivering a message after all.

There was another lightning strike—it was close—and the bay lurched just a few inches but enough to strike the saddle against my injured cheek. I stood there for a moment more with my eyes closed, breathing through the pain, and thought about the ferocious burst of the big owl's wings on the trail and at the trailer—but it wasn't the owl, it was something else, something similar.

I guess my mind wasn't working.

I stowed the Colt in the holster at my back, fixed my hat and pulled the dead man's canteen from the saddle horn, unscrewed the top, and took another draught. It still tasted bad but with more of a bitter, metallic taste than mud puddle—it was probably from the liner. I replaced the canteen, looking at the beads on its face with the twin bird insignia. I thought that what was bothering me was about a bird but not about an owl, and I thought about the meadowlark I'd seen sitting on Kyle Straub's sign outside the hospital when I had been questioning Mary last week.

It was something about the meadowlark, something about it not sounding right.

One strike of lightning followed another in succession, and I felt the tingling of intimidation in being the tallest point on the big mesa; then I slipped a boot into the stirrup and made myself taller.

The bay behaved and only took a few steps to the left to avoid the smell of the dead man. I swayed in the saddle for a moment and felt a mild nausea. It must have been a drop in blood pressure from the exertion and the exhaustion. I'd seen enough dead bodies, but maybe Hershel had deeply ingrained himself in my psyche in the short time I'd known him. One thing I knew was that the world was a little bit poorer from his loss and that it was my job tonight to right the scales.

I yawned, cursed, and thought about the meadowlark

again. Why was it my mind had suddenly decided to mimic the horse I rode and jump left?

I thumbed my eyes. Was it Hershel's dead body the horses had sensed at the trailer or was it something else?

Maybe it was the meadowlark. . . . Why the hell was I continuing to think about the damn meadowlarks? I started with a jerk at the thought, so that the bay stopped and looked back at me.

I pulled the reins through my fingers, kneed him just slightly to get him going again, and looked at the canvas cover of the canteen, at the stenciled letters faded from the years.

I was tired.

It was two meadowlarks.

I looked down, and my head began nodding with the rhythm of the horse as he continued on. The next volley of lightning struck even farther south, down near the tip of the mesa, so the horse didn't pay too much attention.

Two meadowlarks.

One's voice was right, the other was not. There are two types, eastern and western, and they do not sing the same song—similar, but not exactly the same. Where had I heard an eastern meadowlark lately? Evidently I was thinking of Cady and my trip to Pennsylvania and, more importantly, the conversation we'd had on the phone at the bar. I kept riding south but was having trouble remembering why. It wasn't about birds. It was something about a boy, a dead man, and a horse.

It felt like I'd been traveling a long way. My head kept

nodding until my chin poked into my breastbone. I yanked my head up and opened my eyes, and I was unsure if it was real or a dream.

The road was gone, and a thin layer of snow, less than an eighth of an inch, covered the ground and vegetation for as far as I could see into the gloom, except for a perfect circle of dark ground where there was no snow and where nothing grew. The bay stopped and looked at the scene with me. There were no struggling tufts of grass, no sage, nothing. It was as if some flying saucer had landed on top of the mesa, burned all the undergrowth and the thin skim of snow, and then had gone.

I exhaled and my head dropped again, but when I forced my face back up I could see something in the middle of the circle, like the center of a clock with both hands pointing toward midnight.

I knew it was a hell of a lot later than that.

I thought about the teepee circles that were part of the landscape in our portion of the country, but I couldn't see any of the rocks that the Indians would have used to mark the periphery. And the circle was too big. Even the Crow and Cheyenne family-sized teepees wouldn't be this large in circumference.

Crop circles maybe, but there were no crops.

The bay pulled up a little way from the edge, then pranced toward it and whinnied. I was just beginning to wonder if it was really a hole and that my tired eyes were playing tricks on me when another lightning strike hit no more that a hundred yards to our right. My horse had had enough, and he bolted to the left. I tried to hang on, but this time he pivoted, slipped, and fell.

I hit on my side like a load of firewood and felt the air push from my lungs with the impact and a sharp pain in my foot as the bay landed on my boot with an audible crunch. I lay there for a second to get my bearings, assess the damage, and generally feel embarrassed about falling off my horse. For a westerner, coming unmounted is as shameful as wearing your pants inside your boots, asking somebody how big their spread is, or pissing on the floor of the Alamo.

The only good thing about the fall and the excruciating pain in my foot was that it cleared my head enough to think about what I was going to do now that the bay was hightailing it north across the hardpan range and disappearing into the darkness. I watched the stirrups bouncing off the horse's sides in a comical interpretation of a TV western and allowed my head to fall back on the crusted snow. "Damn."

The hammer of the .45 was digging into my back, and I started to roll over, when another streak of pain ran up from my right foot. My eyes watered with the hurt, and I wiped at them.

It was then that I saw something at the far edge of the circle. It was something dark and big, and it was rapidly moving my way. I thought it was the owl again, even though it was the wrong color and didn't seem to be flying, and figured maybe he thought he'd found a culinary bonanza.

I tried to raise my head, but the pain in my cheekbone made it hard, so I just watched as the big creature stamped the ground and rushed forward to snake out its long neck and snap at my head with huge clacking teeth.

Pain be damned, I yanked back and looked up at a thousand pounds of unrivaled fury. It was a horse, but only in the sense that the headless horseman's horse was a horse. I could hear the clanking of chains where the thing had come unfettered from hell, and I expected fire to blow from its nostrils at any moment.

Unable to move any farther, I lay there on my back and watched as the black beast reared on its hind legs and crashed its hooves to the ground only inches from my foot; it stamped at me over and over again.

I had found Wahoo Sue.

I discovered a reserve I didn't know I had and dragged myself back on my elbows as the horse screamed at me and whinnied and snapped the air in an attempt to get free from the nylon halter around her head. She was close enough that I could see where it had rubbed her raw and where the dried blood had stained her dark face. The harness was connected to a heavy, rusted logging chain that was in turn connected to a rock in the middle of the circle, and the length of links had torn and chafed the chest, barrel, and rump of the tortured animal.

October 26: four days earlier, afternoon.
Mary Barsad's hands had come up again, and she had tried to aim an imaginary rifle despite the restraints at her wrists.

"His voice kept telling me to do it, and when I looked at his body lying there on the bed it was as if I already had shot him. It was as if the blood was already there, that I'd already shot him, but the voice was telling me to do it again."

I moved to my right, placed my hands on the foot rail of the hospital bed, and looked into her face. "You fired the rifle?"

Tears spilled from her lower lids and highlighted her high cheekbones. "Yes."

"How many times?"

Her head went back as if she'd been struck and then stayed at that odd angle. "Three times."

I don't think the expression on my face changed, but the facts had. "Three times."

"Yes."

Wade Barsad had been shot six times.

She turned her head toward the light. "He said that he deserved it, said that he deserved to die."

"Wade."

"Yes."

This time she didn't move. "But the voice that told me to kill him—it was Wade's."

October 31, 2:30 A.M.

"She likes you."

The voice came from the darkness to my left. I could see his outline as I lurched up on one elbow, but I was still having trouble focusing. "How can you tell?"

"'Cause she would have killed you if she didn't. Okey?"

I stared into the darkness. He had come closer, and I could see his shape more clearly. I'd figured it out, but now that I heard the hard nasal voice like flat stones falling and the signature word, it was confirmed.

"How are you, Wade?"

He laughed. "I knew you'd find out; it was just a question

of when." The horse strained against the chain, but this time she directed her fierce aggression toward him. He walked closer but was careful to stay outside of the circle where Wahoo Sue had licked the snow and nibbled everything else in a desperate attempt to stay alive. "She doesn't like me much, but then the feeling's mutual." He squatted down in the running shoes and was holding a roll of duct tape. "Just out of curiosity, when did you know it was me?"

My head slipped to one side, and I could just make out his face. From the photographs I'd seen, it was indeed Wade Barsad. I flexed my foot and caught my breath again as the pain clamped inside my boot—broken, no doubt about it. "Meadowlarks."

"I beg your pardon?"

Despite the pain, the horse, and the appearance of Wade Barsad, I had to fight against a mounting exhaustion and mumbled. "Meadowlarks."

He smiled and made a sucking sound with his teeth. "I'm still not following you." He reached out and shook my shoulder. "Hang in there, Sheriff, I've been dying to have this conversation."

"Different song."

Wahoo Sue continued to stamp at him, but since he was the one who had staked her, he knew her range. "What?"

I took a deep breath and let it out slowly, and I think I was drooling. I tried to wiggle my foot again in an attempt to wake up, but the pain had subsided to a throbbing, and my eyes started to close. "The eastern meadowlark has a song that's different from the western one."

He stared at me. "So?"

I tried to concentrate, but my neck muscles had dissolved somehow. "On the phone. . . . Supposed to be your brother back in Ohio, but I heard a western meadowlark."

He sat back on his ankles. "You're shitting me. On the cell phone?"

"Yep."

He was laughing again and leaned back to sit beside me. "Okey, so you're John J. Audubon."

I lay back, thinking that it might be my only chance to keep my sidearm, and stared into the heavily clouded sky. "It was your brother, the dentist, in the house—burned up."

He nodded. "I was getting pressure from my old business associates, and the FBI wanted all of the names and account numbers that I'd written down in exchange for further protection, so I decided to do away with Wade Barsad. I got my brother to fake the dental records for a cut of the insurance money, but I needed a body. Unfortunately for him, it turned out to be his."

"You walked Mary through it, while she was on the pills—"

"You know, I was worried about the mob and worried about the FBI, but then you showed up and I don't even know your name. After I saw you with Vanskike and the boy, I figured I'd better dope you up before taking you on, that's why I didn't just wait for you at the trailer."

"Hershel."

He nodded again. "Yeah, I'm sorry about that. I didn't want to kill him, but he ran. And let me tell you, he was some kind of fast when he got going. I had to throw a bullet into him to stop him, and then I thought that I wouldn't want him to suffer." Barsad laughed and looked at the horse, whose chains clanked against her efforts to get to him. "So, I finished the job." He reached into the pocket of his jacket and pulled out the 9 mm semiautomatic. "And now I have to shoot you and make it look like you shot him, and do something with the kid and try to find my missing kite, and I don't have time for all this."

His voice touched something off in Wahoo Sue, and she stamped at him again. I turned from the horse and could feel my eyes getting a little wobbly. "Sorry to inconvenience you."

"Yeah."

"The boy."

He gestured with his chin. "He's in the truck with an old friend of yours."

"Dog?"

He laughed. "No, not your damned dog. I tagged him with the four-wheeler, so I thought he wouldn't be any more trouble. Besides, he wasn't worth a bullet so we drove off and left him."

I'd allowed my arm to fall to my back and made an attempt to roll toward him as if I were interested in the conversation. "The canteen."

"Yeah, I wrote the note. It was a calculated risk, 'cause I wasn't sure if you'd seen the old guy's handwriting." He studied me some more. "How are you still awake? It must be your size."

I could feel my Colt, but I had to get my jacket out of the way to reach it. "I am a little drowsy."

"You should be; I put enough sleeping pills in that canteen to drop a buffalo." He started to rise, and I froze my hand. "Anyway, there's somebody that wants to meet you before you knock off for the night. Okey?" He looked back into the darkness to our left and shouted. "Hey, hurry up if you wanna talk to him." He looked down at me. "He's going to love seeing you again—"

Cliff Cly came out of the dark and stood there with Hershel's Henry rifle in his hands. I was happy to see that he was in pretty rough shape. He ignored me and looked at Barsad. "Where the fuck did you get this?"

A quiet second passed. "I got it off the cowboy."

Cly looked at the old repeater and then back to Barsad. "You kill him?"

Wade shook his head, and I wondered why he was lying. "No. I told you Cliff, I don't kill people unless I have to."

Cly walked over closer and looked down at me. I noticed his face was pretty messed up and he was wearing a neck brace. I could see the individual knuckle marks on his forehead, and the swelling and discoloration around his eye was far worse than mine. I felt a little better.

I looked up at him. "How's your head?"

He glanced at me in a dismissive manner. "Fuck you." He turned and shouted to Barsad. "What about this asshole here?"

Barsad's voice sounded a little farther off, and he must've been going toward the truck. "He's got enough product in him that he'll overdose, but we'll shoot him with Hershel's gun and come up with a story later." The rodeo cowboy leaned down, holding the .44 Henry on his thighs with one hand, and started feeling around my jacket with the other. "Check him for a gun. Okey?"

Cly's face was very near my own. "That's what I'm doing." His hand froze against mine as I clutched the Colt at the small of my back.

Barsad's voice faded. "I'll get the kid."

Cly's eyes and mine locked, and I could feel my muscles tense as I got ready to make one last, desperate move. He didn't blink and leaned even closer. "Don't hit me again, you big son-of-a-bitch; the last time you practically took my head off." He winked and then glanced over his shoulder, looked back at me, and smiled. "Relax, Sheriff, I've got us covered, just don't shoot me. *Okey?*" He was grinning now. "Hey, ki-mosabe, can you understand me? I'm on your side." He studied me for a moment more, and then stood and shouted. "He's clean."

I wondered what the hell was going on as Cly stood up. There was a lot of noise, and I listened as at least two doors were slammed. Barsad's voice carried from the left. "What the hell . . . where's the kid?!"

"What'a ya mean?"

There was more noise, and it sounded as if something was slammed into the bed of the truck. "He's not here, Cliff!"

I tugged at my jacket and pulled the .45, clearing it from my body but continuing to keep it hidden.

Wade came into my sight, and my ant's-eye view made them look like giants. "Did you tie him up and put him in the truck?"

"No, there wasn't time. I just taped him and left him on the four-wheeler."

"I didn't see the four-wheeler when I was just back there. Where'd you shittin' put it?"

He gestured. "It's back at the . . ." Just then, I figured I wasn't the only one who heard it start up. "Oh, fuck."

Out a couple of hundred yards to the west, I could see the lights of the ATV as it turned and sped away on what I assumed was the road. Barsad took a few steps in that direction but then stopped and looked back at the two of us, then at just me. "Kill him, and I'll get the kid."

Cliff shook his head and fumbled with something in his pants pocket as he took a step toward Barsad. "I don't think—"

Wade must have seen the move; he wasn't a man to take chances, so he lifted the 9 mm and fired, the bullet hitting Cly squarely in the trunk of his body. He shuddered for a moment, then the big Henry repeater hit the ground and went off, the bullet going into the air, and he collapsed. As he did, I lifted my wavering arm and fired the .45. I was wide and to the right but kept firing as Barsad made a rapid retreat in the direction of the truck.

I continued to throw rounds in Wade's general direction, but he didn't fall. I finished off the clip with a solid thunk as a round hit the truck. I watched as the cab lights came on in the Dodge, but the motor didn't start. I guess he was fumbling for his keys.

I hit the button and watched as the empty magazine slipped from the Colt, and I slammed in the other one that I had put in my jacket pocket. It was like an out-of-body experience, as though somebody else's arms raised and fired just as the big Dodge started.

I saw the passenger side window explode as I emptied the

clip. Wade Barsad disappeared but only for a moment, and I was monumentally disappointed to hear the motor roar and the duellie spray dirt as its lights bobbed, and he sped away.

The horse was going berserk but was at the far side of the circle and out of sight. I watched as the chain, embedded in the rock, heaved and straightened in a direct line into the darkness. I fell back flat and lay there breathing and thinking—what the hell else could go wrong? I could feel my eyes closing and knew that if I didn't get up soon, I wasn't going to be getting up at all.

I looked at the spent semiautomatic in my lap, the slide locked in the open position. I ejected the clip and began refilling it from the loose rounds in my jacket pockets, the cartridge spring making a slight metallic sound as I reloaded.

With each breath I listed a little further, and I might have even fallen asleep if not for Cly, who spoke from the gloom, his words accompanied by a light giggle. "Don't you think we've had enough shooting for one night?"

I'd thought for sure he was dead.

I rolled over on my stomach and began crawling toward him. He was clutching something over his chest. He was still giggling and spitting up a little blood with it as I leveraged an elbow—his face only a couple of inches away. "You should stop laughing; it can't be good for you."

He giggled some more. "How bad is it, Deputy Dawg?"

There was a fair amount of blood, but it was low and to the left—intestines, I hoped, not a lung. It was difficult to tell how bad, but he'd live, for a while, at least. I looked at his face. "Who the hell are you?"

He kept giggling and pulled his hand up. I noticed that he was holding his wallet, which he flipped open exposing a badge. His voice was singsong, and he sounded like he was an announcer on a bad fifties TV show. "Why I'm Cliff Cly of the FBI."

14

He wasn't giggling anymore. "How long do you think I've got?"

"Longer than you're going to want."

He swallowed underneath the neck brace and dropped the wallet. "God damn it, this hurts. I showed the kid how to drive the thing and told him that if I didn't get back in a couple of minutes, to just gas it the hell out of here and stay off the roads." His eyes closed, and he clutched his stomach. "Fuck, fuck, fuck, fuck, fuck!"

I looked at the young man's face. I had to admit that he was good; I hadn't made him, but now, seeing the symmetry of his features under the stubble, and his general demeanor, even after being shot, it all made sense.

It also explained why Sandy Sandberg had called off the polygraph.

Another wave of exhaustion swept over me, and I started getting a little panicked about all the things I had to do before I fell over. I touched his arm, and he grimaced. "You have to let me take a look."

"Fuck you, you one-eyed bastard. No way."

I casually wondered if he'd looked in a mirror lately. "We have to put something in there to staunch the bleeding—your hands aren't doing the trick."

He ground his teeth, and I could hear the crunch of the enamel from a foot away. "No."

"Look, I've got to roll you over and see where the bullet went."

He shook his head violently. "No fucking way." He glanced up. "Why? There's nothing you're going to be able to do for me, so just go get help."

"If I don't stabilize the wound, you're going to bleed to death." I continued to look at him. Something in my head started reciting organs along with percentages—kidney 22 percent, stomach 18 percent, bladder 12 percent, and small bowel 12 percent. Something stuck in my mind that these were bad numbers, and we should root for the smallest percentage.

He studied me. "What the fuck is wrong with you anyway?"

I tried to remember. "I think I've been drugged." My cheekbone ached, and my neck muscles were still doing a pretty good imitation of a boneless chicken. "As a matter of fact, I know I've been drugged. Barsad said he put something in Hershel's canteen." "And I think something in my foot's broken."

"Get the fuck out of here."

I could feel my eyes starting to close again. "Could you say fuck some more; it's really helping."

"Fuck you, I'm the one who's shot in the gut."

I fought with my jacket while trying to get the .45 back into my holster with my other hand. I couldn't really feel my fingers, which didn't bode well for my fixing Cliff Cly of the FBI.

I tried to focus on the case, figuring that the cipher effect might keep me awake—that, and the thought of a man who was possibly dying. But he could still talk, if with a limited vocabulary, so I was starting to think that his lung hadn't been nicked after all. Some more facts leapt up about a collapsed lung—something about air sucking into the chest where it can't escape, which in turn pushes the heart aside, so far, in fact, that the vessels to the heart are pinched to the point that they are closed and there is no blood flow to the heart.

I thought about it and came to the conclusion that that was bad, but it was like somebody else was talking inside my head, somebody I'd once been other than the sleepy person I was now. "So, what's a nice bureau boy like you doing in a place like this?" I attempted to move his hands again. "Let me see."

"Fuck you, Deputy Dawg." His chin planted against the brace, and I watched as he tried to concentrate on not clutching the wound. He relaxed just a little, which I'm sure was for the best, and allowed his head to return to the ground. "He was ours in the witness relocation program, but after the fiasco in Youngstown we let him dangle, in hopes that he'd give us the information on his pals back in Jersey since they were looking for him. He was in Vegas, and then here."

With his hands out of the way, I slowly unbuttoned his shirt and then carefully tore open the T-shirt at the wound. There was no sucking sound, and the blood was pooling at the depression in his skin.

"Well?"

Trying to keep my eyes open, I stretched my entire face in spite of my cheekbone. "It's not as bad as I thought."

"Yeah? Well, I feel so much fucking better."

The voice was telling me things, and I wondered how smart was the guy I used to be? Now he was telling me about how, if it was a low-velocity, low-caliber weapon like a 9 mm, then most of the tissue damage was confined to the bullet tract, as opposed to a high-velocity, high-caliber weapon like a rifle that would result in a lot of damage to tissues and organs just by passing by them. "Energy dissipation."

"What?" His voice was gargled, but I was pretty sure it was just mucus.

I leaned forward. "We're hoping for no major organs or large blood vessels."

"Well, if it's a major organ, hopefully it's my liver; the little fucker's indestructible."

Liver—30 percent.

"I think we can stop the bleeding, but you're not going anywhere and we're going to have to get you medical attention pretty quick." I looked around and noticed that Wahoo Sue had moved off to the far side of the ring, probably because of the blood. She wanted nothing to do with us. The lightning had moved to the east, and it appeared that all we were going to get now was wind. "I don't think I can move you."

"I don't want you to."

"Deal." I pulled off my neck scarf and looked at it, hoping it wasn't too full of bacteria, and began folding it up in preparation for placing it over the wound. I thought about Martha, who had given me the silk bandana, and sighed. It was then that I saw the roll of duct tape that Wade Barsad must've dropped.

I reached over, picked it up, and ripped a length from the roll. Maybe it was being witness to someone else's suffering, or having a task, or all the voices in my head, but I was actually feeling pretty good—still sleepy, but more on the dopey side than the passing-out side. I attached the one-foot piece to my scarf and ripped off another. "This stuff is great; you can use it for everything."

He shook his head. "Oh, God."

I completed the makeshift bandage, took a deep breath, and wished I had some whiskey. "This is going to hurt."

"Uh huh."

I planted the bandage squarely on the wound, pressed down, and wrapped the duct tape in all directions. He didn't move. "There, that wasn't so—"

"Jesus-fucking-Christ!"

I thought I'd been gentle.

The old me in my head was talking again and said that, with the ambient temperature, the blood around the wound was coagulating quickly, but the drop in blood pressure would also increase his susceptibility to hypothermia. I smirked a little to myself but then thought about the fact that no matter how smart the old me was, it was the new me that was going to have to do something about the problem. I took off my coat and carefully placed it over him.

I sat there for a moment, listening to him breathe and feeling as if I'd accomplished one of my tasks. Now, if I could just remember the others. The chain clanked and moved left.

Horse.

Dark horse. Three horses. One rider.

The boy, Benjamin.

I leaned over. "Where do you think he'll go?"

The FBI man looked at me with one eye opened and one closed. "Who?"

I thought it was a reasonable question. "The boy . . . Benjamin."

He took a couple of shallow breaths and then answered. "I told him to stay off the roads, but I didn't go into it much further than that."

"Why did Wade take him?"

He moved a little and immediately regretted it. "Fuck . . . Wade said something about a list that he'd written and that he thought his wife had taken, but he couldn't find it so I think he thought maybe the wife had given it to the girl at the bar; then he wanted to back you off, but I guess when it became apparent that the old cowboy was headed down the mesa, all bets were off." He looked down at the stalled blood at his abdomen. The duct tape bandage was doing a grand job. "I really didn't think I was going to get shot; he just didn't seem like the type."

I thought about that and the old me said something important, which I repeated out loud. "He killed his brother."

He scowled, and there was a little bit of blood staining his teeth. "Yeah, I guess I misjudged him. I started getting really suspicious when I found the old cowboy's gun in the truck."

Reminded of the Henry, I reached past him and picked it

up, checking to make sure the muzzle wasn't blocked and that it was still loaded. Loading and checking the Henry was a tedious process because the magazine tube was under the barrel, but Hershel Vanskike wasn't the kind of man to load a weapon with only one round. "Well, he's dead."

"Vanskike?"

"Yep."

He shook his head. "I was afraid of that. I brought the boy down here, but Barsad stayed back to wait for the old guy."

"Hershel."

He nodded. "Hershel. Said he just wanted to tell him he had the boy."

"How did you find Barsad?"

He sighed. "Caught him returning to the motel after making one of his liquor deliveries to Bill Nolan's place. I guess Wade couldn't get used to keeping a low profile, so he schemed up this idea for getting Bill's truck on a regular basis. Nolan told me about those mysterious whiskey deliveries, and it sounded like Wade."

"So, he was staying in one of the rooms at the motel before I got there?"

"Yeah, I'm pretty good at hiding people even in a town of forty. I waited for him one night and even brought him into the bar when Pat was the only one there. Pat poured us a drink and vouched for me. That's how we all got to be partners."

"Speaking of drinking, that was quite a show you put on at the motel."

"Show, hell. I was drunk."

"Who was the girl?"

"Just a girl, but she figured out who you were before I did."

"What about the fight?"

He laughed and then groaned. "They were getting suspicious, because I was backing away from the more severe aspects of the partnership."

"Like?"

"Killing you." His eyes shifted to mine. "I convinced them that I could just run you off." He raised a hand and tapped the plastic brace at his neck, and even in my stupor, I could see his movements were starting to slow. "Then I convinced him to let me come up here and keep an eye on the three of you, but he came along because he wanted to check on that horse—wanted to see it die. Patience is not a strong suit with Wade, but torture is."

"I'm getting that." I took a deep breath. "So, he did set the barn on fire and kill the other horses?"

"Yes."

I nodded along with him, until I felt myself falling forward again. The old me voice was shouting about abdominal infection, that he only had hours, and that pretty soon Cliff Cly of the FBI was going to start showing more sleepiness and fatigue.

Welcome to the club.

I put the old repeater in my lap, pulled out my .45, and wrapped the FBI agent's hand around the grip. "You've got five rounds, and you're cocked and ready to fire." He looked at me as if I were insane. "You're too weak to handle this Henry, so I'll take it."

Within twelve hours fever was going to set in, his heart

rate and respiration would go up; the heart rate would be unable to make up for failing blood pressure, and as soon as the organs were not getting enough blood they would fail. At this point, the smarty-pants voice was telling me, he would get weak, dizzy, drift in and out of consciousness, and within seventy-two hours, he would die.

"I've got to go."

"What?"

"I'm going to fall over if I don't get out of here, in which case you're going to rapidly follow me into oblivion and Barsad's going to find the kid, none of which are acceptable."

"Your foot's broken—you can't walk out of here."

I rolled to one side and dug a knee up, placed my hands on the ground, and struggled to my feet. I kept my weight on one side, using the Henry as a crutch. "I'm not going to walk."

"Then what are you going to do? We don't have anything to . . ." His voice faded as I stood and hopped, facing the circle of dark ground. "You've got to be fucking kidding."

I pulled my hat down and kept my weight off my damaged foot; I felt like James Arness but probably looked more like Ken Curtis. There was more than just my voice talking now, as I listened to the wind that scoured the top of the mesa. It sounded like phantoms brooding and mourning in a testament to nostalgia and bitterness, and I could almost hear the chattering of the dry leaves in the cottonwoods, moaning and hissing from the powdery river below. Ancient voices pulled me apart from myself and slammed me back together.

I turned my head and looked at Cly over my shoulder. "Cliff, where are you from?"

His voice still gargled. "What?"

I repeated the question and, unsurprisingly, my voice didn't sound like my own.

"Cherry Hill, New Jersey."

"That's near Philadelphia?"

"Just over the bridge."

"That's what I thought." I limped to the edge of the circle. "Remind me to introduce you to somebody—you've got vocabulary in common."

October 31, 3:34 A.M.

I don't know how long it'd been since anybody had stepped onto that dark piece of ground, but the response was what I figured it would be. At first, she stayed at the farthest length of the chain, then she snorted and pawed the ground, and gave one headlong charge toward me.

I just stood there. Horses had charged me before, and it can be some kind of intimidating, but I didn't move. She pulled up about ten feet away, eyes wild, and then reared. The big black mare pawed the air, and I could see the steel shoes that were still on her hooves. She planted and, when I still didn't move, she bounced on her forelegs and planted again; this time she was five feet away.

I held the rifle at my side, took a breath, and held out a hand, fingers in, palm down. She backed away, snorting and shaking her head at me, her tangled mane flying.

I took a step toward her, more of a hop, really, and she rushed forward, turned and sent me flying with her substantial rump. I landed hard on the ground just outside the circle.

After a respectful moment, he spoke. "That went well."

I looked at him and remembered something Lucian, my old boss, used to say in like situations. "You know the difference between an asshole and an anus?"

He spoke from the side of his mouth. "What's that?"

"An anus can't say 'that went well.'"

I could just lie there, but that wasn't part of the contract, so I struggled up on one elbow and felt something fall out of my shirt. I thought it might've been my spleen.

Spleen—8 percent.

I fumbled at it with my stiff fingers. It was roundish and about as long as a short, fat cigar. It was grainy, and I vaguely remembered that yesterday Henry had stuffed a handful of something into my pocket along with my badge.

I glanced at Cly and held it up. "Horse treat."

"Do all you sheriffs run around with those in your pockets?"

"You bet."

I sat the rest of the way up and watched the mare circle the perimeter of the chain. She stamped at me again, then backed away and neighed. I stood carefully, keeping my weight to my good side, and hopped a little closer to her territory. She charged again, but it was a feint—to be honest, I'd thought the earlier one was too and that she had just misjudged her retreat.

At least, I hoped so.

I took another hop-step and raised my left hand again, but this time with the palm up and fingers flat. She was standing near the stake that had been hammered into a fissure in the rocky surface of the mesa, and she didn't move. Neither did I.

The wind rocked against me with the silence of the high

desert, and the ghosts whined their way past but were unable to resist a touch on their way. I felt a chill that had nothing to do with the temperature and wondered if they would be for me or against me.

Maybe it was because I didn't have anything to lose and she could sense my need, maybe it was the keening of the spirits, or maybe it was because she had been starved almost to death, but she took a step forward—what my friends who knew about such things called a try. I took a breath but still didn't move.

She turned her head sideways just a bit, the way horses always do when they really want to see you, and took another step. Another try.

In my life, I have been kicked by horses and bitten by them. I've been stepped on, crushed against gates, and thrown to the ground, but I have also been nuzzled, rubbed against, carried by, nickered at, and warmed by the great beasts. I thought of all the horses I'd known and couldn't think of a bad one. My father had said the beasts of the field didn't feel pain like we did, but I never saw him mistreat one, ever.

You learn by experience, and from my father I learned patience. So, I waited.

She took another step forward, stretched her neck, and tried to smell the grain and sorghum treat without coming closer.

My eyes watered and not just because of the wind. Humans can go for weeks without food, according to size and weight, but all of us perish in about seventy-two hours without water.

Another step, another try.

My arm was getting tired, but I didn't move. The old me

voice was back, telling me that horses don't think like us, they don't hold grudges, and they respond to release rather than pressure.

"Is this going to take long?" I shifted my eyes to him and then back to the mare. "I mean, I'm just asking."

A number of thoughts and responses sprang to mind, but I didn't want to startle Wahoo Sue.

Her neck strained forward, and the prehensile lips with the dark hairs touched the biscuit. You could see the damage the stiff, blood-coated harness had done to the horse's tender nose and cheekbones. The noseband was bloodied and the galled skin around it was seeping fluid. The crownpiece had worn the hair from the poll section of her mane, and what was left was crusted with dried blood and serum. Along with skinning her sides, the unforgiving chain had damaged her legs, gaskins, hocks, and pasterns.

I took a few deep breaths and fought against the chemicals deadening every system in my body.

Her weight shifted, and she took the treat.

Hard to get, but not homicidal, the old me voice said.

I tried to remember what Mary had said when she had been sleepwalking in the jail. I spoke in the softest voice I could muster. "So-o-o girl, so-o-o girl . . ." I watched as Sue took a couple of guarded steps, then aligned her body, and considered me and the second offering.

I could feel myself wavering with each breath, every exhale pitching me forward just a bit. Maybe she could see it, too. Maybe she could tell I wasn't in any shape to do anything, especially hurt her.

Mary's voice prompted again, and I repeated. "S-o-o girl, so-o-o . . ."

Another try, then another.

This time she didn't stretch her neck out but rather took that extra step. I placed the rifle barrel against my side, then rolled my hand up around the treat and only let her nibble on the end.

I raised my hand and touched under her chin. The big mare started in slight outrage, but then settled. I allowed her most of the treat from my hand and ran the other under her jaw line and readjusted the halter in a casual manner.

She lowered her head to me, and the old me voice said something about Hershel's horse at the burned house and at the corral on Barton Road.

I leaned in very slowly and exhaled.

Wahoo Sue stuck her big, velvety nose out to me and inhaled, just as the old cowboy's horse had. We stood there like that, exchanging breath, and I could feel the anxiety start to leave her.

It was as if I'd thrown a switch, and she stood there, stiff-legged but in a small way compliant. I slipped the rest of the treat into her mouth and took hold of the logging chain, careful to hold it away from her skinned and scabbed body. Slowly, I took a step in close, trailing the hated attachment to my left and turning toward the trunk of the mare's body. She twisted to look at me but held still.

I was only going to get one shot at this, and even in my doped state, I knew it wasn't going to feel good. I had to do it smoothly and quickly, neither of which were catchwords in my physical repertoire, even without a broken foot and a drug overdose.

It was almost as if she knew my intention, but I wasn't sure if she pawed the ground in anticipation or warning. I took hold of the Henry rifle and then reached up to her withers, spreading my one hand over her spine, set my good foot, and leapt.

My weight caused her to shift slightly to the right and then she stood on stiff legs as I clambered for a seat. I waited and, to my surprise, absolutely nothing happened.

Almost adding insult to embarrassment, Wahoo Sue turned and looked at me with a large, soulful brown eye. Just to be sure, I stroked her neck, careful not to touch her wounds, and repeated the magic words. "So-o-o girl, easy girl . . ."

Cly called out from my left. "Hey, Sheriff, how are you going to get that stake out of the ground?"

Bureau boys.

I kept stroking her black neck, and it was like the wind was blowing inside me. I slumped forward with one of the waves of fatigue, which knocked my hat back. Somehow, I held the rifle across her withers with one hand and, with the other, I held Wahoo Sue's mane. "Good girl, so-o-o good." I took a few breaths and leaned back, kicking my heels down and gigging her toward the center stake to gain some slack.

I looked over the horse's shoulder to the wounded man on the ground and kept my voice in the same soft tone as I had used with her. "I don't know how long it's going to take, but I'll be back for you, so don't go out crawling around and don't lose my sidearm."

His voice was still strong, and my hopes were that he'd

hold out. He was tough, I knew that; the question was going to be how tough. "I'm not going anywhere."

"If Barsad comes back, don't take any chances, and do what you need to do."

I saw him reaching with his far hand and pulling the weapon up and onto his chest. "Don't worry, I'm not going to let him have another crack at me." I could see a light spot in the darkness where his face must've been. "You're talking like this is our last conversation."

I rubbed my hands up the mare's neck. "Just for now, because once I unbuckle this harness, I don't think I'm going to have time to say anything."

"What do you think she's going to do?"

I stretched my eyes in an attempt to get a clearer view of the harness buckle. "I think she's going to go for water, and that's off the mesa and toward town."

"Do me a favor?"

The nylon was stiff with blood, but I finally got it loosened enough so that I could move the flap under the keeper and through the buckle. "What's that?"

"Don't run over me."

I nodded and slipped the rest of the strap out, and the harness dropped about an inch on Wahoo Sue's long muzzle. I leaned in close and spoke softly into her ear. "I know you're sick, I know you're tired, but if you don't get us both out of here, an awful lot of bad things are going to happen. They say you can run, so you show me."

The halter fell away, and it was all she needed. She dropped her head, lunged back and to the side away from the chain, and was out of the circle. I felt the lift as my chest crashed against her withers, and I clutched the rifle and the big mare's mane.

She crow-hopped to the right, then gathered her big haunches and launched in one great leap. And she was like a missile. I held on as we veered to the right and away from Cliff Cly. He screamed after us as we rushed by.

"Hi-yo Silver, away!"

15

Two quick strikes, and we were at speed.

I'd been on fast horses or what I thought were fast horses, but nothing like Wahoo Sue. I felt like my ears were going to touch behind my head.

We'd veered back west and had collided with the road like it was a wall, the big mare's hooves hammertoeing into the hard surface of the mesa like twelve-pound sledges. I had never been on a horse whose pace was so ferocious, yet whose gait was like a twenty-dollar shave. I could feel the blood and energy that passed between us like an electric current, and it was almost as if the poison was being pulled from my body and cast to the dirt and dust flying behind us. I was enhanced and could feel the wind on my skin unlike I had for some time.

I had never succumbed to the idea of a horse as transportation and was always quick to point out that machines, when you turned them off, stopped eating.

But they didn't have a heart.

As I'd slung my two-hundred-forty-odd pounds onto the mare's back, I'd been worried about her weakened state, but I shouldn't have been concerned. Feral and unfettered, Wahoo Sue was doing what she did best, what came natural to her—running within an inch of her life and mine.

I could see the road stretching to the horizon north like the tensioned string on a gigantic basalt banjo. I slipped my heels in and down, and I rode close, like some grotesque jockey, and dipped my head at her withers to catch my breath—she was that fast.

We galloped past a smattering of rocks that were scattered across the surface of the two-track where something had run into them; I only hoped that it was Barsad and not Benjamin. The road canted slightly to the left, and I assumed that in less than twenty minutes we would be heading into the final furlong with the horse trailer as the finish line.

I became aware of something breaking trail across the gnarled brush of the mesa to my right. I had a brief twinge of panic, thinking it might be Barsad in the truck, and thought about trying to raise the Henry rifle, but there wasn't any way he'd be off the road. I thought it could be Benjamin, but there were no lights, and finally, in the slight sliver of moonlight, I could see it was another horse.

My horse with no name.

He was doing his best, and you could see the stirrups, reins, and even the canteen bouncing with a comic effect. He tried to close the apex of our trajectory, but she was just too fast. I was glad to see he was still alive and unhurt, but the last I saw of him, he had joined the road but was falling away. Wahoo Sue must've been aware of him also, because she shifted into an even higher gear, and I thought about the old cowboy and how happy he'd be if he could see her now. I settled in for the straight shot to the trailer.

The voices were back again, the old me and everyone else; as fast as Wahoo Sue was, she couldn't escape my anxieties. Where would Benjamin go?. Where could he go to escape the truck? He'd have to stay off-road; it was the only advantage he'd have in avoiding the much faster vehicle, but how could he when there was only one way down?

A quick jarring as Sue stumbled for a single hoof strike, and I almost dropped the heavy rifle. I had to pay attention so that when we got to the main road, I'd be able to steer her to the water buckets at the trailer.

As near as my rambling mind could tell, we'd been at a full gallop for miles, so I tried to pull her back into a canter. At first she wouldn't hear of it, lunging forward whenever I pulled on her mane and repositioned my feet. Wahoo Sue had two speeds—fast and damn-well faster.

I tried a second time and could feel her relax a little and finally loosen into a comfortable lope, but after a few more minutes I saw the four-wheeler in the middle of the road. I could only hope that the damn thing had run out of gas. I pulled the dark horse up as close as she'd go and looked down.

There were truck treads beside the ATV, but also a pair of miniature boot tracks leading off into the sagebrush. There were no other footprints, especially ones from running shoes, and it looked like Barstad hadn't even bothered to get out of the truck when he had passed.

That cagey kid had gone to ground and had been smart enough to get away from the road. His Cheyenne half was showing again.

Now, where would he go?

October 31, 4:15 A.M.
I could see the regular shape of the horse trailer. I knew there wouldn't be any feed left, but I was hoping that the grulla and the packhorse hadn't gulped all the water. As we made the turn onto the main access road leading to the cliffside trail down from the mesa, however, I could see that the other horses were gone.

I pulled Wahoo Sue up beside the line where I'd tied the two animals. I could see the fresh tracks where either Benjamin or Barsad must have retrieved them. I was betting on the kid, as the horse tracks scattered toward the road and continued back down from the mesa, but there were marks from the truck as well.

Damn.

First things had to come first or Sue might collapse under me, and I'd be ineffectively afoot. I directed the big mare over to the black rubber buckets that still hung on the side of the trailer. As I'd suspected, the ones that had held the grain were empty, but as I had hoped, the water containers were three-quarters full. I watched as she submerged half her nostrils and sucked in the water like a sump pump.

I patted her neck and then slipped off the side, took one half-step, and collapsed, dropping the rifle and slamming my head against the trailer only to slide down and lay there propped against one of the tires.

I'd forgotten about my broken foot.

Sue skittered away only a short distance to the next pail, and I listened with my hat over my face as she emptied the other bucket. After three deep breaths, I could feel the pain in my foot lessening, but I felt like I was sinking into the hard ground. In my mind's eye, I could see the surface growing farther and farther away as I slipped through the hardpack of the mesa, passing through geologic time, each layer sporting one of those nifty little signs that WYDOT plants along the cut bank sections on the highway: Quaternary, present-day; Tertiary, 1.8 million years ago; Cretaceous, 65 million years ago; Jurassic, 144 million years ago.

Something moved my hat and water dripped in a practical deluge onto my chest and face. I raised a hand to readjust it and looked up at her. "Did you swallow any of it?"

She moved to my right a little, rustled a few oats that the other horses had dropped on the ground, and pulled up a few stalks of dry grass. She chewed and watched me.

I took another deep breath and could feel another wave of exhaustion. I could see myself rolling over and passing out. The boy. The dead man. The bleeding man. The jailed woman.

I crunched my abdominal muscles with a substantial effort and pulled up my good foot, digging the heel of my boot into the ground and pushing myself along the side of the trailer. I propelled myself up and over the wheel well, pushed back on the fender, and sat there.

I looked off to the south expecting to see the bay, but there was nothing there and he must've stopped to take a break. Lazy bastard; he didn't deserve a name. Wahoo Sue continued to nibble at the ground. I wasn't looking forward to hauling myself on her bare back again and remembered that Hershel had that McClellan saddle in the trailer stall. It was old, hard, and likely dry-rotted, but it had to be better than my ass.

I picked up the Henry and pushed away, hopping around the trailer to the back gate, which still hung open, attached with the rubber strap. I pulled the extra blanket out and looked at the torturous device. It was surely intended for someone half my size and even then looked like it would rend a man in two. George B. had seen the Hungarian model used in the Prussian service and made a few modifications; in 1859, the United States adopted the McClellan saddle. It had afflicted cavalry soldiers all the way to the Second World War.

Wahoo Sue had followed me, and I felt for the last horse treat in my shirt pocket. I pulled it out and said the magic words, "So-o-o girl, good girl."

She nuzzled me; I gave her the treat and then draped the blanket onto her back. She didn't move but just stood there, chewing. I reached in and lifted the light saddle with one hand, flipping the far stirrup up over the seat. There was a hand-plaited riata attached to the far side of the saddle that looked like it might've been from a more modern age, but not by much.

Wahoo Sue looked at the primitive saddle and then back to me.

"I know it looks like it came from a rummage sale, but it's all we've got." I leaned the Henry against the doorway, ran the single strap of the McClellan carefully underneath her belly, and said a silent prayer. I pulled the strap up and attached it at the disclike fender. Now that I was handling it, I felt that the leather was supple and soft and saw a patina of saddle soap. I thought again about the old cowboy and glanced south; of course he had taken care of it.

I felt another relapse of chemical fatigue descending from my head into my upper chest like a cold rain, and rested my head against the side of the leather seat. After a moment, I took a deep breath and hopped to the back gate of the trailer to see what we had in the way of bridles.

The only thing I saw was an ancient, plaited, rawhide hackamore, but at least it had reins and a headstall and might not rub her in the same spots as the stable halter had.

I looped the reins over her head, adjusted the fiador so that it rested on the ungalled portions of the horse's skin, and picked up the rifle. There wasn't any horn on the McClellan, but there was more of a rise than that on an English saddle, so I grabbed the fork and cantle and pulled myself up with one quick hop and a lot of scrambling.

She didn't move.

I looked east and could see the solid platinum of the rising sun, which looked like the horizontal filament of a halogen lamp. The force of the flat light illuminated the underside of the clouds, and they looked like gray crinoline. The heavens were giving me a quick look up their skirt.

I looked south, where one man was dead and another was dying, then pulled the reins and wheeled the black toward the road off the mesa. With one quick "hyaa" we took off, and brother, at speed. I'd needed superhuman assistance and had gotten it from her, even if it was like driving a Ferrari with a shoelace.

We turned the corner and dropped off into the darkness of

the mesa's west side, where the sun hadn't yet made an appearance and, as far as I could see, there was nothing on the horizon.

The scoria road was rough, but the larger chunks of red rock had been kicked off to the sides, and Sue was making full use of her speed and of gravity. In the far distance, I could see the dusk-to-dawn lights of Absalom and, with so much happening, I almost couldn't believe it was still there. I knew Wahoo Sue's thoughts were the same as mine, and we shifted into that rarefied speed that no other horse in the surrounding counties, and maybe no other horse in the country, could match, especially in a straight line at distance.

October 31, 6:30 A.M.

We made the Echeta Road without incident, and I still didn't see any traffic, so I eased Sue into a comfortable canter and we loped our way north and west toward Absalom, the power poles on the side of the road contrasting darkly against the gray sky like six thousand crucifixes leading from Capua to Rome.

About halfway to town, I could see a truck sitting on the side of the road, but even with the gloom of early morning, I could see it wasn't the Dodge. I rode up beside the battered '63 and looked around for the Cheyenne Nation. The windows were up, but I could see my thermos on the seat, along with a sleeping bag, a canvas sack full of grocery items, and a small backpack.

I shook my head. Evidently, Henry, following his pinpoint intuition, had been on his way to the mesa; unfortunately, it appeared that Rezdawg had decided to take a rest on the way. This close to Absalom, Henry must have decided to hoof it back to town or had caught a ride with either man or beast. Knowing Barsad's knack for self-preservation, I was sure he hadn't picked up the big Indian, but Benjamin might have.

Wahoo Sue pawed the ground; she was in a hurry to get going, but my exhaustion was catching up to me. I shook my head and studied the raw dirt.

I could still see the hoof prints where the little grulla had stayed on the right track, and the packhorse and Hershel's gelding looked to have followed. I could also see that the horses' tracks were over the duellie's, so Benjamin must have followed Barsad. That was a good sign.

October 31, 6:39 A.M.
I was sure that Wahoo Sue would have tired, but she must have been so happy to be free of her shackles that she continued on at a brisk clip as we topped a rise that looked across the triangle of land where the abandoned old town, deemed too-wicked-to-survive by the railroad, had existed.

There were a few old stone foundations and a broken-down and partially petrified wagon missing two wheels which had augered into the soft bottomland, and there, in the old cemetery that Hershel, Benjamin, and I had passed on our way out of town what seemed like a century ago, were two horses.

It was Hershel's dun and the packhorse.

I slowed Sue and, even though the mare didn't want to diverge from our path into town, she turned, and we approached the other horses at a trot. They were both munching on the grassy hillside but raised their heads to look at us as we rode up.

My eyes played over the surrounding area in hopes of see-ing another horse with a boy astride or Henry Standing Bear, and also hoping that I wouldn't see a red Dodge duellie, but there was nothing to indicate where anyone was or where they might've gone. There was only the faint glow of yellow dawn on the cardboard cutout hills with the clouds still press-ing close from overhead. After being on the mesa, everything in the valley felt close and looked like a page out of a child's pop-up book.

Sue wanted to get back to the main road, but I gigged her up the hill toward the cemetery. The old iron gate that stretched across the opening was still closed and, with the current atmosphere, the gothic letters that spelled ABSALOM probably should have had another line for ABANDON HOPE ALL YE WHO ENTER HERE.

There were markers, mostly the small, set-in-the-ground type, but there were also a couple of larger mausoleums with elaborate stonework. A few sun-faded plastic floral arrange-ments were bowed by the wind and lay close to the ground—they looked like leftovers from the original Memorial Day, if they'd had plastic back then.

I walked the black beauty along the iron fence with the pointed stanchions and then looked at the two roads—the one that continued on to town and the one that shot due west toward the Barsad place. Nothing.

I'd just started to turn the mare when my eye caught some movement in the gully that ran underneath the large culvert that circumvented the road a couple of hundred yards away. I steadied Wahoo Sue and looked hard into the shadows, saw movement again, and a familiar figure.

The Cheyenne Nation.

I smiled and watched as Henry stood there long enough to make sure I saw him; then he turned and went back into the wide mouth of the corrugated steel opening. I checked the horizon, urged Sue into a quick canter, and then slowed her to a trot, staying on the walking path that brought me down to the drain.

Henry stood there with Dog, who was sitting on his foot with the nonchalance of a man waiting for a bus. "You have been out stealing horses?"

"Bringing them back from the dead." I slowed Wahoo Sue to a walk. "Have you seen the boy?" He looked behind him at a diminutive figure on a small horse in the circular end of the culvert. "Benjamin?"

He approached, but his horse was limping. The boy raised his hat and looked at me. He was crying, and the tears made rivers in the red dust on his face. I nudged the big black and pulled up opposite him as he reached out with both arms. I swept him up and planted him facing me on my lap. "Are you all right, Mister *Bandito Negro de los Badlands*?" He nodded but didn't say anything and buried his face in my shirt, the battered cowboy hat falling backward to hang from his neck by the stampede strings. I wrapped my arms around him and pulled him in close as Henry reached up and patted his back. "It's all right, Benjamin, everything's going to be okay."

He shivered and sobbed some more, but his face turned sideways and looked up at me. "The dead man, he chased me."

"Yep, I know." I took a breath and smiled. "When's the last time you saw him?"

He blurted the words out in a bunch. "I saw his truck and

tried to outrun him, but Concho hurt himself, so I brought him under here."

"Smart thinking." I looked down at Henry. "Have you seen the truck since then?"

He nodded. "He drove over the bridge—twice."

"Which direction, the last time?"

He pointed east toward the road to the Barsad place. I figured about a half-mile in the other direction from town. It would be the safest thing to leave the boy here with Henry rather than risk Barsad catching us on the road, especially with Benjamin's horse being lame and mine sure to tire.

Benjamin was staring at the antique rifle in my hands: "Is that Hershel's gun?"

In the distance I could hear a train whistle as I nudged the boy's head back with my chest and looked down at him. "I borrowed it."

The little bandit knuckled his fingers into his eyes and wiped them with a sleeve.

I glanced at the narrow path on the other side of the culvert that clung to the banks of the Powder and could hear the BNSF approaching. I plucked Benjamin up and lowered him into Henry's waiting hands. "Does this trail go all the way into town?"

The Cheyenne Nation shook his head. "No, it joins the road at the railroad crossing."

"I was afraid of that. How far does it go?"

"A quarter-mile."

A half-mile to a phone but, even with a train between us, my odds were getting better. I just had to keep from getting trapped between Barsad and the train.

Henry watched as I thought, and as usual, he was reading me verbatim. "We will stay here."

Benjamin's legs straddled the big Indian's side as Henry continued to hold him, but the boy's voice carried concern. "Stay here?"

He looked unsure as we listened to the train pass the crossroads and begin rocking through town. "Henry Standing Bear is Cheyenne. I'm sure you two have a lot to talk about."

He looked seriously at Henry and finally nodded. "Okay."

I gave him one last squeeze on the shoulder. "You've done really well, and we're all really proud of you." He continued studying me with the dark eyes, and just for a moment, I studied the likeness between the boy and the man who held him. "You've impressed me so much, you know what I'm going to do?" He didn't say anything until I pulled the piece of metal from my shirt pocket that had been tucked away with the horse treats.

He looked at it, dull and heavy in the just morning light. "Is that a badge?"

I nodded, the sound of the train matching the pulse of my blood. "Raise your right hand." He did as I requested. "Now repeat after me: I, Benjamin Balcarcel, promise to stay in this culvert with the Bear until the sheriff comes back and gets me." He repeated it. "So help me God." He repeated that part, too. I pinned the gold-plated star onto his shirt. "But if you leave the culvert, you go back to being a regular citizen and I'm going to be really upset." He looked uncertain. "You don't have to repeat that part."

"Okay."

"You're deputized; just stay here."

"Okay."

Henry smiled and lowered Benjamin to the ground and watched as he put his hat back on, walked over and took Dog by the collar, and returned to his horse. Dog wagged, and the bandito saluted and looked down at my badge as the Bear thumped his chest with a fist and then pointed his index finger down—Cheyenne sign-talk for hope/heart.

I made the same gesture and walked Wahoo Sue past them and onto the narrow, dirt path into the diffused light of the morning where I could see the cars of the coal-laden BNSF flashing by. I glanced back over my shoulder and into the culvert and could see that the boy hadn't moved from Henry's side. I turned in the saddle, the mare tripped off into a quick trot, and in no time we were moving briskly.

The path followed the river pretty closely, and the reflection of the sunrise broke in the shallow and lazy water. We gradually climbed to the surface of the road above and the railroad tracks. Gradual was good because it would give me a chance to look back toward Wild Horse Road and the direction from which Wade Barsad would most likely be coming in his quest to find Benjamin.

Wahoo Sue wasn't completely happy with the proximity of the hopper cars pounding by on the elevated tracks, the clanging bells, or the hooded, flashing red lights, and was even unhappier as we grew closer. The trail, thankfully, drew up a good forty feet from the tracks themselves, and I was just as happy to wait a sensible distance away on a slightly skittish horse anyway.

I turned and looked back east, but the road was empty.

With the noise of the train and the claxon bells, there wasn't much chance of my hearing him, even in the diesel, but I would be able to see Barsad from a long way off. If he did appear from that direction, I'd pretty much made up my mind to shoot right in order to lead him away from the boy, follow the tracks in the opposite direction of the train until I got to the end, then jump across and find a cross-country route into town. That's what I was planning to do; what Wahoo Sue was planning might be something entirely different, but she'd been awfully well-behaved up to now.

I glanced past the protective barriers that sat lowered across the road, and then at the cars, trying to gauge how many remained, but with the curve in the tracks I simply couldn't see. Some of the damn things were four miles long, but a substantial number of the coal hoppers had already passed, so I figured at most I was only a minute or two away from crossing.

I looked back over my shoulder again, but with the rising sun, it was getting hard to see through the diffused light from the east. I threw a hand over my brow but, as near as I could tell, the road remained empty.

I pivoted in the saddle again, and Wahoo Sue took it as a command and turned with me. I took advantage of the situation to give Wild Horse Road my undivided attention. The mare took a few steps, and then planted, to give the road as much study as I had.

Nothing.

I looked at her and leaned down to stroke the side of her neck. "So-o-o girl, good girl." I glanced back, could see that the last hopper car was approaching, and wheeled the dark horse around. She misinterpreted again and thought I wanted to advance into the tail end of the passing train, so she took a few crow-hops sideways and slightly reared.

"So-o-o girl, easy girl. Don't worry; we're not going until the train passes." I patted her neck with the knotted, black mane blowing over my fingers, and she quieted long enough for the final coal car to rock past, with the small electronic device that had taken the place of a caboose attached to the last coupler.

And there, idling on the other side of the track, was the red Dodge and the late, great Wade Barsad.

16

October 31, 7:00 A.M.

Wade Barsad looked up at the same time I did, and as surprised as I had been to find him alive, he was just as surprised to see me not dead. Evidently, he'd circled around.

The bells were still clanging, and the arms of the railroad crossing were still down and blockading the road. In that tiniest of seconds before they rose, I considered the two options open to me—raise the .44 or get moving. Evidently, the FBI wanted Barsad alive, so just pulling the Henry and doing more ventilation to the cab of the Dodge was a choice, but one not without possibly unseen consequences, both legal and mortal.

At Berkeley, during his aborted college career, Henry Standing Bear used to race automobiles on foot for a hundred feet. He would almost always win. He explained to me that unless the vehicle is set up and properly geared for that type of short-distance racing, a relatively capable human being is faster. A driver has the delay of human response but also that of the vehicle. A car weighs at least a ton, so you've got to get its weight up and moving, whereas the human being just runs. Henry says he got beat only once, and that was in an ill-advised, tequila-induced race with a '64 Fairlane T-Bolt.

I'm not as fast as Henry, never was, but I had Wahoo Sue, and I don't think I've ever moved my heels faster, despite the pain in my foot, than when I drove them into the mare's sides. We shot forward like we were racing to beat two minutes at the Kentucky Oaks.

There was only one direction to go and that was the way Sue and I were already headed—it would take Barsad away from Benjamin and Henry, cause him to have to turn, and get me into town where I might be able to either stop him or get help.

We shot diagonally through the blockade arms and flashed past the Dodge, the dirt and gravel surface of Upper Powder River Road matching well with the dark horse's steel shoes. In the blur I could see him scrambling for something in the seat and figured he was going for his pistol, but we were too fast, and the last I saw of him, he'd abandoned that thought and had thrown the big Dodge into reverse.

There was a slight rise in the dirt road leading to the town proper, the shadow of the grain mill and twin silos overlooking the rest of the place from their roost alongside the railroad tracks. There were a few abandoned buildings on the south side of town, ramshackle structures that had long ago decided to join the horizontal landscape, but the only lights that were on were the few dusk-to-dawn lamps that overhung Absalom's three blocks.

Wahoo Sue barreled up the rise, and I took the time to

give a glance back toward the tracks to see the Dodge spraying gravel in pursuit. It was at least another three hundred yards to The AR and the center of town, but what was I going to do then? Leap off the horse and run into the bar, leaving her to the mercy of Wade Barsad? As I felt the pain in my foot, wedged in the metal stirrup, running might not be the best option anyway.

I'd worry about it if I got there.

I crouched against Sue's neck, loosened the reins completely, and gave her her head. The mare gained speed as we hit the flat, and she must've seen him or smelled him because, even though she should have been absolutely worn out, Wahoo Sue accelerated into that breath-snatching velocity that she'd exhibited on the mesa.

I shot a look over my right shoulder and felt my right hand stealing onto the brass receiver of the .44 Henry. Barsad was less than a hundred yards away and gaining, the roar of the turbocharged Cummins diesel clattering up the isolated streets; it sounded as if the train had made a U-turn.

I looked back at the road ahead and the remaining distance.

No way.

We were not going to make it and, if we did, he was going to be on us as we got there—we'd just be crushed by the grill guard and run over.

My mind raced along with us and thoughts streaked across my brain like the chain lightning on the mesa sky. The railroad tracks were to my right, with the majority of town to the left, so there was no chance there, but the interior doors of the granary hung open with a ramp leading inside the cavernous building, and there was a chance there.

I glanced back again and could see the truck was now only a hundred feet behind us. He'd think we had to stop or that we'd have to veer left and up one of Absalom's side streets. Instead, I yanked the reins to the right and sailed Wahoo Sue up the ramp. One of the doors hung loosely while the other rested on its side against the building, providing an opening you could drive a horse through or a truck driven at a sensible speed.

Wahoo Sue trusted my judgment implicitly, and we blew from end to end without hesitation with the diesel breathing down our collective necks.

Wade wasn't as lucky—he was going too fast, and with the added wideness of the duellie and the lift of the elevated scales, he clipped the hanging door and a compressor just inside the opening, causing the Dodge to carom off the opposite side and shed a fiberglass rear fender. He fought to correct his trajectory, but with the force of his speed, he tipped a wheel off the ramp and slid sideways another fifty feet with his brakes locked.

I reined left at the other side, gave the mare her lead again, and we galloped up the road beside The AR toward the tiny library/post office. Another quick glance behind, and I could see the headlights of the Dodge in the sedimentary streams of airborne dust, and the diesel bellowed as Barsad extricated himself from the granary.

The pay phone outside the log building that served as the library/post office was clearly too far in the open to use. I wheeled Sue around the corner across the dried-grass lot and headed back south out of view of the main street. I pulled her up short. There was no way I could outrun Barsad on the open road, but in the confines of the little town I figured I could use the maneuverability of the horse against him.

I settled the mare, lathered in sweat and snorting, and I couldn't help but think that she knew who he was and what the consequences would be if he caught us. She raised her head with the large, soft ears pivoting and listened along with me. We could hear the diesel as it sped up the hill; then I saw the red Dodge pass between two buildings and slow down on the street I'd just left.

I walked Sue, trying to cool her down a little, countering Barsad's progress by continuing back around the log structure and down the hill. If I could make it to the bar, I could possibly find a safe place for the horse and make a call.

I stopped Wahoo Sue at the lower side of the building, and we listened as the diesel continued up the hill and, as I'd hoped, turned left. I continued down and tracked Barsad by listening to the sound of the Dodge's engine as he turned again, but somewhere a block south.

I gently kicked her to a canter as I got to the next alley and turned toward the back of the bar. If I could hide Sue behind the building and get inside to make a phone call, I'd be able to get help to all the people who were counting on me.

I guided her into the lot behind The AR just as the red truck drove by the end of the alley we'd just been on. I wasn't sure if he'd seen us, but I pulled the horse up to the back-door mudroom and hoped not. There was nowhere else to go. We stood next to one of the decayed, lath privacy fences that sided the dry-grass lot, as well as the thousand-gallon propane tank, which was the size of a small Japanese minisubmarine, sitting along the side of the fence to my left.

The racket of the diesel continued to echo off the hills and through Absalom. It sounded as if he'd stopped somewhere to my right and was now idling. I pulled my hat down and thought about using the Henry rifle on the Dodge's tires.

Sue pivoted her head and began backing up. I hadn't asked her to do that, and I ducked under the eave of the building as she continued to back away into the narrow walkway between the bar and the unconnected rooms. I wasn't sure what she was up to, but she hadn't failed me so far.

We stood there, and I could feel her legs stiffen. What if Barsad had parked the truck and was now pointing the semi-automatic at us?

Enough was enough; I raised the .44 and jacked the lever-action. I wasn't sure what Wahoo Sue's response to gunfire from close proximity would be, but it had to be better than being shot or run over by a seven-thousand-pound truck.

I heard the bellow of the diesel, so he hadn't parked; I pivoted Wahoo Sue in the direction of the alley, but he sounded much closer.

The fence to my left blew apart as the Dodge crashed through and veered. I spun Sue into a rearing turn at the other side of the walkway as the duellie slid through the lot, occupying it with the front wheels turned toward us. Barsad had the 9 mm out but he miscalculated the distance to the propane tank, and I watched as the impact forced the pistol out of his hand and onto the floorboards where he would have to take the time to look for it. I could see that the utility tank had lurched off its concrete blocks and sat at a thirty-degree angle.

In a movie, it would've blown up. But we weren't in a movie and it didn't, and I could see Wade throwing the Dodge into reverse and swinging back.

I realized that I was trying to lose a truck in a three-block town, but my options were limited. I could get off and shoo the mare away, but my mobility was questionable to say the least, and once I got off the big black horse, there wasn't anything to say she'd let me back on her.

Shooting the truck from the moving horse was an option but not nearly as easy as it appeared in most westerns. I'd known many an individual who had learned that by shooting either themselves or their horse; besides, the FBI wanted him alive, so it was a last resort.

I looked back up the paved main street that headed north when I suddenly remembered the Range Co-op phone jack at the junction box next to the bridge. Would it still be there? Would the bridge still be there?

If I were trying to outthink myself, however, that's the direction I'd go.

I started to gig Wahoo Sue, but she'd already read my mind. It would take a while for Barsad to disentangle himself from the propane tank and the fences and get back on the road, and by that time I hoped to be up the rise and out of sight. Wahoo Sue was at an immediate disadvantage on the blacktop, so I reined her to the right, where there was a broad dirt walkway for horses—an advantage of small-town Wyoming.

I looked back as we got to the top of the rise overlooking Absalom and could see no activity in the streets below. The population must've slept like the dead or more likely didn't want to be involved. The early morning sun was throwing a diffused glow through the clouds at the horizon, and the shadow of the mill cast across the town like a closed door.

By my calculations, it would take us less than two minutes to get to the bridge, but you can travel a lot of distance fast in a turbocharged pickup truck. We started around the long, guardrailed bend that led to the bridge, and I could feel the big mare gaining speed as she went into that extended gallop that felt like she was rotating the earth. Maybe she knew, maybe she could sense that this was our last shot—the only way we were going to get away. "So-o-o girl, go-o-od girl. Go-o-od girl, go-o-od."

It was my father who had taught me to talk to animals. I wondered who had taught Mary Barsad. He said they understood a hell of a lot more than you think they do. I remember him speaking to the horses he shod in a low and reassuring voice, explaining what he was doing to them; he said it was one of the things we owed them for their absolute, unreserved, unswerving loyalty. He said the outside of a horse is always good for the inside of a man.

In spite of the pressing circumstances, I could feel the ascension of my spirit as we galloped alongside the two-lane strip that led away from Absalom, and that feeling doubled when I saw that the old kings-bridge system of girders still spanned the Powder River and that the Range Co-op trailer that Steve Miller had been working from was still parked by the pole.

I wasn't sure if the water coming from my eyes was in relief or from Wahoo Sue's velocity, but either way we now had a shot. The dirt trail beside the asphalt was growing narrower, and by the time we got within a hundred feet of the bridge we were forced onto the pavement, so I slowed the big dark horse to a canter.

The sun had stopped making much of an effort to get through the overcast, and the flat light of the Powder River country was doing its best to rob me of the slim glimmer of hope I'd been stoking. It became completely quelled as I slowed Sue at the blinking yellow lights that had been attached across the chest-high, wooden fence with which they'd blocked off the bridge.

There was a large banner that had been strung across which read DO NOT CROSS—IMPORTANT STRUCTURAL ELEMENTS HAVE BEEN REMOVED—DO NOT CROSS.

I looked at the other side of the river and could see that the blue plastic auxiliary phone was still attached to the junction box and was gently tapping against the pole.

I sighed deeply, and then Sue did, too. I looked around, but the hillside to our left was too steep to ride. I walked her over to the edge of the road, where an old, creosote-poled guardrail stood against the edge of the drop-off. It was a good hundred feet to the surface of the slow-moving river, which looked like zinc in the gray light. There were large slabs of sedimentary rock but no trail and no way down.

I sighed again, and Sue turned her head to look at me, possibly wondering what it was we were going to do next. I wondered about that, too.

I walked her back, the ghostly sound of her hooves echoing

off the hardtop, and looked at the surface of the bridge. The warped, weatherworn planks were still the same color as the water below and looked as they had when Bill and I had driven across them only a few days ago. The only thing that looked different was that the giant rivets that held each plank had been undone, and I wondered about the support trusses and the joists underneath.

It was possible that the only things they'd removed were the attachments to the concrete buttresses and that the structure was basically intact. It was also possible that, although it wasn't capable of supporting the weight of a modern vehicle, it could support the weight of a man and horse.

The thing to do would be to dismount, break through the barricade, and walk Wahoo Sue across on the loose planks. It would provide some excitement of its own considering my broken foot, but there was no way I was leaving her on this side, not by herself, not after we'd come so far together.

I started to disengage my swollen foot from the stirrup when, from the road leading back to town, I heard the distinctive clatter of the Cummins diesel. I turned in the thin saddle, looked back, and could clearly see the reflection of the headlights on the vintage guardrail.

After not finding us in town, he'd taken a chance and headed north.

As Vic would say, fuck me.

Wahoo Sue knew what was coming and pivoted on the hard asphalt to meet it head on. I raised the .44 Henry repeater from its comfortable resting place on my lap but then stopped.

I looked at the height of the barricade and got that light-in-the-balls feeling I always had when I was thinking about doing something colossally stupid. There was a barricade on the other side as well, and the length of the bridge between.

About sixty feet—it would have to be enough.

Hell, I knew she could do it; damn, I wouldn't be surprised if she suddenly sprouted wings and flew us across. The question was the bridge, and whether or not it would not only hold the weight of the two of us but the weight of the two of us at impact and speed.

I trotted her back toward the hillside to give us a straight trajectory and could feel the big mare stiffen as I gave her time to consider what it was I was asking her to do. Could she jump? Would she? If not, I was looking at a lonely header into the thick wooden planks and a possible crashing descent into the twelve-inch-deep water a hundred feet below.

I spoke to her in the same steady voice I'd used on the mesa. "I know you're tired, and I know you're sick, but we've got another hundred feet between us and safety. If we can make it across, then we're done—I promise." I swiveled my head to look back down the road and could see the damaged Dodge wheeling around the corner. "I promise."

I dug my heels into Wahoo Sue and let her rip. "Yaaah!"

I almost fell off but got myself positioned as the barricade and bridge swallowed the view. I was in close, but when the mare gathered herself and leapt, I was even closer and was pressed hard against her withers. In that one brief second, we were flying.

From my perspective, it felt as if we'd cleared the blockade by fathoms, and the next instant we were clattering across the length of the bridge. I was expecting the world to fall from beneath us, and I remembered a blood spatter and another saddle with a smooth and shiny surface, worn by both human and beast in a sacred bond of speed. At that one moment it came to me that if we died like this, there could be no bitter or better end.

I felt the pressure of her second leap, the world was silent, and it was almost as if we hung there between heaven and earth while the spirit of Wahoo Sue decided which firmament we would join.

We pounded onto the pavement of the Powder River Road like sledgehammers on Rodin's doors to hell, and I could feel her steel shoes sliding on the slippery surface of the worn and cupped road.

She slowed to a canter on the dirt and grass that made up the supply lot where WYDOT and Range had parked their equipment. Dust floated up from the dry ground as I reined Wahoo Sue into a tight turn and looked back across the bridge through the clouds of talcum scoria that filled the air.

Barsad hadn't seen the blockade or had decided to ignore it, and scattered the sawhorses, two-by-fours, and signs in every direction as he charged across the bridge in the three-ton vehicle. I watched as the surface separated with the lateral movement and the planks split and began falling into the water. The truck's undercarriage dropped, and his momentum stopped as the wheels fell and the Dodge became high-centered on its axles while the diesel motor wailed like some *Tyrannosaurus rex* buried in tar.

He gunned the motor in desperation, but the three-hundred-and-fifty horses couldn't do what my one had.

I drifted Wahoo Sue back toward the end of the bridge and

looked down at the Henry rifle, which I had lost on the side of
the road with the impact of our landing and which, with my
broken foot, might as well have been on the other side of the
Bozeman Trail. I turned the big black horse sideways so that
we could both watch the show.

The motor loped into an idle, and we all waited, unmoving. I didn't know if he'd had time to retrieve his 9 mm from
the floor of the truck; even if he had, it wouldn't shoot through
the windshield, so he was going to have to come out.

Barsad attempted to open the door, but with the listing
of the massive truck it only lurched about two inches and
then jammed into the wooden planks.

I motioned with my chin and raised my voice. "Shut it off."

Dutifully, the diesel went silent, and it was eerie how I
could all of a sudden hear the flow of the river below. I listened as the bridge creaked, and the electric window on the
driver's side whirred and went down. His hand came out
holding the 9 mm, and it was one of those wicked little Smith
& Wesson autoloaders. I watched as he extended his arm out
the window and glanced at the Henry rifle lying between us.

He finally looked at me with one hand stretched across the
top of the cab, the other pointing the pistol. His voice was a
little tight. "This is an interesting situation, don't you think?"

"Not for me."

He smiled. "You know, I really hate that horse."

Wahoo Sue didn't even give him the benefit of a glance.
"That's all right; I don't think she cares that much for you, either."

He smiled again, but it was more of a smirk. "You know, I
didn't really want to kill you."

"Is that so?"

"Then why would you want to kill me?"

"There's Hershel Vanskike as a starting point."

He shook his head. "That wasn't me, that was Cliff."

"Cliff Cly is a federal agent. You're lucky at least *he* wants you alive."

There was another squealing creak, and one of the planks under the mighty engine gave way, dropping the truck's cab at an even more drastic angle and lower into the surface of the bridge. Barsad scrambled to get both hands over the cab but still managed to hold the semiautomatic on us.

Wahoo Sue took a quick two-step back with the noise and then sashayed her substantial rear for a moment, but that was all. I wondered if she wanted to remain close because she was rooting for the truck to fall into the river and, once and for all, kill the son-of-a-bitch.

Again, nobody moved, and again the only sounds were the twisting load of the bridge and the water beneath.

Barsad's one hand was flat against the roof of the cab, the other, still holding the 9 mm, was hooked on the window channel. He didn't look quite so smug.

"You know, I don't know how much longer that bridge is going to hold."

His eyes flicked up at me, and it was as if he were afraid to move his head for fear of causing the final collapse. "Well, maybe we can make a deal, okey?"

I thought about the old *Bidpai* parable about the scorpion that makes the deal with the frog to carry him across the river. "I doubt it."

He studied the gun in his hand. "I've got an awful lot of leverage here."

"No, you don't."

"Well, I've got a lot of money."

"So?"

"A lot of money, and even more tucked away." When I didn't respond, he breathed a quick but careful breath out. "You can't tell me that—"

"You know, the longer this conversation is, the greater the chance that you, that truck, and the bridge are going to collapse into the river." I listened to him breathe. "Now, I don't particularly care, but maybe you do, seeing as how you went to all the trouble to come back from the dead." I started untying the riata from the saddle strings of the old McClellan. "From my perspective, it looks like you've only got one choice. I'm going to throw you this lariat, but I'm not going to do that till you throw that nifty little Smith & Wesson into the river—and I want to hear the splash."

He glanced up at me, and his fingers tightened on the pistol. "This is an eight-hundred-dollar gun."

I smiled. "That's okey, you've got plenty of money and more tucked away, right?"

I thumbed the comforting surface of the plaited rawhide in my thumb and forefinger, rolling out the leather hondo and trying to think about the last time I'd thrown a riata. "You know, one of the worst images perpetrated on society is the idea of a cowboy with a gun—you give a real cowboy a choice between a gun and a rope and he'll take the rope every time, because that's how he makes his living. No self-respecting cowboy makes a living with a gun." I tossed the loop out with one hand, uncoiling it through the burner to a sizable length. "Now, I'm no cowboy and it's been an awful long time since I threw the hoolihan, but you can more than double my chances by grabbing it." I threaded more of the rope out and kept looking at him, his hand still holding the Smith & Wesson. "It'll take a basic, flat loop with a good wrist twist, finishing with a palm-out release."

His voice was sounding high and tight. "Look . . ."

"This old McClellan doesn't have any horn to dally to, so I'll just have to brace it off the fork and hope for the best. I don't know when the last time this rawhide was oiled, so it could just snap like a piece of brittle cottonwood—maybe it'll hold, maybe it won't."

I watched him swallow the last tiny bit of courage he'd been holding between his teeth, and his knuckles whitened around the black plastic grip of the 9 mm. If he was going to do something stupid, then now was the time.

I thought about two dead men, a dying man, a terrorized boy, my dog, a tormented woman, and the tortured horse I now rode.

I leaned a little forward in the saddle and more emphasis came into my voice as my right hand, still holding the coiled lariat, touched Wahoo Sue's wither and the mare shifted for the first time to consider her tormentor. The black beauty placed a hoof forward and relaxed a rear, kicking the two of us into an almost insulting stance. "And then you're going to have to depend on this horse; and she may pull, or she may not."

His fingers twitched, and the butt of the 9 mm autoloader made the slightest of tiny noises against the sleek red surface of the truck's bodywork. "You know, mister, I never caught your name."

I straightened in the creaking hundred-and-thirty-year-old saddle and took final aim on his head with the rope. My voice sounded very conversational. "That's because I never threw it."

EPILOGUE

November 7, 11:00 A.M.

I nudged Dog, readjusted my crutches, and propped my Velcro-wrapped broken foot onto the rocks as I sat on the guardrail. I tried not to think about the three-hundred-dollar pair of Olathe boots that had been ruined when the Campbell County Memorial Hospital doctors cut the one off of me. Of course, I could always give the orphan to Lucian and let him stuff some socks in the toe to get it to fit or let them hang it off the gutters of The AR.

The new and improved railing turned the corner where the old car-bridge used to span the distance over the Powder River. I had to admit that what the new bridge lost in dramatic design, it made up for in solid, steadfast boredom. A steel-reinforced, continuous concrete slab with a thick, galvanized pipe railing running about three feet high on either side, it looked like it would survive a direct hit from a cruise missile, but it wasn't anything I'd want to ride a horse over.

Wahoo Sue stamped a foot. She was in the refurbished horse trailer that I had bought for Hershel and Benjamin that Vic had detached from the Bullet. "Relax. She's on her way."

It was cool this afternoon and, even though the sun was shining, it hadn't overcome the chill of the day. I was wearing my duty jacket, the one with the embroidered star, which protected me from the weather and provided another layer between the crutch pads and my armpits. Doc Bloomfield said I was stuck with the crutches for another two weeks and that I was supposed to keep my weight off of the proximal avulsian fracture of my fifth metatarsal, which sounded a lot more serious than the broken bone attached to my pinkie toe.

I propped the crutches onto the guardrail opposite Hershel's Henry rifle and hooked the underarm pads on the edge of the metal so that they wouldn't slip and slide into the water. I studied the bruising that had encompassed my foot and that showed in the exposed part of my nifty little space boot. Dog had gotten up and had saluted each of the guardrail supports before switching to the horse trailer that was parked behind us. He was fine, having only strained his leg when Wade Barsad had hit him with the ATV.

Cliff Cly of the FBI would live and was recuperating in Denver. The DOJ had come down pretty hard on him, but I'd gone to bat for the wayward and inventive agent, explaining that if he hadn't done what he'd done, I probably wouldn't be here. He'd been replaced by a more businesslike man who was now up at the Barsad place supervising a crew that was sifting through the debris in an attempt to find Wade's kite.

The bureau was still attempting to put pressure on Barsad to give up his friends, but so far he wasn't talking. Evidently, with two life sentences hanging over him, Wade wasn't feeling any need to be cooperative. Maybe he was looking for a plea bargain, but with the two murders, that was a stretch.

He'd most likely spend the rest of his life behind bars, but the Feds still wanted the names to pursue racketeering charges against those on the list. As we might all well imagine, Wade's memory had gotten a little vague since being arrested.

The missing kite was still missing.

I yawned and covered my mouth with my hand as a metallic sand-colored Escalade came into view and made the turn across the river.

Bill Nolan was innocent, except for taking a few too many sleeping pills with his nightly gifts of rye and leaving the keys in his new truck for anyone to drive. The thing had been totaled, and the last I'd heard he was still going to Denver and was buying a hybrid.

Pat, the bar owner, was so far only charged with conspiracy. I guess he thought he was going to get a lot of money being in business with Wade Barsad, but like everybody else, all he would get was time.

I thought about Sandy Sandberg as the Caddy rolled across the new bridge. I'd have pinched his neck there in the hospital, but he raised a hand, smiled down at my broken foot, and explained how he'd been sworn to silence by the FBI division chief. I forgave him but told him I found it interesting the confidences he chose to share and the ones he chose to keep. Anyway, I'd called in a favor, and Boss Insurance was found liable for the claim on the Barsad place, in light of the fact that the sheriffs of two Wyoming counties signed affidavits saying that the probable cause of the fire was most likely lightning.

I rested my foot back on the ground and pivoted as best I could to greet the SUV. Dog stopped sniffing guardrails and began wagging his tail in anticipation of its arrival.

The Escalade pulled to a stop at the other side of the road and, before it could be put into park, the passenger door flew open and a four-foot sheriff's deputy scrambled out. Benjamin and Dog met at the middle of the road where Dog jumped and put his paws on the boy's shoulders, sending the two of them tumbling to the surface of the road.

I raised my voice. "Easy, he's not completely indestructible."

Juana climbed out of the same door. "Who are you talking about, Benjamin or Dog?"

I watched as a tall, blond woman got out on the other side of the Cadillac. She answered the question. "Both."

The Guatemalan bandita walked straight up to me. "You get left here alone?"

I nodded. "Dog and me; Vic ran Henry down to his truck with a new fuel filter."

She looked at my face and my foot. "You're a mess."

"Yep. How're they treating you up at ground zero?"

Her face immediately animated. "It's really interesting. They're going through everything, because they're pretty sure the list was in the house. They're sifting through the ash and that's not so exciting, but—"

"She's asking so many questions they can't get anything done."

I looked at the tall woman as she rested her hands on Juana's shoulders and then grazed one down to pet Dog's broad head as he and Benjamin joined the group.

She looked a lot better out of the orange CCDOC jumpsuit, and she had put on a few pounds but still looked thin enough to make the wind whistle. Doc Bloomfield had removed the last bandage from her throat, and she had tied a silk scarf that was covered with yellow poppies around her neck as camouflage. Her hair was down and pinned with a hand-etched silver barrette, and it looked as if she had put on a little makeup. In an attempt to augment her lack of body fat and insulation, she had put on a down vest which she wore over a turquoise fleece that made the blue of her eyes bluer somehow. You could see why the old cowboy had plastered his walls with her photographs. "How are you doing?"

"I'm living in a sheep wagon until they get through with my house, but I'm okay."

I smiled as the horse nickered behind her. "Hershel would've liked that."

Mary glanced down at the rifle, which was still leaning against the railing. After a moment, she smiled back up at me, and it was heartfelt. "He didn't have any family that I can locate, so I thought I'd scatter his ashes on the bluff overlooking the river."

"He'd like that, too." I stood as the horse nickered again, this time more persistently. I carefully lifted my leg over the guardrail, moved to the right, and adjusted my crutches under my arms. "If you don't mind grabbing that Henry, I think there's somebody back here that wants to see you." Second smile, possibly even brighter than the first. Wahoo Sue stamped her hooves, banged against the sides of the trailer, and whiffled in full voice. "I had the veterinarian, Mike Pilch, check her out, and he said she was in surprisingly good shape, considering all she had been through."

Mary's hands went up to the openings in the side of the

trailer like leaves attempting to find sunshine. The big mare stamped again and began running the sides of her head against the long fingers that now twined their way into the trailer. I could still see the pulsing, blue blood of the woman's temples as it coursed its way back to her heart. Her voice was soft. "So-o-o girl, good girl."

I rested the rifle in my lap and gave them a little while. "So—"

She turned to look at me. "So what?"

"What are you going to do with the ranch?"

There was no hesitation. "Rebuild it." She continued to stroke Wahoo Sue. "It was always my dream, my place—not his." She glanced over her shoulder toward Absalom. "It's a good little town; it just had a few bad characters in it."

The bandita leaned against the trailer and looked at me. "There's just one thing I can't figure out."

Leave it to the associate degree.

"What's that?" I ran my hands over the old repeater and adjusted my hat.

"Why did Wade try to kidnap Benjamin?"

"Wade couldn't afford to have very many of those kites around, but it was the only insurance he had for when he resurfaced again—and with his track record he would have. Without it, the mob would've eventually killed him, so he had to stick around till it turned up. Even drugged, Mary knew that list was important and took it and then passed it off to Hershel, but as near as I can figure there must've been a witness. Wade couldn't get at Mary, Hershel wouldn't tell him, so that left only one person who might know where the information was."

I studied the boy as I wrestled my pocketknife from the front of my jeans and laid the historic, lever-action carbine in my lap. "Or maybe Benjamin here knew something." I smiled at the boy. He ducked his head and started chewing on the stampede strings. "Am I right?"

He looked at all of us. "I'm not supposed to say."

"Because you promised?" He nodded, looking more serious than I'd ever seen him. "But the man who made you promise is gone, right?" He nodded some more but didn't say anything. "Now, as a sworn deputy of Absaroka County, you're not supposed to keep secrets from your boss."

He finally spoke. "Yes, but a promise to *el hombre muerto* is a sacred trust."

I put up a hand. "That's okay, you don't have to say anything. I wouldn't want you to betray him." They all watched as I placed the point of my knife in the slot of one of the tiny screws that attached the commemorative brass plate to the stock of the .44 Yellow Boy. "One of the things a man holds very dear is his fortune." I looked into the dark eyes of the boy. "Right?"

He nodded. "Right."

I loosened the one screw, handed it to Benjamin, and started on another as I looked at the name on the brass plaque. "The fellow who originally had this rifle didn't fare too well in the end, but your fortune is your fortune."

The boy watched as I unscrewed another and handed it to him. "The next fellow that had it didn't end up too well, either, but he was a heck of a guy while he was here, wasn't he?"

Benjamin nodded solemnly.

"And when he used to say that his fortune was in this rifle, he meant more than the amount of money it's worth, didn't he?"

The boy continued to nod as I handed him the last two screws and used a fingernail to delicately pry up the small brass plaque. There, embedded in a carefully routed groove, was one of the tiny scrolls that Hershel used to pick up from the checkout line at Kmart.

I used the point of my knife to lift the end of the plastic encapsulated fortune and pulled it out into my hand. I put the knife on the surface of the horse trailer's fender, carefully slid the tiny roll of paper from the cellophane sleeve, and unrolled it from end to end, holding it with my fingertips.

The writing, so small you could barely make it out with the naked eye, stretched from end to end, front and back.

I glanced up at them and then carefully rolled Wade Barsad's kite and slipped it back in the clear plastic sleeve.

Mary backed up the Escalade and guided the hitch to my horse trailer. Juana watched as I carefully placed the paper fortune into my shirt pocket and then reattached the plaque onto the repeater that had first belonged to a buffalo soldier and then to a cowboy. "How long have you known about the rifle?"

"Since we camped on the mesa. He kept repeating that line about his fortune being in this Henry, and I think that was his way of telling me without telling me."

She looked stymied. "Why didn't he just tell you?"

I thought about it as I lifted the Yellow Boy and propped it on my knee. "I don't know. He was careful, and he didn't know me, at least not well enough to actually tell me, I guess."

She looked at Benjamin, who was playing with Dog in the dry lot across the road. "But he knew you were a sheriff."

"That didn't count for much in the old cowpuncher's worldview." She still looked confused. "Hershel was like a lot of the old boys from this part of the country—he didn't trust a title. With him, you had to earn it."

She smiled the perfectly formed smile. "Well, you did that."

I looked toward the hills east, and to the Battlement at Twentymile Butte rising above the Powder River plain. "No . . . if I'd really earned it, he'd be here with us." Before she could say anything else, I continued, "So, any of those bureau types giving you a hard time about being illegal?"

She glanced over her shoulder as Mary got out to hook up the trailer electricals to the Cadillac. "No, I've got a protectress, and she has lawyers who are working for my citizenship."

I nodded. "So what are you and Benjamin going to do?"

"Benjamin is going to go to school, and I'm going to work for Mary and get my degree. Then I think I'll go down to Laramie and finish up—maybe work for the FBI someday." I didn't say anything, waiting for her to throw the signature fist to her hip just as she had on the first day I'd met her. "What?"

I shrugged in the face of Latin attitude. "I wouldn't be surprised."

As Juana went to collect Benjamin and Dog, Mary came back to open the upper hatch of the trailer's Dutch door so that Wahoo Sue could hang her head out. Mary stepped up on the railing at the fender, and I watched as the horse stuck her muzzle out to her as she exhaled. I smiled to myself as Mary gently slipped her arms around the big mare's neck. Sue, in turn, dropped her head and pulled the woman against the side of the trailer in a sort of armless hug.

"Hell of a horse."

She turned to look at me. "Yes, she is."

Her eyes stayed with me, even as I studied the brass plaque on the heavy rifle. "Mary, I've got a question about the list. I think Hershel got it from you."

It was quiet for a moment, and the only sound was the mare's hard shoes on the wooden surface of the trailer floor. "Me?"

"I can't be sure, but I'm pretty positive. You were the only one who knew what that list was other than Wade, and I doubt he gave it to Hershel." I could tell she was thinking. "You might've done a lot of things you weren't aware of under the influence of those sedatives."

She didn't move, and even her slender hands, which were still entwined in the horse's mane, were still. "Including kill a man?"

I took a breath and felt tired. "Nope, not that. I'll tell you what I think happened, and then you can decide about it and see if it finally falls into place." I swallowed and started in. "I think Wade drugged his brother and shot him, then brought you in there and had you shoot a dead man, a man who looked remarkably like Wade and a man, deep down, you wanted to be rid of."

"But how did he get his brother out here? He hated Wade."

I shrugged. "He had financial problems of his own, and Wade convinced him that they could extort more money from their old business partners. That's the problem with dealing with people like Wade Barsad—once they get something out of you, they've got something on you, and they're always go-ing to come back for more." I thought about the man's brother. "At least, that's one scenario."

She stepped down but kept a hand on Wahoo Sue's nose. She looked at me, but said nothing.

I crutched my way back across the road and sat on the guard-rail with the newest addition to my ever-growing collection of priceless weapons in my lap and watched as the Escalade crossed the bridge and pulled away. I was really tired now and hoped that Vic would be back with my truck soon so that I could go home and take a nap.

I called to Dog and followed the trail of dust as Mary rounded the far corner of the Powder River Road and she and Juana and Benjamin and Wahoo Sue disappeared. I held my star in my hand and allowed my eyes to travel toward the mountains. The diffused clouds dappled back from the Bighorns and abandoned the sky to the pale blue of fading fall.

"You lost?"

I'd been so caught up in my musings that I hadn't even heard the old five-ton GMC 500 pull up. I leaned the Henry against the guardrail and sat there holding on to Dog's collar. "Nope."

Mike Niall had another load of hay and surprised me by cutting the engine on the big flatbed. I listened to the motor tick and waited.

His strong profile looked toward the mountains. He was empty of emotion but full of dignity. He had yet to actually look at me, but I suppose he'd noticed the old Henry as he'd pulled up. "Expectin' trouble?"

I tipped my hat back. "Always."

He worked his mouth but didn't say anything else. It was another load of good-looking hay, and I could smell it from twenty feet away even with a crosswind. He spat in the road like he had before and finally spoke. "I heard that sheriff over in Absaroka County got reelected yesterday in a landslide."

I took a deep breath and flexed the muscles in my broken foot. "Yep, it's getting so that people will vote for anybody these days." I could feel his eyes on me, and I tried to think of something else to say, but I was so tired I just sat there. Twenty-four years in office and now at least two more. I started wondering if I'd make it, but he saved me from my thoughts.

"I believe I'll drive this truck across that new car-bridge."

I smiled as I studied the vintage vehicle and its substantial load. "Think it'll hold?"

He leaned forward and spat again, the sepia-colored stream shooting through the rust holes of the truck's floorboards. "I'm not sure." He stared hard at the new structure. "But I'm a man who likes to take chances." I could feel his eyes on me again. "How 'bout you?"

I turned back toward the river, released Dog's collar, and began petting his broad head. "Me, I'm the cautious type."

I heard a soft snort before the starter on the big truck ground, the aged motor coughed and caught, and the lumbering vehicle crossed the bridge, turned the corner, and was gone.

Holding my badge in my open hand and looking at the river, I sat there thinking about what Juana had said that night in the motel room about how some of us aren't meant to cowboy-up. I thought about how many times the heavy piece of metal might skip on the surface of the Powder River if I got the angle just right. I palmed it in my hand and felt the weight of its bond, then opened the back clasp and pinned the six-pointed star to my shirt.

I rubbed Dog's head again and took off my 10X, turned it over, and studied the sweat stains and the patina of red dust that had gathered on it in the last week.

I flipped it back over and held it by the brim, then suddenly pitched it like a Frisbee. Dog started and made a move to fetch it, but I grabbed his collar, and we both watched as the black hat hung over the void of the Powder River, pitched to one side, and disappeared into the northbound water below.

Craig Johnson's sixth novel featuring Sheriff
Walt Longmire is now available in Penguin paperback.
Read on for the first chapter of

JUNKYARD
DOGS...

1

I tried to get a straight answer from his grandson and granddaughter-in-law as to why their grandfather had been tied with a hundred feet of nylon rope to the rear bumper of the 1968 Oldsmobile Toronado.

I stared at the horn pad and rested my forehead on the rim of my steering wheel.

The old man was all right and being tended to in the EMT van behind us, but that hadn't prevented me from lowering my head in a dramatic display of bewilderment and despair. I was tired, and I wasn't sure if it was because of the young couple or the season.

"So, when you hit the brakes at the stop sign he slammed into the back of the car?"

It had been the kind of winter that tested the souls of even the hardiest; since October, we'd had nothing but blizzards, sifting snowstorms, freezing fogs, and cold snaps that had held the temperature a prisoner at ten below. We'd had relief in only one Chinook that had lasted just long enough to turn everything into a sloppy mess that then encased the county in about six inches of ice with the next freeze.

It was the kind of winter where if the cattle lay down, they weren't likely to get back up: frozen in and starved out.

I lifted my head and stared at Duane and Gina.

"Yeah, when I hit the brakes I heard this loud thump." She shrank into her stained parka with the matted, acrylic fur of the hood surrounding her face and tried not to light what I assumed was her last Kool Menthol. We all sat in the cab of my truck with the light bar revolving to warn passing motorists of the icy roads. The roads, or more specifically the thick coating of ice on the roads, was what probably had saved Geo Stewart and, if it hadn't been for the numerous 911 calls that my dispatcher, Ruby, had fielded from passing motorists and the stop sign on state route 16, the seventy-two-year-old man would have made the most impromptu arrival into the town of Durant, Wyoming, in its history.

"I guess he slid into the back." Gina Stewart nodded the same way she had when she'd told me she'd been after cigarettes, Diet Coke, and a box of tampons from the Kum & Go, where she worked part-time.

I looked at the bubblegum-pink lipstick that stained her lone smoke. I'd warned her three times not to light up in my truck and tried to ignore the vague scent of marijuana that wafted off the pair. If she was down to her last cigarette, it smelled like they still had plenty of something else.

"He's a tough ol' fucker. That isn't the first time he's come off the roof."

We all listened to the static and random calls of northern Wyoming law enforcement on my Motorola, and I stopped scribbling in my duty book. "The roof?"

"Yeah."

I looked at Duane, but he'd yet to utter anything more than a grunting agreement to whatever Gina had said. "Yunh-huh."

I studied the two of them and thought about resting my head on the steering wheel again. "The roof of the car?"

She shook her head inside the hood and pulled the unlit cigarette from her mouth. "Roof of the big house."

"The big house."

"Yeah."

It was quiet. I thought about the Stewart family's compound, comprising a Victorian house and a number of single- and double-wide trailers. "And what was he doing on the roof of the big house?"

She pulled the hood back from her face; the heater from my truck was just beginning to bring the temperature inside the vehicle to past the ice age. For the first time, I noticed she had enormous brown eyes and a lovely, heart-shaped face. It was spoiled by dirty-blond hair, but she was pretty in a shop-worn way.

She had learned that to captivate men you must treat them with the utmost attention. I'd only been in the cab with Gina for ten minutes, and I was already dizzy; of course, that could have been from the less-than-legal fumes floating off the two.

She looked at Duane, and so did I, figuring that the rest of the saga was his to tell.

Duane Stewart had dropped out of school at the age of fourteen with his parents' consent, because he was, in an internal combustion sense, gifted; if you had any type of motor-driven vehicle produced before 1972, Duane could fix it. He and his uncle Morris had a ramshackle mechanic's shop that was on the road to the junkyard, which was the family's other going concern.

Thickly built, he had a few pimples scattered across his face that reminded me of how young he still was—early twenties at best. His eyes hunted mine, but he ducked away and cleared his throat. "Yunh-huh, we was cleanin' out the chimney."

I watched the blue and red lights from my truck that joined with the yellow ones from the EMT van behind us as they raced across the hillsides. "In February?"

He looked at his new wife again and then back to me. "Yunh-huh."

I took a breath and leaned back in my seat. "Maybe we need to start at the beginning."

The young man tipped his grease-stained cap back on his head—it read HEMI. "The chimney of the big house gets stopped up in the winter after you burn it for a few months, so we dip a mop in kerosene and force it down the flue to clean it out."

"Kerosene."

"Yunh-huh." He warmed to the story and began gesturing with his hands, the old dirt and grease embedded in the swirls of his fingerprints and nails. "I'd a done it, but I'm afraid of heights and Grampus's agile. He can climb out that top window on the gable end and get a hold of the gutter and swing a leg up onto the roof." He made the statement as if it should have settled everything.

It hadn't. "So, the rope—"

"It's slippery up there with the ice, so he tied it to his waist and slung it over the peak and I tied 'er off to the Classic."

It was coming all too clear now.

He nodded as he studied my face. "Yunh-huh. I was in the backyard watching Grampus when Gina come around the house and said she was going to the store and did we need anything. I told her no, and then she left."

I covered the smile that was creeping onto my face with a hand. "The Classic is the car that your grandfather was tied to—the Oldsmobile?"

"Yunh-huh. We heard the car door slam and the motor catch, and that's when Grampus and me looked at each other. It was about then that the rope went tight." His calloused hand smacked the palm of his other and leaped forward. "Grampus fell over backward, and then he shot up the roof and over the other side."

"Duane, you stupid prick, how'm I supposed to know you've got Grampus tied to the back of the car?"

His neck stretched in indignation. "We . . . we do it every year." He turned back to me. "We dump snow beside the driveway, so I figure he landed on that, but with the forward momentum I don't figure he hit anything solid till he took out the mailbox at the end of the driveway."

I went ahead and rested my head on the steering wheel anyway.

Gina rejoined the conversation. "We always park the car facing forward so you can see both ways when you pull out." Then there was an accusation, just to even the score. "People drive too fast on that road, Sheriff."

Duane reached a hand out and played with the coiled cord that led to the mic clipped to my dash and then gestured toward his partner in crime. "I guess we're lucky nobody ran over him before she got stopped."

I raised my head and nodded. A local sculptor had made the first 911 call when the junkman had slid by him. "Mike Thomas says your grandfather waved as he passed him going the other way."

Gina nodded her head. "We like Mike."

They both smiled at me. I sighed and placed my pen on the aluminum clipboard. "So, what did you do then, Duane?"

"I jumped in one of the wreckers, but they ain't near as fast as that 455 in the Classic, and it's front-wheel drive so it took a while for me to catch up—especially with the roads bein' as slippery as they are, and by the time I got here that deputy of yours already had Gina pulled over."

Gina nodded. "And she used some really rude language."

I brought my face a little forward so that the young woman would know I was addressing her. "Did you hear the thump again, the second time—after Vic stopped you?"

She fingered the fur around her neck. "No, he kinda swung into the barrow ditch back there after I made the turn."

I nodded and slipped the clipboard back into the pocket of the driver's side door. The Stewarts were a drama waiting in the wings. It seemed as far back as I could remember the clan members had been involved with some form of misadventure or another, usually resulting in a visit to the Durant Memorial emergency room.

"Duane, didn't your dad die falling off a roof?" The young couple sat there unmoving, and I didn't say anything either. It wasn't like I was accusing him; I just wasn't perfectly sure. "About five years ago, wasn't it?"

Duane's eyes stayed still, and his head dropped a bit. "Nunh-uh, it was a heart attack."

I assumed that *Nunh-uh* was the opposite of *Yunh-huh* and nodded at him to encourage the rest. "After he fell off the roof."

"Yunh-huh."

I was sorry to keep at the boy since it seemed to sadden him, but I figured I had a certain amount of leeway in the interest of public safety. "He wasn't cleaning the chimney with the kerosene mop, was he?"

The young man took a deep breath. "Nunh-uh." He cleared his throat. "It was in September, and he was patching a hole. He slipped and fell—then he had the heart attack."

Charging any member of the Stewart family with reckless endangerment smacked of delivering coals to Newcastle, or to Moorcroft, for that matter. I nodded and pulled down my new hat, buttoned my sheepskin coat, and flipped the collar up to defend against the bracing February wind that was slicing down the foothills of the Bighorn Mountains.

I opened the door and lodged myself in the opening just long enough to speak to Duane one more time. "You know, Duane, maybe your family should stay off roofs."

We were in the process of enduring our second week of subzero temperatures for the third time; in the day it was no higher than a balmy one, and at night it plummeted to as low as forty below. Everybody was getting tired of it, and I was threatening to move to New Mexico again.

I passed the '68 Toronado, which I considered the ugliest car to ever roll out of Detroit on bias-ply tires. It was a gold-colored beast with more than a few rust patches but, as my deputies could testify, the drive train had been modified to the point that it wasn't your father's Oldsmobile anymore, and it ran like a raped ape. Ever since they'd gotten married a little less than six months ago, Duane and Gina had taken turns doing public service and going to driving school in attempts to keep their respective licenses.

I noticed the untied yellow rope still leading to the ditch, felt the onset of another headache, and trudged on.

I'd broken a bone in my foot back in October, and it was still giving me a little trouble. Struggling against the wind and attempting to get a good footing and a half on the ice, I lurched one of the back doors of the EMT van open. The vehicle was parked in the drive of Deer Haven Campground beside Vic's unit and I almost knocked myself out on the vehicle's headliner.

Vic stood by the other door. I looked at my undersheriff. Second-generation law enforcement, Victoria Moretti was the personification of the fact that ferocious things come in small packages. After five years in the Philadelphia police department, she'd landed in our high-altitude, currently perma-frosted neck of the woods and had slowly begun defrosting my heart. She looked like one of those women you see draped over the hoods at car shows; that is, if you've ever seen one with attitude and a seventeen-shot Glock.

Santiago Saizarbitoria—Sancho, as Vic had christened our Basque deputy—was seated on the wheel well and was watching as Cathi Kindt swabbed road debris from a few scratches and burns on Geo Stewart's ear where he'd collided with one of the chrome-tipped tailpipes of the Olds.

I looked at the assembled deputies and EMTs—it was either a slow day for civil service on the high plains or everybody was looking for a place to get inside. I put my gloved hands on my knees and leaned in for a look at the junkman. "You know, in this country we usually reserve this kind of treatment for horse thieves."

Geo smiled, red-faced and glassy-eyed. He was a ball of tendons and stringy muscle, tanned by the scorching Wyoming summers and freeze-dried by the winters into a living jerky. He had pale blue eyes, and the edge of his pupils looked like rime ice.

The aged Carhartt coveralls hung from him like shed skin with torn openings that exposed a red lining looking like a subcutaneous wound. His logging boots were double-tied, and he sported a welder's undercap in a faded floral print. A huge key ring, attached to a loop at his hip, jingled as he spoke. "Hey, Sheriff."

George "Geo" Stewart's great-grandfather was one of the original founders of Durant and said to be the first Caucasian baby born in the territory, but it was Geo's father who started the junkyard after the Second World War. When a mild amount of suburban sprawl overtook his collection of discarded automobiles and trucks in the early sixties, the county commissioners persuaded Geo the elder to take his rusting inventory and swap his in-town spread for a larger one farther east that they had acquired from Dirty Shirley, the last madam to do business in the county.

The commissioners had retained some of the land next to

the junkyard and had made it the town landfill, so when Geo the elder died, Geo the younger inherited the junkyard and the part-time position of maintaining the weigh-station scales and the municipal property.

He had a knack for such things, and I only heard from him when people tried to dump without a city water bill, when they tried to skim on the amount of refuse they unloaded, or when kids got into his junkyard and tried to make off with vintage goods. "Hey, Geo, how are things up at the dump?"

His expression took on a serious quality, but he was nothing if not unfailingly polite. "With all due respect, Walt, Municipal Solid Waste Facility."

I shook my head at the old man. "Right."

"He won't go to the hospital." Cathi looked back at me. The Absaroka County sheriff's department might not have too much to do besides stay in out of the winter wind, but Cathi Kindt was another story.

I avoided the paramedic's gaze and sat next to Sancho. "Does he need to?"

She sat on the gurney next to George and folded her arms. "He's seventy-two years old and just got dragged behind a car for two and a quarter miles."

I took off my hat and studied the inside band to gain a little time and let Cathi cool off. Mike Hodges up at H-Bar Hats in Billings had been kind enough to build me a fawn-colored one, since I'd pitched the last one into the Powder River after I decided that I was not a black hat kinda guy.

I leaned forward and looked past the irate EMT. Geo was still smiling at me, and I figured his teeth were the best part on him. "He looks pretty good, considering." The grin broadened. "How do you feel, Geo?"

He looked around the interior of the van and took in the expensive equipment. "I ain't got any of that gaddam insurance."

I figured as much. "Geo, what part of you hit the mailbox?" Everybody in the van looked at me, Cathi started to speak, and Vic covered a grin and snorted a quick laugh.

"M'shoulder." He moved it, and I could see its alien position and hear the joint grind. "Little stiff."

"Why don't we get it X-rayed?"

He shrugged with the other shoulder. "I told ya. I don't have none of that insurance."

I smiled back at him and shook my head. "It's okay, Geo, the county's got plenty of money."

"I want a raise." Vic walked along beside me as the glass doors of Durant Memorial's emergency entrance closed behind us.

"No."

We were bringing up the rear of the Municipal Solid Waste Facility entourage. I nodded for Saizarbitoria to follow the gurney into the operating room and gestured to Duane and Gina that they should sit on the sofas by the entryway where Geo's brother, Morris, joined them. He'd evidently heard that his brother had been injured, and the gravity of the situation was partially reflected in the fact that as far as I knew, the man only came into town about three times a year.

"Hi, Morris." I waved at him, but he didn't wave back.

"You just said the county has plenty of money."

I lowered my voice in an attempt to get her to lower hers. "They do for medical services involving recalcitrant, unin- sured junkmen but not for the sheriff department's payroll."

Her voice became more conversational. "I want to buy a house."

I nodded and then smiled just to let her know that she shouldn't take her current annual wage personally. "Then you should work hard and save your money."

"Fuck you."

"It's amazing the respect I seem to command from my staff, isn't it?"

Janine, who sat behind the desk, was my dispatcher Ruby's granddaughter. She looked up at us from her paperback, nod- ded, and scratched under her chin with the large, pink eraser of her pencil. "Amazing."

Vic leaned her back against the counter and crossed her legs at the ankles. "I'm not kidding, at least about the house. I'm tired of living in a place with wheels on it."

Ever since arriving in county, Vic had occupied a single- wide by the highway, and I'd often wondered why she hadn't taken up a more permanent residence. Perhaps my latest re- election and promise to abdicate to her in two years was hav- ing an effect. "Where is this house you want?"

"Over on Kisling. It's a little craftsman place."

I looked past her. "The one with the red door?"

She didn't say anything for a moment. "Okay, who died there?"

I shrugged. "Nobody. I just drove by yesterday and saw a for sale sign. Do you know that the Jacobites in Scotland painted their doors red in support of the Forty-Five Rebellion and Bonnie Prince Charlie?"

"Do you know I don't give a bonnie big shit?"

Janine snickered.

Vic uncrossed her ankles and shifted from one booted foot to the other. "I've got an appointment to go over and look at it again tonight. I guess there's a bunch of people interested."

"Would you like me to go with you?"

She raised an exquisite eyebrow. "Why in the *This Old House* hell would I want you to do that?"

She had a point; my home skills were just short of negligible—I'd only gotten around to having the Mexican tile in my six-year-old log cabin installed this past fall. "It's a guy thing; even if you don't know anything about cars, you open the hood and look at the engine."

"Seven-thirty. Then I'll let you take me out to dinner."

I took the weight off my sore foot and looked down at my boots, which were covered with buckled galoshes. "That's a nice part of town. The houses around there usually go in a hurry. What do they want for it?"

"One-seventy-one, but I think I can get it for one-sixty-two. Alphonse says he'll front me the down, and then I can just pay him back when I can, sans interest."

Alphonse was Vic's uncle who had a pizza parlor in Philadelphia and, other than Vic's mother, Lena, the only non-cop Moretti. "How's the rest of the family feel about this?"

"They don't know about it." As a general rule, the machinations of the Moretti family made the Borgias' seem like Blondie and Dagwood.

Her shoulder bumped into my arm as she changed the subject. "So, your daughter and my brother are getting married this summer?"

I took a deep breath with a quick exhale. "All I know is what I get from the answering machine at home."

"At least you've got a home." She shifted her weight again, this time in not-so-simple dissatisfaction. "Mom says the end of July."

I shrugged. "Mom would know." I thought about Vic's mother, and the brief time I'd spent in Philly almost a year ago. "Did she mention whether they were thinking of doing it here or in Philadelphia?"

She looked up at me. "There was supposedly talk about some special place on the Rez—Crazy something . . ."

I thought about it. "Crazy Head Springs?"

"That's it."

"Uh-oh."

"Why uh-oh?"

"It's where I once helped raise the pow-wow totem; it's a sacred place for the Cheyenne but controversial. Crazy Head was a Crow chief, but part of the break-off Kicks-in-the-Belly band."

"Like Virgil?"

"Yep, like Virgil." Virgil had been one of our holding cell lodgers who, after having been released, had gone MIA. "The Cheyenne don't like the idea of a Crow chief being exalted on their reservation. Henry took Cady along with us when she was seven, and she's always said she wanted to be married there."

Vic shook her head. "We'll see if it lasts till the summer."

"What's that supposed to mean?"

Her eyes met mine, but she diverted again. "So, has the Basquo talked to you?"

I started to yawn and covered my mouth with my hand. "About what?"

"Quitting."

I stopped in mid-yawn. "What?"

I studied her a moment more, but my eyes were drawn to an approaching lab coat flapping toward us from the hallway. I swiveled my head to meet Isaac Bloomfield, surgeon and all-around Durant Memorial physician-in-charge. As a member of the lost tribe, who must've really been lost when he settled in Wyoming, Isaac Bloomfield had set up practice in Absaroka County more than a half-century ago. He had been one of the three living inmates of Dora-Mittelbau's Nordhausen when Allied troops had liberated the Nazi *Vernichtungslager.* "How's the patient?"

"Well, that's the first time we've ever had that happen." He looked up at me through the thick lenses of his glasses, which magnified the multiple layers of skin around his eyes. "His hair has grown through his long underwear."

Vic made an unflattering noise through her nose.

"Probably more than we needed to know, Doc."

He adjusted his glasses and motioned with his almost bald head toward the double doors of the ER. "Walter, I need you to come with me." He glanced back as Vic started to follow. "Alone."

I turned to her as I followed the thin man into the inner sanctums of Durant Memorial. "Stay here. I want to know more about the house and the wedding. And Sancho."

She stuffed her hands in the pockets of her duty jacket and called after me. "I've got that appointment at seven-thirty."

The Doc walked me into the first examination room and closed the door. I glanced around and noticed we were the only ones there; that's why I'm a sheriff, because I notice things like that. "Where's the patient?"

He placed the edge of the clipboard on the counter next to a sink and studied me. "In the next room."

"Please tell me he didn't just have a heart attack." I thought about it. "You know the family has a history."

"Yes, but the patient in question suffers from diabetes, not heart disease."

"All right, then." I looked at him. "What's up, Doc?"

I stood there in his disapproving silence. He slowly brought his gaze up. "You've had a rough year. A very rough year." He peered at me and tapped the examination bench. "Climb up here."

"Isaac, I don't have time . . ."

He patted the clipboard. "Neither do I. I have every intention of retiring soon and handing the responsibility for this place over to the new young man we've hired."

"Who?"

He ignored me and patted his clipboard again. "These are the mandatory examination papers for the county health plan and, if you do not sit down, I will have them cancel the coverage."

I took a deep breath and looked at him; he was studying the contents of the folder that contained a running documentary of my physical misadventures. The doc usually dragged me in for the health insurance examination whenever he felt it was high time and long enough.

Bushwhacked.

"Ruby called you, didn't she?" He didn't say anything, so I sighed, stepped up, and sat.

He placed the file on the gurney beside me, reached out and thumbed both sides of my knee, pressing up on the cap through my jeans. "How's the knee?"

I winced. "All right, till you started monkeying around with it."

He looked up at me, all the world the likeness of some venerated Caesar and just as forgiving. "The shotgun wound to your leg has healed moderately well?"

"Yep."

"No lingering symptoms from pneumonia from drowning?"

"I didn't really drown."

His voice was sharp. "When you have to be resuscitated, you drowned."

"Okay."

"Take off your coat."

I did, and he took my left hand and examined the scar tissue. He held my upper arm and turned my forearm, rotating the elbow. "Does this hurt?"

I lied. "No."

He unsnapped my cuff, raised the sleeve of my shirt, and looked more closely at the elbow itself. "You have some swelling here, under the scar tissue."

I lied again. I didn't usually lie, but with the Doc it had become a habit. "I've always had that."

He shook his head and manipulated my shoulder. It sounded gravelly like Geo Stewart's. "The shoulder?"

"It feels great."

"It doesn't feel great to me, and it doesn't sound so good either." He frowned as he compressed the joint and lifted my arm. "How's that?"

It actually hurt like hell, so I pulled my arm loose. "Not so great, which is why I've dropped mandatory departmental saluting."

"How is your foot?"

"Fabulous."

He studied me with a look, and the only description that might apply would be askance. "You're still limping."

"I've come to consider it a character trait."

"Take off your hat."

"I don't think that's going to help with the limp."

He placed his hands on my head, adjusted the angle, and pulled my left eye down for a look; this was the part I was dreading. He released my head and got a small plastic bottle of something from the cabinet behind him. "These drops are for your eyes; would you like to do it, or would you prefer I administer them?"

"How many drops?"

He held up two fingers, and I did my part for the advancement of medical science. My vision became blurry as he studied his wristwatch and waited. After a bit, he reexamined my eyes. "Well, your pupils don't show any particular abrasion, but it's the damage to the ocular cavity that has me worried." He released me, picked up the file, and stepped back, folding his arms over the folder and his chest. "I can't make out any detachment of the retina, but it's possible that there's some ocular trauma." He thumbed his chin and continued to look at me like a card player would at an inside straight.

"I could'a been a contender, Doc."

"You could also go blind as a bat in your left eye if you get hit there again."

I froze. "What?"

"Just a little medical humor. If you're not going to take your condition seriously, why should I?" He hugged my file a little tighter. "Still having the headaches?"

"Only when I come in here."

I had made the mistake of mentioning to Ruby that I had had a few recurring headaches, which must have resulted in this examination. I started to edge my rear end off the table.

"How often?" He continued to study me without moving out of my way.

I took a breath and settled. "Every once in a while."

"What about the flashes?"

"It was a onetime thing; I just moved my head too fast." Once again, it was a lie, and I was pushing my luck because the Doc was pretty good at spotting them. After those smiling government *Gruppenführers* with black uniforms had taken him away, Isaac Bloomfield had become a walking polygraph test.

"You're sure?"

The trick to a good lie, no matter how outrageous, is sticking to it. "Yep."

He shook his head very slightly, just to let me know he knew I was lying. "Walter, I have a deal for you."

"Okay."

He started to speak but then stopped. After a moment he licked his upper lip and tried again. "I will sign these forms indicating that you are in fine shape, which you are for a young man with this many accumulated injuries." I liked it when the Doc called me a young man and tried not to dwell on the fact that he was in his eighties. "But, only on one condition."

There was always a catch with the Doc. "And that is?"

"You have Andy Hall in Sheridan do a complete examination of your left eye."

"All right."

I had started to get up again, but it was too quick of an answer and he placed a hand on my knee, the bad one, to stop me. "I will set up the appointment."

I hedged. "I can do it, just give me his number."

"No, I will make the appointment for you. What time this week is good?"

"This week?" Even with my blurred vision, I could see his large brown eyes studying me.

"Yes."

Damn. I thought about it and figured the more time I had, the more time I'd have to get out of it. "Friday?"

He produced a pen from his lab coat pocket and scribbled on the top of the forms with a flourish followed by a stabbing period. "Thursday."

"That's Valentine's Day."

He smiled, his mission accomplished. "Maybe your heart will be in it."

I pulled on my coat and put on my hat. "All right, now that you're through cutting me off at the pass, do you mind telling me how Geo Stewart is?"

"Routine dislocation of the left shoulder."

"Well, that would explain why he was waving at passing traffic with only one arm."

Isaac nodded. "I'd like to keep him here for observation, but there's something else that's come up in casual conversation that I thought you might need to know."

"Now why do I not like the sound of that?"

Isaac Bloomfield cleared his throat. "It would appear, that at the dump—"

"You mean the Municipal Solid Waste Facility?"

The Doc continued as if I hadn't interrupted. "They have found a body part."

A PENGUIN READERS GUIDE TO

THE DARK HORSE

Craig Johnson

An Introduction to
The Dark Horse

After twenty-five years on the job, Walt Longmire, sheriff of Wyoming's Absaroka County, finds himself at a crossroads. The recent past has been tumultuous for the widowed lawman. His only daughter, Cady, is trying to get on her feet again after a brush with death, and he's become romantically entangled—albeit reluctantly—with his feisty undersheriff, Victoria "Vic" Moretti. It's also an election year, and the town's smooth-talking prosecutor has launched an aggressive campaign against him, making Walt unsure of whether he wants to continue on the job. Then, Walt is sent a "guest" prisoner from a neighboring county, and—convinced of her innocence—he is galvanized to pursue the one thing in which he's always believed: justice.

It's more than Mary Barsad's beauty and wealth that set her apart in a place where most criminal cases are generally "Bubba shot Skeeter while they were drinking beer in the cab of Skeeter's truck and trying to figure out if Bubba's Charter Arms revolver was loaded" (p. 201). Utterly indifferent to her own fate, the champion horsewoman has confessed to shooting her husband, Wade, in the head six times after he set fire to their barn, which contained her eight beloved horses. However, as Walt teases out threads of her story, he discovers that Mary was so doped up on insomnia medication that she can't actually remember the murder.

So it takes little prodding for Eric Boss, an old acquaintance investigating the fire, to convince Walt to make a few undercover inquiries over in Absalom on behalf of the insurance company. But the Barsad ranch is also near the spread Walt once called home and his return is complicated by unsettling memories. And he isn't there long before he learns that the dead man had a gift for making enemies on both sides of the law.

Born Willis Barnecke, Wade dodged a murder charge by testifying against several Atlantic City mob acquaintances before disappearing into the witness protection program. He'd already embezzled away the good name of his first new identity when he got up to his old tricks as Wade Barsad. To ensure the FBI ignored his more recent illegal activities, Wade strung them along with the promise of further information.

Walt is literally dodging bullets when both Vic and Walt's old friend Henry Standing Bear turn up in town. And since the FBI's trying to warn him off the case and just about everyone in Absalom—from the illegal Guatemalan beauty to the old cowpoke who adored Mary and the ranchers whose cattle Wade stole—harbored a grudge against him, Walt's going to need all the help he can get to bring in the real killer.

In *The Dark Horse*, Craig Johnson deftly explores the devastating wake of one brutal man but leavens it with his western lawman's wry, erudite humor. Fast-paced, smart, and compulsively readable out of the gate, *The Dark Horse* is a surefire winner and a fantastic addition to Johnson's addictive, award-winning Walt Longmire series.

ABOUT CRAIG JOHNSON

Craig Johnson lives with his wife, Judy, in Ucross, Wyoming, population twenty-five.

A Conversation with
Craig Johnson

When you first started writing The Dark Horse, *what was the first scene you envisioned and how did the rest of the novel develop from there?*

I've always looked at my protagonist as a vertical figure on a horizontal landscape, and the opening scene of *The Dark Horse* is no different. The opening scene was always the one of Walt at the bridge overlooking Absalom for two reasons; first, I wanted to begin with the sheriff entering an unfriendly town to get the action going rather than having the reader sit through an elongated exposition. This also led to the split-time narrative that I'd used in *Another Man's Moccasins*. The second reason for using the form is that I like to bookend the novels and have Walt end the book in the place where he started out—in that sense, the bridge became a metaphor and a landmark.

What do you see as the code of the West, and does it still exist— if it ever did—outside of fiction?

There's a great line from *Ride the High Country*, the Sam Peckinpah film with Joel McCrea, where McCrea's character, an older lawman, makes the remark that he just wants to enter his house justified. I don't think there's a geographical aspect to doing the right thing, it varies from person to person. The West is interesting in that it's so physically large and the population is so small, and this makes for a stark ethical background. I think it's easier to respond to society's mores when you have an audience; it's when you are alone that your true character shows—that's when the code of the West becomes interesting to me.

In what ways is Wyoming different from other Western states? Could you—or Walt—ever live anywhere else?

Wyoming is the least populated state in America, and I've got to admit that I like that. I was recently at the National Book Festival in Washington, D.C., and the woman who was in charge of wrangling me was apologizing for the long lines at lunch and then asked me what the lines were like in Wyoming. I told her that we didn't have lines, and that folks tend to bunch up in the front and say, "You first." I like Wyoming best, or else I wouldn't have built my ranch here, but I'm not particularly metrophobic. I like New York, Los Angeles, Paris, Omaha. . . . I think city life provides a stimulus that a lot of people respond to, but I enjoy the isolation of ranch life, it keeps me focused. As for Walt, I think he's the same way; he enjoys the city (see *Kindness Goes Unpunished*), but he also enjoys coming home.

Dog and Wahoo Sue are as rich and developed as any of the novel's human cast. Do animals have a different role in the West than they do in more populated parts of the world?

With animals, I think it's just a question of being around them, not really a question of geography. I'm sure the hansom cab drivers in Central Park have just as close a relationship with their horses as the cowboys of Wyoming. Like Hershel says in *The Dark Horse*, "Animals are the finest people I know."

Cady put herself on a "mystery-a-day" program while recovering from her injuries. Why do you think someone who endured the kind of trauma that Cady went through would enjoy reading mysteries? Why are so many people drawn to this genre?

It appears to be a universal, whether it's simply a voyeuristic glimpse into another world, or a quest for justice that seems to elude us in reality. We live in a time when crime fiction readers are more sophisticated, they expect arc of story, fully developed characters, social commentary, historical accuracy, and humor. I think it's also a question of what my buddy Tony Hillerman used to call "telling a good story." One thing is for sure—you're dealing with life and death and the stakes don't get any higher.

Even though Henry Standing Bear has a relatively minor role in this book, he is a big influence on Walt. Twice in the novel—when Walt is fighting Cliff Cly and when he's trying to outrace a truck— he draws on advice he received from the Cheyenne Nation. Who would Walt be without Henry?

Up shit creek, without the proverbial or figurative paddle. People always refer to Henry as Walt's sidekick, but I think it might be more like Walt is Henry's. I've got a good Cheyenne friend, Marcus Red Thunder, and I draw an awful lot of Henry from him. I think if you're lucky enough to have one good friend in life, you've done well. Walt's done well, too.

When Walt tries to persuade Rose to stop drinking until her baby is born, she tells him, "Mr. Good Samaritan, you're in the wrong town" (p. 89). It must have been difficult for you/Walt to accept the helplessness of his position considering the possible consequences. Could you talk about this?

I think it was intrinsic to the book to have Walt out of his element, away from all of his usual resources, which only amplifies the helplessness you sometimes feel in law enforcement. It's frustrating, sure, but you keep going out there and doing the job because people need you to do that. Walt is something of a knight in that respect—I think it's Ruby who comments on that part of Walt's character.

The Walt Longmire novels are never afraid to tackle issues of social inequity. Is this why you choose to write Juana—the most intelligent resident of Absalom—as an illegal immigrant? What are you trying to say through her character?

She was an outsider in a town of outsiders and emblematic of one of the book's themes—that sometimes the rules aren't meant to apply to everybody. That's the big question here—what society is and what happens when it breaks down. She says it best herself when she addresses the myth of independence in the West. There is a dichotomy in the structure that she embodies.

Cowboy movies have been around for as long as Hollywood, so it's difficult not to compare fictional cowboys with their cinematic counterparts. Is Walt's character influenced by, say, Jimmy Stewart or Clint Eastwood? Who would you cast as Walt in a film adaptation?

It is, but I don't. I avoid using actors as characters, simply because I don't know any. I prefer to use real people from my life. I get asked that question a lot, though—Gary Cooper, but he's not returning our calls.

Walt's adventures seem to strike increasingly closer to home. Where will Walt Longmire's boots take him next?

The next book, *Junkyard Dogs*, is very loosely based on a story I actually took from my little town of twenty-five. There's this junkyard to the south of Durant and when a new housing development is built nearby, the conflict leads to a modern day range war. I realize it doesn't sound like it, but it might be the funniest Walt book yet.

QUESTIONS FOR DISCUSSION

1. Who is the novel's dark horse?

2. Is Walt willfully trying to lose his reelection campaign? Would his life be easier if he were no longer sheriff of Absaroka County? Why do you think he chose to become a lawman instead of a rancher?

3. If Cady marries Michael Moretti, Walt and Vic would find themselves in an even more complicated relationship. Does Walt owe it to Cady to break things off with Vic?

4. Do you agree with Walt's prediction that the potential jurors for Mary Barsad's trial would find her guilty because she shows no repentance?

5. In what way does Absalom's bloody past affect the course of the novel? How would you answer Bill Nolan's question to Walt: "If nobody remembers the history, did it still happen?" (p. 131).

6. Does the Powder-River-Pound-Down-Tough-Man Contest help Walt work through his anxiety about Cady? Is physical violence simply an inextricable part of male genetics?

7. For a Wyoming lawman, Walt's distrust of horses comes as something of a surprise. How does it affect your opinion of the good sheriff? Do you believe that animals have an intuitive sense of human intentions?

8. Walt remembers his father saying "the outside of a horse is always good for the inside of a man" (p. 296). What do you think he meant?

9. How much responsibility does Walt bear for Hershel's death? Did his actions needlessly endanger Benjamin's life?

10. Do you approve of the witness protection program? Is it fair that criminals—perhaps murderers themselves—can escape punishment for their crimes by testifying against more serious offenders? Is Cliff Cly's behavior acceptable for an officer of the law?

11. Do you think Wade's brother invited his fate? Why or why not?

For more information about or to order other Penguin Readers Guides, please e-mail the Penguin Marketing Department at reading@us.penguingroup.com or write to us at:

Penguin Books Marketing Dept.
Readers Guides
375 Hudson Street
New York, NY 10014-3657

Please allow 4–6 weeks for delivery.
To access Penguin Readers Guides online, visit the Penguin Group (USA) Inc. Web sites at www.penguin.com and www.vpbookclub.com.

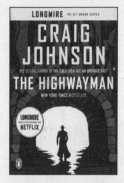

THE HIGHWAYMAN

When Wyoming Highway Patrolman Rosey Wayman is transferred to Wind River Canyon, she starts receiving "officer needs assistance" calls. The problem? They're coming from a legendary Arapaho patrolman who met his end a half-century ago. With an investigation that spans this world and the next, Sheriff Walt Longmire takes on a case that pits him against a legend—The Highwayman.

WAIT FOR SIGNS

Ten years ago, in one of the earliest appearances of Sheriff Walt Longmire, Craig Johnson wrote his first short story, "Old Indian Trick." Each Christmas Eve thereafter, fans rejoiced when Johnson sent out a new story featuring an episode in Walt's life. Now, *Wait for Signs* gives fans a chance to own these stories in a single volume.

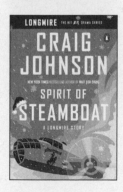

SPIRIT OF STEAMBOAT

Sheriff Walt Longmire is in his office reading *A Christmas Carol* when he is interrupted by a ghost of Christmas past: a young woman with a hairline scar and more than a few questions about his predecessor, Lucian Connally. Soon he finds himself in a story that takes them all the way back to Christmas Eve 1988.

 VIKING   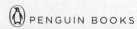 PENGUIN BOOKS

Ready for more Craig Johnson? Let us help. Visit prh.com/craigjohnson

Depth of Winter

A Longmire Mystery

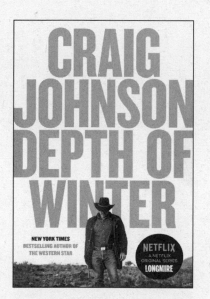

In Craig Johnson's latest mystery, *Depth of Winter*, an international hit man and the head of one of the most vicious drug cartels in Mexico has kidnapped Walt's beloved daughter, Cady. The American government is of limited help and the Mexican one even less. Walt heads into the heat of the Northern Mexican desert alone, one man against an army.

VIKING

PENGUIN BOOKS